POETIC JUSTICE

POETIC JUSTICE

Nigel Tranter

Hodder & Stoughton

First published in Great Britain in 1996 by
Hodder and Stoughton
A division of Hodder Headline PLC

British Library Cataloguing in Publication Data

Tranter, Nigel, 1909–
Poetic Justice
1. English fiction – 20th century – Scottish authors
2. Scottish fiction – 20th century
I. Title
823.9′12 [F]

ISBN 0 340 62581 3

Typeset by Hewer Text Composition Services, Edinburgh
Printed and bound in Great Britain by
Mackays of Chatham PLC, Chatham, Kent

Hodder and Stoughton
A division of Hodder Headline PLC
338 Euston Road
London NW1 3BH

Principal Characters in order of appearance

Archibald Campbell, 7th Earl of Argyll: Great Scots noble.

William Alexander of Menstrie: Laird of small estate, poet and tutor.

Ludovick, Duke of Lennox: The king's cousin.

James the Sixth, King of Scots.

Sir William Erskine of Cardross: Commendator of Glasgow, brother to Earl of Mar.

Annabella, Dowager Countess of Mar: King James's foster-mother.

Prince Henry: Elder son of the king; Duke of Rothesay.

Janet Erskine: Daughter of Sir William.

Lady Agnes Douglas: Daughter of the Earl of Morton.

Patrick, Master of Gray: Acting Chancellor.

John, Earl of Mar: Foster-brother of the king.

Sir Robert Carey: English courtier.

Queen Anne of Denmark: Wife of James.

Alexander, Lord Fyvie: Later Earl of Dunfermline.

Prince Charles: Younger son of the king.

Robert Cecil, Lord Cecil: Principal English Secretary of State.

William Herbert, Earl of Pembroke: Great English noble.

Ben Jonson: Poet and playwright.

Ailie Graham: Daughter of the miller of Cardross.

Count Gondomar: Spanish ambassador.

James Hamilton, Lord Abercorn: Scots noble.

George Villiers: Royal favourite, later Duke of Buckingham.

Princess Elizabeth: Daughter of the king, later the "Winter Queen".

Lady Arabella Stewart: Possible claimant to the throne.

Robert Kerr or Carr: Later Earl of Somerset.

Sir Randall MacSorley MacDonnell: Later Earl of Antrim.

Sir Thomas Hamilton of Binning: Secretary of State for Scotland.

Sir Thomas Hope of Craighall: Lord Advocate of Scotland.

Duncan Drummond: Shipmaster of Dumbarton.

Mary Gray: Mistress of the Duke of Lennox.

John Stewart of Methven: Illegitimate son of Lennox.

Sir Robert Gordon of Lochinvar and Kenmure: Deputy governor of Nova Scotia.

Queen Henrietta Maria: Wife of Charles the First.

Claude de la Toure: French Huguenot, deputy governor of Nova Scotia.

William Laud: Archbishop of Canterbury.

William Kerr, Earl of Lothian: Warden of the Middle March.

PART ONE

1

The two men eyed each other, one doubtfully, the other almost mockingly, there in the doorway of the small fortalice of Menstrie Castle, while the group of retainers in Campbell colours stood by their horses in the courtyard and watched. They were two very different men, in looks and in temperament, in rank and status, and in much else, although much of an age, both youngish. Despite the differences, they were friends, and had been for long.

"I will take you to him, present you, Will," the dark one said. "They tell me that he has been writing this poem of his for weeks now. How he whiles away the time, when he is not hunting, until Elizabeth Tudor dies! He is like a man smitten with the plague, two plagues! A plague of desire for the woman's throne. And a plague of words, rhymes, couplets, at which he scratches himself."

"And you would have me go to him? In such state? What is behind this? I know you, Archie! There is some ploy you are at!" the other declared, fairer of head and skin, keen of eye, slenderly built but wiry.

"No ploy, man. This will be good for you, of benefit. Another poet. Time that you were brought to his notice. He is seldom in Stirling these days. He is come from his hunting at Falkland for this meeting of the Privy Council, and goes on to Edinburgh thereafter. Here is opportunity. Come with me."

"Is that an order, my lord?"

Archibald Campbell shook his dark, saturnine, proud head. "Be not such a fool, Will!" When his friend spoke in that fashion, he, even he, had learned to be careful, over the years. "I but seek your weal, man."

"And something else, no?"

"Not so. Be not so ready to suspect. Why?"

"Say that I have known MacCailean Mor for long enough to be wary of such sudden gestures."

"What ails you at it? He will not eat you, slobbering monstrosity as our liege-lord may be! Perchance you will be able to serve him. Teach him how to pen his poetry, you the master at it. Put him in a better mood for the rest of us. James's moods are the bane of all who would serve the realm."

"Or serve themselves in it!"

"You are sour this day, Will. When I but seek your good. This, I judge, will get us into James's presence, privily. You should be grateful."

"Ah, so that is it! The privy presence! You require this?"

"Well, I would welcome it, yes. In this state of affairs, with Elizabeth of England dying, at last! There will be much to settle. And he should have much on his mind, beyond poetry!"

They were talking about James the Sixth, King of Scots, the Wisest Fool in Christendom, the self-proclaimed Lord's Anointed, and a much concerned monarch in that year of Our Lord 1603.

"Very well, Archie. I will come. Although what good it will serve, I know not. But I must dress myself. I cannot appear before the king clad thus."

"James cares naught about clothes, man. He wears anything that comes to hand, himself, in whatever state. He will not care how you are dressed."

"Yet *you* are clad finely, I see, my lord Earl of Argyll! Am I to shame you before all, even if not our sovereign-lord?"

"As you will. Go change gear. I will ride on. Join me at Stirling Castle hereafter. You will be admitted if you give my name."

"My lord!"

The chief of Clan Campbell pursed fairly thin lips at

4

this small laird and feudal vassal of his, who could speak to him as few others did, then shrugged and turned away to join his waiting henchmen and the horses.

William Alexander of Menstrie watched him go, with a smile. If MacCailean Mor had looked back he would have perceived that it was a warmer smile than might have seemed likely after that exchange of views. They *were* friends.

Presently then, Will was riding, alone, westwards along the levels of the Carse of Forth, the Ochil foothills on his right and the meanders of the Forth, suddenly changed from estuary to river, on his left, with the towering bulk of Stirling's castle-crowned rock four miles ahead. Menstrie Castle, with its little village, lay directly under the steep slopes of Dumyat, the most shapely of the Ochils, facing the two-mile-wide strip of flat and fertile land between the escarpment and the water, still salty as far as Stirling; whereas Castle Campbell, his friend's and all but master's Lowland seat, soared some eight miles eastwards along these hillfoots, near his township of Dollar. These locations were significant, and strange also, for Lowland as they had their domicile, both these men, both nearing thirty years, were Highlanders by blood, Argyll chief of one of the largest and most important clans, with his "capital" at Inveraray on Loch Fyne, and William, calling himself Alexander, really a MacAllister, a sept of the great Clan Donald, hereditary enemies of the Campbells. Two or three generations before, that acquisitive clan had dispossessed the MacAllisters from their lands in Kintyre, and taken them over. The first Earl of Argyll, on becoming Chancellor of the realm or chief minister for James the Fourth, had built this Lowland Castle Campbell to be near to Stirling from which the king ruled, and brought the dispossessed MacAllister with him, giving him the small Menstrie property as sop for the wide but lost lands of long Kintyre. That practical individual, instead of seeking to rebel at fate, had accepted the situation, proved himself a useful aide to Argyll, and changed his surname to Alscinder, or Alexander, the English-language form of the Gaelic Alastair, thus becoming a small Lowland laird instead of a Highland chieftain. Perhaps some echo of all this was apt to sound in Will's attitude towards his feudal lord. That, and the fact that he had been chosen by the present earl's father as tutor for his son, although only two years older, this because he had had a superior education at St Andrews whereas the young Campbell had not. Indeed Will had accompanied the new earl, on his father's death seventeen years before, on the lengthy Continental tour which was all but obligatory for Scots of high birth.

As he rode past Cambuskenneth Abbey where the great Bruce had received the surrender of the captured English lords after Bannockburn, below the Abbey Craig from which William Wallace had directed the only slightly less famous Battle of Stirling Bridge, Will's mind was not so much on any possible audience with his present odd monarch, as on a form of words. For he was, at this juncture, nearing the end of a long poem which meant a lot to him, his ninety-eighth, and it was his ambition, his determination indeed, to publish the entire sequence once the hundredth was finished, not in prideful self-esteem but because he looked on his gift for words as something that God had entrusted to him and would expect to see used and presented as pleasure, enjoyment and interest for others. Just how he might achieve this he knew not, but somehow he would, that he was sure. This present piece, to be entitled *The Tragedy of Darius*, had gone well enough in the main; but now, near the finish, he was having difficulty in winding it up sufficiently dramatically. It *was* a tragedy, after all, and Darius, who had created the ancient Persian Empire, triumphant as had been most of his life, had scarcely died gloriously; and although Will could not change that, he had somehow to end his epic on a high note. Not easy, after the stirring lines which had gone before. So he turned over in his mind a variety of words and phrases and sequences which could lead

6

up to a final flourish, without striking a false note nor being inept.

Thus preoccupied he reached Causewayhead and turned southwards to ride along the mile-long raised causeway itself, whereon Wallace had won his victory, with the soft bogland still there on either side into which the mounted English knights and heavy chivalry had been forced into floundering and mired defeat. And so on to cross the high-arched ancient Stirling Bridge, the first and only way over Forth, other than by boat; for eastwards stretched the seventy-mile estuary, and westwards, for twenty-five miles right to the mountains around Ben Lomond, lay the waterlogged and impassable plain of the Flanders Moss, which had confronted and defeated armies right from Roman times, five swampy miles in width, with only the MacGregors, lately decimated and even their name proscribed – this by Campbell machinations – knowing secret and devious ways across it. So Stirling Bridge, overlooked by its rock-top royal fortress, had for centuries been the cockpit of Scotland, where invaders could be held, and access to the north and the Highlands denied. Darius the Mede would have appreciated the significance of this, the mighty strategist of long ago.

> The Median hero all his life surveyed
> From great Persepolis palace strong;
> As on his death-bed he was laid,
> And weighed where worth had ousted wrong.

No, that would not serve. The triumphant emperor, dying, would scarcely so spend his last hours, contemplating failures, even though he had suffered them, like lesser mortals, in especial the sore defeat of Marathon, five years before, at the hands of the Athenians. If he could bring in the later wiping out of that episode, at the end, on a high note?

Debating with himself thus, he entered Stirling town and set his mount to the narrow, climbing streets which led up steeply to the fortress, streets thronged with the idle retinues of the great ones attending this Privy Council, already some of them drink-taken and coming to blows with rivals, in typical Scots fashion. Up at the jousting-ground before the towered gatehouse, Will dismounted, to tie up his horse among the many tethered there, and went to present himself to the guards.

"Alexander of Menstrie, to join my lord Earl of Argyll," he announced, and was admitted without question.

Within the walls of that skied citadel with its far-flung vistas, he climbed over cobbles and naked rock to the palace block, past the famous Chapel Royal which had seen so much of history enacted. More guards beyond barred the way, but again yielded to the confident manner of the new arrival and the mention of Argyll's name.

The great Outer Hall was crowded and loud with talk, lords and barons, lairds and chieftains and churchmen thronging. Why so many of these? After all, this was a meeting of the Privy Council, was it not? A comparatively small and select body. What brought all this company, however lofty?

Looking around him as he worked his way through the press, Will could see no sign of Argyll. Nor indeed of sundry others whom he would recognise as Privy Councillors and Lords of the Articles. Presumably, then, these greater ones would be in the further Lesser Hall, lesser in size only. Reaching a communicating door into this, he asked the guards there whether the Earl of Argyll was within. And at a shrug which might mean anything, he used the sort of voice which could give even MacCailean Mor pause, instructing to go and inform his lordship that Alexander of Menstrie sought word with him, important word.

That had its effect.

Argyll appeared after only a brief interval and, taking Will's arm, led him over to a vacant corner.

"James is not down yet," he disclosed. "He is up in the royal apartments. Best thus, that we may see him alone."

"If he will see us?"

"I think that he will see me, if I refer to further MacGregor trouble. Naming Roro in Glen Lyon."

"Are the MacGregors not sufficiently punished?"

"That is neither here nor there. My deplorable kinsman, Duncan of Glenorchy, has contrived to obsess James with hatred and fear of the MacGregors. He will believe anything of them. That will win us into his presence, I think. Then – you and your poetry. And his."

"M'mm. I do not know that I like this. This device."

"With James Stewart, devices are necessary. As all who have to deal with him find out. Come."

Heading through the press for the outer door, Will remarked on the numbers present and wondered the reason; in February, and many evidently from afar, when travel conditions were at their worst.

"It is this of Elizabeth Tudor. The word has got around that she is near to her end, at last, and all know that James is itching to be off to London to take over her throne. Many will undoubtedly wish to go south with him. There will, therefore, be great changes in Scotland, many vacant positions and offices. So, they seek to bring themselves to the royal notice."

"As would yourself!"

Argyll frowned, but could scarcely deny it.

Out in the courtyard, they moved on round the palace block to a wing which housed the royal quarters. More guards barred their way.

"The Earl of Argyll to see His Grace!" That was all but a bark, and MacCailean Mor, without waiting, pushed his way past the sentinels authoritatively and made for the stairway, Will somewhat doubtfully following.

They climbed to the first floor, at the landing of which two more guards stood. The monarch was well protected.

"Argyll. With especial tidings for His Grace," these were informed. "The king will see me." That was a statement, not a request.

One of the men, bowing, went within; but the other remained, barring entry.

"I do not see why you wanted to have me here," Will said, low-voiced. "You appear to be able to gain the presence without my aid."

"Wait, you," he was advised.

And there was quite a wait before footsteps sounded behind the closed door. Then two men appeared, not one. Argyll stiffened.

"Ah, my lord Duke!" he got out. "Here, here is a pleasure!" He hardly sounded overjoyed nevertheless. "I . . . we have word for His Grace."

"Indeed, my lord. Perhaps your word will keep? His Grace is not for audience yet. He is . . . engaged." The speaker was a stockily built man of early middle years, plain of feature, undistinguished in appearance but bearing himself easily, Ludovick Stewart, Duke of Lennox, the king's cousin and the only duke in Scotland, he who had acted viceroy while James was over in Denmark collecting his bride, Queen Anne.

Argyll hesitated. "The word is anent the MacGregors," he said, less than confidently now. "That *might* keep until the council. But knowing His Grace's concern with, with matters of the muse, shall we say, I judge that he will be prepared to see our friend here, Alexander of Menstrie, privily. Before affairs of state take all his attention. Will Alexander is a poet, you see, a notable poet. And would wish to talk of poetry, verse, balladry, with his liege-lord who is also a poet."

Will could scarcely deny that, there and then, however he felt.

"So! And you consider that this is the time to do this, my lord?" the duke asked − but it was at Will that he looked, consideringly.

"His Grace is seldom . . . available. To such as our friend. And, and he seeks the royal guidance in what he is presently writing. One poet with another, as you might say."

This was the first Will had heard of his seeking royal guidance. He shook his head. "My lord Duke, I would not wish to trouble His Grace with my poor scrievings! It is my lord Earl's notion, not mine . . ."

"Knowing His Highness's great concern with the muses, in especial poesy and prosody," Argyll added.

"Poetry would seem to be a sore affliction for those so inclined!" Lennox observed. "*I* have been spared it." He smiled at Will. "I will inform the king."

They waited, eyeing each other.

After an interval the duke returned. "His Grace will see you. But only for a brief time. He has much on his mind."

They were led through an anteroom to another closed door, no guards on this one. Lennox opening it, he announced, "The Earl of Argyll and the Laird of Menstrie crave audience, Sire."

Bowing, the new arrivals found themselves in a bedroom. Will had heard that the monarch was apt to favour his bedroom, indeed often conducted interviews from the bed itself, in various stages of undress. Now, at least, he was fully clad, and wearing the high hat which seldom left his head – allegedly for fear of bat droppings landing upon him. He considered the visitors sorrowfully from great lacklustre eyes, these said to be the best feature of James Stewart.

Certainly he was an odd figure of a man, of medium build, shambling, knock-kneed, anything but handsome, a dribble almost always running from his lips, for his tongue was too large for his mouth, and seeming as untidy in his make-up as he was in his clothing. He made the most unlikely son for the beautiful but ill-fated Mary Stewart, whoever his father had been – and there were questions about that, the Queen's Italian secretary David Rizzio being the favoured choice rather than her second husband, the Lord Darnley. But woe betide those who judged by appearances and underestimated the Wisest Fool, for those large eyes were shrewd, however mournful, and

11

missed nothing, and his tongue, whatever its size, could be biting.

"Aye, aye – so here's a mannie who ettles to scrieve lines and rhymes, aye, lines and rhymes, eh?" he said thickly. "Ambitious, just!" The king always spoke braid Scots from childhood, his foster-mother, the Countess of Mar, always insisting, here in Stirling Castle where he had been reared. "Menstrie, eh? Yon's just doon ayont Blairlogie, is it no'? Hielant folk, I am told. But no Campbells!" And he glanced at Argyll.

Surprised that the monarch should be so well informed, Will bowed again. "Your Grace honours me by knowing of my poor house and line," he said.

"Hech, aye – there's lines and lines, mind! And some worse than others, I'm thinking! No' only the written sort. I jalouse that if Argyll brings you to me, man, it'll no' be for lack o' purpose! Campbells being that way! Eh, my lord?"

Argyll, clearly disconcerted by this prompt and telling challenge, shook his dark head. "Your Grace's love for poesy is known to me. And, with the council, and matters of state hereafter, I judged that there would be no opportunity for my poet friend here to gain your royal ear. When he lives so close by."

"Aye. I'ph'mm. Nae doubt. So, what's your trouble, my mannie, that you seek my aid? It maun be fell important to you to come yammering at *my* door!" It was at Will that he looked.

That man cleared his throat. He sought to adjust, to arrange his thoughts and words to meet this curious situation. Obviously he had to play this the king's way. "Sire, I am at present seeking to indite a quite lengthy measure. Of epic proportions. Not of epic worth, I hasten to say. But epic as to subject also. I think to call it *The Tragedy of Darius*. On Darius, Emperor of Persia . . ."

"D'you think that I dinna ken that, man! Darius the Mede, who united Media and Persia, aye and Athens, Babylon and Egypt forby." A whinnied royal laugh. "As

I am about to unite Scotland and England, with Wales and Ireland too. Maist appropriate! Him who slew Gaumata the usurper – aye, and a wheen others! And wed yon Atossa, when the rightful king killed himsel', she who was his ain sister and wife, forby! Right shameful folk they were, but before Christ, mind, before Christ's right teachings."

Blinking his surprise at this detailed royal knowledge of ancient times, Will nodded. "Your Highness is renowned for your erudition. So, no doubt, you will perceive my problem, Sire. I am at the end of my poem, and I wish to finish on a strong and lofty note, in keeping with what has gone before, all the glories of the imperial triumphs and campaigns. But Darius died in his bed, of a lingering sickness, scarcely the tone and tempo that I would seek to end on. You will understand, Sire, I am sure."

While Will had been speaking thus, James had gone to sit on his bed. No doubt with those knock knees he preferred sitting to standing. But the move gave no hint of boredom at what he was hearing, indeed he looked interested.

"Aye, weel, endings are important, to be sure. I grant you that, Alexander man. But this is a tragedy, you say? No' a triumph. So you'll no' need a flourish at the end. Mair o' a cry o' sorrow, for what might ha' been. No tears, no wails, but a call to whatever god he worshipped – a bull, was it no'? Can you credit it, just, worshipping bulls? Mind, they have fine long cockies, bulls! He had Persian stane bulls at yon palace o' Persepolis. A bit roar to his bull for the price he had to pay, eh?"

"Sire, you overwhelm me! Your interest, your perception! On a theme which you cannot have been considering . . ."

"Och, weel, see you, I ken your need. For I hae something of the same problem my ain sel', in this pass. I am scrieving a piece on yon Elizabeth, whose throne I'm to mount any day now. The Tudor woman who's been ower-long a-dying. I'm naming it *Gloriana*.

It's for her English court and lords, right arrogant and prideful crittus, mind! But I'll hae to work wi' them. So a bit ode to Gloriana, as they called her, will dae nae harm. But she's no' been á' that glorious these last years. Aye, and she slew my mother! Now she's but a mumbling hulk, the Maister o' Gray tells me, mouthing on her bed. So I ken your trouble for an ending. But mind, yours is no' so sair a problem as mine, for yours is a tragedy you say. And mine is a celebration o' sorts. So I hae to end wi' a flourish."

"I see your difficulty, Sire. Do you wish to bring in your own succession to her throne? Indicate that you are the heir to Gloriana, and will continue and enhance her glory?"

"There you have it, man. That is needful, at the end. But no' easy to put down when it's mysel' I'm writing aboot! But these high and mighty English lords maun learn who's master now, or any day now. And no' to look doon their prideful noses! Difficult."

"Could you end on the note, Sire, of Gloriana no more? Gloriana passes on. Now succeeded by Grace. Play on the English usage of majesty for their monarchs, and the Scots grace. Gloriana's Tudor majesty passes to more ancient Stewart grace? Something of that sort?"

James was fingering his wispy beard, and gazing with those eyes which now had become almost soulful. "Man Alexander, I might just use that, aye! Gloriana's Tudor majesty passes. To mair ancient Stewart grace! That's no' bad. No' bad, ava'. Forby, ancestral might be better than ancient, see you. I'm no' that auld! They might pin the ancient on to me, instead of my crown! Better still, patriarchal, which speaks o' man, rather than deid woman! Aye:

> Gloriana's Tudor majesty passes,
> To patriarchal Stewart grace.

Better still, no' passes, but reaches oot. Reaches oot to patriarchal Stewart grace. That right telling, is it no'?" James looked at the two listening lords. "See you, reaching oot means *they're* doing the seeking! The Englishry. Seeking mysel' to come and rule ower them. In patriarchal fashion, as in Scotland. No' just a change but an improve on Gloriana's majesty. You see it?"

"Excellent, James!" his cousin agreed. "Very subtle. Together, you and Menstrie have it."

Argyll applauded likewise.

"I'ph'mm. That's for *Gloriana*. But this o' Darius a-dying. We maun gie it a guid finish, right enough. What hae you thought on, Alexander?"

"Well, Sire, I was thinking along these lines, but without satisfaction. As you will perceive:

> The Median hero all his life surveyed
> From great Persepolis palace strong
> As on his death-bed he was laid
> And weighed where worth had ousted wrong."

Will's voice tailed away, his dissatisfaction the greater for having to speak the words in such distinguished company.

"Ummm!" the monarch said. "'Worth ousted wrong.' Man, that's no' just a high note, no. We could dae better than that, I'm thinking. To rhyme wi' strong, is it? Throng? Song? Along? Och, strong's no' just easy. See you, if you changed it to great, palace great. You'd have to change great Persepolis palace then. So, fine Persepolis palace great. Then you could end your verse wi' fate, maybe. And weighed his reign in Persia's fate. How think you o' that?"

"Much better, Sire, to be sure. Better. Persia's fate. That tells, yes. I thank you.

> The Median hero all his life surveyed
> From fine Persepolis palace great,
> As on his death-bed he was laid
> And weighed his reign and Persia's fate.

That sounds well."

"Aye, weel – is there mair to come?"

"Perhaps another couplet, Sire, that is all. Something of this sort.

> He closed his eyes on this world's view,
> And faced the next, and challenge new.

That is not quite right. But something thus."

"Challenge new isna' just apt, no. Nor view either, I'm thinking. If you were to change view to scene, maybe – and faced the next, and pastures green. No?"

"Pastures green?" Monarch or none, Will could not pretend that he liked that. "For a warrior emperor, Highness, pastures green sounds too, too pastoral, I think."

"You say so? Maybe so. Then make it yestreen. And faced the next, forgetful of yestreen. That would serve."

"To be sure. Yes, Sire. Forgetful of yestreen is good. You are kind. That will round it off well." He hoped that he sounded grateful and honest, not risking a glance at the two listeners.

"Words are the stuff o' wonder for them as hae the gift. Aye, and hae the sensibilities!" James looked almost accusingly at the duke and earl. "No' all hae these!" He turned back to Will. "So your bit task will be finished? This o' Darius. What do you think to dae wi' it, man? Your tragedy? So folk can read it, hear it, savour it? You have scrieved other verse?"

"Well, Sire, it is but one of a series, a long series, I fear. It is the ninety-eighth, no less! Although most of the others are less lengthy."

"Guidsakes! Ninety-eight! Man, you're no' begunking me, *me* your ain sovereign-lord! I'll no' be gulled, mind."

"No, Highness. It is truth. I have been at it for long. Years. I planned, perhaps foolishly, arrogantly, to make a book of them. Of one hundred poems."

16

"A book! Here's a notion indeed. One hunnerd! In a book. You're no' feart, Alexander man! And this is ninety-eight. So you've twa mair to do yet?"

"Yes, Sire. One on Julius Caesar and another tragedy on Croesus. But shorter than on Darius."

"But Croesus was before Darius, man!"

"Yes. But I do not write them in order of years, Sire. But just as the spirit moves me. Perhaps unwisely. But so it suits me. Perhaps, when I publish – if I can – I will set them in due order."

"You dae that." Suddenly the king altogether changed his stance and tone. "Now, I've mair to dae than mak poesy, for you or mysel', mair's the pity! There's this council. Off wi' you. Or, first, we'll hear what my lord o' Argyll brought you here for, this day! No' just to hear verses, I swear! He'll be wanting something o' me, that's for sure."

MacCailean Mor looked less comfortable at that than the son of Great Colin should have looked. "I, ah, I believed that you would wish to hear of my friend's project, Your Grace. But, as well . . ."

"Aye, oot wi' it, man."

"Well, Sire, the word is that you will be going off to London soon, to take over Queen Elizabeth's throne. Many will be going with you from Scotland, undoubtedly. To assume high positions in that realm. Including, no doubt, my lord Duke here. So . . ."

"Aye, and *you* would be one o' them, Argyll! Is that it?"

"No, Your Grace, not so. I would stay in Scotland. I have large responsibilities here. A clan to lead. I sit on your Privy Council of Scotland. And I am Admiral of the Western Seas."

"Ooh, aye. So what do you want, man? What are you at?"

"I have served Your Grace in the field. Against the Catholic lords, the Earls of Huntly and Erroll and others. I led at Glenlivet. Forby, both my father and my grandsire were Chancellors of your realm . . ."

17

"I canna mak you Chancellor, Argyll man. The Master o' Gray acts Chancellor. Acts, mind, no' right Chancellor. But he sits in the chair, does oor Patrick!"

"Not the Chancellorship no, Sire. But the duke here is Lieutenant of the North. If he goes with you to London he can scarcely fill the office adequately. If *I* was Lieutenant of the North, as well as Admiral of the Western Seas, I could keep the north and the Highlands in order for Your Grace. For these northern Catholic earls, Huntly, Erroll and the rest, will think to rise again, with Your Highness away in England and so many Protestant lords with you – nothing more sure, I would say. I am experienced in warfare. And have large number of men at my command. I could serve you, and Scotland, well, Sire, as Lieutenant of the North."

"So that's it! I kenned there was something. Lieutenant and Admiral baith, eh? You'd be the king o' a' the Hielants, Campbell man? A right monarch on your ain!"

"Never that, Sire. *You* are my king and monarch. I would be but your faithful and leal lieutenant and servant. For I judge that you will need someone such!"

"You do? Maybe aye, maybe no. How say you, Vicky?"

The Duke of Lennox shrugged. "If I am with you in London, James, as my lord says, I cannot act Lieutenant of the North. Someone must do so. I cannot think of anyone better than my lord. Or who can field so many men as Clan Campbell and its allies."

"You reckon that they'll be needed? A' the men? Against Huntly and the rest?"

"The Highlands are largely Catholic yet. And with their Protestant monarch gone south they could see opportunity."

"I've forgiven Geordie Gordon much. And Erroll, the Constable. Aye, and Angus forby. Och, they'll no' rise again, I'm thinking. But I hear you dinna name Huntly marquis, man. I made him marquis near a year back. He has his pairts, mind, even if he is a Papist."

"Your Grace's generosity to the Gordon is well known, Sire." Argyll glanced at Lennox, for the duke's sister had been married off to Huntly as a child bride, although it was known that he and the Gordon chief were unfriends. "But Huntly is said to keep close touch with Philip of Spain, who seeks a restoration of the Catholic faith here. So . . ." He left the rest unsaid.

James, who had a soft spot for Huntly, said nothing either. The duke spoke.

"James, if the council has to be got over before the banquet planned, it would be as well to get it started, I say. There will be much discussion." Lennox, among his many other offices, was Lord President of the Council. A practical man, the king owed him much.

"Aye, but they can wait. They a' can." The monarch nodded at Argyll and Will. "You hae my permission to retire. Aye, leave us. But you, Alexander man, you can sit up near me at this repast. In case I hae words for you, some matter to speak on. See to it, Vicky. I'm no' just happy on yon patriarchal grace. Patriarchal's a gey unchancy word. The meaning's right, mind. But I dinna like patriarchal. Noo, off wi' you."

They bowed themselves out.

Past the guards, Argyll looked at the other. "I hope that you are sufficiently grateful to me, Will, for all that!" he said. "The man is next to crazed, to be sure. But he has taken to you and your rhymes. What a creature to have as Scotland's sovereign-lord! And like to be England's too, it seems. What have we done to deserve that! And now you are to sit up on the dais at this banquet. All because of a few rhyming words! Are you not pleased that I made you come?"

"As to that I am unsure, Archie. It is no wish of mine to be sitting in high places. Nor to attend any banquet. And you? Are *you* satisfied with your device? Have you gained what you wanted, by getting into the presence, think you? I knew it was for something of the sort you planned it. And so did the king! He is not so crazy as you deem him. Will you be Lieutenant of the North?"

"I *should* be that. I am the obvious choice. But Mar might seek the position, and he is James's foster-brother and crony. Why I wanted it brought up before the council meets. Fortunately Lennox has a sound head on his shoulders. And much influence with James. He could counter Mar."

"This banquet, Archie? I am not clad for any banquet of kings and lords. Have I time to ride back to Menstrie, to change into better gear? While the council meeting takes place."

"Nonsense, man. You are well enough as you are. You will be as well clad as your liege-lord, I swear! Besides, many there will be in like case. In travelling garb."

"But, sitting up on the dais. I wish that he had not ordered that. And all because of a word – patriarchal!"

"Tush, Will! You will do very well. Be thankful that you do not have to sit at the council. It will be all about the English situation, and members seeking positions and places and offices."

"Unlike MacCailean Mor!"

2

So Will had quite some time to wait there in Stirling Castle, before the banquet, while the council was in session. Many others were in the same situation, of course; and because of the outer and larger hall having to be prepared and seated for the feast, most of the company had to be disposed elsewhere, meantime, in various quarters of the great fortress, which in this cold February weather could be less than comfortable. Fortunately Argyll's position enabled him to proceed right through to the lesser hall, and he took Will with him, among the nobles.

There were still quite a number left, lords and chiefs who were not Privy Councillors, when a herald came to announce that the Secret Council, as he named it, would meet in the council chamber forthwith to await His Grace's arrival; and there followed an exodus of the great ones. The residue consoled themselves with the plentiful liquid refreshment. Will, who felt that he did not belong to this company, would have taken himself off for other premises, wishing that he could just have returned to Menstrie, but found himself approached by an acquaintance, hardly a friend but the father of a friend, two friends indeed, Sir William Erskine, Commendator of Glasgow, no less. And in this citadel of Stirling he was one to be heeded, for he was a brother of the Earl of Mar, hereditary keeper of the castle, foster-brother of the king, and one of the most important men in the realm. Sir William himself was important, although not on the Privy Council, and rich, one of those who had profited exceedingly from the Reformation, for his uncle had been Bishop of Glasgow, and the great Church lands thereof had been, as so often the case, manipulated into the hands of the bishop's family, his nephew being granted the style of Commendator of Glasgow. Sir William's son Robert had been a long-time university friend and companion of Will's; and his daughter Janet likewise, something of an accomplice, a lively character.

"I see that you are with Argyll, Menstrie," the older man said. "Your one-time pupil, eh? How does he think in this of the English crown? It seems that there is now no doubt that James will succeed to it. My cousin Mar was envoy, with the Master of Gray, to London, to settle it all with Cecil, Howard and Sackville, Elizabeth's lords. Does Argyll mean to go south with the king? Like so many?"

"I think not, sir. He has his clan to lead. And sundry Campbells not averse to stepping into the chiefly shoes! He must remain in Scotland, I think."

"Aye. Glenorchy, Ardkinglas, Lochnell and those other rogues! He has his problems with that crew. Yet hereafter so much, I fear, will be decided in London. Those who would hold sway in Scotland will have to go south for their authority. That is why this council meeting is so important."

"I can see that, yes. You, sir? Will you go to London with the king?"

"I judge not. I have much to keep me here. The Glasgow properties to see to. And if Cousin Johnny Mar goes with James, as he may well, then I would probably become keeper here, in his stead, acting keeper of Stirling Castle. So, London is not for me." Erskine tapped Will's shoulder. "Lad, who does Argyll think to be ruling Scotland, for James in London? Himself, perhaps?"

"H'mmm I do not know, sir. He has not confided in me."

"His father and grandfather were both Chancellors, chief ministers of this realm. There is no Chancellor at this present, with Maitland dead. The Master of Gray is acting it, but not having the title. James will not give him it. He does not trust Patrick Gray, I think! Huntly, our only marquis, might aspire to it. But being Catholic, that

22

would not serve. Erroll and Angus likewise. Hamilton is a sick man-ah, he has just been made a marquis also, by this strange monarch of ours, who esteems English titles. So – Argyll?"

All this was beyond Will. "I do not know," he repeated. He was not going to divulge Argyll's aim to become Lieutenant of the North. "In matters of state, my lord of Argyll will keep his own counsel."

"Yet you are close to him, Menstrie. And if he does become Chancellor, you could have influence. There will be great changes in Scotland when Elizabeth Tudor dies. We must be prepared for it."

A little bit uncomfortable now, the younger man wondered what Erskine was wanting from him, or at least from Argyll, for he seemed to be angling for something. There would be a lot of that going on hereafter, it seemed. He changed the subject.

"How is Robert, sir? And Janet. It is some time since I have seen them."

"Oh, well enough. Robert is at Balgonie. And Janet is here, with me, at Stirling. She is to act governess to the young prince, Henry Frederick. No, governess is not the word, for the boy is now nine years. Scarce lady-in-waiting either! It is my great-aunt's notion, the Countess Minnie. She is getting old, and needs a help with the lad."

Almost as though summoned by name, a commotion in the lesser hall heralded the arrival of a group of newcomers, three women, a boy and two menservants, these last carrying musical instruments, a spinet, a lute and a lyre. All turned to eye them, surprised.

And they were worth eyeing, for the hitherto entirely male company. Although the older woman was not beautiful she was as strong-featured as her reputation warranted, an able, indeed dominant female, Annabella, Countess Dowager of Mar, known as Minnie, the king's foster-mother, who had reared him here at Stirling and was now guardian of the king's elder son, Prince Henry, who now came in behind her.

23

He was a slender youngster, a deal better-looking than was his father, eager-seeming and looking about him interestedly, despite being all but a prisoner in this fortress. For, heir to the throne as he was, and apple of his father's eye, he was the victim of a feud between the king and queen. James and Anne were ever at loggerheads over something, almost everything, many sympathising with the Danish young mother in being saddled with so odd a husband, with his curious tastes. She was relegated to her dowery-house of Linlithgow Palace, half way to Edinburgh, where she was allowed to keep her younger son, the silent Charles, and the daughter Elizabeth – but not Henry, whom she was not permitted to see in case she should influence him against his sire. This extraordinary situation meant that the boy was allowed out of Stirling Castle only under guard and for no distances, for fear that the queen might have him kidnapped and taken into her own custody – this a strange reflection of James's own childhood, penned up here on this rock by the Protestant lords lest his Catholic mother, Mary Queen of Scots, should get him into *her* hands.

But it was the two young women who held at least Will Alexander's gaze, both good-looking, eminently eye-catching. One was Janet Erskine, his friend, dark, bright-eyed, vivacious, lissome and carrying herself in almost boyish fashion as befitted her tomboy reputation, a pleasing sight to see. Nevertheless, it was the other beside her who held Will's attention; for this was quite the most beautiful and spectacular woman that he had ever set eyes on, her cascade of flaming red hair, her finely sculptured features and grey-green eyes, her long swanlike neck and superb figure. He stared, biting his lip.

For, although so struck and surprised by what he saw, Will knew this young woman, or at least knew who she was. She had, in fact, been the inspiration and subject of his very first effort at poetry when, as a sixteen-year-old youth, he had seen the Lady Agnes Douglas and had been smitten with a sort of bursting admiration for the redhead, two years his junior but in all else his senior, in rank and status and prominence of family. For this was the daughter of the Earl of Morton who, as Sir William Douglas, had been gaoler of Mary Queen of Scots at Lochleven Castle, where she had been forced to sign a document of abdication in favour of the baby James held at Stirling. Sir William had succeeded the then real ruler of Scotland, the Regent Morton, his kinsman, when that Douglas had eventually been executed, not before time, by his own devised heading-machine, the Maiden, on which so many others had perished before him. Will had seen the young Lady Agnes at Castle Campbell, and had been overwhelmed by her looks and fiery red mop even then, although scarcely daring to exchange words with so wonderful a creature. He had gone straight home and striven to put into penned words what he had been unable to speak, in a headlong spate of youthful worship which he had entitled "Aurora", the roseate goddess of the dawn, his poetic baptism. He still had that paper somewhere. And now, this startling, dramatic beauty, developed into fullest loveliness, still all but overwhelmed him.

Janet had spotted him beside her father, and came over, almost running. "Will! Will Alexander!" she exclaimed. "How good! How splendid to see you! It has been long." She gripped his arm. "Here's joy! What do you here with Father?"

Collecting his thoughts and emotions, Will took her hand, to kiss it. "Janet!" was all that he could find to say.

"He is with my lord of Argyll," Sir William said, "who is at the council. We have been speaking of this of the English move."

"Folk talk of little else!" the young woman declared. "It is scarcely decent, I say, waiting for, wishing for, Queen Elizabeth to die! Why this eagerness to go to England? We have fought the English all down the ages. Why now seek to join them?"

"There is much to be gained, lass. Much of wealth and standing and position. Forby, an end to warfare."

25

"I think that I see it as Janet does," Will said. "Scotland is good enough for me!" But his eye still strayed back towards the Lady Agnes Douglas.

Perhaps Janet mistook the direction of his gaze. "Prince Henry? Now, it seems, to be in *my* charge! You know him, Will? Have met him? He is a friendly, amiable boy. Come, I will present you."

They moved over to where the prince stood with the other two women, Janet smiling on all.

"Highness, here is Will Alexander of Menstrie. Long a friend of mine. He writes poetry and balladry."

"As does my royal father," the prince declared. "Is it very difficult? He finds it so, I think. I must not speak to him when he is at it."

"It can be taxing on the wits, Highness, seeking for the right words—"

Will was interrupted. "Did I hear aright? Menstrie? Is it Will Alexander of Menstrie!" That was the beauteous Lady Agnes. "Sakes, here's a change! And a pleasure. A man of parts, and looks, now, I see! How many years since last I saw you, sir? At Argyll's house, was it not?"

Will bowed, recollected that he ought to have done so to the countess first, and repaired that omission. "Ladies, your servant. I, I am honoured. That I am remembered. Yes, it was at Castle Campbell. Many years ago. Fourteen or fifteen, perhaps! But I have not forgotten either. Nor could I!"

"And what does that mean, sir? Do I take it—?"

The Lady Agnes it was who was now interrupted, and by the older woman. "I ken o' Menstrie. Indeed once I visited it. Lang syne. Yon would be your faither I saw? A Hielantman, was he no'? Alscinder, he ca'd it, as I mind." Here was the source of the king's braid Scots.

"Alexander we call it now, Countess. MacAllister once it was. MacAllisters of Kintyre."

"Aye, before yon Campbells robbed you o' it! Was MacAllister no' a bit sept o' MacDonald?" Clearly here was a knowledgeable woman, from whom James Stewart had learned more than just his manner of speech. She had been Annabella Murray of Tullibardine, from the verge of the Highlands, herself.

"Yes, Countess. The great Clan Donald had many branches: MacIan, MacAngus or MacInnes, MacVurich, MacDonnell, MacRory, Clanranald, even the MacDougalls were originally of the name."

"Aye, and a' scoundrelly caterans, I've nae doubt! But nane sae ill as thae Campbells, heh? Who stole other lands than yours! And by words, forby, no' their swords! Words and clerks' deeds and charters! Aye, words can hae mair sway in the end than cauld steel, mind, as oor present guid liege-lord kens fine. Campbell, I'm tell't, means wry mouth. Twisted tongue, just. And weel it may! You heed that, Henry lad." And she patted the boy's head.

The Lady Agnes laughed. "I did not know that. I will have to tell Archie of Argyll when he comes paying court!"

"You dae that, lassie. But, see you, we didna come here to blether anent Hielantmen! We're here to gie this pack o' lordlings a bit enterteen, wi' music and sang, just. Afore they're a' that drunken as no' to behave themsel's at Jamie's banquet! So, ower there to the bit dais, and we'll dae what we came for."

"Do you *sing* ballads, Will Alexander, as well as write them?" Lady Agnes asked, as they followed the servitors with the instruments over to the raised platform at the end of the hall. "Prince Henry has a good voice. But we could do with a man's strains to give some weight to our female twitterings!"

"Will sings like a bird! Mind you, I will not say what kind of bird!" Janet announced.

"Call it a crow!" the man advised. "But I scarcely came here to sing."

"Nor did we. But the Lady Minnie insists. So we must suffer it. Or *these* must!"

So, on the dais, the countess at the spinet, Agnes at the lyre and Janet at the lute, the two males looking uncomfortable at first, a series of traditional ballads was rendered for the imbibing company. They started with "Red Harlaw", suitably, since Alexander, Earl of Mar, had been the victor two centuries before, and which was well received even though the ancestors of some of those present had been on the losing side, including Will's MacAllister Clan Donald forebears no doubt. This was followed by "The Song of the Outlaw Murray", which the countess asserted did not refer to her branch of the family but to the Border Murrays, an ill lot. The tune of this being better known, some of the listeners sought to join in the chorus, which helped the entertainment along. The countess did not sing, but the two young women had good voices, Janet's the more confident, while the prince's treble was a delight. Will produced a powerful tenor and quickly picked up the melodies with which he was not familiar, as they followed on with "Rose the Red and White Lily", the thirteenth-century "Auld Maitland" and "Cospatrick", by which time the company was beating time with tankards and flagons in appreciation, however little this helped the stories involved to come over.

It was Janet Erskine who then suggested that Will Alexander should give them one of his own compositions. He was less than eager to oblige, since this would have to be a solo and, at least at first, without accompaniment. So he chose "Blairlogie Glen", which had a fairly rhythmic chant, easily picked up by the instrumentalists, and he soon had his companions joining in the refrain. This being applauded enthusiastically, he gave them a very different "MacAllister's Lament" for the lost lands of Kintyre, and the price the Campbells had exacted – as well that Argyll was otherwhere – a sorrowful but stirring piece sung to a traditional West Highland cadence.

Then Prince Henry was persuaded to give them "The Lord John", which apparently appealed to his father and which he rendered most movingly, to much praise.

They finished up with Will's "The Dream of Dumyat" and the ancient and lengthy "The Well at the World's

28

End", soprano, tenor and treble voices alternating between the well-known refrain.

All voted the performance a success, and there was much congratulating of the ladies in especial, the young ones' looks remarked upon, before they retired, with the prince, to prepare themselves for the banquet. Will took the opportunity to escort them to their quarters in the separate Mar tower.

The two young women appeared to be sharing a room next to the prince's, and at their door Will was told how much they admired his ballads, the words and the singing. Janet rewarded him with a kiss, admittedly only on the cheek, and Agnes promptly followed suit, to the sniggers of the heir to the throne.

Distinctly bemused, the Laird of Menstrie found his way back to the lesser hall.

The council presumably over, a herald presently arrived to announce that all should take their seats for the banquet in the outer hall. There followed a somewhat unseemly exodus, with considerable pushing and passing, for, apart from the very lofty ones either up on the dais or immediately below it, men had to find their own seats, and few wished to be the humblest. Will, who would have been quite content at the lowermost end of one of the lengthwise tables, had to wend his self-conscious way to the head of the hall and mount the platform, by royal command. He noted that, as well as the dais table itself, throne in the centre, there were two secondary tables, shorter, set endwise a little way apart at either side, and he was much pleased and relieved to see two young women already seated at one, his friends of the ballad session. Also there were the Countess Annabella and Sir William Erskine her kinsman. Whether or not it was there that Will was intended to sit, he made straight therefor. And he received a co-operative welcome, sufficiently so for the two girls to move a little way apart on their seating to allow him to place himself between them.

"I am to be up here by His Grace's orders," he hastened to explain. "On account of poetry! We are . . . he is writing an ode to Queen Elizabeth, or about her. And asks my, my aid."

"Lord!" Agnes exclaimed. "Our crow flies high!"

"Will's verse will much enhance the king's, I vow!" Janet declared. "He is known to write. But can he make up fair poetry, Will?"

"Oh, yes, he has been inditing verse since boyhood. He has a fair ear for words, there is no doubt. But who am I to judge? There is a word now concerning him in especial at this time. The word patriarchal. He likes not the sound of it, although the meaning is right. Patriarchal Grace. 'Gloriana's Tudor Majesty passes to Stewart Patriarchal Grace.'"

"Patriarchal! What a word to get tongue round! In verse. Especially that royal tongue!" Agnes said, head ashake in dazzling, gleaming red. "Little wonder that he likes it not. Trust James Stewart to think on a word like that!"

"In fact it was *my* suggestion," Will admitted. "As I say, it has the correct meaning, but sounds . . . unwieldy."

"It means of ancient line, does it not?" Janet asked. "Of ancient family rank? Of the fathers. Would fatherly not serve?"

"H'mm. Scarcely that. Stewart *fatherly* Grace is not just what he seeks to render for the English lords he is wishing to rule. He will himself be younger than most of them – and hardly paternal!"

"Then time-honoured? Elder would be little better . . ."

"What of ancestral?" Agnes put in.

"I had thought of venerable, myself. Time-honoured is overlong to scan."

"Senior?"

"Would patrician not do?"

Their debate was interrupted. A herald came to blow a trumpet to announce the arrival of their sovereign-lord, and all must stand. The king entered by the dais door, high hat still in place, leading young Henry by the hand and followed by a distinguished train, all save the Duke of Lennox more richly dressed than himself, privy councillors, earls and prelates. James was heading, in his shambling walk, for the throne-like chair at the centre of the main dais table when he thought better of it and veered to bring the boy over to this side table, at the head of which the Countess Annabella stood, this sudden diversion, apparently unpremeditated, causing some confusion in the file of dignitaries behind.

"Here, laddie, sit you beside the Lady Minnie," he announced thickly. "Best there. Behave yoursel', mind." He eyed the others standing thereat, at which the ladies curtsied and the men bowed, his so liquid glance settling on Will Alexander.

"Aye, sae you're there, man Alexander," he said. "Hae you the right word for me?"

"I have thought on it, Sire. I, we thought of one or two." There before all, Will felt not a little embarrassed at being thus singled out by such sudden demand. "Venerable, perhaps? Or ancestral? Patrician?"

"Patrician? Na, na, patrician means noble, o' noble blood just. We need better, higher, than that. Ancestral? That'll nae dae either. A' folk's forebears are ancestral. This is a deal mair than that. What was the ither?"

"Venerable, Sire. To Stewart's venerable grace."

"Better, aye better. Venerable. But no' just right yet, man. Venerable minds you o' grey-beards and the like. I'm no' that, yet!" The monarch whinnied a laugh of sorts, then frowned. "I'll consider it. But think again, man. Think again." And, to the relief of his patiently waiting train, he left the prince at this table and ambled off to the long, main board, to ease himself into the chair.

Argyll, a few paces behind, lifted an eyebrow at Will as he passed. And just behind him, quite the most handsome man in all that assembly looked thoughtfully from Will to his two companions as he strolled on.

The Lady Agnes tapped Will's arm. "Patrick, Master of Gray," she said. "Said to be the handsomest man in Christendom! And one of the cleverest. How think you?"

"He is good-looking, yes. I have heard of him, to be sure. But never before seen him. Argyll says that he is too clever altogether!"

"My father names him the most able rogue in Scotland," Janet observed. "Says that he it is who has contrived that the king will succeed Queen Elizabeth, when she was considering another woman, Arabella Stewart."

The other privy councillors ranged themselves in order of precedence right and left of the king's seat, while the clerics went over to the other side table.

Now all could sit.

Young Henry, Duke of Rothesay, to give him his due title, grinned at Will and squeezed in between the countess and Sir William Erskine, across the board from Will and the younger women.

"I told him about our singing," he called over, and was shushed to silence by the Lady Minnie as the Archbishop of St Andrews rose to say grace before meat, at some length, with especial reference to the honour of the royal presence.

With the servitors hastening in with the steaming viands, talk resumed. Low-voiced, in the circumstances, Will mentioned to the companions whom many men there must be envying him, that he noted that the prince, in the care of the countess as he might be, was not apparently being reared to talk in the braid Scots which his father favoured. To which Janet answered, with a little laugh, that this was the king's sole concession to his wife. Anne, being Danish, had sufficient difficulty in learning and speaking English without having to cope with the Scots Doric dialect.

"Poor Anne!" Agnes sympathised, in something of a whisper. "She must wonder at her fate, at being Queen of Scotland, wed to so odd a husband. And soon, it seems, to become Queen of England also. God be praised that such is never like to come to us!"

"You mean never wed a poet?" Janet asked.

"There are poets and poets!"

Will looked from one to the other, but said nothing.

"I am surprised that Queen Anne did gain that concession," Janet went on. "In the matter of words. Since she lost the first. His name."

"Name? What mean you?" Will wondered.

"You have not heard of this, Will? Of young Henry's name? His christening. The king, wishing to please Elizabeth Tudor, to help forward his eventual claim to her throne, wanted his heir named Henry, after *her* father, Henry the Eighth, of ill fame. But Anne wanted him called after her own father, King Frederick of Denmark. Neither would give way. Even at the font, in the Chapel Royal here, they fought over it, for Anne has a will of her own. She told Bishop Cunningham of Aberdeen that he was to christen the child Frederick Henry, while the king insisted on Henry Frederick. The poor bishop was much concerned. But the king was the king, and he muttered Henry Frederick, and splashed the holy water. And then, with another splash, he named him Frederick Henry! So our Duke of Rothesay was christened twice, Henry Frederick and Frederick Henry. Think you that has ever happened to anyone else?"

"I had not heard that. He is always called Prince Henry."

"Here, yes. But if he was at Linlithgow Palace he would be Prince Frederick! One reason, I think, why the king keeps him from her."

"Does the boy miss his mother, think you?" Agnes asked.

"I know not. Possibly he does not, in truth. For he scarcely knows her. The countess has always acted not so much mother as grandmother. He is fond of her. Nor do his brother and sister mean aught to him. He never sees them. It is a strange family, indeed."

"With James as its father, it could hardly be otherwise," Agnes asserted. "And with his grandsire too."

"You mean the Lord Darnley?"

"No, I mean Davie Rizzio! My father's kinsman, the previous Earl of Morton, who was regent, always said that Darnley could not father a bairn! And that Rizzio, Queen Mary's Italian secretary, was James's father. Which would account for much."

"Illegitimate!"

This intriguing conversation was interrupted partway through the venison course by the said doubtfully fathered character himself banging on the table with his goblet and turning in his chair to jab a finger towards the lesser table, and clearly at Will Alexander. Rising, and hastily seeking to swallow the meat in his mouth, that man made his way across the platform, to the surprised stares of all.

Behind the king's chair, with Lennox on the right and Mar on the left, Will stooped low. "Yes, Sire?" he said.

"Aye. See you, I'm nae mair content wi' venerable than I am wi' patrician, man. I'm thinking on primal, just. Primal would scan. And it's simple, but right telling. Primal's the first, aye, first of all. Taks the mind back to the beginning o' a' things. How deem you primal, man Alexander? Stewart primal grace?"

"Good, Sire, good! Primal sounds well. And means well. Yes, I like that. Primal grace."

Leaning over the royal shoulder, Will had to swallow more than venison. For the smell of unwashed humanity was strong. James was known to look on washing with disfavour, asserting that water was bad for the human frame, taken externally or internally – perhaps another reason for the queen's disenchantment with her spouse.

Another voice spoke up, this from Lennox's right, melodious, all but amused. "If I heard aright, the problem is to do with ancient Stewart grace? Since we all so revere you, Sire, why not revered? Revered Stewart grace?" That was the Master of Gray. Was there something of mockery in that seemingly casual suggestion?

"When I require your advice, Patrick Gray, I'll ask for it!" the king jerked.

34

That was acknowledged by a silvery laugh.

"Awa', you, Alexander. I dinna think you'll better primal. Awa'."

Thankfully Will returned to company considerably more to his taste.

"The highly favoured one!" Janet remarked. "How does it feel to have become suddenly so close to our sovereign-lord?"

"I think I would prefer not to be quite so close! However, that will be the end of it, I judge. He seems happy with the word primal." He nodded. "That Master of Gray? Does the king mislike him? He spoke sourly to him."

"My father says that he does not trust him," Agnes declared.

"Yet he makes him Chancellor of the realm."

"Only *acting* Chancellor! The beauteous Patrick's only sure office is Master of the Wardrobe."

"I have heard that he seeks no other than that," Janet added. "That he desires freedom of action. Only to have the responsibilities which he chooses to assume. Master of the Royal Wardrobe gives him access to the king whenever he so desires, but does not saddle him with unwanted duties. He is as clever as he is handsome, that one."

"You sound admiring?" Agnes suggested. "But then, who would be otherwise!"

"You are not?"

"I would be wary of that one! As is our James. And so says my father, who went with him to London as envoy over this of Elizabeth Tudor. He believes that Master Patrick has set his eyes on high position in England. That is why he has worked hard for this accession for the king. Scotland is too small for the Master of the Wardrobe! My father calls him the Machiavelli of this realm!"

Will wagged his head over all this. "I am unversed in the affairs of state, for which I thank my Maker!" he said. "As for much else."

"Hear him!" That was Agnes. "Our poet. Could a poet be an innocent?" And she tapped his arm.

35

Janet did not comment.

The repast continued, course succeeding course, their host, Mar, or at least his mother, having excelled themselves for the occasion, which might well be the last such before great change overtook Scotland and its ruling families. Suitable liquor to go with the meats and sweets was equally plentiful, and it became evident that it was having its effect on at least some of the company, no doubt the long wait and refreshment, while the council had been sitting, contributing. Despite the royal presence the occasion was becoming ever more noisy, and behaviour, especially down towards the lower end of the hall, verging on the rowdy. The king was something of a drinking man himself, able to imbibe copiously but never seen drunken; but presently, while not making any move to order quiet, he did turn again to look towards the lesser side table, and beckon.

Will, assuming that more poetry was to be discussed, groaned internally, but dutifully rose and went over to the monarch.

"Och, it's you again, is it," James said, looking up, so evidently it had not been for him that the signal was intended. "But you'll dae. Hae them tak the laddie to his bed – Henry. It's getting ower noyous here, for him. There's them as canna hud their drink! Off to his bed wi' him. The women tae hae my permission to retire. Awa'." And a dismissive hand was waved.

Will went back to announce the royal command to the countess, who nodded and said that it was not before time. She stood and beckoned to Janet, who rose and came over, Agnes Douglas electing to do the same. Young Henry was more reluctant, but did as he was told when Janet took him by the hand.

Will decided that, present company departing, he would be as well to do the same himself, whether the royal dismissal included him or not. The banqueters could do without him, that was for sure. So the three women, the boy and the man bowed to the back of their liege-lord and made their exit.

Over at the Mar tower, when the young women went upstairs with the prince, Will continued to accompany them, none seeming to object. This time, deliberately or otherwise, Janet took Henry to his own room first, with instructions to wash well in the warm water which was there provided, and to get to bed quickly. With goodnights from all three, he had his door shut on him.

Opening the other door, Janet turned to Will. "I think, since there are the two of us, it would not be unseemly if you were to come in for a minute or so, Will? How say you, Agnes?"

"To be sure. If you judge that we will be . . . safe!" Laughter.

Nothing loth, the man followed them in.

A fire blazed in the lamplit chamber, a tub of steaming water nearby. There was a great double bed, canopied – all the palace beds were thus covered, for James had a horror of bats' droppings, however few bats were likely to gain access to the rooms – so evidently the young women were sharing a bed. There was a flagon of wine on the bedside table, and two cups – only two.

"Possibly we have all had sufficient wine for one night," Janet observed, going over to this table. "But just a sip, perhaps? For good company's sake. That is, if Will does not object to drinking from my cup?"

"So long as your lips grace it first!" he declared gallantly.

"Mine also," Agnes said. "Be not so greedy, Janet!"

Thus honoured, the man bowed to each, while Janet filled the wine-cups and moved over to the fireside with them.

With the firelight making a flickering, gleaming glory of Agnes's flaming head of hair, they sipped, smiled at each other, and in fact passed the two cups round, and round again, a peculiarly pleasing and at the same time unsettling experience for the man, torn between varying and conflicting emotions with these two, in so intimate a setting. They said little, but eyes were busy as well as lips. They took their time, and emptied both cups.

Eventually Will felt that he must make the move, however unwillingly. "I am loth to leave you, leave you both," he said. "But needs must, I fear. You will be weary, and have had a sufficiency of me for one night! Forby, I have to ride back six miles to Menstrie."

"You do not bide in this castle tonight?" Agnes asked. "Near us?"

"No. I fear that it will be packed full, with all these lofty visitors. Even you share a bed, I see. And, and bliss, I swear!" That was as far as he might go.

"Aha, there speaks our poet!"

"If go you must, you take our kinder thoughts with you," Janet said.

"Kinder?"

"Kindest!" she amended, and reached up to kiss him, this time full on the lips.

He was savouring that when he found the other to be embracing him also, and her kiss was not only slightly the longer, but her lips opened and stirred beneath his own.

Bemused, he did not release her hurriedly – until he saw Janet eyeing them both consideringly. He drew back.

"I, I thank you. Thank you both. For kind, for kindest thoughts. And . . . all else. I shall not forget it. Ever. I may even celebrate this night in my poor verse. However inadequately."

"Do that."

"We shall await it, Will."

They both accompanied him to the door to say their goodnights, with pats and squeezes. He jerked himself away from them almost roughly and was off downstairs in a hurry; he had to, in the state he was in, a man much affected.

Was he over much so? he wondered, as he rode home through the night. More than there was cause to be? He was no mere impressionable youth any more. Was it the poet in him? Too much of feeling, challenge, beauty, emotion? The price he had to pay?

This of poetry. He had meant what he had said back there in the bedroom. He would put this evening into verse. For himself rather than for the others, he thought. And more than that. He would finish his lengthy collection, his hundred poems, and dedicate it all as he had done his very first effort at rhyme, to Aurora of the flaming hair, the rosy dawn – Aurora! He had decided that as Agnes's lips had moved under his in yonder bedchamber. But this night's verse he would entitle "To Janet".

He had the first few stanzas compiled before ever he reached Menstrie.

3

It was only two afternoons later that Will had visitors at Menstrie Castle, quite a visitation indeed, for Henry, Duke of Rothesay was not permitted to ride any distance from Stirling Castle, by the king's command, without an escort of armed retainers of the royal guard, this in case of kidnapping. James himself had been kidnapped, as a boy, more than once, and this had much affected him – even though it was not his mother who had been responsible, as was in this case his fear. Janet Erskine brought the boy.

She was looking happy, flushed with the cold February riding, and very attractive, as she reined up where Will was engaged in repairing a fence to prevent his cattle-beasts falling down an undercut bank into a burn draining from the nearby hillsides.

"Ha, the muse gives place to the mallet!" she greeted him. "How fares the king's collaborator?"

"Sufficiently well – but the better for seeing you! And His Highness."

"You will be seeing a deal more of His Highness, Will. And possibly even of my poor self! By royal command." She dismounted. "His Grace desires that you become tutor to the prince here. How say you to that?"

Will blinked. "Tutor? Me!" He swallowed. "Do I hear aright? Tutor? You, you are not cozening me, girl?"

"I am not. Am I, Henry?"

The boy, grinning, dismounted also. "It is so, yes. My father says it. He says that I need a man to tutor me now. That I am old enough for that." He made a face at Janet. "Not just women! A man. You."

"But, but . . ." Will stared from one to the other. "How

40

can this be? The king – His Grace scarcely knows me! Only once has met me, seen me. I am but a small laird . . ."

"Clearly he thinks well of you, Will. And he will know that you were tutor to Argyll," Janet said, "when he was the Lord Lorne."

"That was different. I was vassal to his father, old Argyll. But to the prince, Duke of Rothesay, heir to the throne!"

"Perhaps it is because you are a poet, and being a poet himself, he approves of poets."

"Will you teach *me* to write poetry?" Henry asked.

Wagging his head, the man took up his mallet. "Come. Come within." He waved the escorting group towards the courtyard at the side of the small castle. "Here is a wonder! As wonder I must!"

"You cannot refuse, Will. It is a royal command, no mere suggestion."

"But I have this Menstrie to see to. The house, the lands, the folk. I am not rich, to pay others to do it. And am not used to courts."

"No doubt His Grace will make some . . . provision. And Stirling is nearby."

"I could come and live here," the boy said. "I like it here. Those high hills. And the river . . ."

"I think not, Henry," Janet said. "Your father requires that you dwell secure in Stirling Castle. But we will come here often." She glanced at Will, as they began to lead their mounts towards the castle door.

"I would not be expected to dwell at Stirling?" he asked.

"As to that, I do not know. The Lady Minnie only told me to come and inform you of the king's command. He left yesterday for Edinburgh. What else he ordered you will have to learn from her. So you will have to come and see her."

"What will you teach me?" Henry asked. "I do not like the Latin. Nor the French. My father says that I should learn of the ancient Greeks. Why? Why these old things?

Of dead people. I would much liefer learn of hawking and hunting, of the bow and arrow. Of running races. Aye, and singing more ballads. Ballads of fighting and battles and slaying the English."

"Hush you, Henry!" Janet chided. "The English are to be our friends now. Your royal father, we believe, will soon be King of England as well as of Scotland. In which case you will be going to England, no doubt."

"I do not want to go to England. I *will* not go!"

"I think that the first thing that William Alexander will have to teach you is to do what you are told by your elders, Henry!"

"I do not know why my father wants to go to England. It is much better here."

Will sought to improve the atmosphere by changing the subject, as he led the way into the tall L-shaped tower-house with its angle-turrets and steep crowstepped-gabled roofs. "I have written a little piece about two nights ago," he told Janet. "As I said then that I might. Just a few lines. For you! Come into the withdrawing-room. There is a fire there. Some wine and cakes. Honey wine for His Highness."

Will had lived alone at Menstrie since he had come back from his lengthy tour of the Continent with Argyll, and returning, had found his father recently dead. He was an only child, his mother long departed. Perhaps this solitude had been a factor in his poetic development.

In the private withdrawing-room off the hall on the first floor, he rang a bell to summon his motherly housekeeper, Meg Graham, who in fact required little summoning, having observed their arrival from the downstairs kitchen, and was ready to produce the required refreshment. While they waited, Will piled logs on the fire, sat his visitors down, and went to a desk to produce a paper which he handed to Janet.

"My apologies for the quality of this," he told her. "I rushed it off, most of it on the way home when I left

42

you, with the urge on me. No doubt I may improve on it hereafter – if it is worth the improving."

She took the paper, and read, after glancing up at him, her eyes questioning.

TO JANET

You womankind make men so blind,
　　With beauty, art and excellence.
You tantalise us with your eyes
　　And empty our significance.

You steal the heart, our wits depart,
　　For sight of you we yearn;
Your persons far outwith compare
　　Our dreams of longing burn.

When one of you to man extends
　　Her glance, her lips, her hand;
How can he then resist the urge
　　As manhood he defends?

But if perchance there's two of you
　　What rescue can he crave?
He's lost, he's lost, in helpless bliss
　　His very soul to save.

Oh, womankind of grace refined
　　When man you eye and mindest;
Have mercy when there's two of you
　　And treat him at your kindest.

"Will!" she cried. "This, this is brilliant! How did you do it? Sakes, here is a wonder! Wicked, mind you! Women are not so unkind as this – not all of us, leastways. Some may be. Nor men so feeble! But it is a marvel. And you composed it in the saddle as you rode here? That is extraordinary. You must have felt very strongly to do that?"

"Could I feel otherwise? Leaving the pair of you in that bedchamber. Two so lovely and cruelly kind women!"

"Cruel? Surely not! Kind, I know not. But cruel, no. Why say you that?"

"Do not tell me that you are so innocent! That you do not know how you can arouse a man. With your eyes, your lips, your bodies . . ." He glanced at the boy sitting there, and coughed. "A woman can tempt. Eve was only the first! And *two* women!"

"I did not mean aught like that, Will. I cannot speak for Agnes Douglas. But . . ."

"You cannot be unaware of your powers, girl!"

"What powers?" Henry put in, interestedly. "Do women have power that men do not have? I do not think so. Men are much stronger."

"Power of a different sort, Highness. They can sway, persuade men to act, to do what they seek. You will discover!"

"You will teach me about that, then? And, and the hurlyhackit? I want to do hurlyhackit. It is played at Stirling, they say. But none has showed me how. You know of it?"

"Oh, yes. It is a game, a sport. Sliding down the hill on a kind of slype or sled. Made out of a cow's skull and horns. A very rough sport, Highness."

"I want to do it. No one has shown me."

"Well, that may not be what your royal father requires of me! But we shall see . . ."

"So you will come to see the countess, Will? She will tell you fully what are the king's wishes – which I think will hardly include hurlyhackit! I wish that we could stay with you now, at this your fireside. But the daylight goes so soon, and I have to have Henry back before dark, by order!"

"To be sure. Is the Lady Agnes still at the castle?"

"No. She went with her father, with the king, to Edinburgh. She will be biding at the Morton house of Dalkeith, I think. Does that distress you?"

"Distress? No. Think you that it would?" He did not wait for a reply to that. "Yes, I will come to Stirling to see the countess. In a day or two. Meanwhile, I will ride with you as far as the Causewayhead."

So they all trotted together the four miles to the start of the long causeway across the Forth's marshland leading to Stirling Bridge, in the gloaming. Will asked whether Janet, who had her little poem tucked into her bodice, had decided on what she was to be called now, since the prince's governess sounded wrong and lady-in-waiting was scarcely suitable for a boy. She said that lady-attendant was the countess's suggestion. That sounded apt enough.

Goodbyes were said under the steep crags from which William Wallace had directed his famous victory, always a preoccupation of Will's. He turned to ride back, with something of another preoccupation on his mind: this of Janet asking him whether Agnes Douglas's departure distressed him. Had he given that impression? Did it, in fact? Were his feelings, his strange admixture of feelings, his torn-two-ways emotions, so evident? These two women! Janet, his old friend since childhood, of whom he had always been more than fond and whom he had all but taken for granted; and Agnes, whose extraordinary beauty had so impressed him as a youth, and now almost overwhelmed him, swept perhaps the poet in him off his feet? Aurora! Out of reach? Despite those lips moving and opening beneath his! As well, it might be?

Even as he mulled it over, his mind was beginning to compose more words, a sequence of words, rhyming, telling words, to put his dilemma into verse.

Two days later, then, Will Alexander presented himself at Stirling Castle again, seeking the countess dowager. It was noteworthy that this was who ruled the great royal citadel. Her son was hereditary keeper thereof, as her husband had been, but he was apt to be away with the king, his foster-brother, and although he had a wife and children, he kept them at Alloa Tower nine miles away, this despite her lofty lineage, for she was the sister of the

Duke of Lennox; so his formidable mother was left in charge.

The Lady Minnie, so-called because the infant king had named her that, Annabella being too much for his difficult tongue, received Will with a sort of stern civility.

"So, young man, you have come! Why the king deems you suitable for his son's tutoring, I do not know, ask, nor question. But it is a notable honour, you will realise?" That was part question, part warning.

"I esteem it so, Countess, although I by no means sought it. Indeed, I would have preferred . . . otherwise."

"You say that! Why?"

"I like the prince well, lady. And Janet Erskine, his attendant, is an old friend. But I have my property to manage and none other to see to it. And I am no courtier."

"You will learn, then – as well as teach! And Menstrie is no great lairdship demanding much attention. So you will not allow such distraction to interfere with your duties here."

"I am still my own master, Countess. I could refuse this appointment."

"You are not and could not! King James is your master, master of us all. And this is his royal command." She eyed him keenly. "You mislike this duty? You, who tutored Argyll. This of the heir to the throne should be to your benefit. What have you against the prince?"

"Nothing. He seems to be a fine lad. It is not that. But I have my own life to live, and had not thought to live it thus!"

"Then you should not have commended yourself to His Grace, as you seem to have done, young man! So, to your duties. The king wants Henry schooled in all subjects suitable for a prince, the clerkly ones but not only these. How he should carry himself before men. Sports. To know the Scriptures. To esteem the philosophers and the ancient law-givers, since one day he will himself be a law-giver. Speech, and the use of words, well chosen.

46

James judges you effective in that – why he chose you. That, he hopes, will induce a love of poesy in the boy. Myself, I do not esteem verses so highly, but then, I am a mere woman!"

"Women can be poems in themselves, Countess!"

"Do not cozen *me*, Menstrie! I am not one of your light hizzies, who twitch their skirts for you! Like those two who sang with you – and more than sang, perchance? So, you will commence your task at the soonest. And I will look to see results in the boy."

"I will do my best. Since it seems that I must. But, Countess, I hope that it will not be necessary for me to lodge here in this castle? Menstrie is not an hour's ride away. And I have much to see to there."

"M'mm. Sometimes you should bide here, I think. But mostly it will serve. If you spend most of the days with Henry. You will ride abroad in the country around with him, to be sure, teaching him sporting skulls. So far he has had little or nothing of that. So you can do it from your own Menstrie. But always under sure guard, see you – His Grace insists on that. He fears that the prince may be the object of attack. To get him into wrong hands! You understand?"

"You mean, the queen? That she may seek to take him into her care? *Her* son, as well as the king's."

"We shall leave that. It is not for others to judge in this. Now, be off with you. To Prince Henry. I will be watching your progress, and his, with some heed."

Thus warned, he took his leave.

Will heard his charge before he actually saw him, the lad's treble coming down the stairs of the Mar tower to him, accompanied by the notes of a lute. Whatever the duties of a lady-attendant to a young prince, singing practice appeared to be one. Knocking at the door of the boy's apartments, he entered.

There proved to be two chambers here, intercommunicating, the further one the bedroom. In the first, an anteroom, Janet sat playing, while the prince paced

47

about singing. Their smiles of welcome were in marked contrast to the Lady Minnie's reception.

The young woman rose and came to him hands outstretched, and in the presence of the boy she received a chaste kiss on the cheek. Henry laughed.

"Have you come to teach me hurlyhackit?" he demanded.

"That is the least of my duties," Will said. "I am told that you are to be taught all the clerkly subjects, the humanities, the philosophies, the ancients' wisdom, the Scriptures and more. Hurlyhackit was not mentioned, Highness!"

The lad's face fell. "Must I learn all that?"

"Oh, and more. But some sport and games also, it seems. Even poetry!"

"Poetry! I do not greatly like poetry. My father sometimes reads me his poetry. So many big words! But, sport! Hurlyhackit is sport, is it not? What does it mean? It is a strange word, is it not?"

"He keeps asking me that, Will," Janet said. "I cannot tell him."

"Strange, yes. I have never considered it. But hawkie or hackit means a cow, a white-faced cow. And hurly will just refer to hurtling down a slope, I suppose. So that would make sense, no?"

"Will you please show me, Master Will? I want to see hurlyhackit. Do it. No one has done it for me."

Recognising that this was going to be a consistent plea which was not going to go away, Will looked at Janet, who shrugged. He nodded.

"Very well. Since I have not started your tutoring yet, Highness, we might go and look into this matter now. If we can find the sleds, the cows' skulls. I did this once, here, many years ago."

"I think, Will, that you should stop calling the prince Highness, now that you are to be so close. Name him Henry, as I do."

"Yes, Master Will. Highness is a silly word, I think. I do not feel high, at all! I do not think grace is very good either. My father is called that, but has not much of grace, has he?"

"M'mm. I think that we had better not make judgments on that, Henry! A king can be gracious without being graceful. Come, we will go and see if we can find someone to tell us where they keep the skulls, the hackits. You will need a cloak for the cold; you also, Janet . . ."

The young woman, doubtfully, came along.

Will led the way up to the highest north-east corner of the rock-top where, instead of the sheer crags of most of its faces, there was a steep grassy slope, scarcely smooth or unbroken, dropping down for over one hundred feet to a green terrace, on which two or three cows grazed, the descent thereafter continuing as naked rock to normal ground level.

"That, down there, where the cows are, is called Ballengeich," Henry announced. "My great-grandsire was sometimes called the Gudeman of Ballengeich. I do not know why."

"That was because King James the Fifth used to go out among his ordinary people, not saying that he was the king but acting as the gudeman, or farmer, of Ballengeich, the terrace down there, his very small farm. He much liked hurlyhackit, it is said," Will explained.

At least there was no problem in finding the cows' heads for sleds, for there was only the one building near the slope-lip, a shed, its door open, and inside among bales of hay, milk buckets and the like, was a heap of horned skulls, discoloured and caked with dried mud, no lower jawbones attached and the upper jaws smoothed off to act as runners. Excited at the sight, the prince ran to grab one, but had difficulty in dragging it clear, the curling horns catching in others.

"There is not much space to sit on one of those!" Janet observed.

"No. That is part of the challenge. To remain seated on that, clutching the two horns, while bumping down over that rough hillside," Will agreed.

49

"Indeed! Then I, for one, will not attempt it!"

"I will!" the boy exclaimed. "Now! Can we do it now?"

"Well, you could try first on a small slope. There is a place there. You have to guide it with your legs and feet. That is not easy. Going fast, over uneven ground, it can even be dangerous. You could injure yourself, break an ankle or the like. You have your legs stretched out, in front. See, I will show you."

They dragged two of the skulls over to the edge of the slope, seeking a spot where it was less steep and where there was only a short drop before some gorse bushes broke the descent at a ledge.

"Sit you like this," Will demonstrated, crouching down on one of the skulls, legs on either side, and gripping the horns. "You have to sit well forward. Then push yourself on with your heels. I will go down to those bushes. Do not follow me. I will come up again, and start you. The grass is damp in this weather, slippery. The danger is if you slew to one side or the other. Then you can go awry, and off down where you do not want to go, and over ledges and falls. It takes skill and care. I have not done it, myself, for years."

"Should you now?" Janet asked.

"I have chosen a safe place, I think. How do you find your seat, Henry?"

"There is not much room."

"No. So watch how I start. And how I steer it – or try to!"

Edging his unwieldy seat over the lip of the slope, using both heels and bottom to propel the thing, Will had to push and manoeuvre his odd vehicle for a few yards down before suddenly it took off and went slithering and quickly gathering speed in a far-from-straight course thanks to the bumps and hollows of the uneven ground, having to be guided, if that was the word, nudged this way and that by busy heels and even the outstretched hand sometimes. In a zigzagging and erratic progress, skull and rider bucketed towards those bushes – and being gorse, jagged whins, they were not the most comfortable barrier to crash into; but it was that or hurtling on right down the hill to the Ballengeich terrace, in headlong career.

Will did crash into the prickly bushes, and came to a halt, pitching forward into those thorns. Picking himself up gingerly, he decided that apart from a few scratches he was undamaged. But was this an advisable start for his tutoring of the heir to the throne? What would King James say? But at least it would give Henry warning that hurlyhackit was a sport to be taken heedfully, and, so long as he aimed for these bushes, there was no real danger.

Will dragged his slype back up the hill.

"I do not think much of that for an enjoyment!" Janet commented. "Do you judge it wise to let the prince try it?"

"I will, I *will*!" the boy cried, already astride his skull. "That was splendid! Can I go now, Master Will?"

"Wait you, I think that I had better come with you, for this first time. Alongside. In case you do not find it easy to steer." And to Janet, "On this small slope he will come to no harm, other than a bruise or two and some scratches. And it will teach him the problems of it, before he tries the longer run. If so he wishes to continue with hurlyhackit!"

So Will set the two skulls side by side, close, where he could grab one of the boy's horns if necessary, and sat.

"Now, we go together. Try to keep beside me. If your slype gets out of your control, goes off down in the wrong direction, throw yourself off it. Best if we try to keep together. And try to make for the middle of those bushes. At first it will be difficult to get amove. But once it starts to slide it will go quite fast. But not always straight. Are you ready?"

Henry nodded, knuckles white as he gripped his horns tensely.

They edged forward, the boy getting a little ahead, probably because he was lighter. Will reached out to restrain him, to keep alongside. Once the slope began to take over, however, it was the man's skull which tended to move the faster, and he had to reach for one of the other's horns to hold them together, which had the effect of jerking the prince's skull over a little so that they collided, legs and feet in contact. But at least they kept side by side thus, as they lurched downwards at speed, the boy yelling excitedly.

That is until, with Will steering less expertly than when alone, they surged over to a little ledge not encountered on the previous descent, with a small drop beyond. This was only a foot or so, but sufficient to wrench the pair apart. Not only that but to overturn Will's slype and throw him bodily off, losing his grip of the other horn in the process.

They both continued with their descent, willy-nilly, the man rolling over and over, the boy shouting but still astride his difficult mount.

It was not far to those gorse bushes. Henry crashed into them at speed, and was thrown headlong. Will managed to halt his tumbling career before reaching the whins, although his skull preceded him, bounding on and landing up beside the other.

When he picked himself up, the man found his charge pushing out of the bushes and grinning triumphantly, clearly unhurt and very proud of himself.

"I won! I won!" Henry cried. "I was first. And you fell off!"

"Aye, you are the clever one! Mind, we went a little way off-course. But you hung on well. Better than I did! Are you much scratched and jagged?"

"No. Nothing." The prince licked some blood off the back of one hand. "That was good. We will do it again."

"Well, once more perhaps. It will be cold for Janet, standing up there in the wind." They pulled their two skulls out of the thicket, to drag them uphill again.

The young woman was critical of their performance.

"Of all the fool pastimes!" she greeted them. "If King James the Fifth found that to his taste, then small wonder that he is considered to have been an odd monarch! Are either of you hurt?"

"Only in my pride!" Will said. "To have fallen off. Did not Henry do well to stay on?"

"It depends what you mean by well!"

"I will do still better this time."

"You are not going to do that again?"

"Just once more," Will said. "To ensure that he has the rights of it. The steering, with hands and feet and bottom. The bumps make that difficult. We went over a shelf there, which we ought not to have done. That sill. Went off course. Try again, to better that."

This time they started alongside again but not so close together, with no reaching out to each other. And although, once started, their courses diverged somewhat, with the man going the faster because of his weight, they both kept straighter courses. Once Henry was nearly off, but recovered his seat. By digging in his heels as he neared the bushes, Will managed to avoid a headlong crash therein, although he slewed round sideways. This had the result of the boy landing right on top of him, in a sprawl of arms, legs and horns, with gasps and yelps. But no damage was done, and the mirth unlimited.

Up at the crest again, Henry was urgent that Janet should have a try at this wonderful sport; but both his elders decided otherwise, Will saying that this was enough for the first day, and the woman declaring that she had no desire to be as daft as her two companions. So the skulls were put back into the shed, Henry eliciting a promise that they would have another essay at it, and very soon – on condition, as Will promised, that the boy did not attempt it on his own.

They returned to the Mar tower, the prince chattering without cease, asserting that he would tell the Lady Minnie all about it, although Janet suggested that this might be inadvisable.

After refreshment, Will took his leave, saying that he would come back in two days' time to start with his tutoring.

Unfortunately or otherwise, the boy insisted on accompanying the other two down to the stableyard and Will's horse, so that the farewell kissing had to be as discreet as on arrival. They would have to get this better arranged.

The man rode home to Menstrie wondering what life now had in store for him.

4

So commenced a new stage in Will Alexander's affairs and development, for development it proved to be, with much to be learned as well as taught, new experiences to be assimilated and to cope with, new outlooks and opportunities opening. Although he had tutored Argyll, it had never been as a small boy, and one next in line to a throne. Nor had he ever had to act under the eagle eye of such as the Countess Annabella, and much of the time confined within a rock-top fortress. And, devoid of sisters as well as brothers, never had he been so consistently in the company of a young woman, and a very attractive one, however friendly he and she had been in the past, off and on – for of course Janet was with young Henry most of the time, and penned up in the citadel likewise, with old Lady Minnie the only other well-born female with whom to associate, so that she tended to be much in Will's and his charge's company. Nor did she seek to hide her fondness for them both. All of which had its impact on the man.

They were not always confined within walls, of course, despite the wintry weather, for Will felt strongly that the boy must get out and about, work off his youthful energies, learn sporting pursuits – other than just hurlyhackit – meet people and learn to play the prince. So it was not all study and book-learning, writing and reciting, question and answer. There was much riding abroad, even some hill-climbing in the nearby Ochils, although this last had to be on a very modest scale until the better weather and longer days made it practical. It was a pity that always they had to have the armed escort with them; but with no

55

least hint of interception or interference developing, from Linlithgow or elsewhere, Will did manage to convince the countess that a mere couple of the royal guard was sufficient protection; and he was able to select two friendly and cheerful young men, who in fact became quite good companions and did not obtrude too much on the trio.

One of their favourite rides was to Cardross Castle, islanded in the great Flanders Moss west of Stirling. This was a house belonging to John, Earl of Mar, long an Erskine place, but lent by him to his kinsman Sir William, Janet's father, as being considerably more conveniently placed towards Stirling than was the Commendator's House of Glasgow, which was his own property. Here, near the foot of the Loch of Menteith, was where Janet had grown up, and long known to Will. Some dozen miles away, it made a suitable day's outing, there and back; and Lady Erskine, Janet's mother, like her brother and sister, were always glad to see them; while the Flanders Moss area itself, that vast swampy wilderness between Lowlands and Highlands, scrub forest, lost lochans and hidden tracks, always intrigued the prince, with red and roe deer, otters, badgers, foxes, even the occasional wolf and wild boar to be glimpsed, the last watched out for warily.

In all this, Will's association with Janet inevitably grew very close, so that they became notably intimate, enjoying each other's company and such physical encounters as were possible in the circumstances, and coming to look on themselves as in a kind of partnership. And yet, and yet, always at the back of the man's mind was Agnes Douglas, the lovely Aurora, whose beauteous looks had put their own spell upon him long ago and which recent contact had done nothing to dissipate. Will, almost guiltily, still sought to communicate with her in his own fashion, although they saw nothing of her at Stirling, through his poetry, writing her, or his vision of her, into sonnet after sonnet other than his original offering, improved and polished as even this was, and all without actually naming her or identifying her to anyone but himself, brilliant, glowing womanhood personified. It made a strange dichotomy in him, two women competing for heart and mind of a man who was not of a promiscuous or devious nature.

Thus the winter months passed into a belated spring, until one day at the end of March, when the three of them were returning from hurlyhackit, now using the full hillside slope with fine expertise, even Janet having ventured the upper trial slope, they found a messenger from Edinburgh's Holyroodhouse Palace with the countess dowager, with the news. Elizabeth Tudor was dead, at last, James had been declared by the English Houses of Parliament to be her lawful successor, and he would be going south to take over his new throne at the soonest. All was to be changed. History for the two kingdoms would never be the same.

The messenger, sent by the king and the Earl of Mar, brought intriguing details. Elizabeth had died, after fighting this life's extinction for a full week, on 24th March. Sir Robert Carey, youngest son of one of her prominent statesmen, Lord Hunsdon, given the long-awaited signal by his sister, Lady Scrope, throwing a ring to him from a window of Richmond Palace, had ridden forthwith for Scotland, to be the first with the news for the new monarch, reaching there in three days of punishing horsemanship and killing three mounts in the process, to find James in his bed; and on receipt of the long-awaited tidings, being created therewith a Gentleman of the Royal Bedchamber and promised the viscountcy of Falkland for his pains. The new double monarch was reportedly getting packed and ready to be on his way south at the earliest, to ensure that no other would-be occupant of the throne sought to make an attempt on it in his absence. He would be off at the beginning of April, with a large company, but not including his wife and family. They were to come on later, when sent for.

Will and Janet, of course, wondered about their own positions in this new state of affairs. Neither had any desire to follow the court to London; but the Lady

57

Minnie said that they might well be ordered to do so. They must await instructions. Needless to say, they were both distinctly concerned over this.

So commenced a period of uneasy waiting upon events. They tried not to allow their perturbation to communicate itself to young Henry, who did not seem to be greatly exercised one way or the other. Will's worry, of course, was anent his property, should he be required to take the prince to London. He could not just leave Menstrie with no one in charge, and, this situation never having crossed his mind previously, he had nobody in mind to entrust with the charge. And he just did not *want* to leave his home and homeland. He wished that he had never agreed to accompany Argyll into the royal presence that day.

It was Argyll himself who arrived at Stirling one day about a month later, bringing news and some guidance for his friend. He had accompanied the king when he had left Edinburgh on the 4th of April, with a large train, but had turned back at Berwick-upon-Tweed two days later, after being duly appointed Lieutenant of the North, in room of the Duke of Lennox who was going on south with James. So he had got what he wanted, and was now, as Admiral of the Western Seas as well, more or less viceroy of all Scotland north of the Forth and Clyde, with his Clan Campbell in a dominant position.

There had been a remarkable scene at Berwick, when the monarch crossed the wooden bridge over the Tweed into his new kingdom. James had sunk down on his wobbly knees when he had reached the far side, not so much out of devotion to his acquired realm's ground but in thankfulness in getting safely over that bridge, for it had moved and shaken under him and his followers, and he had a terror of falling into water, as he had of many other possible disasters, declaring it to be shamefully shoogly, and to be replaced instanter by a good strong brig of stone, the first new charge upon his English treasury. There had followed another extraordinary episode when, with Argyll himself and a number of other earls and lords taking their leave of the monarch before turning back for Scotland, James had rounded on the Master of Gray – he who had so largely been responsible for manipulating this accession to Elizabeth's throne by skilful political and diplomatic manoeuvring, and who had clearly expected to be rewarded by high office in England – and told him to return to Scotland also, that he no longer required his services, and that he was sure that he would find plenty of other clever rogues in London without Patrick Gray! This to astonishment of all present and the obvious consternation and anger of the usually so urbane and assured Machiavelli of Scottish politics, the acting Chancellor of the realm and Master of the Wardrobe.

James had then ridden on into Northumberland, being met by a huge welcoming company of English nobility and gentry under the earl thereof. Gray had ridden off northwards alone, in his rage and humiliation, clearly desiring no company for himself. Argyll judged that James Stewart had been unwise in this, for Gray, whatever else, was clever indeed, subtle, crafty and experienced as he was handsome, and he would not forget nor forgive this insult. The king, Argyll feared, had made a dangerous enemy.

As to the likelihood of Will being summoned to London with Henry, he had no knowledge. But he did have some small comfort for his friend if that did happen. He would send an able young man, newly wed, one Wattie Campbell, son of his steward at Castle Campbell, to act steward for Will at Menstrie. He would serve to manage the property in Will's absence, possibly be even better at it than its laird was himself, being well trained!

With that Will Alexander had to be as content as his concern allowed. It was of small comfort for Janet.

Two weeks later they had another visitor with news, none other than the Earl of Mar himself, who had apparently turned back from the king's company at York. His account of the royal progress that far was astonishing, all the English magnates and squires turning out to welcome their new liege-lord, receiving him with

59

magnificent banquets at their great houses, large numbers accompanying him onwards, no doubt largely in the hope of gaining positions, appointments and privileges in the new regime; so that even by then he had a train of over one thousand, highly unmanageable and requiring to be sustained *en route*. How many more he would collect before he reached London was anybody's guess. James was clearly revelling in it all. He had already created over one hundred new English knights, for no particular reason, although it was being indicated that His Grace was apt to receive a donation of one thousand pounds for such advances in dignity. And he had not yet reached the most populous and richest parts of his latest realm. The only rift in the lute was the report that the plague had struck London, most unfortunate at this auspicious moment.

Mar brought word with a more personal impact. The king desired Queen Anne now to join him in London, bringing with her young Henry, now to be styled Prince of Wales it seemed, also the Princess Elizabeth; but not the younger Prince Charles, who it appeared was to be left in the care of Sir Alexander Seton, Lord President and brother of the new Earl of Winton, at Dunfermline, this until the child could speak, for although only three years, the boy had not learned to enunciate words, and his father found this deplorable and wanted no offspring of his to be looked at askance, in England or elsewhere. So poor little Charles was to be cooped up in Dunfermline's ancient palace until he became presentable. Meantime, Will Alexander and Janet Erskine were to accompany the queen and her other two children to London. And this without undue delay.

So the blow fell.

Will thereafter had to go to Castle Campbell, to tell Argyll that he would indeed be requiring that steward to manage Menstrie for him; and Janet to Cardross to inform, and pack her belongings required for a stay at court in London town, neither of them happy at the prospect. They took Henry with them on both errands, the boy much impressed with Castle Campbell perched on its pinnacle above the township of Dollar, or Dolour as many said it should be called, the former Castle Gloom standing as it did beside the Burn of Sorrow before this drained into the Black Devon. Small wonder that Argyll's grandsire had changed the name to Castle Campbell. Something of all this was mirrored by at least two of the visitors.

They learned some interesting but sad news from Argyll. Mar had gone to inform the queen at Linlithgow that she was to be escorted by him to London. There had been a furious altercation, for Anne much disliked Johnnie Mar, calling him her son Frederick's gaoler, and refused utterly to allow him to conduct her southwards. When he had insisted that this was the king's command, she had in her anger thrown something of a fit, as a result of which she miscarried of the child she was presently bearing, and was now lying abed ill.

Will and Janet, who had not known that the queen had been pregnant again, went off bemused.

It was mid-June before the queen was in a fit state to make the journey to London, and the arrangements made for it. This included sending up the Duke of Lennox to replace Mar as escort. Anne liked the easy-going duke; and his younger sister Henrietta, Marchioness of Huntly, was her principal lady-in-waiting. So Ludovick of Lennox arrived at Stirling to collect young Henry, and with him, his tutor and lady-attendant said farewell to the Lady Minnie, without tears, and Lennox led them the score of miles south-eastwards to Linlithgow, regaling them with extraordinary stories of the impact of King James on the late Elizabeth's stiff and starchy court, and the changes there being made.

Janet had never seen the handsome redstone palace rising beside the lovely Linlithgow Loch; nor could Henry remember it, although he had been there as an infant. It was the dower-house of the queens of Scotland, and a vastly more comfortable and attractive residence than was the king's main seat of Stirling, although of course not so defensively placed; a splendid quadrangular edifice, with towers at the corners, enclosing a paved courtyard of notable size, it had been the scene of unnumbered dramatic events, including the birth of Mary Queen of Scots. And beside it rose the famous church of St Michael, almost as handsome and storeyed, wherein James the Fourth had been warned, in 1513, by that weird spectral figure, not to ride with his army into England, to break a lance for the Queen of France as she besought him; and which warning that romantic monarch ignoring, all had ended with his death and the disaster of Flodden Field.

Once she learned that the Earl of Mar was not with them, Queen Anne welcomed the visitors well enough. Her embrace for her son, whom she hardly knew, was dutiful rather than motherly, she naming him Frederick of course. Anne of Denmark was a somewhat strange young woman, not yet thirty – although not so strange as was her husband – perhaps this being inevitable in the circumstances, wed at the age of fifteen to her oddity, who was not really interested in women, whatever his other tastes. She had been used thereafter merely to produce the necessary heirs – this latest miscarriage had been of her sixth child – and to produce a handsome dowry from the King of Denmark. She was not beautiful but was well formed and not unattractive, although sharp-featured, and with a will of her own. She probably would have made a satisfactory wife for someone less peculiar than James Stewart.

The visitors had assumed that Anne was no more anxious to make this journey than Janet and Will were, but this proved not to be the case, her objections having been only to going in the company of Mar. She had, of course, been informed of the arrangements and timing for their departure, but she announced that she was by no means ready yet to leave Linlithgow, that she had still much packing to do and gear to assemble. She would inform them when she was ready – all this in a very foreign accent.

62

Meantime, the visitors would be accommodated in the north-east tower of the palace; that is, except Prince Frederick, who would remain in her own quarters, and this produced friction, with young Henry announcing that he would rather stay with Master Will and Mistress Janet. His mother frowned, then shrugged, and gave a wave of dismissal.

The duke's sister Henrietta conducted them across the courtyard to their tower overlooking the loch, Henry declaring that he did not want to be called Frederick and that he did not greatly like the queen – at which, of course, he had to be instructed that he was to behave very nicely and respectfully towards her, that she was his mother, and had not been allowed to visit him at Stirling. He would, they were sure, come to be very fond of Queen Anne, Ludovick of Lennox raising his eyebrows.

This prediction, however admirable, was scarcely speedily fulfilled, certainly not in the five days they all spent at Linlithgow before the queen was prepared to set forth. Lennox went off on affairs of his own, and the Stirling trio spent the interval exploring the countryside around, visiting Pictish sites on the hills to the south, and fishing in the loch. In none of these activities did the queen join them, and the boy's meetings with his mother did not engender much mutual empathy. However in these days Will and Janet came to know something of the other two royal children, Elizabeth, a lively, dark-haired girl of nearly seven years, and the frail-seeming three-year-old Charles, big-eyed and silent. Henry found them uninteresting.

Lennox arrived back, having apparently been to Edinburgh to prepare a reception there; and at last the queen conceded that she was almost ready to move. But there were two unlooked-for developments. One was the fact that she assembled a great train of pack-horses laden with her belongings – and of course mounted men to lead them, nearly two score of them – which would greatly complicate travel, it was feared, both as to pace and feeding, plus accommodation. Anne was notoriously extravagant, loving expensive clothing, gear and jewellery – indeed she was always in debt to Geordie Heriot, the king's jeweller and banker, James refusing to pay her bills; she appeared to be taking most of her garb and belongings with her to London. And second, she was determined to go to Dunfermline on the way, over in Fife as it was, to see young Charles safely installed in the old palace there, to ensure that his quarters were suitable and that Sir Alexander Seton, the keeper, was given fullest instructions as to the child's care and welfare. This diversion would be highly inconvenient, of course, going north instead of south, and over the Forth estuary. But the queen was definite, indeed peremptory, and Lennox amiable.

So a great and lengthy procession set out at last, its principals, the escort of guards Mar had provided from Stirling, and the pack-horse train, and this at no very swift pace, with a maid-in-waiting having to carry small Charles in her arms, and the Princess Elizabeth scarcely a practised horsewoman at six, indeed the queen herself less than expert, although Lady Huntly was better. Skirting the loch, they took the road northwards over the shoulder of Grange Hill in the direction of Linlithgow's port of Boroughstoneness, before turning eastwards by Abercorn to reach Queen Margaret's Ferry, where the Forth narrowed to a mere mile across, a journey of less than a dozen miles but which, at their so moderate pace, took them over two hours, after a late start. Clearly this was going to be no speedy journey.

There was no point in taking all their numerous cavalcade across the ferry and on to Dunfermline, so the principals' group took ship, all the rest being billeted, in the king's name, on the township of South Queensferry, little as this was appreciated by its folk. Lennox said that it was another six miles to Dunfermline thereafter, so that clearly, at this rate, they would not get back to the Lothian side that night, annoying delay as it was.

A flat-bottomed scow, necessary for the horses, took

them across the estuary to the steeper Fife shore, where-
after they rode on past the small castles of Rosyth and
Pitreavie to what had been Malcolm Canmore's capital,
where his second wife, the saint-to-be Margaret, had built
the first Roman Catholic stone abbey in Scotland, beside
his rambling palace.

Here they were received by Lady Fyvie, for her
husband, absent at the law courts in Edinburgh, was
preparing the Palace of Holyroodhouse for their reception,
at Lennox's instigation. He was still being called Lord
President Seton although he had been created Lord Fyvie
not long before, the able lawyer and judge who was to be
little Charles's guardian until the boy was in a fit state
to send south to join the rest of the royal family, by
the king's express command. This lady, formerly Lilias
Drummond, had six daughters of her own, so she was
a very experienced mother, and suitably motherly in her
character as in her appearance, which no doubt helped the
queen to accept a situation which she found distressing in
the extreme. The quarters and conditions provided here
for the wordless prince proved to be satisfactory, indeed
better than at Linlithgow, as was the accommodation
and fare offered to the visitors. All the little girls made
a fuss of the small boy, who was probably bewildered but
retained his strangely detached attitude. Janet herself had
become quite motherly towards him, his brother however
remaining critical.

Lady Fyvie made an excellent hostess and they had a
comfortable night.

A delayed start in the morning and some hold-up at the
ferry saw the reunited entourage as far as Edinburgh by
mid-afternoon, where a salvo of cannon from the castle
greeted them as they made for the abbey-palace of the
Holy Rood, and Lennox had arranged for the provost of
the city to present the keys thereof – treatment the queen
had never before received.

In the event they stayed for six more days in Edinburgh,
although the duke had not bargained on so long a delay; but

Anne was not to be hurried. A new coach was being built to carry her and her daughter onwards, and she insisted on supervising the finishing details for herself. Also she ordered fine new clothes for herself and her children, Henry to get a purple satin doublet and breeches and Elizabeth a red taffeta bodice and brown skirt, the pride of the queen's own being a figured taffeta gown, with a white satin and purple velvet-lined mantle. Her ladies also did well, the Edinburgh tailors busy, even the odd character who acted as her jester gaining a new coat.

Will and Janet took the prince for walks in the hilly, crowded city, where it stretched up the mile-long spine of a tenement-clustered slope, with narrow wynds and closes on either side, right to the rock-top castle so like Stirling's, the boy agog at all that he saw, and being taught the necessity of keeping to the crown of the causeway, as it was called, in the Canongate and High Street, to avoid the filth on each side overflowing the gutters. As well, they all agreed, that Edinburgh was so hilly and therefore windy a place, otherwise the stench would have been all but overpowering. They also climbed the dramatic heights of Arthur's Seat which soared above the palace and abbey, the boy having to be instructed on the life and achievements of that all but legendary High King of the Britons, who had used Dunedin, as Edinburgh was then called, as a base for his campaigns. They went riding around the base of the hill, among its woodlands, saw St Margaret's, Dunsappie and Duddingston Lochs, and even followed the Figgate Burn down all the way to where it flowed into salt water amid fine sands.

At length the queen was satisfied, and to Lennox's relief they were preparing to set out, now with a carriage drawn by six horses to add to their cavalcade, when of all things another entourage arrived at Edinburgh from the south, a group of English nobles with six court ladies and two hundred horse, sent to escort the queen to London – presumably by the English Privy Council, since James himself would never have thought of such a thing. So there

66

had to be another day's delay while this group rested. It was a bemused Duke of Lennox who eventually led what amounted to a small army off on the four-hundred-mile journey southwards. Henry was now mounted on a fine French thoroughbred.

A host of such numbers can never travel fast, and despite the coach which ought to have speeded up the queen's and her daughter's riding, they only got as far as Dunbar, where the Norse Sea took over from the Firth of Forth, that first night, and where the so forceful Bothwell had taken and raped Henry's grandmother, Queen Mary – this only some thirty miles through the fertile East Lothian countryside, by Haddington. Lennox had hoped for better mileage than that. And on the morrow, when they had to climb over the knuckle-end of the Lammermuir Hills and then the heights of Coldinghame Muir, to the former priory thereof, now a Home seat, that was a mere score of miles. Obtaining quarters for the night for this host was a major headache, despite the use of the royal command. When they won only another twenty miles the day following, to Berwick-upon-Tweed, it was evident that this would be about an average rate of progress. And with another three hundred and forty miles to go that meant over two weeks' riding. They noted that, so far, no work had started on the building of a stone bridge to replace the king's shoogly one.

But at the other side of Tweed another great concourse was clearly waiting for them, and an illustrious one. It proved to be another welcoming party sent by the king to greet his heir, and incidentally his wife, to English soil, and included the Earls of Sussex and Lincoln, the Countesses of Worcester and Kildare, Sir George Carey, who announced that he had been appointed Queen Anne's chamberlain, and the Ladies Walsingham, Scrope and Rich. For how long these had been waiting there was anybody's guess. They had brought with them the late Queen Elizabeth's jewellery, or some of it, and a selection of her vast wardrobe of dresses, many allegedly never worn. Anne's reaction to this display of her husband's care and thought was less than enthusiastic. No doubt she guessed, knowing James, that it was not all done to please her, but to emphasise his new power and wealth and to impress his English courtiers. She accepted the jewels, handing them over to Lady Huntly, but rejected the clothing, saying that she was not in the habit of wearing others' cast-offs, and frowned upon her new chamberlain, waving this welcoming party to fall in behind her Scots group and the ones who had come to Edinburgh earlier. Anne was showing that she could play the queen without any help from her spouse.

So the progress down through England commenced, overdone as it was, reaching Alnwick, Morpeth, Newcastle and York, where the lord mayor and aldermen conducted the queen round the city, to cheering crowds, and presented her with a silver chalice filled with gold coins, Henry and his sister getting lesser cups each with twenty pounds in gold.

The great company were entertained for four days in York, while their horses rested, before proceeding on southwards. In it all, Will Alexander's and Janet Erskine's positions were odd and uncomfortable, among all these high-born ones yet not *of* them, yet because of their charge of Prince Henry, and his demands to have them close to him always, indeed the queen's desire to keep the lofty English folk in their place, they were always up at the front of the processions and entertainments. They sought to look on it all as something of a holiday jaunt, an experience, an exploration, and part of their own education as well as the prince's, new territory for them all in more than just the terrain. The pair became even better companions than ever, although they were seldom able to be alone together in these circumstances. And thanks to the hospitality showered on them by the magnates, civic dignitaries and churchmen as they went, they ate too much.

5

It was well into July before, weary with continued travel, most saddle-sore and gorged with food from almost nightly banqueting, they reached the Thames valley. They saw the smoke of London from Hampstead Heath, but did not actually enter the city, being informed that the plague still raged there and King James and his court were presently staying at Richmond Palace. So it was south-westwards up Thames further miles, before they learned that their destination now was to be Windsor Castle, almost a score of miles further west, presumably the monarch desiring to distance himself from any possible germs of disease carried on the wind. This was too far to proceed that day, so it was decided still to make for Richmond Palace for the night, where there would be ample accommodation for their large company, and on to Windsor next day.

By this time the Scots travellers were used to the difference in size and splendour of English seats and mansions compared with their own, so much more extensive and richly furnished and less defensively fortified, if at all. Did the English not require to protect themselves against their neighbours on occasion, as they did in the northern kingdom? It looked like it; and yet English history was reputed to be almost as bloody as Scots. But even their experiences so far had not prepared them for the size and magnificence of Richmond Palace in its acres of parkland, almost a small town in itself. Here it was that Queen Elizabeth Tudor had died.

But on reaching Windsor the next day, they were all but overwhelmed by the immensity and dimensions of it all, allegedly the greatest fortress-castle in Christendom, covering acres of an eminence above the Thames, amid its ornamental pleasure-grounds, known apparently as the Slopes. Started by William the Conqueror and added to by almost every English sovereign since, from its huge Round Tower or Keep to its innumerable subsidiary and flanking towers, its battlemented curtain walls enclosing its Upper, Middle and Lower Wards, its chapels and halls and gatehouses, it dominated the scene. Absurd that men and women should feel almost oppressed by the stone and lime handiwork of their predecessors, but that was the effect of it all on the newcomers as they neared it.

Another strange process developed at Windsor. Gradually their great concourse of coaches and horsemen and women melted away, until as they approached the first of the many gatehouses, only the very loftiest remained, and even these tended to drop off as they proceeded deeper into the enormous establishment. And thereafter the Scots party began to wish that they had not done so, for they found the successive groups of Yeomen of the Guard eyeing them ever more suspiciously, however authoritative the Duke of Lennox sought to be. There appeared to be unnumbered barriers, guards and checks to get past before they could reach King James; and these arrogant underlings were hard to convince that the visitors had any right to claim an audience. They were clothed for the road, of course, travel-stained and less than splendidly clad anyway, the queen's fine apparel still packed in her carriage, so that she was looked at doubtfully indeed, in fact Henrietta, Marchioness of Huntly being accorded more respect for some reason. The duke had never been to Windsor, so that he was unknown as the king's cousin. Anne grew the more indignant.

Once they won into the royal quarters matters did improve, for here, among senior courtiers and ministers, Lennox was known, and those with him treated more respectfully, even though it was still not recognised that one of them was their queen. But there was still a seemingly endless succession of corridors and antechambers to get through before the final presence-chamber was reached, with two more yeomen standing at the door. These did not recognise the duke, but a spare, stooping but keen-eyed individual, dressed quietly but expensively, happening to emerge therefrom did and, looking at the women and children, came to the right conclusion.

"Can it be, my lord Duke, that here is our gracious queen?" And his gaze went from one woman to another.

"I am Anne," the queen said. "And you, sir?"

"Ah! Robert Cecil, Your Majesty – your humble and devoted servant." And he bowed deeply, and reached out to kiss the royal hand.

Anne had never been styled majesty before, and looked a little doubtful. Lennox presented the other man. "This is the Lord Cecil of Essendon, Principal Secretary of State and Chancellor of the Duchy of Lancaster, Your Grace. He has been very prominent and helpful in the transfer of the throne and its powers to James." The duke and Anne were the only two persons who could call the king by his Christian name.

"His Majesty is busy with his pen," Cecil informed. "After much signing of charters, deeds and documents, he is ever glad to indite more scholarly and enlightening words!" And he turned to throw open the door.

Will Alexander groaned inwardly. Not more poetic interchange?

Something of a blast of hot air, by no means perfumed, met them, for James liked warmth, even in high summer, and a well-doing fire blazed on the chamber's hearth. The king sat at a table, slovenly dressed as ever, high hat on head and a quill in his hand. He looked up, frowning, at this interruption; and even when he saw who was there, his expression did not greatly change.

"Och, it's yoursel' Annie!" he said. "Aye, and Henry. And the lassie, Bessie."

All save Anne bowed, if Henry only slightly.

James almost reluctantly laid aside his pen, and rose. "You have taken your time," he declared. "I was waiting at yon Richmond for you, Vicky. You should hae hastened mair than this, aye hastened." He did not come forward to greet them. "I sent plenties to help you on your way."

"The larger the company, the slower, James," Lennox said. "And Her Grace received much welcoming and entertainment as she travelled."

"Ooh, aye. Nae doubt. I commanded it, mind."

Anne advanced, Elizabeth by the hand, Will pushing Henry forward also. She brought the children up to their father, who made some gesture of clasping her to him, very brief and scarcely an embrace, stepped back to their mutual relief, patted his daughter on the head and punched his son on the shoulder.

"Laddie, you've grown, I declare, since last I set eyes on you." And to his wife, "So you've lost another bairn, Annie, I hear!"

"To my pain and sorrow, yes, James. It was . . . grievous."

"Aye, and brought on, I'm told, by your spite at Johnnie Mar, was it no'? That was ill-done. And you wouldna come south wi' Johnnie, either! I had to send Vicky for you. What ails you at Johnnie, woman?"

"Everything!" the queen said briefly.

Lennox made so bold as to step in, the only one who could have done so. "It has been a difficult time for Her Grace, James. And, to be sure, for you awaiting her. But now she is here. With your family. Prince Charles is safely bestowed at Dunfermline with Seton. We rejoice at this happy occasion."

Rejoicing was scarely evident in that overheated room, but some smiles and nods were produced, if not from the royal pair.

"Aye, weel," James said. "It's guid to see you all – even if no' before time! Bessie's grown too. Aye, and Henry, you're learning your lessons to mak a right prince o' you?" A glance over at Will.

"Yes, Father. Master Will has taught me the hurlyhackit."

"Hech, you say so! That fell ploy! You could break your

neck at that, boy!" The great royal eyes accused Will. "I'd hae thought that you, a poet, would hae had mair sense, man Alexander!"

"I . . . we did it carefully, Sire. Slowly at first, learning day by day. He, Prince Henry, is now very skilful at it." That was anything but confidently declared, in that company.

"Mebbe so. But yon hurlyhackit is no' what I tell't you to teach the laddie."

"He is well forward in his studies, Your Grace. In the humanities, the Latin . . ."

"Majesty, man – it's majesty noo, no' grace. *You* should mind o' that!"

"Was not Stewart grace to outdo English majesty, Sire?"

"Och, weel, it's the custom here, see you. They a' say majesty, canna get their English tongues round grace! Eh, Cecil man?"

Robert, Lord Cecil bowed. "Your Majesty's presence is grace itself, Sire! The one includes the other." That was smoothly said.

"Aye. So that's the way o' it. So Henry's coming on wi' his learning, is he? I'll be trying him oot on that, mind. And soon. It's no'—"

"James, I did not come all this way to stand here while Frederick's education is discussed!" Heavily accented as that was, Anne made her point very clear. "I am weary with travel. And so is Elizabeth. Where do we find rooms and refreshment in this, this monstrous place?"

"What would *you* ken aboot education, woman! But och, there's a whole tower here set aside for you and your womenfolk. Rob Cecil will show you. It's a right spread o' a fortalice this. Did you esteem a' the fine women I sent up to greet you, Annie? Some o' the best bred and notable in a' this England, mind. They'll mak a right guid court for you."

"I require no such train, James. I am well content with my own Danish and Scots ladies."

"You'll hae the court I provide for you! You're Queen o' the United Kingdom o' Great Britain, Ireland and maybe a bit France too, mind. And Henry's Prince o' Wales. Aye, and nane o' that Frederick nonsense! Cecil, man, show them to the women's tower."

"Yes, Majesty. If Her Highness will come with me . . ."

"Henry, you bide here wi' me."

As the company began to break up, Janet glanced at Will, clearly indicating that she must go with the queen. That man, feeling utterly out of place there, deciding that he ought to bow himself out with the ladies rather than remain with the prince meantime, found himself halted by a thickly worded but definite command.

"I havena' gien *you* leave to retire, Alexander man! You'll bide, forby. I want a bit word wi' you."

Cecil was about to escort the ladies out when the door was thrown open from the other side and who should enter, unannounced, but John, Earl of Mar, clad more finely than anyone had seen him hitherto. He sketched a mock genuflection, looking from James to Anne, grinning.

"I have only just heard the good news, and who was here, Sire," he said. "And came hot-foot."

"Aye, weel, you're just in time to hear my Annie gie her regrets that you werena wi' her on her journey, Johnnie."

Queen Anne, pushing Lord Cecil aside, swept out of the chamber without so much as another glance at anyone. In the silence, and bowing uncertainly, the ladies and the one man followed.

"So that's the way o' it!" the king said, frowning. "We'll hae to see aboot this. She can be a right besom, that one!"

"Perhaps, James, I should go after Anne," Lennox suggested. "And my sister. Help them to settle in?"

"As you will, Vicky. Women are the devil! You can tak Henry, forby, see you – no' to his mother, mind. Find him a bit room some place near to me here. Go wi' the duke, laddie."

"Will I accompany the prince, Sire?" Will asked, uncertainly. There were only the four men and the boy in that room now.

"No. I tell't you I want a word wi' you – plenty words!"

That sounded ominous. Presently Will found himself alone with the monarch and Mar. The latter looked at him fleeringly. "So you got her down here at last!" he commented. "A sair trauchle, I'll be bound."

"Her Grace was well entertained all the way, my lord."

"I'd have had her here a deal sooner—"

"Nae doubt, Johnnie. But I've matters to discuss wi' Menstrie here," James interrupted. "Much o' wordage – aye, wordage."

"Then I'll leave you to it!" his foster-brother said, grinning. "I'm less thirled to words! With Your Grace's – no, Your *Majesty's* – gracious permission, of course!" And Mar made for the door.

"Johnnie's no' great on the writing," the king observed, and gestured Will over to the table. "Sit you doon, man." He waved at all the papers. "I'm right throng, wi' a' this."

Will swallowed. "Is it another poem, Sire?"

"Na, na. I hae another on the go, mind. But this is no' it. I'm working on two ploys, see you, at this present. I'm repenning my piece on *The True Law of Free Monarchies*. You'll hae heard tell o' that? No? Och, weel, and you only a bit lairdie! I wrote it four or five year back. But yon was for Scotland, in the main. Here in England there's different notions and customs that need putting richt – aye, they do! They'll hae to learn. Sae it needs a bit altered and added, just. But I dinna need the help o' the likes o' you, in that! But there's this other and right major and God-appointed task – aye, God-appointed. It's the Bible, nae less. The Haly Bible, nae less, man!"

Will blinked. "The Bible?"

"Aye, Haly Writ. The Writ was writ in the Latin until

75

the Reformation, mind you. Still is, for maist folk. And maist folk canna understand it. Sae maist dinna read it. And it's no' been properly translated into oor ain tongue, since. Och, there's been attempts at it, aye, by different scrievers, or bits o' it. Mainly by oor ain Scots divines. But it's no' been right done. And no' a' o' it. And here in this England it's worse. I soon discovered that, attending their services. Mistaken. Misinterpreted just. Misread. Sae, I jalouse that the guid Lord has put this duty upon me, as the Lord's Anointed, to set this to rights, to mak Haly Writ true and understandable for a' folk, no' just Latin scholars. I'm going to translate the Bible, just!"

Will stared, sovereign-lord or none. "But, but . . . that is . . . that is . . ." His voice trailed away as he wagged an incredulous head.

"Aye, it's a big task. Ooh, aye, I ken that fine. But I've set mysel' to dae it."

"The whole Bible, Sire? All of it? The Old Testament and the New? From the Greek and the Latin? Hundreds and thousands of words, *thousands* of thousands! Is it, is it possible?"

"Aye, it is. I'm set on daeing it. Mind, I'm going to need a deal o' help. That's whaur *you* come in, Alexander man. It's no' poetry, forby there's much o' poesy in it. David's psalms and the like. And yon Solomon's proverbs. But you hae the gift o' words, like mysel'. And you hae the Latin. You taught Argyll, and noo young Henry. Sae here's a right new duty for you. You're to aid me in this great ploy."

Will drew a long breath. "Sire, how can I? I am no divine. I did not study theology at St Andrews. This will require learning far beyond mine. The learning of a host of biblical scholars and ministers of religion. Not such as myself."

"You'll dae it fine, man. And I'll correct what you dae! A' them *should* hae done it, but havena – the divines, the bishops and the doctors. I'll shame them, and hae it done. Dae some o' it mysel'. I'm at it a'ready. I started at the beginning, just. Genesis. Adam and yon Eve – a right typical woman, that! The Garden o' Eden. It's richt enough that *I* should start this great work, see you. For I'm the true heid o' the Celtic royal line, which started frae Adam. You ken aboot that?"

Will had assumed that they had all started from Adam, not just James Stewart, but did not say so. "I am very ignorant about such matters, Sire."

"Then you ought no' to be! You're o' the Hielant blood yoursel', are you no'? MacAllisters. Weel, then! Adam, see you, was the first right man whae the Almighty decided had arrived at His godly image. There had been plenties o' men before him, doon the ages, mind – the folk o' the Land o' Nod. Them that yon rogue Cain went to, after he'd slain his brother Abel. Aye. But Adam, his faither, was the one God saw as coming up to his ain image. Sae it was to be a new dispensation. The Land o' Nod folk were different. You understand?"

His hearer nodded, if doubtfully.

"Aye, weel, as Adam's seed grew and multiplied, they outgrew yon Garden o' Eden. Mind, yon was no small plot, but a' the land between the Rivers Tigris and Euphrates. You'll hae heard tell o' them? What became Babylon. Ower many o' them for the bit land, his descendants had to move oot as the ages went by. They were the Celts. And they moved on and on, ever westwards. Aye, westwards. Until they came to Ireland and then Scotland; their leaders, their kings, are my ain ancestors. And then, wi' the great ocean, they couldna move any mair. Sae there you are!"

Perhaps Will Alexander was not very good at hiding his disbelief, for his liege-lord poked him on the chest with a stabbing finger.

"You dinna credit it, man? Then follow you the gal names o' places – that's frae the Gaelic, the language o' your ain folk. Gaelic was what they spoke, so Gaelic's the language o' heaven, just. You pick them oot, the gal names on any cartograph and mapping. On frae the Euphrates through the lands o' the Syrians and the Anatolians –

yon's the Turks – and round the north shores o' the Middle Sea, yon Mediterranean; aye, the gal or Gaelic names. Galata and Galindire and Gallipoli, to Galaxid in Greece, and Gallerate and Galdo in Lombardy and southwards to Galatina. You get Galicia in Castile and Gallego in Portugal till you come to Gaul, the auld Romish name for France. Aye, and so ower to Galway in Ireland and then Galloway in oor Scotland. Mind, St Paul preached to the Galatians. Sae that's the road they came, frae the Garden o' Eden. Aye, and left their traces a' the way, Celtic carvings on stane, still to be seen, I'm tellt. Interlacings, crescents and V-rods and Celtic beasties." James nodded complacently. "And noo they hae a Celtic-line king in this England, which they havena had since Arthur o' the Britons. And he'll gie them the Bible so's they can understand it!"

"Your Grace, this is beyond, beyond all. All in wonder!" Will had almost said beyond all belief but stopped himself in time. "A venture beyond all in conception, in understanding and planning. But the whole Bible! It will take years to do . . ."

"No if I hae enough o' the richt folk on it. Daeing the different books o' it. I'm thinking o' setting up a conference o' churchmen, to plan it. They hae colleges here tae, mind – Oxford and yon Cambridge. I'll hae them at it. But it will require a deal o' checking and correcting, I'll grant you that. You'll aid me in that, man Alexander. Aye, and there's another mannie whae's to help – he's a poet, tae. Harrington. Sir James Harrington. He's no' bad, for an Englishman! We'll a' work it together, you and me and him."

Will sat silent now, practically dumbfounded at the enormity of what was so confidently proposed, more than proposed obviously, commanded. The Bible, the whole Bible! And he, it seemed, to play a major part in it.

James clearly did not see him in any way inadequate for the task. "You'll start wi' the psalms, just. Yon David was a poet, sae you'll manage them fine. You'll hae a Bible in the Latin, man, for teaching young Henry? Teaching him the Scriptures. Aye. Weel, off wi' you, then. You'll hae to work at it, aye, and on Henry forby. While we a' traipse aroond these parts. For we'll be moving hoose, as you might say, trying oot different palaces because o' this plague in London town. I'd liefer be at Whitehall at this present, but we daurna go there. They say there's thirty thousand deid. Vicky Lennox will find you and Henry a room here meantime. We'll ca' you Gentleman o' the Bedchamber to him noo, no' just tutor. Och, I'll get back to Genesis, noo . . ."

Will bowed his way out, to go in search of the duke, wits in a whirl.

6

So commenced an unsettled and unsettling period for Will Alexander, as for others; for others, because of the great numbers who thronged the royal court, they could not reside for long in any one palace or mansion for reasons of sanitation and provision, even at the enormous Windsor Castle. So for what remained of the summer it was constant moving of quarters, as though some of them had not had enough of movement on their long journey down from Scotland. Admittedly they visited some magnificent houses, the seats of great nobles as well as royal palaces such as Nonsuch, Greenwich, Hampton Court and Woodstock, where their hosts sought to outdo each other in hospitality, and to impress their new monarch with their loyal service, usually in the hope of preferment, position and honours; and this did include more than just feasting and accommodation, for James's fondness for the chase was known, even though he rode in as ungainly fashion as he bore himself in all else, and hunting expeditions were frequent, deer even being imported from neighbouring parks for his benefit. Not that Will Alexander was apt to take part in these, for he was much too busy tutoring Henry and translating the Book of Psalms into English.

In all this moving around, scarcely conducive to the prince's formal education any more than to scholarly translation as it was, Will suffered a sad development. Janet's services were to be dispensed with. James saw no need for a lady-attendant for his son, and Princess Elizabeth had her own ladies-in-waiting now. Janet's appointment had been the Lady Minnie's idea, not the king's. So now she was to be sent back to Scotland. She would go with the Earl of Mar, her kinsman, who was also returning, more or less to take over the rule of the southern part of the land, while Argyll ruled the north, the Master of Gray's position now being unclear. But at least some stay of execution was granted, for Mar wished to attend his foster-brother's coronation ceremony, and James would not deny him that. So Janet stayed on, vaguely attached to the queen's entourage meantime. Not that Will saw a lot of her, for Anne kept her court very much apart from her husband's, apparently to their mutual satisfaction, even though they visited the same palaces and mansions. Seldom could there have been a royal family so divided as this one.

The coronation situation was much on the king's mind. He could not feel really secure on his new throne until he had been crowned; and the only conceivable place for an English coronation was at Westminster Abbey in London. Yet London remained in the grip of the plague, with seven to eight hundred people dying daily, it was reported. And the king's advisers were urgent against taking the risk of entering the city. But, as weeks passed, James decided otherwise. It was strange for one so fearful in so many other respects; but in this, James was the bold one. He declared that since he was the Lord's Anointed, and the coronation service was another anointing and due act of worship, he would be quite safe from the Evil One's plague on such occasion. While this may not have relieved others of anxiety, it seemed to do so for the monarch – and Anne was not consulted. So, one brief sally into London town, for half a day, at the end of this July, 1604, and then back to safety at Windsor and elsewhere.

Before that Will, Gentleman of the Bedchamber to the prince, was involved in a different ceremony, and in which Janet also took part. This was a special investiture of Knights of the Garter, the first to be conducted by James Stewart, and at which the heir to the throne was to be so honoured. And Henry, who was fond of Janet, insisted that she and Will should be present on this great occasion for him.

It was a colourful affair indeed, in St George's Chapel at Windsor, Henry being very pleased with himself in his fine velvet cloak. He was not the only one to be so honoured, Lennox also being admitted to the prestigious order, the visiting Duke of Wurtemburg likewise, and the Earls of Southampton and Pembroke, James's brother-in-law, Christian of Denmark *in absentia*. The king's less than impressive appearance and the untidy way in which he wore his splendid robes hardly added to the occasion; but his son at least behaved well and enjoyed the feasting and entertainment thereafter, although at one stage causing raised eyebrows by leaving his place at the dais table and going down to talk to Will and Janet in their lowly places far down the hall.

Thereafter James decided that Will would get more psalms translated, and Henry more tutoring, if they were to remain in one place instead of parading round the countryside visiting great ones and inspecting palaces. So they were despatched to a modest royal property called Oatlands, near Weybridge and Brooklands in Surrey, a dozen miles south of Windsor, this having been built by Henry the Eighth out of the stones of Chertsey Abbey nearby, demolished by him at his Reformation. Here their scholarship and study could be pursued with a minimum of distraction. Summoning up courage, Will asked the monarch whether he might take Janet Erskine with them there, to assist on the domestic side of things where a woman would be a help. To which James acceded, asking whether Will had a fancy for this young female, and warning him that women were apt to be a menace, leading men astray; and that he was not to let the creature get between him and his labours with the psalms, as she might well seek to do. He, the king, would be expecting a good swatch of them ready for his inspection – there were one hundred and fifty of them, mind. And the laddie's education not to be neglected either.

So, all much pleased with this development, the trio took their leave of the courts and rode off the dozen miles to Oaklands, Janet thankful to get away from the queen's entourage, where she had been treated as something of an outsider imposed on Anne by James. Unfortunately the king insisted on them being accompanied by half a dozen of his royal guard to ensure his heir's safety.

They found Oatlands to be a pleasant place in its own parkland, larger than they had expected, with outbuildings, stableyard, even a laundry, so with ample accommodation for the escort without having them in the main house. There was a caretaker and small staff, who also ran a farmery attached; and these had been sent word of their new responsibilities. So all was ready for the newcomers.

This was, needless to say, a highly satisfactory arrangement for Will and Janet, a house to themselves, or almost, and no longer any problems in being alone together, once Henry was off to bed of a night. They chose to occupy three adjacent chambers, with a comfortable withdrawing-room nearby and an anteroom off as study, the staff being at the other end of the establishment. Janet remarked that it was almost like being a married couple with their son – and then clapped a hand over her mouth in simulated concern. Will did not contradict her. Henry hoped that they could stay here always, and had to be reminded that Janet was having to leave for Scotland after the coronation, whenever that might be, sad as this was. The boy got over this disappointment by wondering whether there was anywhere in this flat landscape where they could do hurlyhackit. The skulls might not be difficult to procure, although the cattle-beasts these English had were not like their own long-horned Highland ones. Will doubted whether this was a practical pastime in these circumstances but imagined that there would be compensatory activities.

That first evening at Oatlands, after Henry was belatedly settled in bed, the man and woman went for a stroll in the July dusk, companionably arm-in-arm. At first they talked of their various and varied recent experiences and the strange direction their lives had taken; but presently their converse died away, and they walked together silent but with their own unspoken communion. Where a stile crossed one of the farmland fences from the park, and Will assisted Janet over, he held on to her and they kissed, and kissed again. Hand-in-hand now they walked on, still without words.

When they returned to the mansion, and checked that Henry was asleep, after closing his door quietly behind them, they eyed each other in the lamplight. Janet it was who said it.

"Will, help me to be strong. As I ought to be. It would be so easy, so much to my pleasure, to, to take you in through this door of mine! I should not – but would! I am weak. You must be strong enough for both of us, Will. And say goodnight here."

"Think you that I am so strong, woman! That I do not wish to go with you? Equally as you may. More so, I swear! I am a man, and you are loved and lovable and, and more. You draw me to you. My whole being aches for you. And you call me strong!"

"Stronger than am I. For I will not say you nay if enter you do! But . . ."

"But you would not have it so?"

"I would, oh I would! That is the pain of it. My wish, my desire, my woman's body, would have you in. Only my mind, or some part of it, says that it should not be so. Not yet. One day, one night, I pray – yes, when it would be your right, *our* right. But not now. And I need help, Will."

"As though *I* do not! But, yes, you are right, to be sure. Or that part of your wits that so tells you. I suppose that I must heed it, to my sorrow. Janet, to put the charge on *me*? Is that a woman's wiles?"

"No. No it is not, my dear. Not that. I need you. Your love and caring and, and embrace. But I need your

84

strength also, for what is best for us. We should not start . . . a-wrong."

"Start, woman! We have been close for long, for years."

"Close, yes. But not thus, to move into a, a unity. As it would be. Oh, what use are feeble words, Will? You know, and I know, what we are at. And you know that if you choose to follow me through this doorway, I will not thrust you back. But . . ."

"Aye, but! Go, then – while I still have some will to summon up! Go, I say!"

Strangely she did not go, but instead threw herself bodily into his arms, to all but wrestle with him there, gulping incoherences. And he responded as manfully as he had made that sore decision for them, his hands seeking her breasts, her hips, his lips as active where they might, his urgent person hard against her.

For long moments they stood thus. Then she broke away, with some panted exclamation, flung open her room's door and fled therein. The man it was who closed it behind her, and all but wondering at himself, went to open his own, to slam it shut behind him.

Was King James right, then, that women were a menace and apt to lead men astray? As Will threw off his clothing and sought his bed, he was all too aware of what was like to be taking place so nearby, just through that wall, his imagination's pictures vivid. And yet, as he lay staring up at the canopy of his bed, another image of white loveliness took shape before his eyes, that of red-haired alluring beauty, Aurora. Heaven help him, Aurora also!

As well that Will Alexander had so much to keep him busy in the days that followed, with an eager and lively boy to school, not only in book-learning and study but in outdoor pursuits as well, even though not hurlyhackit, for the prince was energetic and loved the outdoors, as indeed did his tutor. They found a room in the mansion stacked with sporting equipment, bows and arrows, spears, quarter-staffs, fishing gear – the Thames was nearby – even discus and quoits and bowls, Henry Tudor's favourite game. Presumably Oatlands had been in the nature of a recreation palace for the monarchy. At all of this, and more, young Henry perforce must try his hand. Archery particularly captivated him, and he proved to be very good at it, with a keen eye and aim. Throwing the discus demanded a similar ability, and he easily beat both Will and Janet at this.

Then, to be sure, there were the psalms. The king had lectured Will on the intricate matter of the languages of the Scriptures, how most books of the Old Testament were written in Hebrew, some in Aramaic, whereas the New Testament was entirely in Greek, before being translated into the Church's Latin. Oddly, the Greek versions of the Old Testament books, or some of them, were more ancient than the Hebrew; Origen, a Christian, having translated them in the third century AD, whereas most of the Hebrew and Aramaic writings surviving dated from as late as the ninth century, based of course on more ancient scripts. All this greatly complicated the task of making authentic transcriptions into English, especially as one Wycliffe had attempted it in 1382, and Tyndale as late as 1525, this with the Reformation text known as the Breeches Bible produced in 1568. But none of these was wholly accurate or entire. James had lent Will some texts and allowed him to scan others. The psalms, he explained, were not all King David's. Seventy-three of them were, twelve being by Asaph and eleven by the Sons of Korah, he who had rebelled against the authority of Moses and Aaron. King Solomon himself wrote two of the psalms.

Will did not really take in all this, but gained sufficient understanding of his task at least to make a start, learning that not all the lyrics fell into the same category, some being praise, some prayer, some song and some lamentation, but all imbued with allegiance to the Almighty.

He got on reasonably well with the first six. But the seventh was introduced as a shiggaion of David concerning

86

the words of Cush the Benjaminite, whatever that might mean. Research proved that shiggaonoth, presumably the same word, meant a variable tune or versification, just as selah, which occurred in the text, meant a pause in the singing or reciting. This did not help him much, especially when he got to verses twelve and thirteen, and translated them as:

If he turn not he will whet his sword, he hath bent
    his bow
    and made it ready.
Behold he travaileth with iniquity and hath conceived
    mischief
    and brought forth falsehood.

This did not seem to make sense, as a song of praise to the All Highest and righteous God. Will could only conceive that King David had intended the previous verse to apply. It ended: "God is angry with the wicked every day." So that, if he made all but the final he in verse twelve to have capital Hs, and both hes in verse thirteen, but none in verse fourteen, it would make sense, these with the capitals relating to God and those without to the sinner. Would this be understood by the reader or singer?

This was fairly typical of Will's problems, although there were others which quite eluded him, and which he would have to leave unfinished until he could consult King James. Why the monarch considered that because he, Will Alexander, was a poet of sorts he could adequately translate and interpret the thoughts, faiths and writings of long-dead religious zealots, he was at a loss to understand. But then, so much about their extraordinary liege-lord was equally beyond understanding.

After that first night's taxing debate at their bedroom doors, the prince's attendants sought to avoid any repetition. Not that they held each other in any way at arm's length or denied their affections and mutual attraction, kissing and embracing as opportunity offered, sometimes quite comprehensively; but they did not allow it all to go too far, and said their goodnights elsewhere. The situation admittedly was not satisfactory, and Will knew very well what was required to right it. But something held him back – and he knew equally well what that was, yet could not by some effort of will banish it from him as he told himself what he ought to do. It was a waterfall of red hair and those magnetic grey-green eyes responsible, of course.

In the event, this bitter-sweet problem was of short duration, for, after a bare week at Oatlands, a messenger arrived from Hampton Court Palace requiring Prince Henry to be brought there instanter for the coronation ceremony. Nothing was said about Janet Erskine going along, but Will took it upon himself to include her in the summons. So trio and escort set off down Thames for Hampton Court without delay, eight miles.

They found that palace in a state of some tension. James, against the advice of all his statesmen and courtiers, had decided to go ahead with the coronation at Westminster Abbey the very next day, plague or no plague. He would heed the others so far as to omit the traditional ride through the city to let the citizenry see their new king and queen; but they would go by boat down Thames to the Whitehall Stairs at the waterside, and so to Westminster, thus avoiding any passage through the narrow and disease-ridden streets. Admittedly this would much affect the numbers attending, but this did not greatly concern James. The important matter was that he should receive the English anointing and crowning, too long delayed already, to add to the Scottish ones. So long as the necessary clergy and officers of state were present to play their parts, the rest did not signify. The fact that Queen Anne was apparently against the project only made her husband the more determined. They would be in Westminster Abbey for only an hour or so, and thereafter safely away to Windsor again, not here to Hampton Court, too near to London evidently, for two of the royal servants were already plague-stricken – hence part of the tension.

It was quite late that night before Will was ordered to attend on the king, with Henry already in bed and Janet reluctantly attaching herself to the queen's separate court again. He found James also in bed, but very much awake, pen in hand and hat on head, the covers littered with papers. The Earl of Mar was in attendance, but when he saw Will, he grimaced and departed.

"Ha, there you are, Alexander man," he was greeted from the bed. "I heard tell o' you bringing young Henry. Aye, and yon woman." Their liege-lord did not miss much. "Hoo are you faring wi' the psalms?"

"None so ill, Sire, although it is slow work. I have reached the twenty-second. But that is a long one, all complaints . . ."

"Is that a'? Twenty-two! And there are one hundred and fifty. Man, you are dilatory, aye dilatory!"

"I have the prince's tutoring to pursue also, Your Grace."

"Ooh, aye – fine, that! What is taking you sae long at it? Only twenty-two done."

"It is the comparisons, the various texts, in Greek, Latin and the earlier English translations. Trying to ensure that I have the rights of it, accuracy. They vary much, Sire. Wycliffe and Coverdale differ notably. Tyndale and Rogers changed much . . ."

"Yon Wycliffe was a heretic, just! Pay nae heed to him. And these other translations, man. Hold to the original Greek – I tellt you that at the start. You get it doon as best you can, and leave it to me to go ower it and correct. You dinna think I'm leaving the final version to *you*, Alexander! Noo, I havena much time for you at this present. But gie's a look at one or two o' your problems . . ."

Will drew some papers from his doublet pocket. Smoothing them out, he started with that seventh psalm, and the hes, with his insertions of capital letters to make sense of it. James approved of this, at least. Then he moved on to psalm eleven, where in the first verse he could not understand what "Flee as a bird to your mountain" could mean. Yet that was the literal translation.

"Och, man, dinna you ken that? Yon's a mistake. It's no' a bird, it's a flea. Aye, a bit flea! Read you the first Book o' Kings – yon's Samuel, mind, no' what's been wrongly called the first, when it's really the third." At Will's look of mystification, James tapped his arm. "In chapter twenty-six o' Samuel One, if I mind aright, it's there, and David quotes it. Aye, here's how I mind it. 'For the King o' Israel is come to seek a flea.' Aye, a flea. 'As when one hunts a partridge in the mountain.' A bird, mind. Whae'd have thought they'd have partricks in yon Holy Land. Sae, you see the translation's a' agley."

Wagging his head in astonishment, not so much at this mixed-up wording as at the monarch's extraordinary knowledge and memory, Will went on, "The same psalm, further, gives a verse that seems to say 'Upon the wicked shall He rain down snares, fire and brimstone and an horrible tempest.' I do not see how God could rain down snares, traps to catch birds or coneys . . ."

"Na, na, snares isna right. He means temptations just, to trap the sinner. I'd hae thought you'd see that, man."

"This is the trouble, Sire. I can make guesses as to such. But are my guesses what is required? I believed that I was to *translate*, not to make my own assumptions and guesses."

"Man, Alexander, are you forgetting *me*! Mysel'. You're no' the arbiter, just. I will go ower your work, never fear. You leave the decisions o' these difficult bits to me. Aye, and others, mind, for I'll hae plenties o' divines and the like at it, in due course, to check and check again. Your task is to get the main verses into fair English; aye, and *poetic* English. That's your part, no' making judgments."

Not so much humbled as relieved, Will nodded. "That, Your Grace, is a comfort to me. I shall not trouble you with more of this." He put his scraps of paper back in his pocket. "Do you wish to see what I have done so far? Not now, but later? Or wait until I have done more."

"I havena time to be at the checking, no' at this present. Later. I've this of the coronation to see to, and a wheen else! I just ettled to hear hoo you are getting on wi' it – that you *are* getting on! I'd ha' deemed you further on than this! Sae, off wi' you. Aye, and hae young Henry in guid state for the business the morn. We board the boats at nine hours. Awa', man Alexander."

Thankfully Will bowed out, passing Mar drinking in an anteroom. They did not exchange more than glances.

In the morning, quite a fleet of barges and boats were assembled on the Thames for the odd voyage downstream the fifteen miles to London's centre. Unfortunately it was raining heavily, and awnings had not been provided for all craft – and even on such as had them, leaking was general, so the handsome velvet cloaks worn by the great ones, although welcome for their cover, were scarcely improved in appearance. The king, it seemed, cared nothing for the rain, and himself took charge down at the waterside, detailing who should sail in which of the fully a score of vessels. They would pick up further boatloads down-river, to be sure, including most of the clergy; but the majority of those attending the coronation had been housed in the extensive quarters of this Hampton Court. Most of the great ones, of course, were used to travelling on horseback or in their carriages, and did not take kindly to this of being crowded into the vessels with their subordinates and retinues. Normally, in any major function, the more important the noble or statesman the larger his "tail" as James put it, his accompanying train. But today numbers were being strictly curtailed, earls being allowed only sixteen attendants, lords and bishops only ten. Even so, the boats tended to be packed full, the king insisting that each magnate board with his own retainers, much as they would have preferred to travel with their peers.

Then the queen's entourage was late, and her husband fretted – indeed he sent Mar to hasten them on, hardly the wisest choice. Anne was to have a barge for herself, her

91

daughter and her women, Henry to travel with his father in the first and decorative scow, with its royal standards hanging wet and limp. As the prince's attendant, Will found himself on this leading craft, in fact closer to the monarch than all but Robert, Lord Cecil and Johnnie Mar, who had returned to say that the queen was nearly ready, but refusing to come down with himself.

Under the dripping awning of the second scow, a band of musicians was ordered to strike up, while impatiently the monarch and all others waited.

So restless and irascible did James Stewart become that Will feared that he was going to command a casting-off and start to be made without the queen; however, eventually the women did appear, unhurrying, and were directed to the third vessel, Janet among them, Henry, spotting her, declaring that she should come in *this* boat, to be flapped to silence by his father.

The voyage commenced, to music, the oarsmen seeking to pull in rhythm.

Rowed by Kingston, Richmond, Kew and Fulham, they picked up sundry adherents, these falling into line behind. The rain continued and the musicians played on.

At Wandsworth they began to come into the outskirts of the city, and quickly thereafter the buildings and houses and docks proliferated, until by Chelsea and Vauxhall they were deep in London town. The king's ideas as to the topography were somewhat vague, and, although he had suggested that they made for the Whitehall Stairs landing, Robert Cecil pointed out that there was a pier at Westminster itself, for the former palace and Westminster Hall, and much nearer the abbey; and they would come to this first. Since they all would have to walk, in this rain, it would be an advantage.

So at Westminster Pier the first of the flotilla pulled in and moored, disembarking their complements. There was no room for more than four craft to berth at one time, so that the unloading process was delayed, and King James was not the one to hang about waiting for lesser mortals,

having already had enough of that at Hampton, over his
wife's delay. So he set off straight away, with Cecil, the
Earls of Pembroke, Southampton and Montgomery, and
young Henry – therefore with Will Alexander also, plus
the royal guard of course, leaving Anne and her ladies, and
all others landing, to follow on at their own convenience.
James was not much of a walker, with his ungainly gait, so
the pace was moderate. There were no crowds to welcome
them, the few citizens they saw eyeing them without any
particular interest, unaware who they were. It made a
wet walk.

As Cecil had said, it was not far to Westminster Abbey,
a handsome pile, although no finer, as the monarch
remarked, than some of those his ancestor King David
had erected in Scotland. They entered by the great west
door between the two soaring square towers. At first it
looked as though they were quite unexpected, with the
splendid fane all but empty. However some individual
must have played the scout, for presently out from one of
the transepts hurried a group of handsomely clad figures,
mostly prelates obviously, who were loud in their apologies
for not being at the door to welcome their sovereign-lord,
whom they had not expected to arrive thus unannounced,
an embarrassing performance. Clearly they had looked
for a more resounding advent from the new head of
the Church of England. A chubby, bustling little man,
gorgeously robed and chained, declared himself to be
the Lord Mayor of London, and then presented the
Archbishops of Canterbury and York and sundry other
bishops.

James, who had met most of these before, was more
interested in his present surroundings than in the regrets
expressed, and was intent on making his way forward to
the main choir or chancel area. There, before the high
altar, was placed centrally a gold-painted, high-backed
wooden chair, with a box-like seat, other chairs to right
and left. He called his son thither, and pointed.

"See you that, laddie. Yon's the coronation chair the

93

rascally Edward Plantagenet, or Angevin – that was his right name, mind – the chair he had made in 1296. You'll ken aboot that limmer? It was to be o' gold, see you, but och, he changed his mind!" That with something of a hoot of laughter. "For he was right tricked! See what's in yon box beneath. His lump o' stane! Yon came frae Scone. He jaloused it was the Stane o' Destiny! It wasna. The right stane was hidden awa' frae him, and this lump put in its place, in Scone Abbey. But he kennt nae better. Sae the kings of this England hae been sitting on this cheatrie ever since!" Another hoot.

"Master Will told me about the true Stone of Destiny," Henry said. "He thinks that it is in the Highlands somewhere. In the Isles, he says."

"Nae doot. Yon MacDonalds hae it, I'm tellt."

"And will you sit on this one, Father?"

"Ooh, aye. Even though it's no' the right Scots one, it's the English coronation stane. They've had a' their kings crowned on it since yon Edward. That's three hunnerd years. Sae, since I'm the king noo, I'll hae to sit on it." He leered over at Cecil, who had come up and was listening. "It'll dae me nae harm!" He chuckled, and turned to Will. "Eh, Alexander man?"

Will bowed, but discreetly forbore comment.

"This interests me, Sire . . ." Cecil began, when a commotion at the other end of the abbey heralded the arrival of the queen's party. The prelates hurried down to greet her.

Cecil had to swallow his interest in the coronation stone meantime, and conducted the king and Henry through a side chapel and into the Chapter House from which the clergy had emerged, and where they could wait in some comfort and privacy while all was arranged for the ceremony. Will, Henry clutching his hand, had no option but to go in with them, unsuitable as this was for such as himself.

James found sundry items of interest to examine, magnificent vestments, silver chalices and platters, golden candlesticks, even a Breeches Bible, which he explained to his son was so called because of the Reformers' odd preoccupation with decency, so that, in the illustrations therein, they had covered up Adam's and Eve's privy parts with breeks, king and prince sniggering equally over this. Will was being advised to have a look at the psalms section when the queen and the remainder of the chancel party trooped in, to much chatter and disorder. He took the opportunity to escape, and went out to find a modest place in the body of the main church, where presently Janet joined him, having noted his exit.

"This must be the strangest coronation ever!" she declared. "I am soaking wet! You will be also? Even if we do not all catch the plague, we may die of the chill!" She gestured around them. "The abbey is half empty!"

"I do not suppose that will concern our James! He is, I'd say, only anxious to get this anointing and crowning over and done with, so that he can feel secure against any rival claimants. He says that there is a plot by some dissident lords, Catholics mainly, to put the young Lady Arabella Stewart on the throne, the king's cousin. Queen Elizabeth at one time favoured her. She has always lived in England."

"I saw her at Windsor. The queen likes her well. I do not think that she now aspires to the crown, Will."

"Probably not. But James wishes to be sure. Once this coronation is over, however odd and unusual it may be, he will feel secure – the Lord's Anointed, for England equally with Scotland."

"England, I fear, has won a strange monarch!"

As they waited there, Henry came out, looking for them, and spotting, came almost at the run. "Why did you go away?" he demanded. "I wish that I could be with you. My father says that I must stay with him. But he says that it will not be long. He has told the Cecil man that all is to be made short. I have to go up there and sit beside him. He is going to sit on that chair with the stone underneath. And I am to sit next to him."

"What of your mother, the queen?" Janet asked.

"I do not know. I am all wet . . ."

The musicians had arrived and, moving on into the side chapel, struck up somewhat raggedly at first but soon produced something more solemn-sounding than what they had provided during the rowing down-river.

"I think that you had better go back to your father," Will said. "It sounds as though matters are going to start soon now. Especially with the king requiring haste, and to get all over as quickly as possible."

Reluctantly the prince departed.

Presently the music changed from the hymn-like to something resembling a march, and out through the side chapel issued a procession, not very precise nor ordered, led by the Dean of Westminster carrying a white linen garment over his arm, followed by the little lord mayor. Then two Yeomen of the Guard, bearing aloft banners with the leopards of England quartering the lilies of France. A group of lords came thereafter, each carrying on cushions and trays items not identifiable at a distance, presumably all having some official status, then the bishops, notably not wearing their mitres. After a pause came the earls, some, as officers of state, bearing the various symbols of regality, four swords, held upright, golden spurs and batons of office. The Kings of Arms followed on, Garter, Clarenceux and Norroy, then the two archbishops, bearing the ampulla and the anointing spoon. Behind these was borne the great two-handed sword of state, carried not as it should have been by the Earl Marshal, the Duke of Norfolk, for, a Catholic, he was forfeited, but by the Earl of Pembroke, flanked by the orb on the right and the sceptre-with-dove on the left. All this before the king appeared, behind Southampton bearing St Edward's crown on its cushion.

James shambled out, looking about him interestedly, critically, caring nothing for dignity but concerned seemingly with the other participants' behaviour, even glancing behind him to see that Queen Anne followed on, her hand on the arm of the Duke of Lennox, and behind her young Henry with the Earl of Mar. The musicians' marching beat he ignored, as indeed did his wife.

If it all seemed rather less august and stately than it was meant to be, it had to be remembered that there had not been a coronation for forty-five years and, owing to the circumstances, there had been no rehearsal.

All had to make a right-angled turn to climb the few steps up into the chancel area where the chairs were arranged before the high altar, this having to be carefully negotiated by those carrying the various precious burdens. And when the king's unsteady gait all but produced a trip here, Will for one held his breath. But the manoeuvre was completed without disaster, although thereafter there was some shuffling about, with not all the company quite sure where they ought to be placed. However, the dean, acting as master of ceremonies, got everyone approximately in place, and bowed to the Archbishop of Canterbury to take over.

James, having trouble with his lengthy crimson robe, was taken by the arm and led up to the altar, where he had to kneel on a faldstool. He there muttered something after the prelate, and then, searching in an inner pocket, made difficult by that velvet robe, produced the required nugget of pure gold, one pound in weight, as the traditional oblation, this to be put on the altar as indication of the new king's support of Holy Church. Then the queen was led to his side, to do the same. They knelt there while the dean read out the litany.

The royal pair rose, and all the regalia was brought forward, piece by piece, to lay on the altar also, the musicians signed to play, since this took some little time, the various bearers having to do it in due order. The sermon dispensed with, the archbishop administered the coronation oath, phrase by phrase, which James repeated thickly. He then had a Bible from the altar given to him to kiss.

All this over, the monarch was divested of his long

crimson robe and led to the coronation chair, that over the stone, to sit thereon, the queen being given the chair on his left, Prince Henry on the right, this amid a certain amount of confusion, for four Knights of the Garter had to come up and hold a silken pall over the king while the archbishop anointed him with the holy oil from the ampulla, using the spoon, with a finger dipped therein to apply to the royal head, breast and the palms of both hands. This achieved, the dean, also with some difficulty, placed the white linen garment which he had been carrying throughout over the king's head, James less than co-operative and the Garter knights distinctly in the way.

Then, at last, the St Edward's crown was carefully placed on the royal head, to shouts of "God save the King! God save the King!" from all present.

But there was more to come. Repeating after the archbishop, the monarch had to swear to preserve the Protestant religion as established by law, to govern the realm also according to the law as enacted, and, oddly, to promise to sign the declaration against the doctrine of transubstantiation – all this inevitably in a moist gabble, details of which did not reach most of those present.

There followed the presentation of the spurs, the girding on of the sword of state, the investing with the armil or stole, the fitting of the ruby ring on the fourth finger, the receiving of the orb and sceptre, and finally the presentation of a glove by the lord of the manor of Worksop, the significance of which was lost on most, including the monarch obviously.

James was rising from that chair, having had a sufficiency of it all, when he was pressed back, to receive kisses and tokens of allegiance. All present in the chancel were apparently entitled, indeed required, to come forward, take the monarch's hand between their two palms and swear fealty, then to kiss their sovereign-lord's left cheek. One of the first to do so was the dandified Philip Herbert, Earl of Montgomery who, after that somewhat lingering kiss, bent further over to kiss the right cheek also – to the indrawn breaths of the watchers, and James's slap on the offender's cheek, and guffaw.

The final ritual was for the newly crowned monarch and his queen to receive Holy Communion. But here there was a hitch, for although James took the bread and wine, Anne would not, to the consternation of the Archbishop of York, who did the administering. The queen was known to have leanings towards Roman Catholicism, and this appeared to prove it, much to the concern of all who had just heard her husband swear to uphold the Protestant religion. Possibly it was the declaration against the dogma of transubstantiation which had brought her to this. For moments there was dismay, uncertainty, save on Anne's part, none knowing quite what to do, but James took over, flapped his hand at wife and prelate both, indicating that it mattered not what a mere woman thought on such matters, and turned away, gesturing to Henry, clearly having had enough of ceremonial for one day.

All that mattered over, as far as he was concerned, the crowned monarch was not going to be troubled by any more and unnecessary formalities, but evidently was for getting out of the premises and back to the boats without delay, leaving others to do anything that was needful at the abbey, and not even waiting for the queen and her ladies, who were in less haste. Henry darted away and came to Will and Janet. These then became concerned that the boy should rejoin his father, and so went hurrying off after the king's little group, which included the Earl of Mar, while Lennox remained with Anne.

They caught up with James as he was disappearing round Westminster Hall, on their way to the riverside.

At least it had stopped raining.

Considering his odd gait, their newly crowned liege-lord made good time to the pier. Their fleet of boats and scows had now marshalled themselves bows-in to the landing-stage, which took up much less room, so that they all could be moored alongside; but this did entail rather awkward embarking, and James spluttered reproofs as he was assisted inboard. In twos and threes his entourage arrived, proud English earls and lords seldom having had to hurry afoot like this previously, even Robert Cecil, usually so calmly assured, looking somewhat offput. Once Cecil was aboard, the king gave orders to cast off, not waiting for the queen or any of the other boat-parties. Janet proved to be the only woman on the royal barge. Henry was obviously enjoying this part of the programme. The musicians had not yet appeared, so the craft's journey up stream was unaccompanied in more ways than one.

Being rowed against the current, they made a less speedy voyage than when coming downstream; and now they had further to go, for James was not making back to Hampton Court but on the extra seven miles to Windsor, those plague victims at the former worrying him. Indeed he announced that even Windsor was probably too near London, and that after a night or so there they would go on much further away. He had heard that Woodstock, north of Oxford, had been a favoured palace of Elizabeth's; they would go inspect that, a good sixty miles, he was told, from London. All should be safe there. He hastened to point out to Cecil and others that it was not himself he was concerned for, the Lord's Anointed, and that twice, but for them all, young Henry here, even that Annie. Cecil said that he feared that Woodstock would scarcely be ready to receive them adequately, not having been much used in late years. His objections were brushed aside.

The prince said that he wanted to go back to Oatlands with Will and Janet, but his father said that he would have to wait for the morrow, for this night, at Windsor, he was going to celebrate and he wanted his son and heir to be present.

At Windsor Castle eventually, with his court and following arriving seriatim as it were, James's notion of a suitable celebration turned out to be more of a prolonged drinking-session. From this Anne and her ladies retired early, and even the king recognised that it was not apt entertainment for Henry, so he signed for

Will to take the boy off at the same time as his mother went, which that man was glad to do. He was less glad about an earlier word from the monarch, to the effect that Johnnie Mar would be heading north for Scotland the next day, having been absent therefrom for overlong already, and who could tell what that rogue Patrick Gray might be up to! And, of course, Janet Erskine was to go with him.

Will, getting Henry off to bed, did not have to go in search of Janet, for she came to them, aware that this would be their last time together, for a period unknown. The prince, late already, was much excited over the day's events and in no mood for sleep, chattering on and on. So his attendants sat with him in his room for some considerable time, knowing that if they did not, the boy would be out of his bed and after them. It was not every day that saw the coronation which was to start an entirely new nation-state, the United Kingdom of Great Britain and Ireland, as James insisted it was to be called, with the heir to it all involved.

When at length Henry's talk and questions began to tail off and yawns become frequent, they concluded that sleep was not far off and that they could leave.

Out in the corridor the pair embraced, but with servitors still in evidence, the celebrating still going on nearby, privacy was less than complete, and Will suggested that they should go and walk together outside. This they did, and hand-in-hand strolled through the gardens and orchards surrounding the castle, thankful that the rain held off.

"What is going to become of us, Will?" the young woman asked, after a silent spell. "Myself sent back home and you remaining here. For how long, think you?"

"I do not know," he admitted. "I have no wish to remain in England. This is not the life I would choose. I am fond of Henry, but tutoring I have had sufficiently long. If I can persuade the king to appoint another tutor and attendant, I will. But he has involved me in this Bible translation also, and that may make him detain me."

101

"Yes. But others could do that. Can you not convince him that your lands require your attention? And that court life is not for you. That your place is in Scotland . . ."

"Think you that James would heed that? And he has the royal command, which none can disobey, even the greatest. If I could offend him in some way? But, knowing our sovereign-lord, he would be as like to clap me in the Tower of London as to send me home! Would that Argyll had never taken me into the royal presence at Stirling!"

"At least he may allow you to return home on visits?"

"I hope so."

Having circuited the castle a few times, they paused beneath a mulberry tree to kiss and caress.

"I am going to miss you, Janet my dear. More than I can say," he told her. "Oatlands, without you, is going to be a different place. Dull. Flat. A nine-year-old boy scarcely the company I would seek, however attractive, not all the time. He is a good lad, but . . ."

"Perhaps you will find some other woman to share your loneliness?"

"Not so! Never think it. You are *you*!"

"But far away . . ."

He stopped her words with his lips, hands busy also.

At length he took her over to the tower which the queen and her ladies were occupying, and they said their goodnights less lingeringly than they might have done had not maidservants kept appearing.

That was indeed the last time that Will and Janet were able to see each other alone, for it transpired that Mar was for off early in the morning, despite the imbibing of the evening, with long riding ahead for his party. So it was a hasty and very public leave-taking, however illustrious the send-off, with the king and Henry among the wavers of farewell.

The day following, with the king and court heading off again up Thames for Woodstock in Oxfordshire, Will and Henry, with their inevitable escort, departed in the other direction, for Oatlands.

7

The months that followed were strange ones indeed for Will Alexander, life seeming in something of a limbo for a young and active man, transplanted from his own land and background to a totally different existence, in the company only of a small boy. Much as he liked Henry, sometimes he felt all but a hermit there at Oatlands, a sense of restriction upon him, which he endeavoured not to display to the prince. He sought to combat this by much outdoor exercise and sporting activities, which suited Henry equally, whatever his royal father would have said; but even so, life for Will seemed to consist almost entirely of teaching and coaching the boy and translating psalms. Long evenings alone did enable him to pursue his own poetic composition admittedly, and he finished his hundredth sonnet, "The Tragedy of Croesus", so that he could now contemplate possible publication. But nothing could dispel the feelings of constriction and isolation. And to say that he greatly missed Janet Erskine was a major understatement.

Meantime, he learned, James and Anne were making an extended tour of southern England, showing themselves to their new subjects and receiving the hospitality of the great ones, the queen revelling in the wealth displayed and the king sampling the hunting available. In the circumstances young Henry was left at Oatlands to advance his education.

So August and September passed. It was early October before the prince was sent for, to join his parents at Wilton House, the seat of William Herbert, Earl of Pembroke, Will to bring him there, and glad of the break in his monotonous duties. Wilton was in Wiltshire, near Salisbury, some seventy-five miles off to the west beyond Basing House, the seat of the Marquis of Winchester, where they had gone from Woodstock.

Wilton proved to be palatial indeed, an enormous house in widespread parkland, but even its proportions and opulence seeming overcrowded so great was the gathering there at this time. Will could not but be impressed by the magnificence of this establishment and the scale of hospitality and entertainment being provided for the royal guests and the literally hundreds of their following. Lennox, whom James always wanted to have with him, and with whom Will always got on well, the least ducal of dukes, said that all these English magnates were vying with each other in the splendour of their receptions for the new monarch; and to the Scots, from no such rich country, this could seem scarcely credible, or indeed creditable, so overdone and extravagant was much of the provision and display. Queen Anne gloried in it, extravagant as she was herself by nature; but James had reservations apparently about all this wealth in his subjects' hands when he himself was, by comparison, poverty-stricken. The Scots treasury had been more or less empty for years; indeed the king, and even more so the queen, was deeply in debt to Geordie Heriot their banker; but he had expected to enjoy quite changed circumstances when he mounted the southern throne. Instead he had discovered the English treasury to be four hundred thousand pounds in debt, to his grave offence, Gloriana Elizabeth in her last years apparently having neglected the monarchial revenues. So all this flourish of riches and power by the nobility of the south all but aggrieved him.

Pembroke, an agreeable character, as courtly as he was open-handed, was himself much interested in poetry and the arts, which commended him to James; but he was also making a great fuss over Anne, who clearly thought well of him. As well she might, considering the scale of his endeavours to please. Will received some demonstration of all this flourish the very first evening at Wilton when, as well as an ambitious masque put on for the queen's benefit – Anne loved such affairs and took part in them herself – there was a different kind of entertainment, a play-acting by a renowned troupe of players brought from London for the occasion, plague or none, known for some reason as the Lord Chamberlain's Men, these under a playwright and actor-manager named William Shakespeare who, it seemed, had been highly thought of by the late Elizabeth. Will had not heard of him nor his group, but clearly he was fairly renowned in these parts. He was a good-looking man of some forty years, with a notably high brow and quite a presence.

Henry was allowed to stay up late that night to see the play, which had the strange title of *As You Like It*, which excited him greatly, the more so in that it went on for a considerable time, keeping bed at bay, with five acts and no fewer than twenty-two scenes. He did not understand much of the speech and allusions, and said so over-loudly; but he did appreciate the wrestling, of which there was much, and the scenery of the Forest of Arden, erected with much ingenuity. The talk of pancakes and mustard left him bewildered, and vocal.

Seeking to keep his charge reasonably quiet, Will was greatly interested in it all, a new experience for him also, a pastoral comedy with a range of characters seeking escape from tyranny and oppressive court life by taking to the forest, where sport and love take over, with some philosophy in the by-going. Nearly all in blank verse, there was included some poetry and song, these inserts connected with Hymen, the god of marriage, and some of the anatomical allusions scarcely convenient to explain to a nine-year-old. It was all notably well performed, the young women, Rosalind and Celia, by no means shrinking from their significant contributions. The writing behind it all intrigued Will, and inevitably he wondered whether he himself could even attempt playwriting. Some of his own work might well adapt, he assessed, to being enacted, if he could discover the secret of this different kind of translating. He well recognised that there could be problems in converting the written and spoken words into action, and to conveying the passage of time. He would have liked to have had a talk with this Shakespeare, but he was much occupied in managing all, and when the performance was over, Henry had to be got off to bed, a lengthy process in the prevailing excitement. By the time that Will got back from these duties, a masque was in progress and the playwright not to be seen. However, during an interval, Lennox brought a youngish man of saturnine good looks, whom he introduced to Will as the deviser of this masque, by name Ben Jonson, another playwright and poet and colleague of the man Shakespeare, who claimed Scots blood although born in London, alleging descent from the Johnstones of Annandale. He left them together, saying that they might well have much in common to talk about.

Will learned from this Jonson, who was friendly and voluble, despite his rather sinister appearance, much that was of interest to him, how he shared the Globe Theatre in London with Shakespeare, how he had been branded on the thumb and gaoled for killing a fellow-actor in a duel, but had been a soldier previously in Flanders, where he had had odd adventures – all this recounted with sardonic humour. It took a little while for Will to get him on to the subject of converting poetry into plays. He declared that it was easier to turn prose for stage presentation, not only in that the actors spoke in prose, seldom in verse, but because so much was implied in poetry, not actually stated, which could not be conveyed effectively in speech or action on stage. So he advised Will, if he had ambitions to be a playwright, first to adapt his chosen poetic theme to prose, and then, visualising the actors' needs in their carrying of the audience with them, turn the words into action, using the scenes and acts to convey the passage of time. Himself, he preferred the composing of poetry, as such, to playwriting, but recognised that there was a much larger audience and market waiting for the latter; not everyone read or appreciated poetry, unfortunately.

Jonson spoke admiringly of Shakespeare, declaring that his plays were bringing a new dimension to the world of entertainment, reaching great numbers who would never previously have dreamed of entering a theatre, street-buskers the height of their entertainment hitherto. Yet he did not play down to the mob, able to hold the attention even of the uneducated. Shakespeare was an actor himself, of course, which enabled him to make his plays acceptable to all and sundry. What did Master Alexander think of *As You Like It*?

They discussed the production admiringly, Jonson critical only of the intricacy of the relationship between so many of the cast, brothers, cousins, uncles, which could be confusing. And he was doubtful about the proliferation of scenes in the forest, difficult to make different.

Will sought his own couch belatedly that night, with much to think on.

Next day James sent for him, to put him through an examination on the subject of the psalms, critical but conceding that he was making some progress. When he had finished them, he was to start on the Song of Solomon, more poetic. Solomon was a better poet than was his father, the king averred.

And what did Alexander think of the play-acting last night? And yon Shakespeare mannie? Will declared that he had been much entertained and impressed, admiring of the way in which the theme had been handled, the speech used to excellent effect and the passage of time well indicated. He had learned lessons watching and listening, and in consequence was feeling distinctly humbled as to his own versifying.

James was not thus troubled. He judged the play worthy enough, and the acting competent, but all that of the wrestling was more suitable for a town's fair than a royal court; and the younger brother ousting the elder from the dukedom was a right improbable contrive. But, och, the mannie was to be encouraged, just, this Shakespeare. He would have a word with him one of these days.

Will mentioned that he had talked with another playwright, Jonson by name, who seemed to be very knowledgeable as to poetry as well as plays, whereupon he was warned by the monarch to watch his step with that one. He had heard that he was a Catholic, and possibly not beyond treason. Pembroke should not have invited him here at this time. But then, Pembroke had some right strange friends, it seemed: that caird Walter Raleigh for one, him that was in yon Tower of London, Pembroke getting Annie to plead for his release. He was getting over far-ben with Annie, Pembroke was – he would have to have a word with her.

Will left the royal presence without any questions asked as to the heir to the throne's progress and well-being.

That evening there was another and more ambitious masque, with Jonson directing and the queen taking prominent part, the king however absenting himself to do some serious drinking with a group of supportive cronies, poor Lennox having to pass most of the time with these, although he managed to escape briefly now and again to visit the more colourful and rousing scene. This was a performance of *The Masque of Blackness*, a great spectacle wherein a large boat was drawn in by alleged sea-horses, with the queen as Euphoria, herself and her ladies with faces and arms blackened, while they were escorted by six sea monsters with torch-bearers on their backs. Not all there approved of the queen thus displayed.

On the second of Lennox's inspections he sought out Will, in converse with Ben Jonson again with whom he got on well despite the royal warning, to tell him that Henry was to be got off to bed forthwith, as this sort of ploy was unsuitable for his son, whatever the boy's mother might think. So King James was kept apprised of what went on, and did consider his heir's situation on occasion, it seemed.

Whether, also, James felt that Anne was seeing over-much of the dashing Earl of Pembroke, as of Jonson, or that it was just in furtherance of his hospitality-sampling progress, the monarch ordained a move onward the day following, to Farnham Castle, the seat of the wealthy Bishop of Winchester. However, this move was not to include Prince Henry, who had been away from his studies for long enough already, according to his sire. So it was back to Oatlands for the boy and his tutor, reluctant as they both were, lessons and psalmody scarcely beckoning.

It was Christmastide before another break was permitted for the pair. They were summoned to Hampton Court, where the festive season was being passed. It was apparently going to be one continuous celebration, not so much of Christ's coming as the infant saviour of mankind as for the start of this new earthly reign. For it was not only James and Anne who were savouring and making much of their new-found monarchial state, however differently they viewed it; their English courtiers were likewise celebrating, for they had in fact been putting up with some ten years of strict rule and non-festivity with Elizabeth Tudor, in her ageing and declining years departing from the Gloriana's reputation she had earned in the previous thirty-five, all but parsimonious and sour. Now they had a monarch who, whatever else, was in favour of parade, spending, flourish and sporting activities, and a queen who loved entertainment and spectacle. So the end of this momentous year for two kingdoms, 1603, was to be signalised more after the fashion of pagan Yule than of the Babe in the manger's nativity.

Conviviality was in full swing when Will, with Henry, arrived on the Eve of St Thomas, the palace and its environs crowded, feasting all but continuous, garb and costume as extravagant as all else, with King James probably the least well dressed present, his wife making up for it. Who was paying for it all was not clear –

the one thing assured, that it was not the monarch himself.

Accommodation being at a premium, son and tutor had to find quarters in one of the stableyards, their arrival and presence occasioning little notice. Nevertheless their strange sovereign-lord learned of it very promptly, for they were sent for surprisingly soon thereafter, the Earl of Montgomery no less appearing to conduct them, in admittedly somewhat superior fashion, to the royal presence, from which he was then dismissed, along with the Lord Cecil, with a flick of an ink-stained hand.

"Sae there you are, the twa o' you!" they were greeted, almost as though they had been absenting themselves deliberately. "You, Henry, you're behaving yoursel'? Eh? Maistering your studies? Your Latinity? See you, what does *non modo hac condicione sed etiam cum grano salis* mean, eh?"

Gulping at being thus abruptly tested, the prince glanced at Will, but, swallowing, got out, "I think it means not to be sure of something, but to take it with a grain of salt, Father."

"No' bad, no' bad. Reservation is the word, mind, not only wi' reservation but wi' the grain o' salt. The bit aboot the salt gave it awa'. But no' bad. Aye, and you, Alexander man? What hae you to say for yoursel'?"

"In what respect, Sire? The teaching and studies? Or the psalms?"

"Psalms, man! Dinna tell me that you're still at thae psalms? It's the Song o' Solomon I'm ettling to hear you on."

"I have only glanced at that, Sire. I have not yet finished all the psalms."

"Eh? What hae you been at, at yon Oatlands? Idling, man? Idling?"

"Not so, Your Grace—"

"Majesty, man – majesty noo."

"Yes, Your Majesty. But idling, no." Will took a risk. "As well as translating psalms, I felt that I must continue

110

with some of my own poetry, Sire. *You* will know how it is. The psalms could, in some measure, stale me. I must keep my own muse from dying, poorly as it may be. I have been able to finish my hundredth piece. So now, save for some polishing and tidying, I can even consider possible publication."

His risk-taking paid off. James nodded, those soulful eyes concerned. "You're right, man. You're right. It's a sin, just, to neglect your bit gift. Aye, yon David's psalms could come between you and your ain versifying, I can see that. One hunnerd, eh? Ambitious! Maybe ower ambitious. You aim to publish?"

"A writer must have readers, Sire. Or where is the point of it all?"

"Uh-huh. Hae you a publisher in mind, man?"

"I have not got that far, Majesty, I know of none here, in England."

"Aye then, I'll seek one oot for you. That is, mind, if I judge they're worth it! Your poems. You'll hae to let me scan them one day. Mysel', I'm working on a book the noo that'll teach this laddie hoo to be a king, just. A book on monarchy. It's a subject no' many hae the rights o', mind." James whinnied his odd laugh. "No' many to compete, eh? It's to be entitled the *Basilikon Doron*. On the art, aye the art o' government by kings by divine right. One day, Henry, you'll hae to dae that. It's *you* I'm scrieving it for. A right notable task."

The boy looked bemused.

"I hae appointed my ain printer doon here in London, see you," the king went on. "Barker. Robbie Barker. I could tell him to print your sonnets, Alexander. You'd hae to pay him, mind."

"I would not so trouble Your Majesty. I will, I hope, find my own printer. Master Jonson will guide me in this, no doubt."

"Aye, maybe. One hunnerd's quite a volume, man. I dinna promise to read them a', see you. But I'll scan some. Meantime, get you on wi' the Song o' Solomon."

111

Clearly that was the end of the audience. Man and boy backed out.

There appeared to be feasting going on in various parts of the extensive palace. Will, with food required after their journey, felt that he should take her son to the queen; but Henry thought otherwise, preferring not to have to account for himself to his mother, whom he scarcely knew, and where he would have to talk to his sister Elizabeth if she was there. He would much prefer to eat elsewhere.

They were told that there was to be an especially splendid masque put on that night for the queen, devised by Ben Jonson; so Will asked where Master Jonson was dining, and was directed eventually to a suite of rooms being occupied by the Earl of Pembroke and others. Here they were welcomed by a mixed company of nobility, players and actresses, Pembroke being very much interested in the arts. The prince was made much of, and responded well, to his tutor's satisfaction. He was an attractive and pleasant-natured boy, even though he was not greatly attracted to his mother and sister.

Will took the opportunity to discuss the matter of printers and publishers with Ben Jonson, who warned him that there were a number of quite unscrupulous tradesmen in London, and to avoid Thomas Thorpe and John Dunter in especial, who would charge exorbitantly and produce shoddy work. He would recommend either James Roberts, on Fleet Street, or Edward Blount, both of whom had done satisfactory work for himself.

As to the evening's entertainment, it transpired that the masque, *The Garden of Circe*, was not going to take place for some time; and after the quite long ride from Oatlands, Henry ought not to be kept up late. So, reluctantly, the boy was presently led off to bed, protesting that he was not tired.

He certainly gave that impression thereafter, with chatter and questions, so that it was late indeed before Will could leave him, asleep, and make for the main ballroom of the palace, where Jonson's masque was to be held.

It had already started by the time that Will arrived. The great hall, all candelabras and mirrors, was packed with richly dressed folk, save for a central space and corridor thereto left clear, this dotted with small trees and bushes in pots. There musicians were playing meantime, and tumblers and clowns entertaining the company between acts of the masquerade which apparently was in three parts. Jonson was not in sight, presumably in one of the anterooms instructing the masquers. Will did not feel it as his place to join Pembroke's or any of the other lords' groupings. There was no sign of king or queen.

With nobody he knew to talk to, he was wondering whether in fact he wanted to remain to watch the proceedings, when a trumpet-blast heralded the next stage of the masque, and he decided to wait.

Out from a doorway into that bush-lined corridor came four gallants clad in silken antique costumes of varied styles, laughing and shouting merrily, one of them the dandified Earl of Montgomery who had led them to James. These capered about among the trees and bushes, tossing balls to each other, to the musical accompaniment. Then out strolled a very different figure, dressed in silver half-armour over a sort of kilted vesture and wearing round his brow the golden circle of monarchy. He announced himself to the audience as Odysseus, King of Ithaca, parading the supposed garden and waving to the frolicking four, who all bowed but continued with their games. He was recognisable as the Marquis of Winchester, from Basing, an impressively built character. Twice he made a dignified circuit of the area.

Then, to another trumpet-call, six young women emerged, fairly scantily clad, in pairs drawing by silken cords a carriage of sorts painted white and gold in which sat a single female in sky blue satin glittering with jewels but otherwise scarcely adequately covered, the cloak she wore over one shoulder doing little to hide the rest of her well-rounded, indeed slightly bulging figure – Anne being pregnant again. For this was the queen. There were gasps of astonishment from many of the watchers at seeing the person of their monarch's wife thus displayed; but such exclamations were drowned by the four of Odysseus's courtiers shouting, "Hail to Circe! Hail to Circe, daughter of the sun god, Queen of Aeaea! Hail, Circe!"

Eye-catching and dramatic as all this was, Will Alexander scarcely perceived or took it in, although staring. For one of the first pair of young women drawing the carriage was not only stunningly lovely, but her cascade of rippling red hair falling to her white shoulders could belong to none other than his Aurora, Mistress of the Rosy Dawn – the Lady Agnes Douglas.

Quite overwhelmed, eyes for no other, Will stood transfixed.

The little procession circled the garden, the young women stepping a dance as they drew the carriage, Odysseus and the other men gazing in seeming awe. Halted centrally, the queen, as Circe, stepped down, having some difficulty in keeping her cloak approximately in place, while making a regal gesture and pointing to one of the gallants.

"Swine!" she declared haughtily. "Earth-bound animals! Hide your faces from the great sun. From swine you came and to swine you return." And she made a dismissive flick of the hand.

The man promptly fell to the floor, and, twisting and turning, rolled away among the potted bushes.

Odysseus protested.

Ignoring him, Circe turned on another of the men and repeated her incantation and gestures. He too fell and disappeared into the foliage.

The young women laughed and pointed. Will tried to catch Agnes's eye, but failed.

When only Odysseus himself remained standing and indeed in sight, Circe turned on him also, going through the same performance. But he did not collapse, standing proudly.

"You cannot cast your spell on me!" he announced. "I

114

am not as other men. Have done, daughter of the sun, have done!"

Circe drew herself up at her most imperious, making various gesticulations. But to none effect. The man stood, smiling.

Then out from the bushes emerged on all fours the likeness of a pig, snout, flapping ears, curling little tail and all, grunting, to be joined by the other three in their porcine guise – this to the delighted cheers of the watchers. They had been quick and effective in transforming themselves, under the cover of the bushes. Now they crept round Odysseus beseeching his aid.

That man drew from behind his breast-plate a sprig of some sort of plant. "See you, Circe, the magic herb moly, given me by Hermes, messenger of the gods. And over this moly, you have no power. I grow it on my island kingdom of Ithaca. Now it can have power over even you! Shall I invoke it against you? Make you in your turn into some creature of the earth? How say you?"

"Not so, O King. You would not offend the sun himself, my father?"

"I would not wish to. And since you are beautiful and fair, I can think of a kinder fate for Circe! So turn these swine back, to be men again. And you shall be safe from my moly-herb's spell."

The young women chorused, "Do, Circe, do!"

Anne inclined her head, and turning waved a hand. And rising from hands and knees, the four men threw off their pigs' costumes, with cries of gratitude, and began to caper once more.

The girls, laughing, threw themselves into the dancers' arms.

Odysseus, bowing, assisted Circe back into her carriage, and then, with a flourish, climbed in with her, to embrace her, she receiving him with every sign of enthusiasm.

The women enrolled the men to aid them in their carriage-pulling, and to somewhat breathless song the

115

masquers circled the garden again and returned whence they had come, to the plaudits of the company.

Hardly had the actors disappeared than Will was making his way through the press after them, out of the ballroom. There were different anterooms beyond. Winchester and the other men were donning more normal clothing in one, and women's voices sounding from the next one. Excited and elated as he was, Will recognised that he could not just burst in on these.

"My lord," he said to the marquis, "that was a notable performance. Is there further to come? I have a message. For one of the ladies with the queen. The Lady Agnes Douglas."

"There is one short scene, yes. But only myself and the queen and one other, Lady Cranworth acting the child Telegonius. So Lady Agnes will not be involved."

Will retired, to wait outside the door, pacing up and down.

Presently raised voices heralded the trio, the queen rather more completely garbed, Winchester in a fine robe, and the smallest of the women dressed as a boy. These proceeded on, as before, down into the corridor for the garden area. Behind them came Montgomery and the other three men, these heading for the ballroom itself. The chatter of women's talk still came from the other room.

Will could scarcely go in. They might still be dressing. Impatiently he waited.

The five of them all came out together, fully clad, however bare of shoulders. The man did not have to proclaim himself. Agnes knew him at once, eyes widening, lips parted.

"Will! Will Alexander! By all that is wonderful! Oh, Will, Will!" And she all but threw herself at him.

The four other ladies looked on in amusement.

Holding her, his lips were too busy for mere words.

"I knew . . . that you were here. In England. With the king . . . and Prince Henry," she got out. "Janet told me. Oh, it is good to see you."

116

"And you! And you! When I saw you come out, in the masque, I could scarce believe my eyes! That you were here. At court. Not back in Scotland. I had no notion of it. How long . . .?"

"Only for a few days. My father required to see King James. All must now come south for office and preferment. I insisted on coming with him."

"To my joy!"

The other four had moved off. Will felt that they must follow them, much as he would have preferred to go off with Agnes alone into other reaches of the palace. He took her arm as they headed for that ballroom.

"I have not seen you about the court, Will."

"No. We, the prince and I, are at Oatlands, a lesser house. Some way off. Much of study and writings! We are here only for Yuletide. And you? How long do you stay?"

"Not for long now. It is a lengthy journey, and my father has his duties at home. Having obtained what he came for, he would be back."

The final scene of the masque, a very brief one, was all but finished, with Circe, a proud mother now and less haughty, showing off her son by Odysseus, Telegonius by name, to the applause of the company, Ben Jonson appearing, to accept his own acclaim for devising it all.

"Are you finished now?" Will asked. "With this of the masquery? Have you other duties?"

"No. My father will be somewhere hereabouts."

"Need you go to him? At once?"

"I suppose not. What have you in mind, Will?"

"We could walk together. It is cold outside, for dressed as you are. But this palace is large. Away from all these people."

Agnes found no fault with that, and they went off arm-in-arm.

They had much to talk of, even though Will's mind was not wholly preoccupied with catching up with events in Scotland any more than with recounting conditions here

117

in England. He did ask after Janet Erskine and heard that she was well, and permanently living at Cardross in Menteith, it seemed. And also of Argyll, who was evidently little at Castle Campbell these days, taking his duties as Lieutenant of the North very seriously, indeed over-seriously for many there, especially the Gordons, who resented interference in their activities, interference which called for armed force, with his Campbell host. So stern were his measures to enforce the king's authority allegedly, that he was earning the by-name of Archibald Grumach, the Grim, although Agnes herself did not find him so grievous, she asserted, when she saw something of him.

Will did not expound at any length on the distinctly humdrum life on the fringes of court, rejecting any suggestion that with the multitudes of attractive women available, he ought to be in his element, no?

They wandered along passages and corridors, through chambers innumerable in that enormous establishment built by Henry the Eighth, and were not the only ones so doing, other couples apt to be more stationary, and often tucked into corners, one pair even on the floor, to Agnes's amusement. They saw servitors too, hurrying to and fro, mainly with trays of flagons and goblets. They did not discover just where the king was, with his drinking companions – not that they were greatly concerned to do so.

When at length they reached the furthest end of the main palace building, and had to turn back, Will felt that pleasing as this strolling was in such company, alternative activity could be worth considering. He had noted one or two reasonably secluded locations as they had come, and at one of these, on the way back, a small room apparently used only for the storage of curtains, hangings, tapestries and the like, he paused, and gestured enquiringly. It was without light, and lacking seating also, but such facilities were not vitally important there and then, to him at least. Agnes allowed herself to be steered therein without protest.

Taking her in his arms, alean against soft hangings, he stroked the torrent of red hair which so fascinated him, kissing it and calling it the Aurora of his dreams, saying that it had stimulated him, that and her beauty of face and figure, to more poetry than just the sonnet so entitled, had done and always would. And since those copious locks and tresses fell down over the white shoulders, gleaming even in the faint light from the corridor, his busy lips found more to linger over, smooth, warm, rounded flesh.

She bit at his ear in this process, but with a gurgle of laughter, declaring that she would have to guard herself against such busy lips, this especially so when they proceeded still lower – for her gown was fashionably low of neck – and with all naturalness they slipped into the cleft of her proudly swelling bosom.

She bit his ear again, a little harder. "Think you that I am so helpless against your advances, Will Alexander?" she asked. "I am a Douglas, you will remember, no timorous, fearful damsel, a prey to men's ill desires!"

"Are they so ill?" he desisted from his explorations sufficiently to ask. "They are but . . . the acknowledgment of my, my worship, woman!"

"Worship is it, now! I have heard such called otherwise! You are glib with your thoughts as well as with your lips!"

Will decided that this delectable occasion would not gain anything by such wordy exchange, so he changed tactics. Raising his head, he effected an end to her speech with a different sort of kissing, and instead of lips investigating lower, slid a hand down where they had been, and somewhat further, to cup one of those delicious full breasts, with its tip which firmed between his fingers. Interested, he transferred his hand to the companion attraction, and experienced a similar reaction. He kept her lips under pressure the while lest there be any verbal protests.

Even if speech was not allowed, her mouth was not quite closed nor her tongue quite stilled, for his own,

119

doing some probing likewise, met with some response other than wordy.

So they stood, and time stood still with them.

The young woman's fingers, somewhat belatedly perhaps, made their own comment by tugging the man's hair at the back, which raised his head somewhat.

"As well . . . that I was not clad . . . as I was in the masque!" she managed to get out. "Or you would have had me . . . babe-naked, I do believe!"

"You would have been the more adorable! But, yes, this gown becomes . . . restrictive! Lower."

"A mercy that you find it so! A woman must have some protection."

"A Douglas scarcely has need of such, I think?"

"This Douglas must needs go seek her Douglas father, Will. He will be looking for me to join him. When I am not with the queen and her ladies. He could be concerned . . ."

"Not if my lord knows his own daughter! We have not been gone for so long."

"We have, you know."

"Has it seemed so long, lass?"

"No-o-o. But . . ." She pushed him away firmly, and hitched up the bodice of her gown. "Take me back, Will." She gave a little laugh. "To think that one hour ago I did not know that you were in this place!"

"You do not regret the finding me?"

"How think you, judge you, halfwit? But, come you . . ."

They found their way back to the ballroom, but in no especial haste despite possible parental anxieties.

Will had rather hoped that the Earl of Morton might well be closeted drinking with the king, and so his daughter would be available for more attentions. But unfortunately he was quickly discerned in the crowd, with a group of other lords and their womenfolk, a big, burly, florid man, redness not confined to features, for it was evident from where his daughter had got her vivid hair, however more attractive her supply. Seeing Agnes, he beckoned her

120

over to present to his companions, glancing distinctly doubtfully at Will.

"You know Will Alexander of Menstrie, Father?" Agnes said. "Tutor to the Prince Henry."

The earl inclined his head only a little. "Here, Agnes, is the Earl and Countess of Dorset. And the Earl of Sussex. And Lord and Lady Knyvett . . ."

Will took the hint and bowed himself off.

After recent delights it would have been anticlimax indeed to have lingered on for further possible entertainment. He wanted to be alone now, to savour what he had experienced, to go over it all in his mind. So it was back fairly promptly to their stableyard quarters, where he could relieve the guard in their watch over the sleeping prince, and he was not long in retiring to his own bed, however active his mind and imagination and aroused his person. He would make poetry out of this night, even though that was not his principal preoccupation there and then.

In the morning, despite his late indulgences, King James was up early, and had others so likewise, for apparently he and all his court who cared to go were invited for this St Thomas's Day to Twickenham Park, three miles to the north, the seat of Sir Francis Bacon, an eminent and wealthy lawyer and cousin of Robert Cecil, where there would be hunting, hawking, archery and other sports for those fond of outdoor pursuits even in winter, with ample indoor activities for those less hardy. So there was much to-do over the transportation arrangements, even for three miles, servants, grooms, drivers, falconers and the like scurrying. There was no royal suggestion, however, that the heir to the throne should be involved nor, therefore, his tutor. And although Will had a hurried look around for Agnes, in all the rush and bustle he caught no sight of her.

Nor did the pair meet that evening, owing to late activities at Twickenham, and when Will did see her the following morning, it was with the young woman actually

121

seeking him out early in their stableyard to say goodbye. Her father was for off, back to Scotland, having been away overlong already, it seemed, and with more than a further week's riding involved. He was determined to be back for Hogmanay and New Year, even though it meant passing Christmas *en route*, a significant indication of priorities perhaps.

So it was but a brief embrace, in front of Henry and the groom with their horses, and farewell, grievous disappointment as this was, for the man at least. Agnes said that she hoped that her father would find need to approach the king again before too long over his various Scottish duties, herself accompanying him.

Thereafter the Christmas festivities fell rather flat as far as Will Alexander was concerned, however unsuitable that was, although he sought to ensure that the boy enjoyed them as far as allowed. But with a royal move to Woodstock after New Year's Day, it was back to Oatlands, studies, translations and poetic composition for man and prince. Such was life.

8

It was March before, the plague over at last, it was considered safe for the king, queen and court to make their long-delayed triumphal entry into their English capital city. James ordered that their heir to the throne was to be on display also, taking part in the procession through the streets to Whitehall Palace. So Will was required to deliver the boy to Hampton Court, and thereafter to remain available, but suitably in the background.

Fortunately the pre-April showers which had been much in evidence held off for this great day, for it was to be a major event indeed, carefully planned and orchestrated, largely by Robert Cecil. An enormous and varied concourse gathered at the Tower of London for the procession, which was to thread four miles of city streets in round-about fashion so that the optimum numbers of the citizens could see the monarch, family and train, and be duly impressed and imbued with the required respect, esteem and loyal fervour. Londoners apparently much sought after this sort of parade and spectacle, and had been starved of it for long, not only because of the plague but that in her declining years and illness, Queen Elizabeth had failed them. Cecil and the other English officials all declared that this was highly advisable, however odd and pointless it would seem in Scotland. The objective also, of course, was for the king and queen to see some of the glories of their new capital, and to meet representative delegations of its population.

So early on 12th March a start was made from Hampton Court, by boat down Thames to the tower, Henry and Will having come there the day previously. Disembarking at the

Tower Pier they found all awaiting them, marshalled and ready, the procession-to-be already extending all round Tower Hill, Byward Street and beyond. However, James upset the arrangements and timing by insisting on entry to the tower itself, asking where the rogue Walter Raleigh was imprisoned – this to embarrass Anne who was known to be in favour of the release of that renowned and handsome traveller and adventurer – and on to visit the lion-pit, of which he had heard much. These great tawny animals, pacing back and forth in their cages, greatly intrigued the monarch, who held forth to those in attendance on the significance of the king of beasts, and the fact that the emblem of the Scots kings was the lion rampant, much superior to the mere three leopards of Plantagenet which had now got converted into feeble short-legged lions passant-gardant, ever looking over their shoulders in fear. If this homily was largely lost on his listeners – Anne had returned to the carriage awaiting her – the actual lion inspection was not, especially for Henry, for James ordered the deputy keeper of the tower to go fetch one of the guard dogs of the prison, to put into a cage so that they might discover whether the lions had lost their kingly prowess by being penned up thus for long, a lesson apparently to be learned therefrom. So an unfortunate mastiff was produced and pushed into the cage, to be promptly sprung upon by the occupant and spectacularly savaged to death. This did not satisfy the monarch however, much as it upset his son; another dog and another lion ought to establish the matter. But when a second hound was brought and led to another cage, it proved to be so fearful as to be got in with great difficulty, and thereafter was still howling to get out when the lion pounced on it from the rear and stilled its yelps in no uncertain fashion.

James, still not satisfied with his experiment, called for a third and tougher mastiff, Henry pleading for mercy. This dog did put up a fight against another lion, more satisfactorily testing the issue and, although injured, continued its defiance, with the prince now hammering small fists against his father's person in urgent demands that the brave dog be rescued. The king relented, and the deputy keeper had to take some personal risks in opening the cage sufficiently to get one animal out and keep the other in. The Prince of Wales threw his arms around the bleeding mastiff which, after an initial snarling growl, turned to lick the boy's hand, and friendship was established. Henry thereupon claimed the creature for himself, and the king, apparently gratified that the lions had retained their majestic powers even when ensnared by the restrictions of enclosure, as must human monarchs hampered by the cares and affairs of state, conceded that his son should have the dog. When its wounds had been treated, it was to be sent on to the palace; and it was to be called Leo, as an ensample to Henry, a monarch-to-be, on regal responsibilities and requirements. James also took the opportunity to read them all something of a lecture on his choice of the name Leo, as emphasising the English misunderstanding over leopards and lions. For these Plantagenet leopards were really lions, if poor ones, the word *leo* so meaning in Latin, and *parum*, feebler. So their English leopards were really only backwards-looking and indifferent lions, unlike the rampant Scots ones.

This authoritative statement delivered, only then was King James prepared to go out and join the waiting procession.

Henry did not want to be parted from his new acquisition, the mastiff Leo, whatever its significance, but since he was to ride a horse in front of his father, and the dog in no condition to trot alongside, Will Alexander was given the duty of seeing that the animal was cared for, and in due course taken to Whitehall.

The great and the good of England had been learning their lessons also, as to patience and respect in waiting upon kings by divine right, not to mention the crowds thronging the city streets. The processional host consisted of representatives of every rank and status, members of parliament, officials of government, officers of state, judges, knights of the shires, nobility, bishops and prelates, Knights of the Garter and the Bath, kings of arms, earls, marquises and dukes, all there in due order of precedence, the least lofty leading – these inevitably far up at the top of Tower Hill. Most were to process on foot, and orders had been issued for the streets to be specially cleaned for them. Bands of musicians would lead and bring up the rear. All this had to be timed fairly exactly or there would be chaos, well over a mile separating first from last instrumentalists; so the delay over the lions had not contributed to the smooth working of the operation.

Nor was all able to proceed forthwith even now. For James had to be mounted on a milk white jennet, while eight Gentlemen of his Bedchamber were to walk alongside holding up on poles a canopy over the royal head; and this demanded not a little trial and error before all could move off in harmony, the queen, in a carriage drawn by two white mules, exhibiting very evident signs of impatience. Nine paces in front of the monarch, to emphasise his nine years of age, was to ride Prince Henry, alone, on a fine Barbary mare.

Even when Will won out of the tower, after making the arrangements for the dog, the long and complicated parade had not started off. Given no instructions as to his place in it all, if any, he was left in no doubt by eager beckonings from Henry to come and walk beside him and his horse. No one appearing to contest this, he found himself in the most prominent and prestigious position of the entire procession, a few paces in front of the monarch, whatever all the magnates thought of this. James at least found no fault apparently, enquiring interestedly whether the canine critter Leo was in fair shape.

At last the signal could be given, the band struck up and forward movement began, somewhat falteringly at first owing to uncertainty in front. Turning away from the waterside, they proceeded up Tower Hill, with the head of the column, out of sight, on the move now also.

Just beyond the tower they passed a choir of three hundred boys from Christ's Hospital singing for them, Anne clapping and waving, James calling to Henry to take heed, and asking whether he could sing in such fashion. They did not halt for this, however, whether that was expected or not.

At Fenchurch Street, crowded with onlookers, they came to a handsome triumphal arch, artistically constructed, where children in the guise of winged cherubs presented the monarch with a model of the city, which James ordered two of his gentlemen to bring up to him for closer inspection – to some upset of the canopy-bearing. Then on through the cheering throngs to Gracechurch Street, where there was a second arch, quite magnificent, the work apparently of the Italian community, the king acknowledging its presentation in lengthy Latin, to the hearers' evident mystification.

The procession was already becoming somewhat fragmented, with the royal party halting here and there and those in front not doing so or knowing of it, gaps appearing. The queen, from her carriage, bowed left and right to the citizenry, the king merely eyeing all with critical interest, architectural features and buildings as well as his subjects.

A third arch had been erected at the Royal Exchange, this by the Dutch merchants, a powerful body allegedly, this representing the seventeen provinces of the Netherlands. Here the monarch was greeted with an address read out in Latin, presumably in recognition of his linguistic powers, which he promptly acknowledged by a speech of thanks in guttural German, for he claimed to be able to speak at least a dozen languages. Whether the Netherlanders understood this was another matter.

On Cheapside where the fourth arch stood, there was an interval, for here a fountain had been contrived to flow with wine, and this had to be sampled, especially as golden goblets were provided, these apparently to be retained as presents, by the king, queen and Prince of

Wales, James concerned to see them safely stowed away in Anne's carriage. Other processionists had got held up here, not unnaturally, at the wine fountain, so that the parade became still further disorganised.

The fifth arch, at Old St Pauls, had more choristers singing from the battlements; and at the sixth, in Fleet Street, the Danish colony produced a brief masque of sorts, and played a march in honour of the Danish-born queen, to her delight.

The last arch was at Temple Bar, where the lord mayor, aldermen and councillors were waiting, more speeches made and the city sword was presented, the king drawing back and barely touching it in his lifelong fear and dislike of cold steel. He cut short the proceedings here, clearly becoming wearied with all this, and waved his entourage onwards, or such of it as was still in sight, for it could hardly be recognised as a procession now. The last speech-maker was left in mid-flow.

They moved on up the Strand, passing Somerset House, which James pointed out to his wife was to be her town-palace, and so on to Whitehall itself, at last. It had taken them almost six hours since landing at the tower, and they had come over four round-about miles. Despite the wine at Cheapside, all probably were thankful to be finished with it, James declaring loudly that he hated crowds, although his wife appeared to have enjoyed it all. The eight Gentlemen of the Bedchamber were much relieved to dispense with their so awkward canopy.

Not for the first time there appeared to be no special instructions nor arrangements for Prince Henry, his father and mother disappearing separately into different parts of the palace, the prince and Will being left to fend for themselves, the boy mainly concerned to know where the dog Leo had been put. It was the Duke of Lennox who came to their rescue, taking them to a suite of three rooms beside what he declared were to be his own, and not far from the king's personal quarters, and finding male and

128

female servitors to attend them. He also promised to find out where the mastiff was and to have it sent to them; a kindly man Ludovick Stewart.

If there was any banqueting that night the pair were not partakers, but were fed adequately enough in their own rooms, Leo, now Henry's preoccupation, being catered for assiduously. The animal did not appear to be seriously injured, the wounds, tears and scrapes demanding much licking. For a guard dog it appeared to be a very friendly disposed creature. Will had difficulty in persuading both boy and dog that they ought not to share a bed that night.

There followed days of uncertainty, as far as pupil and tutor were concerned, their programme and duties vague in the extreme, yet far from free to follow their own devices. Every now and again the prince was summoned to accompany his father on some visit or function in the city, and had to be available, Will not always involved. But most of the time they were left severely alone, and seeing the queen only infrequently. Will got the impression that this was more by James's intention than by Anne's, the king deliberately concerned that she and her son did not become close – why, who could tell.

The pair did get out on their own to stroll through the London streets on occasion, twice oddly enough in the company of Ulric, Duke of Holstein, Anne's younger brother in England on a visit, a graceless youth, little favoured it seemed by either sister or brother-in-law, and with much time on his hands. Henry did not greatly like this uncle either, but was careful not to show it.

Lessons and translations were still the order of the day, therefore. The psalms now were finished, at least as far as Will was concerned, however much correcting and alteration James would desire thereafter, by himself or others. Will was now on to the Song of Solomon, which in one way he found more to his taste, the poetry content being more pronounced. Nevertheless he was at a loss to understand much of it, and what was behind it all. Love, physical rather than spiritual, was obviously a major preoccupation, but to what significance he could not fathom. It did not appear to him to have any due place in Holy Writ.

Since this uncertainty was preventing him from gaining any satisfaction over the results of his work, Will eventually summoned up courage to request an audience with the king, this via the Duke of Lennox, of whom they saw quite a lot. Surprisingly, he was sent for almost immediately, James in the process dismissing summarily the Duke Ulric, with scant courtesy, also Sir Philip Herbert of Montgomery, the favourite, although Lennox remained with them.

"What's to do, what's to do, Alexander man?" the monarch demanded testily. "I'm occupied, fell occupied. Vicky says it's urgent. Aboot the Song o' Songs. I'd no' see you otherwise, mind."

"I understand, Sire. But I am troubled by this translation. Not the words nor the poetry of it – that I like well. But the meaning. I do not get the meaning of it all. And if that is not understood then my translations may be all but worthless. I feel that I am missing something in this, beautifully worded as it is."

"It's an allegory, man. A dramatic allegory. Can you no' see that?"

"Yes, Highness, but an allegory of what? What is King Solomon getting at? All this of blackness. A black woman. Black but comely, fairest of women. Black and fair – surely a contradiction? Yet this is a part of the Holy Bible. It cannot be about merely some black woman whom Solomon found attractive?"

"Weel, it wasna' Solomon who scrieved it, mind. He's named in it, aye, but he wasna the poet. It's him and his kingdom, see you. And the allegory is Christ and His Kirk, just. Solomon was fighting a battle, mind, against backsliders into paganism. His faither had to fight the Philistines, but he fought a different war, against the heathen beliefs thae Israelites were falling back to. Sin,

130

just. Yon black woman, wi' her allure, was the goddess o' fertility."

Will was the more mystified. "But he seems to be in love with her. Was this the Queen of Sheba?"

"Och, man, Solomon had hundreds o' wives, puir soul! No, it was the poet who scrieved this Song o' Songs. D'you no' understand? It's aboot Solomon's war, no' the poet's. Och, I havena time to expound it a' to you. See you, read it again, and seek oot the allegory. And see how Christ's Kirk has to fight its ain war against the harlotry o' evil."

Little the wiser, Will bowed, and was going to ask if he might retire, when James jabbed a finger at him.

"The laddie, Henry. I'm consairned that this London is no' just the place for him. And this Whitehall hoose. Aye, and he's been seeing his uncle, yon Ulric o' Holstein, I'm hearing. And . . . others. He's an ill one, Ulric, a right Dane! Drunken. Nae manners to him. He's young, mind . . ."

"He comes to see the prince occasionally, Sire."

"He was teaching him to throw the dice, I heard tell."

"Well yes, Sire. I saw no harm in that."

"Maybe no'. But you've been oot on the streets wi' him."

"Only once or twice, Sire."

"Aye, weel, you'd be better back at yon Oatlands, wi' Henry. Ower many distractions here for the laddie. See you to it, Alexander. You may go. Off wi' you. And use your wits, man, on the Canticle, the Song o' Songs."

So that was that. Will was in fact not sorry to be returning to Oatlands, however isolated he had felt there. He had never lived in a city before, and did not find the London streets, crowds and smells to his taste. He was an outdoors man and was teaching Henry to be likewise, and Whitehall was no place for that. Whatever the king's reasons for wanting him away, the boy would be better hence. As would he. They would not delay in going.

131

9

Life at Oatlands, by contrast, was reasonably pleasant that springtime, even rewarding in some respects. Henry was proving a worthy pupil, especially in the activities which Will had most satisfaction in teaching, outdoor pursuits and sports. The boy was growing fast.

Nevertheless, to be sure, Will was scarcely a contented man. This was not the life that he would have chosen, however fond he had become of the prince. He should be back in his own Scotland, managing his affairs at Menstrie, not this tutoring and hanging about the fringes of the royal court.

It was high summer, mid-July, when a change in his circumstances was heralded. A messenger arrived from the king, none other than Sir Robert Carey, he who had brought James the long-awaited news of Elizabeth Tudor's death the previous year. He, it seemed, was to take over the care of Prince Henry meantime, and Will Alexander was to depart for Scotland, to Dunfermline, to collect the young Prince Charles, who was now considered sufficiently fit, and able to face the journey south to London. He, Carey, and his wife, would come in a day or two to assume their duties, when Will could set off — this by royal command.

Will did not know whether to be pleased or otherwise. The return to Scotland rejoiced him, even for a brief spell, to his own place and to see his friends, but this of bringing south the sickly Prince Charles was scarcely to his taste. Why had he got the reputation of being a suitable guardian for children?

Carey brought sundry news items from court, the most

interesting to Will being that there had been a great conference of academics and clergy, fifty-four of them no less, to consider the full translation of the Bible, with amendments and additions to earlier translations and progress towards publication at as early a date as was possible. To this end James had set up six commissions, supportive of each other but also in some competition, two based on Westminster, two on Oxford and two on Cambridge colleges. These would meet regularly, and report progress to their extraordinary monarch. Other news was that the king was making moves towards a peace treaty with Spain. England and Spain were not actually at war, but had been at enmity for many years, especially during the middle of Elizabeth's reign, when privateering against the Spanish vessels bringing treasure from South and Central America had become something of a national preoccupation and sport, with expert captains such as Sir John Hawkins, Sir Francis Drake and Sir Walter Raleigh, now in the tower, made Captain of the Queen's Guard, admirals of her fleet, and even governor of Jersey. This activity had largely died away, but James aimed to be a peace-maker, even with the most powerful nation of the Catholic world. Also he had an ambition to found overseas colonies, to gain wealth; and peace with Spain would make this easier. This move of his was less than popular with most of his Protestant English magnates, apparently, but the king appeared to be determined.

So two days later, it was farewell to Henry. Lady Carey seemed a pleasant motherly soul, although what sort of a tutor her husband would make, if that was his role, remained to be seen: a courtier nearing his fifties, he did not seem an apt choice to Will. The prince was distressed and quite emotional over their parting, urging Will to hasten back. He was a little helped by being told to look after the mastiff Leo well.

Will was determined to make the best possible time on his journey north in order to have the longer in Scotland. In fact he was glad of the hard and fast riding which followed,

133

for he had had nothing of this for long, and it produced a great sense of freedom. In summer conditions he ought to be able to average at least fifty miles a day, perhaps more. Seven or eight days, then . . .

In the event he did rather better, without taxing his horse too greatly, and on the afternoon of the sixth day crossed Tweed at Berwick, thankful indeed to be on his native soil again, and drawing in lungfuls of good Scots air. He had always known that he was fond of his native land, but he had scarcely realised how much it meant to him.

Another day and he was back at Menstrie, to find harvest about to commence. His steward, who appeared to be managing all in order, rendered a fair account of the property and his various activities thereon, being especially proud of the excellent spring lambing of the sheep stock on the Ochils. Will was pleased, while noting wryly that his little lairdship seemed to be getting on quite well without him.

He learned that, meantime, the Earl of Argyll was back at Castle Campbell, so he decided to make this his first call, since apparently Archie was only there for brief spells these days. So next morning he rode off eastwards along the hillfoots for Dollar, rejoicing to be back among his homeland hills.

It was good to see his old pupil and companion again, although it was hard to think of him as that, now that he was Lieutenant of the North and Admiral of the Western Seas, all but viceroy of Scotland north of Forth and Clyde, young for that responsibility as he was.

Archie was eager to learn of activities in London and how James was managing his reign of two kingdoms and dealing with the proud English lords. He had heard of this move for an accord with Spain from the Earl of Morton apparently, the which worried him since it was bound to encourage the Catholic party, here in Scotland as elsewhere, and he, Argyll, was having enough trouble with them in the north and Highlands as it was, in especial

Huntly and his Gordons. He had had to teach them a lesson or two, but they were still very much a danger, and any move towards friendship with Catholic Spain was bound to make them more bold and more of a menace.

Will mentioned that he had heard that his friend was now being called Archibald Grumach, the Grim, over his activities in the north, and hoped that this was an unjust appellation, to be told that a strong hand was needed to deal with the clans – other than the Clan Campbell presumably.

MacCailean Mor was interested to hear how his friend had heard of this by-name in England, and Will had to admit that it had been the Lady Agnes Douglas who had told him of it.

"Ah, yes, Agnes mentioned that she had seen you while in the south. She said that you were still Prince Henry's guardian. And working on a translation of Holy Writ, of all things! Do not tell me that Will Alexander has become a religious!"

"Scarcely that! But James has set me on to this, assuming that my poetic leanings, however modest they are, should assist me, especially towards the psalms and the Song of Solomon. I have now started working on the Proverbs. It is no choice of mine, although I see that the Bible ought to be made available to all, not merely those who have the Latin. James is an astonishing man, an odd mixture of clever and foolish, well informed but prejudiced, sagacious, yes, but in my opinion lacking judgment. He has no dignity, yet considers himself God's appointed deputy and spokesman."

"Who was it called him the Wisest Fool in Christendom? And now he has sent you up here to collect his second son, Charles. He must think highly of you, Will, to entrust both his sons to your care. Are you not glad that I brought you to the royal notice?"

"I am not! Much as I like young Henry, this is not the way I would be living, cooped up with bairns. This

Charles is only four years. I could well be saddled with him for long."

"They say that he is backward. Not only in body but in wits. As well that he is not the elder, or we could have an even odder monarch one day! Henry is no dolt, I take it?"

"No, he is a bright lad, with a good head on him. And a heart, too. He hates cruelty, even to animals, unlike his father. He is learning the manly sports well."

"And Will Alexander of Menstrie is his mentor! Are you not a proud man, to be rearing the next monarch of two realms? I can see you becoming a great one, some day! Remember who you have to thank for it when that day comes! So, when do you go to Dunfermline, where Seton – he is Fyvie now, I hear – holds the young prince?"

"I would be in no haste! But cannot delay overlong. A week, ten days hence, perhaps . . ."

Will spent the night at Castle Campbell, and next day would have paid a visit to Kinross and Lochleven Castle, not far off, but learned from Argyll that the Earl of Morton and his family were presently at the other Douglas seat of Dalkeith in Lothian; so instead, he set off on a considerably longer ride, westwards again, for Cardross in Menteith, some fifty miles along the skirts of the Highland Line, a man not a little unsure of his priorities.

Halting overnight at his own house, he reached the Erskine castle, near the shores of island-dotted Loch of Menteith, by midday, a lovely place under the shadow of great mountains, the bell-heather already purpling their shoulders and corries. He could have no complaints about his reception here, totally unexpected as his arrival was.

Lady Erskine greeted him warmly. Always she had been friendly towards him. She was eager to hear his news of the king and Henry and all that went on in the south; and it was only after she had gained quite a full account of affairs that she mentioned that her husband was in Glasgow, as so often, seeing to his wide interests there, and Janet was at home, and was in fact presently down at the loch with her young cousin, Charlotte Erskine from Gogar, who was here on a visit. She had spoken of taking the girl out to the island of Inchmahome, to show her the former priory where the king's mother, Mary Queen of Scots, had spent some time as a child before being sent to France for safety in Henry the Eighth's Rough Wooing attempts.

Will was not long in suggesting that he went in search of the pair. He would row himself over to the island in one of the many boats drawn up on the beach, as he had done many a time in the past.

So it was down to the waterside, a mile away, where as a youth he had spent much time with Janet and her brother, Inchmahome, the Isle of St Colman, a Celtic saint, one of their favourite sanctuaries where they could be secure from adult restrictions and supervision, a distinctly wild trio as he now had come to recognise. The Erskines kept quite a little flotilla of boats drawn up in a bay at the loch-foot, where the Goodie Water emerged, eventually to join the infant Forth, fishing in the loch being a popular pastime. There Will could see the scrape marks on the sand and gravel where another of the boats had recently been pushed out; not that there was any sign of it out on the water.

Selecting one of the craft to drag down and launch, he got out the oars and pulled away westwards. The loch was not far off two miles in length, with three islets in the middle, Inchmahome itself the largest, Inch Talla which held the ruined castle of the ancient Earls of Menteith, and the Dogs Isle, where they had kept their hunting-hounds. So he had a mile to go. It was good to be rowing this lovely loch again, scene of so much of boyhood enjoyments. He actually sang to himself as he pulled.

And, despite the singing and the creak of the oars in their rowlocks, and splash of water, he presently did become aware of another sound rising higher, a calling. With his back necessarily towards the islands, he had not seen the source, but now, turning, he perceived a white

arm waving from the water above a dark head, and none
so far off. Janet. She had always been a keen swimmer;
and there she was.

"Will! Will!" she was crying. "Will Alexander! Here I
am. Here, Will!"

Was he so recognisable, then, even from the rear?
He waved and shouted back, pulling over towards the
swimmer.

Quickly they converged, and the young woman came
splashing, to reach up to grip a rowlock and part hoist
herself out of the water, face upturned, eyes wide and
glowing, lips parted, dark hair streaming on gleaming
shoulders, and shapely breasts free, a picture to savour
and relish indeed. Will did more than savour and gaze;
he stooped to clutch that wet, cool torso and kiss those
open lips, to still the gasped, incoherent questions and
exclamations.

They could scarcely linger thus, delectable as it was for
the man, with Janet's unprotected person getting pressed
against the rocking boat. Releasing herself, she pointed
towards the island, a couple of hundred yards off. He
nodded. She swimming strongly, he rowing alongside,
they headed therefor.

In the shallows of a tiny bay there was another bather
splashing about, equally white but less rounded and
generously endowed, a young girl of perhaps ten years,
fair-haired, laughing, tiny breasts beginning to burgeon.
Paddling about, not swimming, at Will's over-shoulder
glance she put hands down modestly to cover her groin,
giggling.

"Charlotte Erskine, my cousin from Gogar," Janet
called. "Here is Will Alexander of Menstrie, Charlotte.
Heed him not. He has seen unclad females ere this!"

Shipping one oar and using the other to pole the boat
in, he rose and found Janet coming scrambling ashore,
shaking water from head and body almost as a dog
would, actually to come and help to pull the boat up
on to the shingle. She was, of course, completely naked,

and her state of nature seemed as entirely natural as it was delightful.

Will jumped out on to the land and enfolded her in his arms, wet as she was, while the girl in the shallows gurgled with laughter, never before having seen the like. He gasped out, between kisses and hugs, how and why he came to be there, Janet contenting herself with answering if speechless lips.

When they did reluctantly move apart somewhat, but still to gaze at each other, their discrepancy as to clothing set the young woman into laughter to outdo her cousin's. She pointed at him.

"Unfair! Unfair!" she cried. "Come, you. Into the loch with us. Swim, Will, a swim. You used to be a good swimmer. Come!" And she turned and ran back into the water.

He did not contest her command and began to disrobe himself without delay after kicking off his riding-boots. Soon unclad as the two females, he raced into the shallows, past the goggling Charlotte and as soon as it was deep enough surface dived, and went over-arm in pursuit of Janet.

They swam side by side in panting converse, largely to the effect that this was like old times, and wondering how long it was since they had last done it. They decided that it must be a dozen years, at least.

Not to leave the youngster alone overlong, who apparently could not swim, they turned back. Had they been alone, Will would have suggested just lying in the early August sunshine to dry themselves; but somehow feeling that this might seem a trifle blatant to the girl, he suggested a run round the island instead. That was accepted and, picking their way with some care, being bare-footed, they all three trotted off, with much hilarity, the man now the challenger, Janet the hindmost when it came to running.

They passed the abandoned priory buildings, with the quite large church and the twenty-foot-high bell tower,

Janet asking breathlessly what the monks would have thought of this.

Back at the boats they clothed themselves, less than urgently, and then lay in the sun while Will recounted news of the court, his life at Oatlands with Henry and his present mission to collect Prince Charles. They were in no hurry to head back to Cardross.

There could be no intimacies that night, in the circumstances, but they passed a pleasant evening with Lady Erskine, with much talk, out of which, among other matters, Will learned that the Earl of Argyll was seeing quite a lot of the Lady Agnes Douglas – so that was why he had known that the Morton family was presently at Dalkeith.

The information set Will athinking quite deeply ere he slept that night.

In the morning, he felt that he must go to Dunfermline to tell Lord Fyvie that he was going to be relieved of the care of the little prince, and to prepare the boy for the journey and great change of circumstances, giving the Setons a few days' notice, as it were, this being only suitable and courteous. He told the Erskines that he would be back, however, before setting off eventually for England.

It was a fair day's ride from Cardross to Dunfermline, in the Fothrif of Fife, some fifty miles, by Thornhill and Causewayhead, near to Stirling, keeping north of the Forth, and on by Alloa and Clackmannan to enter Fothrif at Carnock.

The ancient royal palace of Dunfermline, at Malcolm the Third's former capital, tended to be overshadowed by the great abbey which his Queen Margaret had erected alongside. It had been little used as a royal residence in recent reigns, and was now more or less home to Sir Alexander Seton, Lord Fyvie, President of the Court of Session, although, a man of wealth as well as foremost lawyer in the land, he had his own fine properties elsewhere, at Fyvie in Aberdeenshire, at Barns in Lothian, and was indeed in process of building a handsome new all but palatial establishment at Pinkie, Musselburgh, near to his brother's main seat at Seton itself.

When Will arrived, the great man was not present, but was expected to be back from his legal duties in Edinburgh that evening; duties which were now going to be the more onerous than ever, according to his wife, for she informed that the king had just created him Chancellor of the Scots realm, that is, chief minister. Word of this had reached them only a few days previously, a major surprise, and the message had also let them know that Prince Charles would be leaving their care; so that was not the surprise Will had anticipated, and perhaps he need not have made this visit.

Lady Fyvie, a daughter of the Lord Drummond, was an amiable woman, motherly as became one with six daughters, all young, a chattering throng. Among these, the four-year-old Charles Stewart could have had difficulty in asserting himself even if he had been so disposed. But he was a strange, silent child, great-eyed, solemn, all but wordless still, capable of only a tottering walk, a pathetic little creature of whom all the girls were obviously very fond. Will was not long in wondering how he was going to be able to transport this frail oddity the four hundred miles to London. Clearly he would be unable to sit a horse.

Alexander, Lord Fyvie, arrived in due course, a handsome, gravely quiet-spoken man of middle years, who greeted their visitor courteously. Nevertheless Will felt himself being sized up for the task and responsibility ahead, and, in the conversation which followed, gathered that the new Chancellor judged that the young prince was by no means ready to make this lengthy journey, nor indeed to be leaving the loving care of Lady Fyvie. But it was by royal command, and he had no option but to let the boy go.

After the evening meal, as they discussed the matter in detail, it transpired that the assumption was that Charles would be in the care of a woman while travelling, indeed two women would be best so that they could take turns at riding with the child in front of them, or pillion behind them, although whether the boy would be safe at the latter was in doubt. He had only been walking, or toddling rather, for a few months, and seemed to have no muscular strength; he might not be able to hold on, riding pillion. Fyvie hoped that suitable women could be provided.

That had Will pondering not a little.

With all the children off to bed, and the usual questions as to the king, queen, Henry and the court life to be answered, a further pondering was aroused in the visitor when, Argyll's name coming up in connection with a meeting of the Scots Privy Council over which Fyvie was to preside in a week's time, and Will's known links with the Lieutenant of the North, it was mentioned that MacCailean Mor was hoping to wed Morton's daughter, the Lady Agnes Douglas. If Will Alexander was less than voluble thereafter for some time, perhaps it was not too noticeable in the host's comments on the problems of governing Scotland in the absence of a resident monarch.

Will had plenty to think about as he rode back to Menstrie next day, after arranging to come back to collect the little prince in five days' time.

Two days later he was back at Cardross Castle. Sir William Erskine had arrived home from Glasgow, and put Will through the now expected inquisition regarding what went on in London, with his own comments as to the situation in Scotland and his surprise at Fyvie, the lawyer, being made Chancellor, declaring that others more senior in status might have been expected to fill the most important position in the land; he had anticipated that his own cousin, Mar, would have been appointed. The king, he thought, might have been ill-advised on this issue – to Will's comment that their liege-lord took his own peculiar advice in most matters.

It was some time before he could contrive to be alone

with Janet, in the circumstances. The girl Charlotte had gone home to Gogar, so there was no opportunity for the pair to make a sally down to the Loch of Menteith on their own, for when Will suggested a fishing trip, Sir William announced that he would join them, a pleasant change from seeing to affairs in Glasgow.

While her father was readying himself, Will did have a word, at last, with Janet. "Lass," he said, "Lord Fyvie insists that I have a woman with me, two indeed, to help look after the child Charles on the journey. He is only four years and feeble indeed. Would you consider the task, Janet? It would be something of a trial, I fear. But . . ."

She gazed at him. "You mean . . .? Ride with you? All the way to London?"

"Yes. It is a big thing to ask. But I know not who else to ask."

"My dear Will, of course I will do it! Think you I would refuse?"

"It is a long journey. Will take much time. For the small prince will not be able to cover many miles in a day. And he will have to be held in front of you. And some other woman. I would take him also, to be sure. It could make for wearisome travel."

"We would be together," she said simply.

Stepping close, he took her in his arms.

Their fishing expedition thereafter was pleasant and quite profitable, although it might have been better still without Sir William, even if they might have caught fewer trout.

It was later, in the evening, when Erskine took Will's arm and led him out into the orchard. "Young man," he said, "Janet tells me that you have asked her to accompany you on your journey south with the Prince Charles, to help look after the boy."

"Yes, sir. Lord Fyvie says that the child must have a woman, two women indeed, to see to the lad. He is used to women's care. And I know no other woman to ask, or who would be better for the task. The king, I am sure, would be grateful."

"No doubt. But this is an unusual request to make to a young woman. To accompany a man on long travel. Even if there is another woman present. There would be talk. Janet's name and reputation could be sullied. I fear that I cannot allow it, Menstrie. Not unless . . . you wed my daughter!"

Will drew a great breath, and swallowed.

"You understand, man? A man and a woman cannot go off together for many days and nights, however friendly they may be. Unwed. Or, at the least, betrothed. You must see that. I have to consider her fame and repute, as her father."

"I . . . I do not know. Do not know if she *would* wed me, sir." That was got out with difficulty.

"That is for you to discover. If she will have you, I am prepared to accede. You are only a small laird meantime. But your care of the princes must mean that His Grace thinks highly of you, and therefore your prospects and position may well improve. So in time you may make a more suitable husband for my daughter. We have known you sufficiently long, at least."

"Yes."

Sir William clearly found this conversation less than comfortable, even though Will was still less at ease. He nodded, and led the way back into the castle.

It was not quite bedtime, and Janet and her mother were working at their tambour frames and embroidery in the withdrawing-room off the hall. Did they know what the men had been at?

Lady Erskine made valiant converse, but her daughter remained very silent. At length Janet declared that she was tired and would say her goodnights; and promptly Will was on his feet, announcing that he would escort her to her own room door. The parents nodded permission, mother looking anxious, father unnecessarily adding wood to a summer-evening fire.

144

Out on the turnpike stairway, it was the young woman who turned, from the higher step, to search the man's face. "Oh, Will," she faltered, "what . . . this is . . . did he . . .? Oh, I do not know what to say!"

"It is myself who has to do the saying," he told her. "You who give answer. *Will* you wed me, Janet my dear? Will you do me the honour?"

She gulped. "This is not . . . as I would have wished it. Oh, Will, Will! To have it forced on you!"

"Not forced, lass, never that. I could, no doubt, find other women to accompany me to London. But it is you I want. Want you for more than that. Will you marry me?"

"Oh, yes, yes! But to win you this way! My father should not have ordered it so. I asked him not to."

"Care naught for that, lass. The fault, if any, is mine. I should have asked you ere this, I think. But . . ." He wagged his head. "With all this of the king and court, and Henry. And now Charles. I have not been thinking of marriage."

"No." She bit her lip. "No, and now you have it thrown at you! It is all wrong."

"Do not say that. Probably I required this. To show me my duty."

"Duty – oh, never that, Will. Not duty. We must not wed for duty's sake."

"No, that is the wrong word. To see my way. To perceive what I should do. And when. Aye, to perceive my great privilege – if you would have me. Of your love . . ."

"I have loved you for long, Will. But you? Perhaps we have been friends, such good friends, for too long? Love, love sufficient for marriage, is a different matter." She paused. "I feared that you were half in love with Agnes Douglas!"

He hesitated. Almost he had said that Agnes Douglas appeared now to be going to wed Archie Campbell, but stopped himself in time, recognising that this was not the

145

occasion to say so, as though admitting that this had some bearing on their case.

"Love," he said instead. "Aye, love, girl. Love is what matters. I love *you*. We love each other."

"You have said it! At last, Will. Said that you love me. Oh, how I have waited for that!" She flung herself down upon him, all but dangerous as this was on those steps. "Oh, Will, Will, my heart!"

Holding her close, her face buried now on his shoulder, he stroked her hair. "But you must have known it . . ." He got no further, as she raised her head and they kissed and kissed, all but shook each other. And something was released inside Will Alexander. Deep within him he knew then that this was right. Suddenly a block had been cleared, a dichotomy which had for so long plagued him, gone. There, on that stairway, he knew it, and rejoiced.

When they found voices again, it was to eye each other wonderingly.

"This is true, is it? I am not dreaming it?" Janet demanded. "Tell me that it is true, Will."

"As true as my heart tells me that it is yours! A dream, yes, but a waking one. We learn . . . that we own one another!"

"Own, yes. You are mine, and I am yours. So, we plight our troth, here on this stair!" She choked as she said that.

"Aye, on these steps I, Will Alexander, take you, Janet Erskine, as my wife-to-be. And I thank your father that he brought me to it. Aye, and the Lord Fyvie also."

"Shall we go and tell them now? My parents?"

"As you will. But, no, I would wait until the morning, I think. Talk now, with them, would . . . detract. No? Let this night be ours."

"You mean . . .?"

"No, I do not mean that! We will not spoil our wedding night, lass! May it not be too long hence to wait. But let us savour this night as we ought, apart in our own beds, yet together in all else. And for always."

146

"Yes. You are right." She took his hand, and led the way up.

Janet's room was on the second floor, Will's on the attic storey above. At her door, she opened it, and turned to him enquiringly.

Smiling, he shook his head. "I must not test myself too hardly! Much as part of me wishes it. Once in there . . .!"

She reached up to stroke his face. "Dear Will! The strong man! How blest I am. But I do not think that I shall sleep this night."

"You will. And dream, perchance. Did you not say that you were tired, back there? Myself, I may have my dreams also, but they will not be so good as the reality."

They embraced then, hands as well as lips eager, but moderate enough in their scope considering that these two had been running about naked together only a day or two before.

They did not linger long, in their good judgment. With a murmured goodnight, Will Alexander went resolutely further upstairs.

Breakfast-time announcements were comparatively formal, and better that way. Lady Erskine did rise to kiss her daughter and smile upon Will, while her husband shook his hand. The happy couple were well content just to eye each other across the table.

Wedding possibilities inevitably fell to be discussed. Obviously there could be no marriage ceremony before the pair set off for Dunfermline and beyond, and Will was due there in two days' time. Yet it might be many weeks before they could get back to wed here in Menteith, with the journey south bound to be slow indeed. They could, of course, marry in England . . .

This suggestion, tentatively put by Will, sparked off considerable debate, not to say controversy. Strangely enough, it was not Janet who spoke against it but her mother in especial, her father only a little less so. Clearly

147

their daughter ought to be married here at Cardross; always it was the bride's privilege to wed at her own home kirk. Will admitted this, but had to point out that such decision would inevitably put off their union for long, an indefinite period. Not only was the journey there and back to be considered, but King James's orders and concerns. After all, he, Will Alexander, was tutor and Gentleman of the Bedchamber to Prince Henry, and might well find himself appointed such to Prince Charles also. This present mission meant that he would have been away from his duties with Henry for some two months. The king might well refuse permission for further leave of absence when it would be possible for them to marry in England.

Sir William, who was a staunch Presbyterian, as befitted one who had gained the great Church lands and properties of Glasgow archbishopric through the Reformation, did not actually assert that a wedding conducted by English Church clergy, Episcopalian, would not be valid, but to be deplored nevertheless, his wife wagging her head unhappily. It was Janet who proposed a solution. Let them wed in England, yes, which would make them lawfully man and wife; and then, when they could contrive to return to Scotland for a visit, have a second ceremony here, as it were blessing the union, and so content all?

Will, needless to say, applauded this suggestion, although the parents accepted it without enthusiasm. Will thought to add that if they could find a Presbyterian minister in London, as surely there must be, to conduct the ceremony, they would.

So it was agreed. They would be off in two days' time. Meanwhile, there was the matter of finding a second woman to help with Prince Charles. Janet thought that she could solve that one also. She would ask Ailie Graham to join them. Ailie was the Cardross miller's daughter, widowed but still quite young, a lively, friendly creature who was at something of a loose end these days since her shepherd husband's death. She would not be used to long days on a horse; but Prince Charles was not either, so that they would not be taxing her too greatly. If she would agree, would that suit?

They went down to the mill that forenoon and Will was much taken with Ailie Graham, a sonsy, smiling, well-made woman in her twenties, not noticeably depressed by widowhood, who showed no hesitation in accepting the proposal, short notice as it was, and not in the least overawed apparently at the prospect of becoming an escort for the king's son. She would be ready to ride in the morning. What gear was she to take?

Janet said that she would be having a couple of pack-horses to carry her own clothing and belongings, and Ailie's would go thereon well enough. Then it was back to the castle to make preparations, with the thought that a wedding had to be provided for. In this matter the men were superfluous, and Sir William took his son-in-law-to-be hawking for wildfowl round the loch, and in the process offering some good advice on the subject of marriage, and women's foibles generally, Will reserving much in the way of comment.

That evening the couple did manage to achieve some time alone and made, if not the most of it, at least considerable enjoyment however much hampered by due restraint. Will told Janet that on the morrow, since they would be passing Menstrie on their way to Dunfermline, he would call in at his house and find one of the family rings to betoken their betrothal.

So in the morning it was leave-taking, with much counsel, admonitions and guidance, but very good wishes also. Ailie Graham was there in good time, and Sir William providing two of his men to escort them as far as Dunfermline and lead the pack-horses. This would probably be the longest day's travel of the entire journey, just over fifty miles, for with young Charles they would be fortunate to cover much more than half that.

Will duly found one of his late mother's rings at

Menstrie, which he placed on Janet's finger, to the applause of the three onlookers.

Passing through the town of Alloa, where there was another Erskine tower-house, which had Janet wondering at its non-defensive situation, so unlike most of its kind, in especial Castle Campbell not so far away, allowed Will to mention, all but casually, that Lord Fyvie had said that Argyll was intending to marry Agnes Douglas, a statement which left the young woman silent for a short while. Will did not continue with the subject.

It took them longer to reach Dunfermline than had Will been alone, but they were there in time for the evening meal, Charles being already off to bed. They were taken to his room however by Lady Fyvie, where the two young women promptly fell in love with the great-eyed, wondering child, not asleep but silent.

All, it seemed, was ready for the departure on the morrow.

Lord Fyvie was concerned that they did not overtire the child on the long journey. He thought that thirty miles in a day would be as much as they should envisage, so about two weeks of travel. He, as Chancellor now, was providing four men of the Edinburgh Castle garrison to act as escort. They ought to have no difficulty in finding overnight accommodation all the way, requiring it in the king's name, in suitably and worthy premises of course, not inns, change-houses and the like. Lady Fyvie gave Janet many instructions as to the prince's diet and care. Clearly husband and wife were much preoccupied with the little boy's welfare. The visitors assured them that they would look after their precious charge with all care and caring.

In the morning there was inevitably some delay in setting off, with the new escorts given their instructions and the Cardross ones sent back whence they had come. Another two pack-horses were added to their train, laden with the prince's belongings, plaids to wrap round him if the weather was inclement, clothes and extra provisions.

Eventually they left the old palace, Charles sitting in front of Janet, indeed within her arms, being no trouble at all, putting up with everything in a sort of calm acceptance and complete trust, which further endeared him to his new guardians. A party of eight, with eleven horses, they bade farewell to a tearful Lady Fyvie.

The six miles to the ferry over Forth presented them with no problems, the boy apparently well content just to gaze at the scenery, look up at Janet when she spoke to him, quite trusting but himself seldom saying anything. Yet he did not give the impression of being dull, stupid or lethargic, but quietly aware, heedful in a placid way. Will occasionally rode close, to speak to him, and once got a smile in return.

The crossing in the scow to South Queensferry gave opportunity for the boy to use his legs; but he seemed little inclined to do so, content to sit on Ailie's lap and watch the water. Exercising body, any more than tongue, appeared to be no concern of this curious son of a differently curious father.

Nine more miles brought them to Edinburgh but, with it as yet only early afternoon, they decided to press on the sixteen miles, by Musselburgh, Tranent and the Gleds' Muir, to Haddington, the boy seeming untroubled, now in Ailie's charge. All were very satisfied with their first day's travel when they reached Haddington, and were able to lodge themselves in the Earl of Bothwell's town-house there, one of his Hepburn kinsmen indeed making a great fuss of them.

Will found the young widow Ailie excellent company, helpful as she was cheerful. Their four armed escorts were no problem, respectful but well able to look after themselves. Janet and himself, they realised, were going to have very little opportunity for any sort of intimacies apt for a betrothed couple. Their time would come.

The child's easy acceptance of riding all day with one or other of the women led Will to reckon that they might possibly make Berwick-upon-Tweed for the next night, forty miles on as it was. The Governor's House there, where he had lodged on previous occasions, he had found comfortable. Being able to require accommodation and hospitality in the king's name was a great help. It would make a long day, at the rate they were riding, but there was little suitable lodging, save in inns and the like, between.

They did reach Berwick, with the prince asleep in Janet's arms for the last ten miles. In the morning they crossed the monarch's "Shoogly Brig", this now being replaced by a good stone one, which James had sworn was to be the very first charge on his new English treasury.

Having proved by this Berwick progress that they could cover at least forty miles in a day without causing the child distress, they began to anticipate that they might shorten the timing of their journey by three or four days; and they confirmed the matter by reaching Alnwick the next night, where the Percy Earl of Northumberland was glad to receive the new monarch's son, despite Charles having far-back Douglas blood in him, the Percys and Douglases being at centuries-old feud.

This set the pattern of their travel, much better mileage than they had feared, some days not far off fifty. Will, Janet and Ailie settled into a routine, acceptable, even though the couple did fret sometimes at the lack of privacy imposed by the circumstances.

They, in the end, made London in eleven days – but only to find that the king was presently hunting at Theobalds Park, in Hertfordshire, thirteen miles north of London, while the queen was at Windsor.

They remained at Whitehall Palace the next day, Will uncertain as to his course now. After some debate, he decided that he ought to take Charles and the two women to Oatlands and, leaving them there with Henry and the Careys, head north again for Theobalds to inform the monarch. Knowing James's curious attitude towards his wife, he felt that he had better do this rather than take the little boy to his mother, which normally would seem the natural thing to do. Dealing with this royal family demanded considerable thought and tact.

The escort was despatched back to Edinburgh.

They found all well at Oatlands, Henry delighted to have Will back, although eyeing his small brother somewhat askance, and Sir Robert Carey as glad to be seeing an end to his unwanted duties there, even though his wife seemed content enough. At least that evening, with ample accommodation available, Will and Janet were able to enjoy each other's company more privately than hitherto.

When Will was for setting out next morning, it was to encounter Henry's clamant demands that he should be taken also – not so much that he wanted to see his father as that he did not want to be parted from his friend again so soon. After some thought, Will came to the conclusion that this might be allowable, and James not too disapproving at a brief visit from his heir. It would be about twenty-five miles to Theobalds, but Henry was becoming a good horseman and this would not tax him.

So it was off again. Will seemed to spend his life in the saddle these days. Henry chattered without ceasing, with much complaint about Sir Robert Carey.

They reached their destination in mid-afternoon, to find the king out at the chase. But Cecil, whose seat this was, and who was no great huntsman, received them kindly enough, and was interested to hear of the arrival of Prince Charles.

When the hunt eventually returned, Will did not immediately try to approach the monarch, but sought out Lennox, who was always with James, in a strange relationship, for they were totally dissimilar characters, seeming to have little in common save their cousinship, the duke sensible, moderate, down to earth and putting on no airs and graces. He was always friendly towards Will, and Henry liked him. He suggested that they wait a little longer now before seeking the presence, for James was in a mood. His favourite, Montgomery, had moved in to kill a cornered stag, which the king considered should have been his privilege. Montgomery would have to learn.

So it was some little time before Lennox came to signal that the Lord's Anointed might advisedly be approached. He had told James that they were here.

Their sovereign-lord eyed his son and tutor with but scant favour. "It's the pair o' you, is it!" he greeted them. "Aye. You, Henry, you're no' at your studies, I see! And you, man Alexander, you're back. You've no' brought the bairn Charles here, I'm hoping?"

"No, Sire. He is now at Oatlands. As I have come to inform Your Majesty. But the prince, here, I deemed deserved a break in his lessons to see his father."

"*You* deemed it! Leave you the deeming to me, man. But och, Henry, yon Carey – does he teach you as weel as this Alexander?"

"No." That was certain as it was brief.

"So! I hope you didna misbehave wi' him?"

"No."

Father and son eyed each other assessingly, and James actually found the hint of a smile. "Hech, hech, sae that's the way o' it! You're no' teaching the laddie muckle o' the civilities, Alexander man, I'm thinking. Uh-huh, and hoo's the other one? Wee Charlie?"

"Well, Sire. He stood the journey south very well. He was uncomplaining. We made good time. I brought two young women to see to him, at Lord Fyvie's advising. One Janet Erskine, Sir William's daughter."

"Ooh, aye. You had a notion for that one, I mind."

"We intend to wed, Sire."

"Is that a fact? We'll hae to see aboot that! Is the laddie talking sense, noo?"

154

"He does not say much, Sire. But when he does, it is good sense, yes. He has a very friendly way with him. Causes no trouble. Do you wish me to bring him here to see you, Sire?"

"*I'll* tell you when I want that, man. He'll dae fine at Oatlands, meantime."

"You do not want me to take him to the queen, Highness?"

"Did you no' hear me? When I want you to dae this or that, I'll tell you. Uh-huh. And hoo goes it wi' the Book o' Proverbs?"

"I could scarcely work on that while I was on the road, Sire. But before that, they went well enough, I think."

"Weel, get you back at it, noo. You're a' ower slow at it, you and the others. Mind, yon Bishop Andrews, he's going ower your translations o' the psalms – he's no' right satisfied wi' them a'. You'll hae to hae a word wi' him."

"I never claimed, Your Majesty, to be a notable translator."

"No, it was the poetry that I ettled you'd reach. So, you keep on at the Proverbs, man. I mean to see the hale Bible finished at the soonest."

Will was greatly daring. "Highness, this of my marriage. Sir William Erskine wishes it to be not long delayed. With his daughter travelling thus with me. If we could return to Scotland, to be wed at Cardross?"

"What ails you, if marry you must, in getting wed here? As weel here as at Cardross."

"It would not be quite the same, Sire. For Janet and her family."

"There's mair to think on than them, man. Your duties wi' Henry. Aye, and wee Charlie tae. Henry's tutoring isna to suffer for the Erskines' convenience, see you. You've been awa' lang enough. You took your time up in Scotland, I noted! Na, na, you'll dae fine wedding here. See you, I'll hae yon Bishop Andrews ca' on you at Oatlands. Aboot thae psalms. Get him to wed you. He'll dae it as weel as the next one. Aye, dae that. Noo, off wi' you baith. We'll

155

be eating soon. Henry can sit by me at table, instead o'
yon Philip Herbert I've made Montgomery! See to it,
Vicky."

So that was that. Majesty had spoken. A bishop . . .!

10

Majesty's voice spoke with equal effect in ears spiritual as temporal, for it was only a few days later that the Bishop of Ely arrived at Oatlands, with two attendants. He proved to be a portly but quite amiable prelate, seemingly more interested in meeting the young princes than in either translating psalms or marital affairs. He devoted most of his attentions to Henry, Prince of Wales.

He and Will got down to considering the psalms eventually. They did not disagree strongly on much, in the main merely minor details; but since this was going to be part of the Bible used by generations, it was important to get it as accurate as possible. Will did not insist on his own interpretations.

During a break from this, he raised the subject of marriage. Bishop Andrews said that he had received the royal command to wed them. Where and when did the couple wish the ceremony to take place?

Will was clear about when: as soon as possible, he declared. But where? He had no special church in mind. He pointed out that he and Janet were Presbyterians, but this would not affect the issue, would it? The bishop raised an eyebrow at that, but not over-high, for the king was also Presbyterian in theory, although he did seem to favour bishops. There was no chapel here at Oatlands, and Will was not sure in which parish they were situated.

The prelate said that he presumed that it was to be a quite quiet and modest ceremony, in these circumstances, and there was no need for it to be held in a church or cathedral, such as his own at Ely. He could wed them here, at Oatlands itself, before the necessary witnesses, if that was acceptable; only, he had his other duties elsewhere, and could not stay more than another day. If this was too soon, insufficient time for preparation, then he could come back, but not for some little while . . .

Will, although he thought that he scarcely required to ask Janet's wishes in the matter, said that he would consult her. She, as he anticipated, was delighted. They would be wed here, on the morrow, bless Bishop Andrews! The Careys, who were for off in a day or two, and Ailie Graham, would serve as witnesses. What could be more suitable and to their taste? The churching could be done in Scotland in due course.

That evening, the couple lingered long after the others had retired, not saying a great deal but thinking their own thoughts and frequently just looking at each other warm-eyed. They did wonder what special preparations they perhaps ought to be making for this great and solemn occasion; but all they could really think of was the joy of being able to claim each other in possession by this time the next day. Were they grievously remiss? Shamefully concerned with the physical and personal rather than the spiritual?

It was harder even than usual to tear themselves apart at their bedroom doors that night.

Before he slept, Will Alexander convinced himself that he had now put Aurora, Agnes Douglas, out of his mind, save as a poetic symbol of beauty.

The wedding ceremony was held somewhat early for such occasions, before noon indeed, for the bishop was intent on getting back to London as soon as possible, duty done. In the event it was not so very private an affair; what with the guards that the king insisted should always be with his heir, the Oatlands servitors, the bishop's attendants, plus the Careys, Ailie and Henry, with little Charles there also of course, quite a congregation assembled to see the nuptial knot tied.

The service was brief, simple, basic – as indeed was

desired. The bishop informed the company that they were gathered to celebrate the coming together of a man and a woman, in the sight of God and them all, into the state of holy matrimony, in which they would become one entity, taking each other for better or for worse until death might part them, a most notable step. He was assured that there was no impediment to this match, and that the two to be made one were fully aware of the solemnity of the occasion and the binding nature of the oaths to be taken. Himself he was the more content to forge the link, in that the man and the woman were together to be guardians and kind custodians of the two royal princes here present, by the king's approval. Indeed he was here by His Majesty's express command.

He then asked the couple if they took each other to be wife and husband, forsaking all others, to cleave to each other here and hereafter, barely waiting for their assurance before pronouncing them wed, according to the ordinance of Holy Church and the laws of the land.

Will had got the Menstrie betrothal ring back from Janet earlier, and now used it for its ultimate purpose as sign and seal of their union. They kissed chastely, and the prelate said a brief prayer, for this marriage and for all present as witnesses, made the sign of the cross over them, and pronounced the benediction.

The deed was done, however improbable it might seem that this could be sufficient to effect all the lawful, personal and irrevocable bindings of marriage, as declared. Lady Carey led the way in congratulation, Ailie embraced them both, and Henry came to ask if that was all. He did not think that they seemed very different from before. Young Charles gazed, but no more wonderingly than usual.

Something of a wedding feast was being prepared for later; but Bishop Andrews was for off, so only a modest repast was provided at this stage, and all bade him farewell, with thanks from the newly-weds.

Thereafter something of a hiatus inevitably developed for the said newly-weds, with the rest of the day stretching ahead of them and the night far off, no one knowing quite what was called for. Will suggested that, despite all the horsed travel done recently, a good ride for Janet and himself might satisfactorily fill the interval. After all, if they had been off on the usual post-marital excursion, this would have been their probable activity. It was agreed, and Janet changed out of her wedding-gown into saddle-clothes. Henry had to be dissuaded from accompanying them.

Horse-riding in the so level lands of private parks, cultivated fields and much population was not to be compared with that in their own Scottish hills and glens; but in the golden early autumn sunshine, with the leaves beginning to turn and the stubble fields yellow, it was pleasant enough. They dismounted more than once, in suitably secluded spots, to embrace, however moderately, Janet admitting that she did not feel in the least like a married woman, and Will assuring her that she would do so later in the day, he would see to that for her.

They returned to quite an ambitious feast organised by Lady Carey and Ailie, Sir Robert made a speech and toasts were drunk, the two princes being allowed to stay up later than usual, although Charles fell asleep in his chair. As soon as he decently could, Will proposed retiral for all, after a momentous day. He was thankful that Carey did not suggest a bedding ceremony, such as was popular in court circles apparently, where the happy couple were escorted by the company to the nuptial couch, the bride undressed by the men and the groom by the ladies, and the pair thereafter seen to be duly joined in more than wedlock before being left to themselves.

They said their goodnights, and hand-in-hand proceeded upstairs.

Steaming tubs of water welcomed them in Janet's room, and quickly they divested themselves. These two having frequently seen each other naked did not engage in the mutual undressing which was so apt to feature on many such occasions. But they did enjoy bathing each other

160

in the warm water, something they had not experienced before, and in which they vied with one another in thoroughness.

Thereafter, it was a matter of not exactly holding back, but of not allowing any headlong consummation, especially on the man's part, in order to savour and appreciate to the full all the loveliness that was at his disposal, to stimulate and arouse – not that much of this was required. Janet it was who reached an initial fulfilment first, and then almost a supplementary one, before Will had to let go in truly major and ardent attainment.

At last, at last . . .!

When they could speak coherently, apart from endearments and fond tributes, they both agreed that it had been worth the waiting for. But the man counselled a little more waiting, only a little. The night was young yet, Janet murmuring only slightly sleepy assent.

Delay, such as it was, could be sweet they discovered, and productive. Man and woman were made to complement each other they now proved and proved again.

PART TWO

11

So a new life commenced for Will and Janet Alexander, a good and fulfilled life, which in a way was strange, because the man had not felt that way before, tutoring and translating. But having a wife to share all with him made the difference. Time no longer hung heavily. Henry, of course, now in his eleventh year, was rapidly developing and becoming the better company, especially outdoors, being sportively inclined and attaining considerable proficiency. As for Charles, that small person, so utterly dependent upon them, became very dear to all, Will included. They understood now why Lady Fyvie had wept on parting from him.

Ailie Graham remained with them meantime. She could not travel home alone, and until the newly-weds obtained the king's permission to leave and visit Scotland again, she was well content with her lot at Oatlands. She had become more than just an assistant nurse for the little prince, a friend for Janet and Will, and a cheerful and valued one.

With the monarch's assertion that *he* would do the deeming and issuing of instructions, Will did not take Charles to see his mother, as he felt that he ought to do; but the word that the child was now in the south had reached the queen, for she arrived at Oatlands one day, with her daughter Elizabeth and the Lady Huntly. Will would have been quite prepared for her to take the boy away there and then, but she made no such suggestion. Presumably James had issued firm orders to the contrary, and Anne contented herself with spending a few hours with the child and Henry, and then moving on. The

165

good-looking daughter Elizabeth it was who seemed most reluctant to part from Charles, although she and Henry betrayed little interest in each other. It was October, and the queen announced that they would be returning to London the following month for the winter. She did not indicate whether this would apply to the Oatlands party also.

In fact, Will was summoned to Hampton Court to see the king in November, to give an account of his stewardship and the progress of the two princes. He was given only the briefest of audiences, his liege-lord being mainly concerned with the translation situation, which apparently was being held up elsewhere, to the royal annoyance. That Bishop Andrews was going to get a flea in his ear! This for not whipping up his team to greater efforts. James had set a publication date for the entire Bible for four years hence, and at the present rate of progress, or lack of it, that would not be achieved. Will informed that he was nearly finished with the Proverbs – to be reminded that this was only *his* version. His psalms had had to be amended; let this later work be better done.

It was only with a deal of resolution in the circumstances that Will summoned up courage, as he was being dismissed with the information that the princes would be expected at Whitehall Palace for Christmastide, to ask whether His Majesty had remembered the matter of recommending a publisher for his *Aurora* book of sonnets? Tutting testily, his sovereign said that he had other matters to see to in the governing of two realms, but had he not indicated that the man Robbie Barker would do it? He could take the manuscripts up to him in London when he came at Christmas. Will, jerking thanks, did not risk asking when he and Janet might go to Scotland for the Kirk's blessing on their union.

So, a month later, it was departure for London. Will and Janet had mixed feelings about this, finding life at Oatlands to their taste now and scarcely relishing city and court life. But the man was eager to see his book published, and this appeared to be the requisite step. Henry was wholly against the move, and had to be consoled by the declaration that they would try to make the visit as short as possible and come back to Oatlands.

Ailie, oddly, was agog to see London town. Would the king allow her to stay on with little Charles at Whitehall?

That anxiety at least was quickly laid to rest. The prince's party was allocated quite commodious although not very handsome quarters at the rear of the palace, and no questions asked as to who was in attendance. It transpired that the queen was at Greenwich Palace down-Thames, and apparently the royal pair were to celebrate Yuletide apart.

Will, by now, knew better than to take the princes to their father without being so commanded, and it was in fact two days later before the summons came, and that in the evening when young Charles was being put to bed. So hurried adjustments had to be made, the boys dressed in their best, such as that was, and Will took the decision to have Janet accompany them, taking the little boy by the hand.

They found James in a fine library, poring over books and papers as always, also as usual with high hat on head, clothing soiled and untidy. For once Lennox was not with him, his companion being Sir Francis Bacon, a talented poet and playwright and patron of Ben Jonson. The four had to wait some time before the monarch chose to notice them, although Henry made their presence very evident. Bacon did rise at sight of the princes.

Eventually James looked up, to prod a finger in their direction. "Aye, then. Sae here's the Erskine woman the bishop wed you tae, Alexander man! Johnnie Mar's bit cousin. I'm hoping neither o' you regret the marriage, heh? Marriages can be regrettable, mind!"

"No, Sire, very much otherwise!" Will averred. "Janet now looks after Prince Charles. Lady-in-waiting, as you might say."

167

"*I'll* say if she's to be ca'd that, no' you! You're ay ower forward, Alexander. Forward." He got up from the table and came over to peer at Charles. "Aye, the laddie's grown a wee. But no' that much. He's still sma'. Near five years he'll be."

"The prince is coming on well. Your Grace." Janet said, dipping a curtsy. "He is speaking more, and is of a very warm and pleasing nature. We all are greatly fond of him."

"Is that a fact! And you, lassie, Majesty it is here in England, no' Grace. I'd hae thought you'd ha' been tellt that."

"I apologise, Sire."

"Aye. And you, Henry, what o' you? Are you behaving yoursel'?"

"Yes."

"Just yes! Or no! You're ay right abrupt, boy. I'm the king as weel as your faither, mind!"

"Yes, Father, I would wish to go hunting deer with you, one day."

"You would, would you! You're no' blate aboot some things, I'll say that for you! Hunting's no' for bairns."

"I'm not a bairn. I will be eleven soon. At Yuletide."

"Sae you will. And you jalouse that's auld enough to go hunting? How say you, Alexander? Is he guid enough on a horse to hunt?"

"I would think so, Sire. He rides well, is good at all sports."

"I can shoot arrows straight. I shot a hare one time."

"Say you so? Was it louping or biding still?"

The boy frowned. "It was running, but it had stopped," he admitted.

"I'ph'mm. Weel, we'll see aboot the hunting." The king pointed at Will. "I'm hearing you've got another woman for young Charlie. Whae's that? No' any laird's daughter either, I'm tellt."

Will never failed to be surprised at the information the monarch obtained, and the details which concerned him.

"Ailie Graham is the miller's daughter from Cardross, Sire. A widow. A kind and most worthy person."

"My father and mother recommended her, Sire," Janet added.

"Ooh, aye. Sae long as she does weel by this wee Charlie. Noo, off wi' you. Frank Bacon and mysel' hae much to discuss. I'm for setting up an alliance o' the princes of Christendom – or some o' them, the guid Protestant ones – tae unite tae keep the Popish ones in their places. Without war, mind, bluidshed. Ower many o' these English lords o' mine are for battle and bluid. Even the man Cecil. Bacon here has mair wits, being a poet, mind. We've got Scotland and England, Denmark and some o' the German states, but aim for mair. Aye, and we've Catholic Ireland to deal wi', forby. Sae, awa' wi' you. And I'm thinking the Book o' Ruth will be the next bit task for you, Alexander man."

They backed out, as ever wondering at the range and priorities of this strangest of monarchs.

They passed a reasonably rewarding Yuletide, seeing little of James and less of Anne, who it seemed was expecting another child. They found some interest in wandering the streets of London, Ailie in particular intrigued, for she had never lived in a city. They always had to have the armed escort with them when they took the princes; but on occasion Will was able to take one or the other of the young women alone, which was much more to their taste.

It was Janet he took with him to Cheapside one day to see Robert Barker, printer, carrying a satchel with his hundred poems. Since he could say that he had come on the king's recommendation, he had little difficulty in gaining an agreement to publish, although Barker did have to emphasise that because of the size of the proposed volume the cost would not be light. Will did urge as modest a price as possible, consonant with a fair production and leather binding, suggesting one hundred copies, at first issue at

169

any rate, calculating that the printer would not overcharge for fear of offending his royal patron. He declared that it was to be entitled *Aurora – Containing the First Fancies of the Author's Youth*, which raised eyebrows.

Barber revealed that he was presently printing a treatise by the king to be entitled *A Counterblast to Tobacco*, the monarch being very much against the new vice of smoking introduced by Hawkins and Raleigh. The printer indeed read out gleefully part of James's Introduction, to the effect that "It is a great iniquitie and against all humanitie that a husband shall not be ashamed to force his wife to the extremitie of having to live in a perpetual stinking torment." Will was interested. He had seen much of the tobacco habit since coming south – he could not recollect ever having come across it in Scotland – and they had had to endure Sir Robert Carey's smoking occasionally at Oatlands. He knew that James was against it, but not that he had written such condemnation.

Leaving his manuscript with Barker, and quite elated at this major step towards publication, Will had to cope with Janet's comments on the title. *Aurora* referred to Agnes Douglas, did it not, linking her red hair and beauty of body with a roseate dawn? She did not actually complain at so styling his first book, but the questions were implicit. He pointed out that he had included the subtitle, indicating that since his very first poetic attempts had been inspired by his boyhood wonder at that head and person, he felt that it was only right to have the succession of outpourings under that heading, although they had nothing to do with Agnes. And *Aurora* did make a suitable title.

Janet wondered whether indeed none of the other writings were coloured by that first vision in some measure. Wondered also whether Agnes was perhaps now Countess of Argyll.

A few days later they had a visit from the queen, looking very pregnant, she having come up in the royal barge from Greenwich. She spent longer with Charles this time, but despite her condition it appeared that her main reason for coming to the city was connected with choosing materials for new gowns to be made for her. Anne had all but a mania for clothing, expensive garb and, to be sure, jewellery to go with it, an extravagance which much concerned her husband, needless to say. Indeed when she came to see Charles and Henry it transpired, through Lennox's sister Lady Huntly, that the queen had been visiting George Heriot, the royal jeweller and banker from Edinburgh, to arrange a large loan, James having apparently seen fit to draw the line over further expenditure, at least for the time being.

By late January not only Henry had had enough of Whitehall and London, but even Ailie. Through the duke they asked permission to return to Oatlands, and this was granted. Thankfully they packed up and headed for the country life again.

It was on Will's and Janet's minds, of course, that they had promised her parents that they would return to Cardross to have their union blessed and, as it were, regularised by the Scots Kirk. The problem was how to gain royal permission and leave of absence. The opportunity for at least the attempt occurred in April, when a messenger arrived from the king inviting Henry to be brought to his new royal hunting-box of Royston Priory in Hertfordshire to try his hand as desired at the chase, or at least his seat. This in two days' time. The excitement generated was intense.

Will took the prince, not much of a huntsman himself, his notion of pursuing the deer being to stalk them on the hill, alone, with a crossbow. On arrival at Royston, for the second hunt of the day, Henry was not slow to recognise that his horse, and Will's also, was not up to the standard of most of the mounts there, good enough for ordinary travel but scarcely fast enough for deer-hunting. He was commenting on this to Ludovick of Lennox as they assembled, awaiting the king, and his complaint was overheard by Juan de Velasco, Constable of Castile, an ambassador from Spain, who these days had become one of James's close associates, after negotiating the extraordinary peace treaty with Spain which was so unpopular with many of the English magnates. De Velasco promptly promised the Prince Henry that he should have a fine Spanish mare such as he was himself riding, much to the boy's elation.

The hunt which followed may have been rewarding enough for the king and some at least of his followers, not all of whom were as keen on the activity as was their monarch, especially as James always liked to reserve the climax for himself; but as far as Henry and Will were concerned, it was all only a gallop through parkland and woods, seldom so much as seeing a deer, however much shouting, blowing of huntsmen's horns and baying of hounds went on. They did arrive at the first kill, to witness the extraordinary sight of the sovereign-lord of two kingdoms, riding-boots off, paddling his feet in the steaming entrails of the slain stag, which James claimed was an excellent remedy for rheumatism and such-like afflictions. The king beckoned to his son to come and observe this, but fortunately did not insist on Henry doing the same, observing that he was as yet ower young to be troubled with the rheumatics. No enquiries were made as to how the boy was making out on his first hunting experience.

A second kill was achieved, with once again Henry's horse being insufficiently speedy to let him witness it, before a return was made to quarters. There, presently, at the meal, all but a banquet, Henry and Will were provided with a side table on the dais, and midway through the many courses were beckoned over to the royal chair and asked how the hunting had gone. Henry declared that his horse had been too slow to keep up with most of the others but that the Spanish man – who was now sitting on James's left – had promised him a fine fast mare like his own, so after that he would not get left behind. His father nodded approvingly at de Velasco, but declared that the chase demanded more than just good horses. There were the ways of the deer to be understood, the best beasts to single out and short-cuts in the run to be anticipated and taken.

They were being dismissed when Will took the opportunity to ask of His Majesty his wife's and his own return to Cardross for a brief visit to fulfil the promise of a blessing on their marriage by the Kirk of Scotland. This had James frowning; but with the Catholic de Velasco on one side of him and the Episcopalian Montgomery on the other, the King of Scots was not in a position to pooh-pooh the separate and superior identity of the Reformed Church of Scotland. So reluctantly he agreed, but pointed out the trouble it would entail in getting the Careys to come and take over at Oatlands in the interim. This had Henry announcing that *he* would like to go north with Master Will, which his sire promptly negatived firmly, declaring that he would do no such thing and that he was getting altogether over-demanding for a bairn of eleven years. The boy's assertion that he did not like Sir Robert Carey was flapped aside. They were turning to go back to their table when the king grabbed Will's arm to ask whether he was finished the Proverbs yet. When told that they were nearly translated, he was commanded to start thereafter on another task: the Book of Ruth would be most appropriate probably – yes, the Book of Ruth.

They got away, the prince making faces.

Will and Janet had to wait for another couple of weeks at Oatlands before the Careys turned up, Sir Robert scarcely pleased but his wife delighted to take over care of young Charles again.

The next day the Scots set off for home, for Ailie Graham went with them; but not to remain there, for she pleaded to be allowed to come back again, much enjoying her life with them and the princes. Good friends as they had become, the Alexanders agreed, the man indeed saying that he would indicate to Sir William and the miller Graham that this was more or less by royal appointment, if there was any reluctance to let her go.

The parting from Henry and Charles did bring a tugging at the heart-strings.

12

It was, as before, good to be back in Scotland, especially with the cuckoos calling their haunting May welcome, the thorn blossom snow white, the gorse ablaze and the bluebells abloom. There were still patches of snow in the topmost corries and scars of the blue mountains, but that only added contrast to the colour and challenge of the scene.

Their welcome at Cardross was warm, despite the reproach that they had taken their time about it, the assumption being not exactly that they had been living in sin in the interim but not far off it.

The parish minister at the Kirkton of Menteith was summoned, and the celebration ordered. They would have it on the Sunday, two days hence, after the normal forenoon service, so that all the local folk could see that their laird's daughter was properly married.

In the event, the confirmation of the union took considerably longer than had the original celebration by Bishop Andrews, Will coming to the conclusion that the Scots Kirk was probably more long-winded than was the English one. It was all but a second wedding, with more declaration, exhortation, admonition and prayer than previously, the proceedings sterner altogether, with even the benediction prolonged and all-encompassing. When they eventually were dismissed, Janet conceded that she now did feel married indeed, so perhaps there was something to be said for all the verbiage.

Oddly, once outside the church, the minister was all smiles and geniality, a different character.

They learned from Sir William that the Earl of Argyll

was indeed now wed to the Lady Agnes Douglas, and as far as was known they were living at Castle Campbell. It was decided that a visit there should be paid; but first they must go and see the Countess Dowager of Mar at Stirling Castle, to inform her of the well-being and progress of her former charge, Prince Henry. And, of course, Will wanted to see how matters went at Menstrie.

So they had a day in the Stirling area, leaving Ailie with her father. They found the Lady Minnie nowise changed by the time passed, autocratic, no-nonsense, but pleased to see them, and demanding in her detailed enquiries after the prince, critical of his father's attitudes and dismissive of his mother's. She declared that the boy would be far better back in Scotland, under her care and that of the Earl Johnnie her son, than growing up at the decadent and foppish English court, of which she had heard little good. Here they would teach him to be a better monarch than was his father. To all this the visitors could only listen and make non-committal if respectful noises.

She also made it clear that she thought that Janet, an Erskine of an earl's family, had rather married beneath her in wedding an Alexander of Menstrie, although she had seen it coming, she averred. As for that red-headed besom Agnes Douglas, she did not know whether to be sorry for her, or for her husband, Campbells being what they were; perhaps they deserved each other.

Will and Janet left Stirling Castle distinctly bemused, after promising to call in at Alloa Tower to inform the earl of what went on at London. They passed that night at Menstrie, where Janet, who accepted that this was now to be *her* house, began to see a number of changes and improvements which she could make therein, Will content to inspect and concern himself with the property and lands. All seemed to be reasonably well with his lairdship, his incumbent competent and giving a fair account of his stewardship. One of the tenant farmers had died, leaving no son to succeed him; but a younger son of one of the others would like to take on the vacant holding, if this was acceptable. Will agreed.

They decided to spend a second night at Menstrie after a day seeing to matters inside by Janet and outside by Will, and next morning set off for Castle Campbell via Alloa.

They found Johnnie Mar affable and interested in all they had to tell him, he, differing from his mother, asserting that Janet had done quite well for herself in wedding Will Alexander for, when young Henry succeeded his father on the throne in due course, he would assuredly not fail to advance in status and position his tutor and guardian. His visitors certainly had not looked that far ahead.

Mar had much to say about the state of Scotland lacking its resident monarch, shaking his head and questioning whether the union of the two crowns was advantageous to the more ancient but less populous realm. Too many of Scotland's best had gone down to London with James; and a ten-day journey each way to gain the royal approval, appointments and signatures for so many matters of state was highly inconvenient. Some sort of viceroy should be installed, senior to the Chancellor and Secretary of State, to act in the king's name; he did not actually hint that he himself might suitably fill that bill, as James's foster-brother. He admitted that Seton, formerly Fyvie and now created Earl of Dunfermline, made an effective Chancellor, but being a lawman was apt to see affairs of state from a legalistic point of view. And he was having trouble, they all were, with Patrick, Master of Gray, one of the cleverest and most able men in the land, whom James had gravely and foolishly offended and who was now working against the royal authority. Argyll had overmuch power and authority, as Lieutenant of the North, all but ruler north of Forth and Clyde, seeking, on the pretext of subduing the largely Catholic Highlands and Islands, ever to extend the influence and possessions of his Clan Campbell. And so on.

The couple left Alloa considerably concerned.

177

Further along the Ochil foothills they came to Dollar, by the Black Devon Water, and climbed the steep zigzag track between the burns of Sorrow and Care to Castle Campbell on its thrusting knoll. But no cares and sorrow greeted them on arrival at the stronghold with its black and gold gyrony-of-eight banners flapping proudly in the breeze. Will, as Argyll's friend and former tutor, was well known to the castle's keeper, or chamberlain as he was now being styled, and they gained access without difficulty, to be told that MacCailean Mor had departed for the north only two days before, but that the countess was in residence. Led up to the great hall, they had not long to wait before Agnes appeared, almost at a run, to hail the visitors with glad cries and come to throw her arms about them, Will first, dancing round, kissing and hugging, as beautiful as ever and as demonstrative.

It was a while before they were able to exchange more than mere ejaculations and gasped greeting, and Will could explain their presence in Scotland, and their determination to come to visit here, Janet adding that they were glad that the new Countess of Argyll was not too grand now to receive them. How did it feel to be wed to MacCailean Mor?

"How does it feel to be wed to Will Alexander, *I* ask! And grand?" She skirled a laugh. "A Douglas does not rise in the world by wedding a Campbell, I'd mind you! Oh, it is good to see you both. Especially with Archie gone." Another laugh. "I mean, myself being left alone here. As so frequently."

"Archie's duties will be demanding," Will said.

"Towards a new wife also, no? Skied on this hillside cliff, roosting like some fowl of the air! You now, Janet, do rather better, I think?"

"I, we, are held down in England, far from home. But we have much to be thankful for, yes. And with the care of the two young princes. We have our happiness!"

The two women eyed each other.

They spent a lively evening of talk, recounting, laughter

178

and a certain amount of innuendo, Will sometimes feeling somewhat uncomfortable between these two, aware of being used as a sort of anvil for them to forge some feminine design upon. Agnes was of course a challenging creature and it would have been a feeble man indeed who did not in some measure rise in response to her provocation, Janet obviously well aware of it.

It was Janet, in fact, who out of her own initiative mentioned the imminent publication of Will's book of poems, and its title *Aurora*, leaving him to make the explanations. This he sought to do fairly carefully, aware of the pitfalls, stressing the youthful start of it all and the intimation thereof in the subtitle, and emphasising that the greater part of the work was on a variety of themes unconnected with the first boyhood flourish. Agnes was clearly much intrigued, clapping her hands more than once, and often glancing at the other young woman.

"So, my fiery locks set alight to your muse, Will Alexander!" she announced. "Or was it more than my hair? My person? Heigh-ho, for what am I responsible? For it was your poetry that commended you to the king, was it not? So Archie says. And this led to your appointment with the prince, and your further steps on the ladder of advancement to who knows what heights! What you have to thank me for!"

"Hence Janet's bringing up the matter, no doubt," the man averred warily. "We are duly grateful."

"No doubt you will be presented with a copy of the volume in due course, as an acknowledgment," Janet said lightly.

"I shall keep that under my pillow of a night!" the other declared, smiling brilliantly. "*Aurora* is a splendid title – the rise of light and warmth and love. I have never greatly liked the name Agnes. I think that hereafter you will have to start calling me Aurora instead of merely thinking it!"

"No, no, that would be to imply that the beauteous early dawn so frequently changes into less fair condition, cloud and rain!" Janet observed. "Are we not told, from childhood, that a red sky in the morning warns the shepherds of trouble to come? Inauspicious, perhaps?"

Rather hurriedly Will changed the slant of the subject. "I am now seeking to polish up, for possible printing, four tragedies: *Croesus, Darius the Mede, Julius Caesar* and *The Alexandria Tragedy*," he said.

"Ah. So now you discover that life is not all love and beauty? We learn that, do we not, in many ways. Even in marriage?"

Her guests left that unanswered.

Later, with bedtime indicated, Agnes said that she would show Janet their room, but intimated that Will should go downstairs to the kitchen premises and bring up a Douglas night-time speciality, hot honey wine with a dash of *uisge beatha*, whisky, which would ensure their prompt and untroubled sleep, The chamberlain would have it ready for them. Will wondered why this could not be summoned up by bell or other signal, but did as he was bidden.

Coming up presently with a steaming jug and three goblets, it was to find Agnes back awaiting him in the hall, alone. She took the tray from him but set it down on a table, and, turning again, came to embrace the man, vehemently, wordless, but mouth open and urgent. Moving her body more languorously than her lips against his, she sought for and placed one hand of his on her breast and, despite himself, almost automatically his other one reached down to clasp her hip.

So they stood for long moments, their breathing deep and hands busy, until abruptly Will recovered himself, however belatedly, and gently but firmly pushed her away from him.

"Enough, lass, enough!" he got out. "This is profitless, unsuitable – however to our pleasure. We both are wed."

She searched his face. "But we are both our own persons still, are we not?"

180

"Not wholly so, no. If our vows mean anything. Vows and, and affections!" To avoid debate and probably further temptation, he turned and picked up the tray with the still steaming jug. "Shall we go up?"

She rippled a laugh, took the tray from him, and led the way upstairs.

At a door on the second floor Agnes threw it open and preceded him into the room. Janet was already in bed and sitting up, her unclad body inviting indeed. She was obviously surprised to see the other young woman entering with Will.

Agnes nodded towards her. "A fair sight," she acknowledged. "My sorrow that I do not offer so much! But at least I can offer this lesser aid to felicity," and she raised the tray.

Janet made no attempt to cover herself. "I do not think that we shall require inducements this night," she observed. "Will you?"

"Perhaps." Agnes put the tray down on the bed, and half sat beside it, to pour out the warm liquor into all three goblets. She handed them over.

Distinctly uncomfortably standing there, Will took his, while the women sipped theirs, taking their time. How long was Agnes going to remain here? Was she proposing to see them into bed, in a sort of bedding ceremony? He would scarcely put it past that one. He made no move to start undressing.

"Where is Archie Campbell gone?" he asked, for something to say.

"He was for Inveraray first, to collect more of his people for some sally into the Isles against the Catholic clans," she said. "He finds such ploys to his taste. You were his tutor, Will, although little older than himself. Was he always the one for strife, struggle, imposing his will on other men? But not on women, I think! Archibald the Grim!"

"No-o-o. I did not deem him so. He would not be imposed upon, was always his own man, but he was no' an aggressor."

181

"And women? On your Continental visiting you must have found many kindly women? How went this with him? And with yourself?"

Will glanced at Janet. "We . . . learned how to behave," he said briefly. He finished off his drink, and set the goblet down on the tray.

But Agnes was not to be hurried. "He would have had me go to Inveraray with him, if only for a day or two. But I do not love those barbarous Highlands. I am glad that I did not go. Or I would have missed this . . . delight!"

Janet finished her potion also. "Perhaps a wise wife should have done?" She suggested. "Is there not a legend, a saying, about red-headed lassies being ever available in Argyll? Descendants of Muriel of Cawdor." She could make her own points.

"He is welcome to them! But, never fear, I will not let him forget that I am Countess of Argyll!"

"Being Countess of Argyll will at Inveraray mean little," Janet suggested. "There your husband is MacCailean Mor, that is all, everything. I have a little of the ancient tongue. You will be but *bean*, wife, woman, to the son of the great Colin. I have lived always close enough to the Highlanders to know their ways."

For some reason that seemed to hasten the other's finishing of her drink, and she rose. "Then I will bid you a goodnight," she declared. "And hie me to my lonely couch. If you dream, do so kindly towards Aurora." She tapped Janet's bare shoulder with quite a flick, and taking up the tray, also flicked an all but mocking kiss on Will's cheek, and left them.

"At last!" the man said, and began to undress.

"A dutiful hostess, is she not?" Janet asked.

He did not answer that directly, but quickly discarding the last of his clothing, made for the bed, she holding out her arms for him.

It was Janet who rather took the lead thereafter – not that the man required much stimulation. They said it all with their bodies, Douglas potion or none.

182

Or not quite all, perhaps. For later, before he slept, Will did think to ask himself whether he had indeed managed quite to purge himself of the pull of Agnes Douglas.

In the morning, she would have had them stay longer, for at least another day; but in the circumstances the visitors felt that they should be gone.

They all made something of a tense parting of it.

13

The eventual return to Oatlands, after nearly three weeks' absence, was highly popular, Henry being overjoyed to see them, little Charles obviously pleased, and the Careys thankful to be relieved, and not long in departing. Before they went, however, they gave the Alexanders the rather ominous news that, two weeks previously, a messenger had come from the king summoning Will to Hampton Court forthwith; and of course he had had to be sent back with the word that Will had not yet returned from Scotland. Needless to say this looked as though James considered that he had been away overlong, and there might well be repercussions from the monarch. Distinctly uneasy, Will felt that he had better be off to Hampton Court the very next day. Nothing was said by Carey about Henry going also, but Will decided that it might be wise to take the boy, since possibly the summons was connected with him; and perhaps his presence might somewhat cushion any royal reproofs. The prince was nothing loth, hoping that there might be hunting to partake in, particularly as he was proud to show Will the handsome new Spanish mare which the Captain of Castile had duly sent to Oatlands, as promised.

So it was off again in the morning, Henry notably mounted and in high spirits.

They found the court in something of a stir, for a variety of reasons, the most evident of which was King Christian of Denmark, Anne's elder brother, come on a visit, presumably to see his sister, who had been delivered of her new child, another daughter, a weakly infant apparently, to be named Mary after the king's mother; but the queen was at her London palace of Somerset House while King Christian was here at Hampton, and making his presence felt. He was a rumbustious character, looking all but a Viking indeed, enormous, loud of voice, more than hearty, seldom wholly sober and drinking and eating to match, ensuring something like chaos wherever he was, undoubtedly a trial to his brother-in-law. But at least, according to Lennox, he was amiable and not intentionally boorish as had been his brother, the Duke Ulric.

A further source of stir was a sort of great ones' alliance at court against James's unsuitable peace treaty with Spain and its consequences, his favours towards the Captain of Castile and his fondness for the permanent Spanish ambassador, Count Gondomar, who had become almost a court favourite, and who was apparently advocating the betrothal of the Prince of Wales to the Infanta Maria Anna, with promises of an enormous dowry, much to the offence of the Protestant lords. All this, they held, was bound to encourage the Catholic cause in England, which was still strong, the more so in that Queen Anne was openly inclining towards Rome, and the Catholic chiefs were on the upsurge in Ireland. The Duke of Lennox was much concerned over all this, for he had been reared a Catholic, although now nominally Protestant, and his sister, the queen's closest companion, was married to the leading Scottish Catholic, the Gordon Earl of Huntly.

None of which, Will judged, had anything much to do with him, and would not account for his summons to the presence.

Lennox did achieve an audience for Henry and himself more swiftly than usual, which in itself was a little alarming. This being a Sunday, James was apparently prepared to bow to Protestant disapproval of sport on the Sabbath. So there was no hunting, and they found the monarch closeted with Robert Cecil, as so often – now created Earl of Salisbury – and a heavy-made, square-featured individual, a fellow-Scot by his accent. These were not dismissed at the arrival of the newcomers.

185

"Sae there you are!" James greeted them, seeming to ignore his son. "You ay tak your time, Alexander man! I didna let you go to Scotland to bide there! You and your woman are Henry's attendants, mind. Aye, and wee Charlie's tae."

"Yes, Sire. I regret it if we were away when Your Majesty expected us to be back. But there was much to see to in Scotland. And since we can go only infrequently . . ."

"There's a deal mair to see to here! O' mair import than just your bit lairdship o' Menstrie, and yon Cardross. Hoo's auld Lady Minnie? And Johnnie Mar, eh?"

"Both well, Sire. And asking after Your Majesty."

"Aye, weel they might. You, Henry. You got your mare, eh?"

"Yes. When will I go hunting on her?"

"We'll see. I'll be oot the morn, belike. You can manage the mare fine, can you?"

"Yes."

"You could teach the laddie better manners I'm thinking, Alexander man. He's ay that abrupt wi' me, abrupt just!"

Will could hardly say that it was only with his father that the prince was so monosyllabic. He merely bowed.

"Uh-huh." The king delved into a pocket of his untidy and never over-clean clothing, and drew out a leather-bound book. "See here."

"A new volume of yours, Sire? Not the treatise on tobacco? Too large."

"Na, na, it's yours. The man Barker didna ken whaur you were, sae he sent them a' to me here, wi' my treatise. One hunnerd o' them! Aye, and one hunnerd sonnets in them. I've no' read them a', mind, but maist. They're no' bad." He cocked an eyebrow. "Was this Aurora lassie your Erskine one? She hasna' red hair."

"Well, no, Sire. It was another, took my youthful fancy."

"You're partial to red-haired women?"

186

"Not particularly, Sire. It was just this one, when I was young . . ."

"Morton's daughter? Yon Agnes – she has right red hair. I saw you wi' her at yon masque o' my Annie's."

"Yes, Sire."

The king eyed him thoughtfully, and then turned, to wave the book at the square-jawed man. "Alexander o' Menstrie's a right philosophical poet, Jamie. And prolific, aye prolific. In his verse, leastwise." And he chuckled. "No' otherwise as yet that I've heard tell o'!" He nodded to Will again. "D'you ken Jamie Hamilton? I've made him the Lord Abercorn, mind. We're at this sair matter o' Ireland, a right trauchle. Thae Catholic chiefs are in right and shamefu' revolt. We'll hae to dae something aboot it, I say."

Now Will knew who the man was, one of the Hamiltons of the earldom of Arran, son of the Lord Claud Hamilton who had so loyally and effectively supported Mary Queen of Scots, the only hero of her last and disastrous battle at Langside.

"His Highness is against sending an army to Ireland," Hamilton said. "But finding other means to enforce order there is none so easy." And he looked over at Cecil, meaningfully.

"I'm no' one for war and battle – I'm ay telling folk that!" the monarch declared. "There's other ways o' ruling a realm. I'm the Lord's Anointed, God's chosen representative, and Christ doesna advocate bluid and killing. Na, na, I'm thinkin' o' colonisation just, no' slaughter."

Mystified, Will glanced at Lennox, who shrugged.

"His Majesty believes that the way to counter these Irish rebels, the Earls of Tyrone and Tyrconnell, the O'Neills, the O'Connors and the rest, is to send over many settlers, from Scotland and England, dispossess the chiefs of their lands, and give them to these new men." He smoothed his chin. "Good Protestants all, to be sure! They will have to go armed, no doubt, but not

187

to do battle unless they are attacked. As they will be, I fear."

"No' necessarily, Vicky. I'll outlaw the earls and chiefs, sae that any supporting them would be bringing outlawry on themsel's likewise. I'll offer the common folk favours, moneys, guids, to support the new lairdies. They're gey puir ower there, starve much o' the time. The Irish dinna ken hoo to use the land. We'll teach them! The chiefs will maybe no' need that much bluid shed to get quit o' them."

"I fear that Your Majesty may not find a great many volunteers to go over and become Irish colonisers," Cecil put in, shaking his head. "What have you to offer them but toil and trouble, danger and enmity?"

"Land, man, land! D'you no' see it? Ever since man crept oot o' the caves, men hae sought for land. It's the abiding need and wealth o' the human race. And the land o' Ireland is *mine*! As is Scotland's and England's. I'm superior o' a' the land, whoever says that they own it. I am that. They only own it frae me. Sae I can gie *you*, Salisbury. And you, Jamie, Abercorn. Aye, and you Vicky, Lennox." He pointed at them all. Even your bit Menstrie, Alexander. Weel, I'll forfeit and dispossess these Irish lords and chieftains. There's plenties o' land in Ireland. Acres by the thousand, the hunnerd thousand. I'll gie it to these colonists, just. At a price, mind, a small bit price, no' for naething! Sae my treasury, that yon Elizabeth Tudor left sae empty, will gain, and we'll get Ireland in order withoot battle. Thae militant Catholic lords will hae to lie low."

There was silence in that chamber, eloquent silence.

"We'll start wi' the north," James went on. "I've been pondering, aye pondering. And conning the maps. Thae five counties o' Ulster, Antrim, Down, Armagh, Derry, Tyrone. Aye, and maybe Fermanagh. Plenties there for a start. And that's whaur the worst o' the rebels hale frae, thae O'Neills in especial. You, Jamie Hamilton, here's your task. Go ower to Ulster. Spy oot the land. Choose a fine whack for yoursel! Get your brothers to aid you. See hoo it should be divided up. Then back to Scotland and enroll folk as colonists. Younger sons o' lords and lairds. Aye, o' merchants and the like tae. Seeking land. Then come back here and gie me your report. And if your report's guid, I'll maybe mak you mair than just *Lord* Abercorn! Meanwhiles, we'll see aboot English colonists. Eh, Cecil? Eh, Vicky?"

The proposed colonisers eyed each other doubtfully, but could not reject their sovereign-lord's orders, however odd and probably impracticable. This new United Kingdom was heading in strange directions.

James pointed now at Will and Henry. "I'm letting you hear a' this, Alexander, so's you can teach Henry hoo to rule a realm, no' by swords and pikes but by wits and guid counsel. We've no' had any battles in Scotland since yon Langside, whaur your faither, Jamie, made a name for himsel'. No since *I* became King o' Scots. Noo, we'll teach the English the same lesson. And the Irish tae. And you teach Henry the trade he'll one day hae to pursue. When the Almighty ca's me awa' to be still closer tae Himsel'! You could mak a poem on that theme, man, while you're at it." A wave of the hand dismissed son and tutor.

"Can I go hunting in the morning?" Henry demanded.

"Say Sire when you speak me, and I'll consider it, boy."

"Yes, Sire. I will be on my new mare."

"Awa' wi' you!"

The next day's hunting was a great success, as far as the Prince of Wales was concerned, although less so for Will Alexander, who was well out-ridden, as indeed was King Christian, who chose to fall out quite early on. The boy had been warned not to outride his father, but he was nevertheless present at the first kill of the morning, after an absurdly early start, although he later confessed to Will, after a long day of it, that the king rode like a bale of straw, and he did not like this messy business of

189

paddling feet in deer's guts. Tired but pleased with himself and his mount, the prince further criticised his parent for not allowing him to hunt again on the morrow, although the chase would proceed, but to go back to Oatlands and his studies. Henry was considering whether to go on calling his father Sire, and had to be read something of a lecture by his tutor on duties towards parents and monarchs. As to preparing the lad for kingly and dynastic functions one day, Will was less than certain, especially those such as the present occupant of the throne would esteem apt and suitable, much less composing a poem on the subject.

They had ninety-nine copies of *Aurora* to carry home with them, their escort assisting.

Will had much to discuss with Janet that night.

Life thereafter returned to normal at Oatlands, with few problems other than those connected with difficult poetry and translations. Little Charles created remarkably little trouble for them, for although he did not develop quickly either physically or apparently mentally, he was a quiet small soul, prepared to sit all but endlessly looking at nothing in particular from those great eyes, his seemingly only inheritance from his father. Ailie Graham doted on him.

As for Henry, his development was quite otherwise, fast and full in almost all respects, and although he preferred outdoor activities to study, he by no means disgraced his tutor. Whether he gained much on the duties of kingship in the process was another matter.

So that summer passed pleasantly enough, with the greater world having but little impact upon them, news indeed being scanty. They did hear that the queen had lost her new daughter, Mary, feeble from birth. This death did not, however, bring her any closer to her surviving children, save perhaps Elizabeth, for Anne did not appear at Oatlands. And there was no further summons to the king's presence until the usual Christmastide call to Whitehall.

Will was not particularly glad to go to London, any more than the others; but he did want to visit the printer, Barker, with his four latest contributions, which he was entitling *Monarchic Tragedies*, of which he in due course ordered another one hundred copies. Or not quite his latest, for he had managed somehow to complete the poem on rule and kingship for Henry, little as he was himself impressed with it – any more than was the prince – in which he sought to emphasise the need to choose wise counsellors, not those merely seeking power and place for themselves; the value of truth in affairs of state, and the dangers of deliberately changing or adulterating it for convenience; the vanity of mere grandeur; the vital regard for the common folk of the realm; and the dangers of abuse of power and pursuit of riches. What James would think of all this remained to be seen.

No command was forthcoming to appear before the monarch for a few days after arrival at Whitehall, although the Duke of Lennox had duly sought them out soon after they reached the palace. He declared that the king was notably preoccupied with the Irish situation, where Catholic intransigence had reached new heights. Lord Abercorn was back from his visit to Ulster, with his findings, both good and less so. He was hopeful about the colonising project, and the lands which could be made available, but this only once the present incumbents were effectively dispossessed, and forcibly necessarily, not merely by royal decree and forfeiture, which they would certainly ignore. He contended that an army would have to be sent to achieve this; but James was stubbornly against the use of force, determined not to besmirch his prized reputation as a prince of peace. He was, in fact, considering himself paying a visit to Ireland, to seek to bend the chiefs to his will by his royal presence. But all his advisers were strongly against this course, stressing the dangers. He could be captured and held hostage, even slain, by the wild Irish. It was unthinkable. All save the monarch were in favour of force, except perhaps, Lennox

191

admitted, such feeble and non-religiously inclined folk as himself, who would be content to let the Irish problem settle itself; after all, there was no real threat to the other two kingdoms and the principality of Wales, that he could see. So it was stalemate at the moment, but the king determined somehow to go ahead with his strange colonising plans. He was now declaring that there were too many people in England and Scotland, and it would be an added advantage to decant some of them across the Irish Sea. No monarch that his courtiers had ever heard of could have suggested reducing his population thus, but then, of course, most rulers looked on the more subjects they had as usefully capable of producing large and powerful armies.

The queen came from Somerset House for a Christmas Eve banquet and masque, this last to be devised and produced by William Shakespeare and Ben Jonson. Anne sent for the two princes, who were both to take part apparently, although what Charles could contribute to any masque was unclear. But at least this represented some royal interest in the boys. The masque was to be entitled *The Dream of a Midsummer's Night*.

At the banquet which preceded it, Will and Janet were in doubts as to their positions. It appeared that the king and queen were to have different tables on the dais platform, a distinctly obvious sign of their curious relationship. Henry and Charles were ordered to sit at the queen's table, Lady Huntly came to tell them, but there was no such invitation for their attendants; and no side table seemingly arranged by the king. So, with Ailie, Will and his wife went in good time to take lowly seats far down the hall, well enough content, although Ailie for one was much concerned about little Charles.

When the two royal groups came in, simultaneously although from different sides of the hall, it was seen that one was all male and the other all female, save for Henry, with Charles being led by the hand by Lady Huntly. The king went to seat himself, with Count Gondomar on his right and Lord Abercorn on his left, an odd juxtaposition, Catholic and Protestant, other lords and courtiers jostling for precedence. Lennox, ever the thoughtful one and healer of rifts, went over to speak to the queen and his sister before taking a seat at the end of the king's table.

The banquet proceeded, to music from the minstrels' gallery.

The splendid meal was halfway through when Will had a surprise. None other than the Duke of Lennox came down to him from the dais to announce that His Majesty desired a word with him. Lennox never seemed to object to his royal cousin using him as a sort of messenger and go-between. Yes, now, he said, and led Will off, the latter, as so often, astonished at their liege-lord's capacity for noting details and acting upon them, as now.

Taken to behind the king's chair, with Henry waving from the other table, Will had to wait a few moments for James to turn his head.

"There you are, then? Awa' doon there. No' wi' Henry and Charlie?" That sounded critical.

Will had no desire to get involved in royal marital crossfire. He merely bowed.

"Alexander o' Menstrie – that's up near Stirling whaur *I* was reared – is Gentleman o' the Bedchamber to the princes," it was explained to the Spaniard. This style and title was something in the nature of news to Will, even though he had been acting the part for months. "He's a poet, see you, and no' a bad one. Hae you composed yon one I tellt you to do, man? Aboot the duties o' a guid king and ruler, eh? To teach the laddie what's what."

"I have, Sire. Whether it is as you would wish, I know not."

"We'll see, soon enough. You hae it here? In this Whiteha'? Eh?"

"Yes, Sire. I brought it. So that you could see it, whatever its quality."

"Aye. Then go fetch it, man. Frae your chambers. When you've finished the eating. Bring it to me. No' here. In the library, just. There's this masque o' my Annie's. Some dream, she ca's it. Mair like a nightmare, I jalouse!" He jogged the ambassador with his elbow. "The count, here, favours masques. *I* dinna. Sae I'll be in the library. Bring you it there, Alexander. After we've eaten." Will was waved away.

So, the banquet over and the two royal parties making their separate exits, Will left his wife and Ailie, while the seating and tables were being cleared to provide open space for the masque, noting the playwrights Shakespeare and Jonson in conference with Montgomery, as he made for his quite distant quarters to collect his so doubtfully compiled verses. It seemed a strange errand to be on on such an occasion; but there was little that was not strange about James Stewart and his requirements.

Back with the poem, he had a word with Janet, who informed him that Henry had come to tell them that he was to play the part of a young man with the strange name of Demetrius, and Charles was to be a fairy called Cobweb. Fancy being named Cobweb! He would call Charles Spider after this! It certainly seemed an odd role for a little boy.

Will, seeking directions, found his way to the library. There the king was already getting down to serious drinking with a group of like-minded cronies, including the Lord Abercorn, though not Gondomar. But the talk was serious, as well as the imbibing. The royal preoccupation with Ireland was foremost, evidently.

Will would have laid the sheets of paper down on the flagon- and goblet-strewn table, near to the monarch, and made his escape, but James picked them up straight away and, interrupting his thick monologue, used them to wave Will to a vacant seat nearby. He then began to peruse the writing, frowning in concentration, while his companions drank and conversed with each other, low-voiced. Abercorn pushed a flagon and goblet over to Will, whom he recognised from the earlier meeting. He indicated that two of his brothers were there, Sir Claud

194

and Sir Frederick Hamilton. It appeared to be almost a wholly Scots gathering.

James presently put down the papers. "I canna read it a' the noo," he said. "But it seems no' sae ill, as far as I've gotten. And scans weel. I like the bit aboot choosing wise counsellors, no' such as are oot for what they can get! Pensions and positions and the like." And he looked significantly round the company. "Aye, and the vanity o' grandeur. The Lord's Anointed doesna need grandeur! Noo, whaur were we? Aye, this o' Strabane. I'm willing for you to hae Strabane, Jamie. And your brothers yon Castle Toome and whaurever it was in Londonderry. And you've got a wheen others to agree to go ower? But no' as many as we'd like, eh?"

"It is inducement, Sire," Abercorn said. "The lands beckon to some, yes. But others require more than that, for they are not assured that the said lands will be available for them, without ample force to drive out the chiefs. They're going to have to take men over from Scotland to gain and work the land, many men. That will cost them not a little. And you want payment. So they seek inducements, we find."

"Uh-huh, I've thought o' that. I'm no' asking ower much in payment, mind. Say three thousand merks Scots for every ten thousand acres – that's only two thousand pounds English. That's fair, eh? And for your inducement, hoo aboot a bit title, eh? I've thought one up. No' a right knighthood – that's only by my personal conferring, as you a' ken," and he jabbed a finger at the knights present, including the Hamilton brothers. "This would hae to be something different. Less than lords, mind. And hereditary, so's older men could see their sons inheriting it, wi' their Irish lands. No' baronies like we hae in Scotland, which used to gie a seat in oor parliaments. It mustna mean that these a' hae seats in an *Irish* parliament. Sae, no barons but baron*ets*, sma' barons. Ca' themsel's Sir, aye, withoot being knights. Something new. Baronet's a guid name, eh? Wouldna that serve?"

195

His hearers eyed each other doubtfully.

"It will not lessen the worth of knighthood, Sire?" Abercorn asked.

"Na, na, it must be different, just. Nae tapping wi' swords on shoulders. And only gien to them as buys a right guid acreage. Hoo say you?"

There were murmurs and nods, but none enthusiastic.

James quaffed deep. "You, Alexander man, hoo say you?"

Surprised at being brought into the matter, it seeming nothing to do with him, Will was at a loss what to reply. "It might well induce settlers, yes, Your Majesty. Men do esteem titles. Their wives would be Ladies? That could tell."

"There you are, then! There speaks a man whae kens what he's at. Kens the influence of women." James all but leered. "We a' hae to be on oor guard against that, eh? *I* am! Sae, we'll mak a wheen baronets, in due course. And mak a wheen merks and pounds for my treasury! And colonise Ulster in the daing o' it."

"Once the rebel earls, O'Neills and O'Donnells and the like, are got rid of!" Abercorn reminded.

"Ooh, aye. Drink up, man Alexander."

There was silence for a little while, save for the clinking of goblets and the smacking of lips. Will had been thinking of seeking permission to retire, but this last royal command rather halted him.

The inevitable theme had to come up. Armed force, cannon, swords, crossbows, pikes, the king shaking his head. None there saw how the rebels were to be dispossessed without such action, or at least the threat of it.

James was adamant.

It was that word threat which Sir Frederick Hamilton had uttered which gave Will the notion. Greatly daring, he raised voice. "Threat, Sire. A threat might suffice. If it was sufficiently strong. And evident. Argyll! The Earl of Argyll."

They all stared at him.

"The earl, Sire. He is not only Lieutenant of the North but Admiral of the Western Seas. Ireland, Ulster, is only some fourteen miles across from the southernmost Campbell lands. He has a great fleet of galleys and birlinns and the like. And large numbers of Campbell men. If he was to parade his fleet all along the northern Ulster coastline, into the sea lochs, threatening landings in force even though not doing so. And you, Sire, threatened armed assault. Might not these rebels take fright? Be prepared to flee? Without MacCailean Mor landing a single man."

"Man, that's right! Guidsakes, why did I no' think on that! Argyll." James waved to the others. "Alexander was tutor to Argyll. Kens him better than any. Aye, he's my admiral o' thae seas. And has plenties o' Campbells – ower many, maist folk say! And ships. He could mak a right threat, aye."

"Would he do it, Sire?" Sir Frederick asked. "The Campbell is something of a law unto himself! It is a large task to set him."

"If I commanded it."

"Aye, but how to ensure that he did it effectively? Use enough of men and ships," Abercorn put in, "to make a threat sufficiently strong to affright the chiefs."

"If Your Majesty offered him some of the forfeited lands?" Will added. "Even the Campbell could covet more land. His line has been doing so for centuries. They took *my* line's MacAllister lands!"

"Aye. Sae they did. We could dae that. Here's a notion. Guid for you! We'll consider a' this. Forfeiture, threats o' force – only threats, mind. Inducements: baronetcies. Payments for lands. A right campaign to enlist colonists, especially in Scotland, guid Protestant colonists. Och, here's the way ahead. We'll drink on it, eh?"

Enthusiasm or none, all were prepared to obey that last. Will, only sipping, for he was no great imbiber, took the opportunity to try to get away.

"Your Majesty, may I leave you now? The princes may need me. Their parts in the masque may be

197

over by now. Little Prince Charles should be in his bed . . ."

"Aye, see to it, man. Guid kens what Annie's up to wi' the bairns! And we'll consider weel what you said aboot Argyll."

Rising and bowing, Will made his escape.

He found the masque in its final stages, this last scene taking place in what was meant to be a wood near Athens. Anne, resplendent as Hippolyta, Queen of Athens, gazing down on the dead Pyramus, and Thisbe – that is, Lady Huntly – mourning, and Henry as Demetrius rather stumbling over the difficult word *videlicit*.

Charles was out of it all, asleep beside Ailie on a bench. Amid all the plaudits and the bowing, Will beckoned to Henry to join them; and presently he led his little party back to quarters, Janet declaring that it had all been notably worth watching, colourful, although Montgomery, as Theseus, King of Athens, had distinctly overplayed his part, even though the queen had not seemed embarrassed at his attentions. And Henry had acted well, in quite a prominent part. The prince said that his brother well deserved the name of Cobweb, for he had clung to one of the potted trees of the wood and done nothing.

Getting their charges off to bed was now the priority, for all had to be at Westminster Abbey for the Christmas morning celebration.

Despite all this activity, the princes and their guardians saw no more of king or queen before the return to Oatlands on Twelfth Night, none particularly disappointed about that however.

14

Will had his *Monarchic Tragedies* delivered to him in due course, his second publication in London, and was bold enough to send an inscribed copy to the monarch himself at Windsor. He received no acknowledgment – not that he expected any – and it was not until April that he was summoned to Windsor. He took Henry again, although he received no instruction to do so.

James was, as usual, out hunting when they arrived, and the prince would have been off on his fine mare to join the chase if he could find it, but Will thought not. On the morrow, perhaps . . .

It was late in the evening, late enough for Henry to be in bed – although now in his thirteenth year, the prince was staying up later – before the anticipated demand came, as so often by Lennox, to attend the presence. The duke warned Will that it was the Irish problem again.

James was in his bed, hatted and robed, papers strewn around, and Cecil in attendance. He got straight down to business without any preamble, talk of princes or even poetry.

"See you, Alexander man, I want you to go to Argyll. Aboot this o' Ulster. Matters are bad there, and it's time we acted. The seas will no' be sae rough frae noo on, for his boats. Summer'll be coming on. I want this Irish venture in process, aye in process. Sae, awa' up to Scotland wi' you, and tell Argyll what's to do."

"M'mm. Yes, Sire. When? And what am I to say to him?"

"Say it's my royal will and command, just. That as admiral he does something to justify the style o' it. Hae ships to go lie off the Ulster coasts, like you said. Mak a bit landing here and there. But nae bluidshed. When he's ready to dae it, send word, and I'll issue letters o' forfeiture and banishment. Then Jamie Hamilton – I'm making him an earl, mind, to gie him my authority – wi' his brothers and a wheen mair, will move ower, and we'll get started."

"Yes, Sire. Can I offer MacCailean Mor, in your royal name, some . . . inducement also? As to lands in Ulster."

"Ooh, aye. Tell him he'll no' be forgotten when it comes to that."

"When do you wish me to go, Sire?"

"At the soonest, just. Wi' the time it taks you to get up to Scotland, to yon Argyll, and he can gather his boats, it'll be into June, I reckon it. Sae, nae delay. I'll hae that Carey to tak your place at Oatlands."

Will hesitated, aware of what he was risking. "Your Majesty, Prince Henry, for some reason, does not, er, respond to lessons from Sir Robert Carey very well. No fault of the prince; nor of Sir Robert. They just do not come together well. Henry is now just turned twelve. Would it be permitted, indeed would it not perhaps be a worthy notion, to take him with me to Scotland? He is, after all, Duke of Rothesay as well as Prince of Wales, and should know Scotland better, I would think. And on the journey, I could continue with his instruction, tutoring, in some measure."

James eyed him, fingering his wispy beard.

"Also, Sire, the prince's presence with me might well give *me* added authority in presenting your wishes to the earl."

That had its effect.

"You'd hae to tak his escort. He has to be right secure."

"Would that not also add to my seeming authority? Men of the royal guard with me. I suggest, Sire, that the journey, and seeing the land, would be good for the prince. He is somewhat confined at Oatlands, now that he is growing older. He is full of vigour, active, eager to see and do new things, as is right and proper. This would, I think, please him. And widen his knowledge of your kingdoms and your subjects. He has never been in the Highlands, has he?"

"I'm no' sure that's any great loss, man! But, och aye, you've got the rights o' it maybe. How say you, Vicky? And you, Cecil?"

Both men expressed approval.

"Aye, then you can take Henry. See you weel to his care, mind. And your wife seeing weel to wee Charlie at Oatlands."

"Yes, Sire. That I promise you. And it will add, I would say, something practical to the verses I wrote for him on aspects of kingship. Seeing, taking part, in the affairs of the kingdoms."

"There's that, aye. On your verses, man, I've read some o' your tragedies. You're improving. Yon *Croesus* was mair like it."

"Thank you, Sire. I have Prince Henry here with me . . ."

"I ken that."

"If you are to be hunting in the morning, may he join the chase, he asks?"

"Weel, for ae day only. For I'm no' haeing you delaying your journey north." He nodded. "You tell the Campbell, when you get to him, that I want his fullest strength on this Ulster ploy. Thae O'Neills and O'Connells and O'Donnells are to hae nae douts that they're right threatened." A wave of an ink-stained hand indicated that the audience was over.

So it was to be Scotland again, and Archie Campbell! Aye, and Archie Campbell's wife!

That aspect of the situation did not fail to occur to Janet two days later when she heard the news – and that she herself was to remain at Oatlands with Charles.

201

"Will you be seeing Agnes?" she asked. "It is likely, no?"

"That I know not. It depends on where Argyll is when I get there."

"She can be . . . difficult."

"I know it, my dear. I will be on my guard!"

"Be so, yes. Having Henry with you might help."

They left it at that.

So, in another couple of days, it was to horse and away, Henry delighted and excited. Whether the escort of six troopers of the royal guard were so also was another matter. They had settled down very comfortably with the estate and farm folk at Oatlands, making their own liaisons.

Will was now accustomed to this northwards journey, knowing the best and quickest routes, how far to aim to get each day, and the places to halt for the nights, greatly convenienced by being able to request hospitality in the king's name, and having the heir to the throne with him assuring them of welcoming receptions. They would have travelled the faster without the escort, of course, their speed dictated by the slowest horseman, which was certainly not Henry, who was quite the best mounted and now excellent in the saddle. He was excellent company, also.

Exactly seven days after leaving Oatlands, they crossed the border at the Deadwater pass of the Cheviots, and Will, arm outflung, demonstrated all that fair, far-flung vista of Tweeddale and Teviotdale and Jedwater, the three peaks of the Eildons, the Roman Trimontium, all the spread of the Merse right to the Lammermuirs, a sight to stir the blood of any returning Scot. The prince was quite affected, and declared that he was Duke of Rothesay from now on.

At Edinburgh next day, they enquired at the castle as to the whereabouts, if known, of the Earl of Argyll. But although they saw the Earl of Dunfermline, formerly

Fyvie, the Chancellor, they won no information. Argyll was seldom in any one place for long, especially during what he named the campaigning season, and it was now May. So there was nothing for it but to proceed on to Castle Campbell and the Ochils, crossing Forth at the Queen's Ferry and on by the Fothrif borders to Loch Leven and Kinross to the Black Devon.

Will approached Castle Campbell with a curious admixture of misgiving and anticipation, well aware of possible tests ahead. Henry was much impressed by the siting of the stronghold, and curious as to the reason for the names of Gloom, Sorrow, Care and Dolour. His tutor was, for once, unable to enlighten him.

Was it relief that man felt when he discovered that not only the earl but his countess were not in residence? As far as the chamberlain knew they were at Inveraray Castle on Loch Fyne-side, having departed thence two weeks earlier.

The visitors spent the night at Castle Campbell, Will taking Henry for an evening walk, to climb two of the neighbouring Ochil hills, a welcome exercise after ten days in the saddle. The cuckoos were calling again, and the new lambs skipping and baaing, and all the land looking colourful as it was challenging.

It was, of course a major journey still to Loch Fyne in mid-Argyll, all the way up Forth almost to its sources, crossing it at Stirling Bridge after a call at Menstrie and on westwards by the south side of the vast flooded wilderness of the Flanders Moss, right to the foot of Loch Lomond, by Drymen, where the Drummond family took its name, Henry having some Drummond blood in him through Robert the Third's queen, Will taking seriously his promised duties of instilling something of Scotland's story into its future king. He had a ready listener.

Up Loch Lomond-side they were into the Highlands proper, the scenery such as to have the prince exclaiming constantly, he wishing to leave their horses and climb some of these great mountains. But at this stage Will could not so humour him although he himself would have liked to do so; they could not be sure that they would find Argyll at Inveraray and might have to go on still further seeking him; so no delays meantime.

Halfway up that long loch, they turned off westwards again, at Tarbet, and over the little pass to Arrochar on Loch Long, Henry's first sea loch, he being struck by the colourful seaweed, which he had not seen before. Then they were climbing, up and up over a pass beneath Ben Arthur, which made other passes seem mere defiles, the boy declaring that he had never been so high in his life. Down beyond, in equally long descent, at length they saw blue water ahead of them which Will declared was Loch Fyne, the longest sea loch in all Scotland, over forty miles of it. But it was quite a long way to Inveraray yet, for they had to go right round the head of the loch and nine or ten miles down the far side. All this, and far beyond, all that they could see was the Campbell's kingdom, where he had had to spend so much of his young manhood, tutoring Argyll.

They passed their third night, after leaving Castle Campbell, at the head of Loch Fyne, and reached Inveraray in mid-forenoon. It was surprising to all but Will to find such a large township here, deep in the Highlands, the largest they had seen since Stirling itself, the Campbell capital, streets of houses, warehouses and stores, a large church and waterside quays at which many vessels were tied up. The castle was some distance inland, on higher ground.

Actually, when they reached there, it was not as impressive as was Castle Campbell, a comparatively modest tower-house in a courtyard for MacCailean Mor's main seat; but Will explained that it was a comparatively new replacement for the great former fortress establishment on Loch Awe to the north, Innischonnel, the traditional home of the chiefs; but this, being set on an island, however suitably defensive, had become an inconvenient base for the earls as they grew in importance on the wider, national scene, with so many comings and goings necessary. Hence this Inveraray Castle.

The gyrony-of-eight banner was flying from its topmost tower as they approached, which looked hopeful for the earl's presence. When they sought admission at the gatehouse, it was to be told that MacCailean Mor would be asked whether he wished to see them, the guards being then informed that the Duke of Rothesay and heir to the throne was not used to being kept waiting outside anyone's house. But even this did not gain them access, until Archibald Campbell himself appeared from the tower doorway, staring.

"Save us, it's yourself, Will!" he cried. "Will Alexander! Here's a wonder! Where have you come from, man? I thought that you were in London now, always. And what is this of a duke?"

"The Duke of Rothesay, Archie. Do you not recognise Prince Henry?"

"Sakes! Is that . . .? I scarce believe it. The laddie I once knew! Come, come you in. Welcome to Inveraray, Highness. I am Argyll."

Dismounting, all proceeded into the courtyard amid exclamations and questions. The escort leading off the horses to lean-to stabling, Will and Henry got only halfway across the cobbles to the tower door when there was further exclamation, higher-pitched this time. There in the doorway stood Agnes Douglas, arm out pointing, beautiful as ever, red hair cascading, but somewhat less graceful of person as hitherto, in fact most evidently pregnant.

"Will Alexander! Yourself! By all that is wonderful!" she called. "You have found me – here in these uncouth Highlands! Oh, Will!"

That man, whatever the significance of that greeting, knew a surge of relief. She was with child. And her husband there. He was not to be tested after all, it seemed.

"Greetings, Aurora!" he could call. "How good to see you. And here is Prince Henry, all the way from Surrey."

"Is not this all but beyond belief?" her spouse demanded. "Come all the way to Argyll. With the prince."

Agnes was not greatly interested in the boy. As they came up, she flung her arms round Will, kissing him, the pressure of her now so fertile body hard against him.

"So good! So good!" she murmured.

"Yes. You are well?" He glanced over her shoulder at the earl. "Both of you?" He might have thought up something better to say than that.

"I am . . . as I have become!" she answered, kissing him again. "Can you not see it?"

"My lord and you will be very happy." He extricated himself gently but firmly. "My . . . felicitations!"

"We are happy also to see you," Archie said. "Happy indeed. But what brings you and Prince Henry all the way to Inveraray?"

"The royal command. I will explain . . ."

"Yes. Come you in. You will not have come far this day?"

"Only from Cairndhu of Ardkinglas."

Agnes looked Henry up and down belatedly, assessingly. "Here is a fine young man!" she decided. Taking both visitors by the hand, she led them indoors, the boy eyeing her bulky figure interestedly.

It did not take long for Will to inform the earl of their errand and the king's requirements that he should play the admiral.

"Ireland! And taking over the land? Here is a strange policy. Whose notion was this?"

"The king's own. He would plant much of the country with Protestant settlers. Forfeit and dispossess the rebel Catholic chiefs. Beginning with Ulster. His English advisers are none so keen. They would have armed invasion. But His Majesty ever seeks peaceful methods. So he does not wish you to make any major landings from your ships. Only the threat of it."

"He would have me sail up and down the Ulster coast, doing no more than that?"

"You could land parties here and there. Burn a thatch or two. Make a presence felt. That is all. Sail into their sea lochs. He says that they have no fleets of vessels to rival yours. There should be little risk to your force. He will send his emissaries, with the letters of forfeiture and banishment. Abercorn – that is, Sir James Hamilton, who is now made earl – will lead in that."

"For how long am I to do this?"

"That the king did not say. When you are ready to sail, he will send Abercorn and his brothers with the ultimatum. He believes that will be sufficient."

"I do not!" Henry declared, listening. "Many men, with swords, will be required."

"You may well be right, Highness," Argyll agreed. "It seems a strange misson."

"You will be well rewarded. With lands over there," Will said. "How long will it take, Archie, to assemble your fullest number of ships?"

"None so long. As it was, I was going to muster my fleet to assail Mull and the other Maclean islands this summer. They have been raiding Islay, which is now *my* island. Jura also. I could do this of Ulster first, if it does not take overlong, and then head north into the Isles."

"It will either succeed or come to naught fairly quickly, I would think," Will said. "So you can do both your endeavours. How long until you can make a start?"

"It is now mid-May. My craft are scattered up and down this coast, from Cowal to the Oban and Loch Etive. And the men have to be summoned from their tasks. Give me until mid-June. A month."

"That will be needed by the king also, yes. For me to get back to London. And Abercorn and the others sent. Say a little later, Archie, the end of June. Then a month off Ulster, and you can go deal with your Macleans and the rest in August, no?"

"Will Alexander, still the tutor!"

"Do I seem so? I but calculate, so as to inform the king."

They had an excellent midday meal, and then the eager prince had to be indulged by being taken to climb a mountain. Not that there were any very lofty ones just hereabouts, but there was a dramatically conical and isolated peak called Duniquaich just to the north, high enough to form a challenge and which would make an excellent viewpoint. MacCailean Mor, of course, was much too important and busy a man to go wasting his time thus; but Will knew the vicinity well. Agnes saw it as a waste of time also, but declared that she would have gone with them but that in her present condition that was scarcely practicable. She would, however, expect the visitors' fullest attentions when they returned.

So a pleasing afternoon was passed scrambling up green corries, over heathery slopes and clambering rocky heights, with the vistas stupendous, mountains to all infinity, save for down-loch, although even there the distant blue heights of Kintyre ranged to hide the Western Sea and the scattered isles of the Hebrides. Henry was disappointed that they could not see Ulster because of Knapdale and Kintyre. But could they see Rothesay? It was somewhere down there, was it not? He had to be told that his ducal seat was far south, with intervening uplands, on the island of Bute, beyond the last of the Campbell lands of Cowal. Could they not go back that way? the prince demanded. He ought to know where his Scots title came from. Did he own anything there? It was a royal Stewart castle and small town, he was informed. It would not be very convenient to visit there on this occasion, well off their return route as it was. Another time, no doubt.

The earl was down at Inveraray town, it seemed, when they got back, and his wife provided her own attentions, sending off the prince to get washed after his exertions on the hill but detaining his tutor meantime, to demonstrate that, whatever pregnancy did for her, it did not detract from affectionate manifestations. For his part, Will could not, with all honesty, tell himself that he did not find this off-putting or over-testing. Perhaps as well that Henry was no enthusiast for washing and returned to them fairly promptly.

Their entertainment thereafter, with MacCailean Mor's arrival, was adequate and friendly, if less personal. Although at bedtime, with Henry already retired, however unwillingly, Agnes did propose to escort Will to his chamber. However, her husband came along also, and at the lingering embrace with which she favoured her guest, beside the door, Argyll did eye the pair thoughtfully, stiffly as Will held himself.

In the morning a change of plans developed, producing both satisfaction and the reverse. The visitors had been intending to remain at Inveraray for another day before commencing their long journey southwards, and Agnes had sundry plans for them; but Henry, mentioning his desire to see Rothesay at the breakfast table had the earl offering assistance to get them there. He would provide a wherry or scow to take them and their horses down Loch Fyne and into the Sound of Bute, put them ashore at Rothesay for an hour or two, and then ferry them across the narrows of the Firth of Clyde to Largs, in Ayrshire, whence they could proceed on southwards by Carlisle and the English Midlands. By water, thus, it was not fifty miles to Rothesay, whereas by land it would be double that, and still require ferrying from Cowal. This suggestion greatly pleased the prince, and to a certain degree his tutor. But it did mean that they would have to leave earlier, for the southwards journey from Largs would take much longer than the usual east-coast route. How long would the scow take to reach Rothesay?

Five or six hours only, Argyll reckoned.

They could do it then, Will decided, but it would mean they must depart from Inveraray this day, by noon at the latest. Could a scow be readied by then? The earl declared that it would, unhesitant. Will got the impression that perhaps Archie Campbell would not be too unhappy to see them go, whatever his wife said. In which case he too would deem it wise to be off.

So there followed hurried arrangements, Agnes indicating disapproval, but not so much so that she failed to give them, or at least Will, a warm send-off, with urges to contrive a return visit before long, preferably to Castle Campbell, when she would be in a better physical state to offer due welcome. Will wished her very well in her confinement and delivery, which, it seemed, must be due in about two months – at which she made a face.

Argyll took them and their escort down to the quays, where a quite large flat-bottomed craft was awaiting them – it had to be sizeable to take their eight horses – to be propelled by no fewer than twelve oars or sweeps plus a large square sail, so requiring some thirty of a crew, with two men to a sweep, seeming a major undertaking just to meet a boy's whim. But the earl made light of it, and, after all, the fact that this lad should one day be his monarch was relevant. He confirmed that he would have his fullest fleet off the Ulster seaboard in about five weeks' time, and waved them off, Will wishing him a son and heir in due course, but calculating to himself that it looked like happening while he was away on the king's business.

That produced no comment.

They made an uneventful and pleasant sail of it down Loch Fyne, although in fact it was mainly rowing rather than sailing, for they were heading south-by-west and such wind as there was was from that airt. But a score of miles down, where Loch Gilp joined Fyne, the main loch made a major bend, being now some four miles wide, enabling them to use the sail more, and ensuring much better speed. Henry was entranced throughout, his first salt-water voyage, and the prospects scenic all the way, mountains, cliffs, coves, bays, reefs and skerries, seals to be seen on these last, cormorants and shags diving, terns wheeling and plunging into the waves, eider-ducks in great rafts crooning their welcome to the summer. Will always

210

held that May was the month when there was most to see and enjoy in the Highlands.

They made even better time of it than Argyll had calculated and were off Ardlamont Point, the southernmost tip of the Cowal peninsula, by late afternoon. Here they had, strangely, to turn due northwards again, for Bute, a narrow island some eighteen miles long, lay just to the east, and Rothesay was situated on its eastern side. So they had to sail up the Kyles of Bute, round the top of the island, and halfway down the other side, the breeze now aiding them. Nine miles down opened Rothesay Bay, fair indeed, their destination.

Henry was less than impressed, however. Presumably he had visualised something like the great fortress-castles of Stirling and Edinburgh as the source of his title; but a building rising out of the middle of a town, on no soaring rock-top but merely among streets, was a disappointment. Admittedly the town itself climbed in unusual fashion up quite a steep hill, in terraces, from the shore; but the castle was very much part of it all, no towering fortalice, at least seen from below. Will explained that although Rothesay was scarcely in the Highlands, it was nearly enough part of the Hebrides to adhere to the Highland tradition whereby the chiefs did not rely on fortresses to protect them from enemies, but on their clansfolk, so that their security lay in their people's loyalty rather than in stone and battlements. More worthy, was it not?

When they had climbed the hill, the prince was better pleased with what he saw, finding the castle quite eye-catching and challenging, however close the townsfolk to it. High curtain walls, unusual in being circular, rising within a deep and wide moat, with towers spaced round it, also circular, and a great gatehouse block, almost a keep, housing the drawbridge and portcullis at its centre.

They had some difficulty in gaining entrance, for although the drawbridge was down and the portcullis up, the massive doors behind were closed and apparently barred; and hammer as they would on these, they obtained no response. But their noise did produce folk from nearby houses, who informed that Hecky MacEwan the keeper, and his wife, seldom if ever used this entrance but had a postern door and gangway round the back, where they occupied one of the round towers. So thither the visitors headed, and had no problem in finding the elderly, grizzled keeper, presumably MacEwan. He was distinctly doubtful about accepting their proclaimed identity, for which he was scarcely to be blamed, since never had the like happened to him before. After all, there had not been a Duke of Rothesay since Mary Queen of Scots' father, James the Fifth, was a boy, and he was only two years when his father, James the Fourth, was slain at Flodden Field and he became king, not duke, a century ago. However, the two members of the royal guard, who had come up with them from the scow, seemed to impress this Hecky more, their garb no doubt making an impact, English leopards and all. The four were admitted to the fortalice.

In the spacious courtyard Henry was all questions. Was that pink-stone building beside their tower a church? It was St Michael's Chapel, he was told. Why St Michael? Not known. Was it all very old? Built in 1098 by a Norse king, Magnus Barefoot, they learned, when the Vikings dominated the Hebrides. Added to later, to be sure; what was called the palace block at the gatehouse erected by James the Fourth. Had anything exciting and important ever happened here? Battles, sieges? Not that Hecky knew of, although Robert the Third had died here, of a broken heart they said, after his son, the then Duke of Rothesay, had been starved to death at Falkland by his uncle, Albany, and his brother, who eventually became James the First, was captured by the English. What did the name Rothesay mean? From the Gaelic *ri-siudh*, meaning the king's seat, he understood. Will queried this last. After all, it had been a principal seat of the High Stewards, not the Kings of Scots, only coming to the crown when Robert the Second, Bruce's grandson, the first of the Stewarts, came to the throne. A Gaelic-speaker himself, Will suggested *rudha-say*, the island at the headland, meaning at the tip of the long Cowal peninsula.

Their tour of the castle thereafter, although interesting, had its depressing side, its unused and neglected air being everywhere evident, under-furnished, bare, empty. Henry soon had had enough. He enjoyed striding round the parapet walkway of the lofty perimeter walling. He declared that when he was older he would come and put the place to rights, live in it, be Duke of Rothesay indeed.

They returned downhill to the scow. The sail out of the Kyles of Bute and across the Firth of Clyde to Largs, with the dramatic mountains of Arran soaring to the south, took only an hour, and it was still only early evening when they landed, Will telling the story of the great Battle of Largs, in 1263, when Alexander the Third finally defeated the invading Norsemen, under King Hakon, and freed the West Highlands from their savage yoke; and how Thomas the Rhymer had prophesied and aided in the victory.

They spent the night on the boat, in the harbour, and in the morning said farewell to the scow's crew, and commenced their lengthy journey southwards.

Will had never travelled this way before, and was interested in all that he saw, viewing places of which he had often heard, and informing Henry of what he had been told. Ayrshire, where the Bruce had been Earl of Carrick; Dumfries, where he had slain the Red Comyn, and changed not only his own life but the history of Scotland; over the border into England at Gretna, to see Lanercost, where Edward the First, Hammer of the Scots, had died cursing Scotland; Carlisle, so often assailed by the Scots, and where Kinmont Willie Armstrong was rescued by Scott of Buccleuch none so long ago; on into the mountains of Cumberland and Westmoreland, with their lovely lakes, which might almost have been

213

in the Highlands; across the Pennines into the Yorkshire dales; and so at length rejoining their previous route at Doncaster. They made long days of it, for Will was very much aware that this was all taking longer than had their northern journey, and that King James required all the time available, and would be critical of any delay. As a consequence, they tended to halt overnight at less than worthy lodgings for a royal prince, riding just as far as they could get each day. It was all an education for the boy, anyway, meeting more of the common people of the realms.

In the event, they completed their journey in only one day more than that of the way up, aided by the fact that, knowing James, Will made enquiries as they neared London, guessing that he would not be in the city but hunting somewhere in the fine early summer weather. They ran him to earth, in the end, at Theobalds Park, Cecil's seat; and sure enough, they had to kick their heels until the hunting-party returned late in the day. And now Will abandoned his usual and suitably respectful custom of waiting for a specific royal summons to the presence, and instead went with Henry to claim immediate audience.

James, being helped off with his long riding-boots by an eager-to-please fair-haired and elegant young man, eyed them critically even so.

"Sae there you are, the pair o' you! At last! You've taken your time, have you no'? It's ower a month since you left. I've been waiting. We've a' been waiting."

"The Earl of Argyll was not at Castle Campbell, Sire. We had to go all the way to Inveraray. We have not delayed, I assure Your Majesty. Indeed we have ridden long and hard."

"Aye, then. And is Argyll going to dae it? As I command?"

"Yes, Sire. He will muster his fullest strength in shipping and men. Will already be doing so. He will be off the Ulster coast by the end of this month, of June. Will do as you say."

"He'd better! That doesna gie me ower long to get a' in train, mind. The Hamiltons are waiting. And I've signed and sealed the forfeitures and dispossessions. Och, I'll hae them off the morn." He deigned to notice his son. "The laddie's been a' right? Nae hinder? Hasna held you back?"

"Far from it, Sire. The best horseman of us all. And the best horse, to be sure."

"I saw Rothesay Castle, Father, where I am duke of. It is poorly kept. It should be tended better."

Will bit his lip. He should have warned the boy not to mention the Rothesay visit, as possible indication of delay.

"Rothesay, eh? That's no' on the road to Inveraray, is it?" But the king let it pass. "Did Argyll say what he wanted in Ulster? His price, eh?"

"No, Sire. But I said that he would be well rewarded, as Your Majesty agreed."

"Rothesay is on an island," Henry went on. "It could be very good there. I would like to live at Rothesay, among the lochs and mountains."

"Dinna be daft, laddie. Yon's no' a place for the likes o' you to bide. Noo, awa' wi' you. I've plenties to see to. Geordie Villiers, awa' and fetch the Earl o' Abercorn tae me. Here, Alexander, pu' off this boot . . ."

Holding his tongue, and also his breath against the stink, and hoping that the prince would say no more, Will retired, with Henry, duty accomplished. It was up to others, now.

15

Be it up to others as it might, it felt strange for Will those many months, reaching into years, as it were, cooped up at Oatlands, living the pleasant-enough if uneventful and distinctly restricted life which fate seemed to have ordained for him, while so much went on elsewhere in which he had had some hand and interest. He was sent no actual news or accounts of what went on over Ulster – James Stewart being scarcely that way inclined – but he did get word of a sort through indirect channels, largely via Lady Carey, who came quite frequently to see little Charles, of whom she was very fond.

So far as he could gather, the Irish venture appeared to be going well. At any rate, there had been no battles, and the Hamilton brothers were sending back good reports; so it looked as though Argyll's threatening coast-patrolling was being successful. Whether the Earls of Tyrone and Tyrconnell and other Catholic chiefs had actually fled was not clear; but at least they did not appear to be taking to arms against the king's edicts. As to would-be colonists and settlers, there was little information, but since this was to be encouraged mainly from Scotland at this stage, that was not to be wondered at.

The Oatlanders saw nothing of the monarch over the months, but they did have a brief visit from Queen Anne, to see her sons. She apparently knew little about the Irish situation and cared less. She did announce that her daughter Elizabeth was to be betrothed to the Count Frederick of the Palatinate.

However galling it was for Will, and to a lesser extent Henry, to learn so little of what had been their urgent business before, Will did have more personal preoccupations, and satisfactory ones. For, when Janet questioned him, on his return, as to how he had got on with Agnes Douglas, and learned that she was very much in the family way, it was with some satisfaction and quiet elation that she herself believed pregnancy was upon her – to her husband's joy and their mutual congratulation. She had missed two of her female monthly recurrences now, so it looked as though the New Year period might see them celebrating more than the Christmas birth.

So those months were rather special for the Alexanders, and one of them having to be taken good care of, even Henry much interested.

Ailie Graham remained with them, now accepted by all, even the queen and Lady Carey, as regular maid-in-waiting to Charles, that prince at last beginning to develop out of wondering childhood into boyhood, and becoming more fluent although never wordy.

It was Yule before, as usual summoned to Whitehall, Will saw the king again, and he somewhat concerned about Janet making the journey to London in her condition, talking about a horse-litter, although she derided any such feeble contrivance, declaring that she would be perfectly capable of riding so long as they took it fairly gently; in consequence making the slowest journey ever, to the amusement of the mother-to-be, Henry watching her as though she might give birth there and then in the saddle.

The royal command to appear came almost immediately upon their arrival at Whitehall, but turned out to be, not as anticipated concerned with the Irish situation, but with Holy Writ.

James had Bishop Andrews of Ely in attendance, that prelate looking distinctly uncomfortable, and relieved to see additional company.

"This o' the Bible translation, Alexander," the king announced without preamble. "There's ower much dispute and bicker aboot the matter. Ower mony views and

217

opinions. Fifty-four o' them! I should hae kenn't no' to let a' these in on it. A' scholars, as they ca' themsel's. They canna agree on aething! Here's me haeing to mak the decisions they should be making. Aye, and the bishops are the worst o' them! *They* canna accept the college men. Theology!"

Will blinked at this diatribe, glancing at the prelate. He did not raise voice.

"You did the Psalms, man." That was all but an accusation. "They dinna like them, the maist o' them. The Proverbs tae. Some say they're ower flowery, no' sufficiently literal. Others that you're mair concerned wi' synonyms and the like, no' the given text. *I'm* no' saying it, mind – and I scanned a' your work when you gien it to me."

"I never claimed to be versed in theology, Sire, only in verse. It was as something of a poet that you gave me these parts to translate. They are in origin poetic, and I sought to render the poetry into English verse which folk here could recognise and understand. I may have made errors of meaning."

"Your critics, Master Alexander, are concerned that sometimes the message may have been lost in the poetic phrasing," the bishop put in. "I do not say that I accept all that some declare. But I do recollect where, for instance, the Latin text says trap or snare and you make it offence. The difference is material . . ."

"Och, man, hud your wheesht! Yon's nit-picking, just. The sense o' it's clear enough. Translating poetry into other poetry is a deal harder than prose, mind. Each poet chooses his fewer words to express his ain conception o' the meaning, no' just using a deal o' words as in prose. *I* ken! David did that wi' the psalms. Then they were translated into the Greek. Then Jerome turned them into the Latin, in his Vulgate. Noo we put them into English. You canna reach a' the different peoples wi' the same depicts, aye depicts – your synonyms."

218

"No, Sire. That is understood. But changes of meaning, for the sake of poetic excellence, in holy Scripture?"

"If I remember aright, that of traps and snares, or offence, was in one where the psalmist says that his enemies' table would be made a trap," Will put in. "That seemed to me a poor translation of what was meant. A table, or a feast as was intended, cannot be likened to a trap or snare with any accuracy. I used offence as meaning the eating would become distasteful, sickening no doubt, therefore offensive."

"Naught wrang wi' that," James said, and pointed at Andrews. "You and your strict literal quibbles! You'd deave the folk wi' lang words and homilies. This Bible is to be a right maisterpiece o' the English language, see you. Yon's been ay my intention. Hech, aye, it might hae been in the *Scots* tongue, no' the English! For I meant to dae it in Scotland afore ever I cam south here. I put it tae the General Assembly o' the Kirk, at Burntisland in Fife, twa year afore I mounted this throne here. But thae meenisters didna tak it up. Aye, you might hae had your Bible in guid Scots! What would you say to that?"

The bishop looked appalled, but did not put his horror into words.

"Do you wish me to go over some of these translations again, Sire?" Will asked. "Where there are questions, objections."

"Some o' them, aye. No' them a', mind." James gestured towards the table whereon were stacked papers. "I'll mark whaur I think you could mak an improve, just. But I want it done quickly, see you. Nae delay. For this great design o' mine has been held up ower lang as it is, wi' a' these disputes and bicker. I want to see it printed, no' endlessly wrangled ower. I'll hae the papers tae you when I've cast my eye ower them."

"Yes, Sire, I will do my best." Will took a chance. "Could I ask Your Majesty how matters go over the Ulster project? Did my lord of Argyll's ships do what was required, serve their turn?"

"Ooh, aye. The plantation – that's what I'm naming it, the Plantation o' Ulster – is going ahead weel enough. I've no' made any o' my baronets yet, mind. I want to see results first, folk actually settling on the land. But thae Catholic chiefs hae gone, fled some place. And there's plenties o' interest in taking it ower, frae Scotland. No' sae much here in England. But I'm no' displeased wi' it a'. Your friend Argyll will dae no' sae badly oot o' it. And we'll mak the Irish sit up!"

The arrival of George Villiers, the new young favourite, whom Will by no means admired, allowed him to make his exit.

So it was to be translation amendments, no choice activity.

It was perhaps with less than suitable care and application that Will scrutinised and sought to amend his translations, on the criticisms of the biblical scholars and prelates; for he was in fact very much otherwise preoccupied with more personal matters. Janet seemed to have miscalculated her delivery dating, and it was well into January before eventually she gave birth, despite seeming about to do so for days, and looking exceedingly pregnant. In the event, moreover, her birth pangs were prolonged indeed, and however bravely she bore them, Will was in a state of dire anxiety, far from able to concentrate on psalms, the prolonging being accounted for, at least, by the production of twin girls.

An exhausted mother apologised to a relieved father for failing to provide a male heir; but Will was quite delighted, declaring that he much preferred the female sex to the male anyway, finding his two tiny daughters something of a miracle indeed, and having to be restrained from carrying them about with him to show to all who would look. Ailie Graham was almost as concerned, and of considerably more practical help; and Henry adopted a sort of semi-proprietorial interest in the twins, while even Charles spent much time with them, usually just gazing appreciatively and nodding his fair head at them.

So Will produced his own psalm of praise for two beauteous daughters, one Jean, who had emerged first, the other Mary, having no difficulty in writing pages on the wonder of it, however scanty and halting his attention to King David's outpourings on alternative themes.

Fortunately or otherwise, King James was also preoccupied with more than Bible matters. He had become locked in a battle with his, or his people's, parliament, and this over moneys. He had, to be sure, inherited large debts from Elizabeth's reign, particularly over the costs of the war with Spain; but although he had put that issue to rights, to his own satisfaction at least, in the Spanish peace, the debts remained. He had instituted many charges and impositions on the nation's trade and wealth, to help clear it – one of the reasons for his Irish venture, although most of this last was aimed to fill his privy purse rather than the national coffers. He had, two years before, set up the so-called Book of Rates, against the judgment of most of his advisers, establishing or increasing duties on what he called tonnage and poundage, on imported goods such as wine and exported trade in wool and the like. Parliament, the Commons at least, where the merchants had much influence with their trade guilds, objected; but James had ruled that his powers in the matter, as in much else, were absolute, and he had forbidden the members even to discuss the subject. Now the parliamentarians more or less rebelled, declaring that free speech was their inalienable right, and not only debated the terms of the Book of Rates but upheld the refusal of certain merchants to pay their duties, notably one John Bate, on, of all things, the import of a shipload of currants. So there was dire conflict between monarch and legislature, with Cecil, as Secretary of State, endeavouring to heal the breach and at the same time solve the king's financial problems by what he called a Great Contract, whereby James would give up his rates in return for a large annual personal grant of moneys, to be paid out of an already all but empty treasury. This all came to a head now, the monarch declaring it impracticable, indeed all but farcical, as well as infringing his divine right. He dissolved parliament. So now he ruled without a legislature, and Cecil was, temporarily at least, out of favour.

The Bible project rather receded in urgency, in consequence, to Will's relief.

In all the circumstances, a return to Oatlands was delayed until the early spring, leaving a London in more unsettled state than it had been since the plague years.

16

James Stewart was not the man to let problems and opposition deter him from his chosen objective, however. Unheroic figure as he appeared, he was in fact a tougher and more resolute monarch, although devious in his methods, than many the two realms had known. Opposition was apt but to heighten his resolution, merely forcing him into alternative ways of gaining his ends.

This was well exemplified in two causes in which Will Alexander had some concern that year, the Irish and Bible projects. The opposition of the parliamentarians, even though they were not allowed to sit in session, developed against other matters than just that of the Book of Rates. They took up the Ulster situation. They claimed that this was being engineered for the benefit of the Scots Presbyterians and against the English Episcopalians, however effective against the Catholics. James, to counter this, collected a number of English supporters who were prepared to become settlers in Ireland, and bestowed on them his new title of baronet – at a substantial price, of course – and gave them the name of the Undertakers of Ulster. This had some effect of stilling criticism; but it did not silence critics on an unforeseen aspect of the situation: Jealousy on the part of gentry who were not prepared to become colonists but who resented others being able to call themselves Sir and their wives Lady while they could not. The monarch's method of dealing with this was simple but effective: he offered knighthoods to such objectors as would pay sufficiently for them, and this being within his personal monarchial authority, the proceeds came to himself in major fashion. It was said that in his first year on the English throne he had created one thousand knights; now he rivalled that, with a certain royal glee.

The other cause to be given the required push was the spiritual one. His committee of fifty-four experts were given until the following year, 1611, to produce and publish the Bible in English, or they would be dismissed and James would authorise his own chosen versions of the texts. And, as a consequence, Will's amendings were summarily suspended, and he had to deliver what he had done to Bishop Andrews, no apology being offered or called for.

So now life at Oatlands developed notably, with Henry growing swiftly towards manhood; Charles, now in his eleventh year, becoming a quite studious boy, rewarding to teach in book-learning and the like, however uninterested in outdoor pursuits; and of course two babies to claim the attention. They all became something of a family, and a happy one, even though they realised that this could not continue for long, Janet a rewarding mother such as the two princes had never really known.

Something of a problem did develop, with Henry becoming almost over-adventurous in his devotion to sport and physical activities, possibly partly in an effort to shame his young brother into some degree of emulation – if so, with scant success. Sometimes he all but endangered himself in his enthusiasm, in horse-jumping, pole-vaulting, running for long distances, swimming and suchlike. Some of all this began to concern Will for, as in the last two, he could scarcely be accompanied, and risks could arise. His royal father would certainly disapprove, and James was undeniably proficient at getting to know of details of all sorts, however distant he might be. Will did not want to discourage the youth, but had to caution him on occasion.

That year, owing to the success of the Irish policy, repercussions arose with the Vatican, where the Pope naturally saw it as an assault on the Roman Catholic faith. This would not have concerned James overmuch had the Pontiff not made approaches to the King of Spain to break off the treaty relations with the new Britain, this concordat being something of a feather James had inserted in his favourite high hat. So there was much consultation, especially with the Count Gondomar, with the king coming to the conclusion that some gesture was required towards the papacy, however opposed his parliament would have been to anything such; but with parliament suspended, James allowed himself a free hand; no point in ruling by divine right if one had to yield one's important judgments to others. Typically, he came up with a most notable if devious project, which ought to cost him and his realm nothing, whatever it might do for Ireland. He would set up an Irish parliament, odd as this might seem when he was having so much trouble with his own English one. He would make sure that it was dominated from Ulster, of course, Protestant, even though the rest of Ireland was almost wholly Catholic. But it had been the Ulster earls and chiefs who had led always, the O'Neills, that line of the ancient High Kings – and these were safely fled, to France it was said. So although the new Irish parliament would undoubtedly have a Catholic majority, that majority would be ever in fear of the tough and king-supported Ulster Protestants. If a suitable balance was not thus kept he, the monarch, could always dissolve the parliament. But meantime it would appear as a notable gesture towards the Vatican, and avoid any rupture with Spain, where there was still talk of Henry being married to one of the infantas.

All this Will learned on a visit by the Duke of Lennox to Oatlands from the court at Windsor, the visit occasioned by the king's concern at information which was reaching him that Henry was being allowed to misbehave, or at least much to overdo unsuitable activities, such as swimming in water. James had a horror of drowning, among other dreads, and was not going to have his heir possibly suffering such fate. Let Alexander see to it.

Will had been afraid of this. He promised to restrain the prince as far as he could; but Henry was now a spirited sixteen-year-old, and not to be treated like a child. Lennox sympathetically told Will to do his best, and had a word with the prince himself.

The fact was that the immurement of the heir to the throne at Oatlands could not go on very much longer. At Henry's age James himself had been ruling Scotland without a regent and by no means always heeding either his advisers or the Scots parliament. Fond as he was of the prince, Will realised that his tutoring and guardianship days were nearly over. The duke agreed to advise the king of the fact.

It took some time for representations to produce positive reaction from the monarch, until late autumn indeed, when Henry and Will were summoned to Royston, where hare-coursing was the order of the day. Their audience was a strange one, even stranger than usual, with the trio involved all pulling in different directions. The king declared that he understood that Henry was now thinking to play the man, leave Oatlands and his studies there, and possibly join the court where he, his father, could at least keep an eye on him and stop all this nonsense of swimming, pole-vaulting, wrestling and the like. The prince declared that, although he did desire to start taking some part in affairs and be given missions about the realm, as in their errand to Argyll, which he had enjoyed, he did not want to leave Oatlands and Master Will's good company; if he could use that good place as a base to sally from and return to, he would much prefer that to life at court among all these proud lords and bowing time-servers – a comment which had his sire spluttering thickly. James, however, seemed to see this suggestion as a possible solution of the problem meantime, of least trouble and inconvenience to himself, and agreed that he would think on it, provided Henry made him a promise to limit his ridiculous and unprincely physical activities. This last was less than firmly given. For his part, Will by no means wanted to become involved with life at court and was happy to remain at Oatlands, looking after Prince Charles and rearing his own brood – that is, if he could not return to Scotland with Janet to his own life.

In the event, it was not long before some results of this confrontation developed. Another summons, to Windsor, produced the royal decision. The prince should have his wish granted to take some part in affairs of state. He could start over the issue of the Ulster colonisation. A number of Scots would-be settlers willing to pay for the privilege had been enrolled and their worthiness checked by the Hamiltons and the Earl of Mar, these to be created baronets. The matter of that creation, or at least their induction and initiation to the style and degree, had been concerning the monarch. Knighthood was straightforward and traditional; the recipients had to come in person, kneel before the king and be tapped on each shoulder by the royal sword, so establishing their status. But this of baronetcies was something new, and must not seem to rival or outdo the ancient knighting ritual, even though it was to be hereditary where the other was not. As ever new Ulster colonists were found, James certainly did not want to have all such coming down from Scotland to be granted audience and given some sort of ceremony; he had plenty to do without that. So he had decided that the bestowal of the rank and title should be signalised by the presentation of a handsome sealed document, heraldically decorated with the Red Hand of Ulster and the royal arms, a parchment for display. James would sign these, but he had no intention of going frequently up to Scotland or having the recipients all attending on him here for the presentation. Yet these recipients would undoubtedly expect some sort of official ceremonial. What better than the heir to the throne making the presentations? Henry could go up to Scotland and usefully serve in this capacity, deputising for the monarchy. Would that suit His Royal Highness?

227

The prince was well pleased with this suggestion and role. When would they start? Obviously he assumed that Will would go with him.

They were told that names were being finalised and parchments prepared. They should be off before winter conditions hampered long-distance travel.

So it was back to Oatlands meantime, Henry's spirits high.

Lennox arrived some two weeks later, with a number of highly decorative scrolls with the royal seal attached, featuring the Bloody Hand of Ulster – which Will felt was scarcely a suitable emblem in the circumstances – above the royal signature JAMES R. Henry and Will were to go to Stirling Castle, where Mar would have the prospective new baronets assembled. Names would then be filled in. No great speech-making was called for, and all ought to be quite a simple and straightforward procedure. Perhaps more than one such investment might be necessary, depending on the numbers of suitable colonists coming forward, and how far they had to come. Mar would arrange it all.

All this prospect pleased Henry, especially the notion that their stay in Scotland might be lengthened by having more than one investiture. The longer the better as far as the Duke of Rothesay was concerned. Will saw the prospect as not unpleasing also, although it did mean that he would be away from Janet for some time, there being no possibility of her accompanying them, much as she would have wished to do so, the twins still too young to be left in Ailie's care for so long. Charles at least was no problem.

Two days thereafter, then, they set off, with the usual hard-riding escort, theirs the freedom of the road again.

They made Stirling in excellent time, indeed before Mar was ready for them and had assembled the would-be baronets. There would be some delay. Not to kick their heels idly, the visitors took the opportunity to make calls at Menstrie and Cardross, and also at Castle Campbell, for Mar said that Argyll, having secured large lands in Ulster in return for his fleet's services, was interesting quite a number of his clansmen in the plantation scheme, some of his lesser lairds and land-holders being on the baronet list. As far as Mar knew, he was at Castle Campbell meantime.

At Menstrie all seemed to be in order. As before, Will knew a longing to be back here in his own place where he belonged, under the shadow of his beloved hills. Would he ever return to live here? What had his poetic urgings landed him into?

At Cardross the Erskines were pleased to welcome Prince Henry and eager to hear of their twin grand-daughters; and Miller Graham proud to have his daughter as maid-in-waiting to Prince Charles. The Ulster project came in for much discussion, not all of it favourable, particularly the idea of creating an Irish parliament, which Sir William felt was bound to encourage militant Catholicism. And these new baronets were likely to get uppish. As a knight himself, he resented them being able to call themselves Sir, just because they had to pay the one-thousand-pound fee. Some of them, he was quite sure, once they had got themselves their new titles, would resile from their Ulster obligations, possibly never so much as visit the place.

Next day their visit to Castle Campbell held a very different flavour, Argyll now very much in favour of the plantation, as he had reason to be. His wife was welcoming indeed, proud to show off her son, another Archibald, but not so much so as to limit her expressions of womanly affection otherwise. Even Henry received attentions, flattering for a youth, slightly embarrassing as he found them.

Argyll said that he had a number of further settlers in view for Ulster, in addition to the ones due to appear at Stirling, not all Campbells but clansmen of lands the Campbells had taken over, Lamonts, MacGregors,

MacNaughtons, even some of Will's MacAllisters. Most of these admittedly could not afford the money to buy baronetcies; but they would make good settlers. The only problem was that some of them were Catholics. Would this debar them from taking part?

Will thought not, probably, so long as they were well warned not to let themselves get involved in religious strife. After all, the population of Ulster at large would remain Catholic, so a few more settlers would not greatly affect the issue. King James was not in any way rabidly anti-Catholic; indeed this attitude was held against him by many of his English advisers, his friendship with Count Gondomar, for instance, indicative.

With the earl favouring his visitors with his near presence fairly consistently, there was little opportunity for his countess to express her kindnesses other than by words and expressions. Evening and night passed without behavioural problems.

In the morning they went back to Stirling, where they found Mar had collected the first batch of postulants for the new order of under-nobility, fourteen in all, three of them Campbells. An interesting development now became evident. This was that of the aspiring baronets no fewer than four were Englishmen, who had come north to seek inclusion in the order, presumably under the impression that there would not be a similar opportunity in England, admittedly two from just across the border in Cumberland and Northumberland. Mar found no fault with this, so long as they paid their due price.

In the fine decorative hall with its carved monarchial heads, erected by Henry's great-grandfather, James the Fifth, a little ceremony was enacted, the prince making his short introductory speech, emphasising his father's intentions and goodwill for the concerns of his realms, his pleasure in establishing the Order of Baronets of Ulster and his good wishes towards all present; Henry, who had rehearsed this a few times, doing it very well, even though with one or two pauses and spurts over slight gaps in memory. Then Mar introduced each of the postulants, one by one, to be handed his parchment and, bowing, kiss the princely hand, Henry being whispered the name of each as he came up, so that he could thereafter address him as Sir Donald Campbell, Sir Anthony Coke or whatever. All went smoothly and Will, watching, was well satisfied with the results of his tutoring.

Mar and his mother, now looking her age, provided a meal for the new baronets, who thereafter all departed whence they had come. How soon all these might be making their larger departure for Ulster was uncertain.

Discussing a further investiture with Mar, Will learned that if the prince and himself could delay their return south for, say, another ten days, this would be advisable, to let some of the more distantly dwelling further applicants reach Stirling, not only Campbells and the like but lairds from the Isles, Moray, even Caithness. This was accepted, joyfully by Henry.

So now they had ten days to dispose of as they liked. The prince was in no doubts as to what he wanted to do with them: a return to Rothesay and then a visit to the adjacent Isle of Arran to climb some of those great mountains he had seen there. Will agreed, although he did say that he would like to have a couple more days at his Menstrie property, which he felt distinctly guilty about neglecting, however well his steward managed without him. But they would head west first.

They spent a not very comfortable night in Rothesay Castle, the first time a Duke of Rothesay had bedded there for centuries probably, Henry being concerned to make a detailed survey of what should be done to the premises to put them into suitable state for his frequent visits.

Then in the morning they were all ferried over the Sound of Bute to Arran – for they still had their escort of half a dozen armed guards to take with them everywhere, by royal command. Will thought, however, that they need

231

not drag these characters, pleasant enough as they were, up the mountains with them.

Arran was a Hamilton possession, indeed the Marquis of Hamilton had been Earl of Arran previously. He had castles all over the island at Brodick, Lochranza and Kildonan, but nowadays these were little occupied. The visitors were advised, at Rothesay, not to seek lodgings at any of these castles but to go to the house of Kilmichael, where lived a Fullarton family, hereditary coroners of Arran, who were in essence stewards of the island.

It made an impressive approach. Arran proved to be much larger than Will had realised, the boatmen telling them that it was almost a score of miles long and about half that in width, mountainous indeed as was evident, but with the mightiest peaks in the northern half, ten or more of them towering hugely and already snow-capped, these having Henry exclaiming. They landed midway down the eastern shore at the wide Brodick Bay, where three deep valleys opened like spokes of a wheel. They were directed to the southernmost of these, Glen Cloy, where they found Kilmichael of the Fullartons, a sizeable establishment. As usual, the presence of the heir to the throne ensured them a respectful welcome from the elderly coroner and his three sons, quite comfortable quarters being found for them, much better than in Rothesay Castle.

Henry was for setting off for the heights straight away, but they were warned that these mountains were not to be tackled lightly, especially when snow-topped, having their dangers, with cliffs, sudden ravines and clefts, steep screes and, in snow, cornices which could collapse under them – all of which but made Henry the more eager. John Fullarton, one of the sons, offered to act as guide on the morrow, and this was gratefully accepted. Meantime they could climb a more modest summit, A'Chruach, which rose just south of Glen Cloy and which, although not a spectacular eminence, because of its isolated position offered notable and far-flung vistas.

This Henry and Will did, finding the ascent not

difficult, with a minor glen to take them much of the way up. They were rewarded with magnificent views in all directions, westwards across the Kilbrannan Sound to the long Kintyre peninsula, southwards down the Firth of Clyde, eastwards to mainland Ayrshire, but above all northwards over the ranked array of mighty peaks and ridges, glowing white pinnacles slashed with dark shadows cast by the slanting late-afternoon sunlight, challenging indeed.

In the morning, then, their escorts left to their own devices, John Fullarton led Henry and Will up the northern of the three valleys from Brodick Bay, Glen Rosa, to climb Goat Fell, the highest summit of the island, although, as Fullarton told them, it was not the most difficult to climb. He also said that Goat Fell was not its true name, which was the Gaelic *Gaoth-ceann*, the windy height, well named as they would discover, its three mighty shoulders converging to two all but conical peaks, out of a crescent-shaped crest half a mile in length.

The approach up Glen Rosa was itself spectacular, the walling thereof steep-sided, little more than a defile presently, and its rushing river, with its cascades and falls, having to be crossed and re-crossed time and again. They covered two miles of this, mounting all the way, red deer most evident on either side, before Fullarton guided them off right-handed to start the real ascent.

It was a taxing task they had set themselves, not only on account of the gradient and its extent but because of the pitfalls and obstacles, the sudden crags and escarpments which had to be negotiated where they could not be avoided, the cataracts from the melting snowfields above, the tumbled rock confusions to be clambered over, the ledges, the crannies, the slippery screes of loose stones. The round-about ascent took them almost two hours; but the triumphant finish, even ploughing their way through softish snow in swirling wind, more than compensated for the effort, for the prospect from here was as breathtaking as all else, so vast were the distances opened before them and dramatic the scenery. They could see even to Ireland, much of the southern Hebrides, the Paps of Jura standing out, Ben Cruachan, the Campbell mountain, far to the north, and Ben Lomond shapely to the east. Even Will had to be warned to keep his eyes on where he was treading lest the treacherous snow-cover plunged him into depths, overhanging cornices being an ever-present danger.

Henry for once was speechless.

They descended by the almost more precipitous north-western slopes, going carefully indeed, into the upper reaches of Glen Rosa for the quite lengthy walk back, the prince tired, as was Will, but ecstatic, fulfilled.

Next day, to give their leg muscles some rest, they explored the southern perimeter of the island on horse-back, much impressed by the sea cliffs of Bennan and Dippin Heads, and the offshore isles of Pladda and St Molaise, to be ready for the following day's further climbing.

John Fullarton warned them again that this next venture would demand even greater care than on Goat Fell, for it would entail a dramatic narrow ridge-walk, known as A'Chir, the Comb, between the peaks of Ben Tarsuinn and Cir Mhor, a mile of it, with mighty drops down each side, the most challenging feature of the entire range of mountains. But first they had to climb Ben Tarsuinn itself.

This, the way they were taken, was less difficult than had been Goat Fell although a longer ascent, and the peak only a couple of hundred feet less in height. But heading northwards thereafter along A'Chir was quite the most exciting event of Henry's life, all but Will's also, for this was the traversing of an elongated crest so narrow that it was possible to look down both sides, in many places, at one time; and with snow cornices and extensions apt to project, almost each step had to be surveyed and tested. Fullarton led heedfully, his shepherd's crook prodding and probing, their progress slow indeed. But no haste was desired, so stupendous and riveting were the sights, so extraordinary and exhilarating the experience, something never to be forgotten. They were indeed scaling the heights of living, Will acknowledged to himself; never had he felt more alive, and somehow worshipping. Their Creator knew what He was about when he formed these mountains. What the Lord's Anointed would have thought of his son venturing hereon was not to be considered. Especially when they came to a gap in the comb, as it were between two teeth, admittedly narrow, only a yard across, but having to be jumped, once their guide had ensured that the rock was clear of ice, he then using his crook for them to grip as they leaped over after him.

The peaks of Cir Mhor and Caisteal Abhail at the northern end of this tightrope of a ridge made a rewarding finale, but they did not rival the stimulation, the challenge, of the ridge itself. Their descent to the glen, and return down it, had them gazing upwards and wondering.

After that, anything else on Arran would have been anticlimax. Will therefore suggested a return to the mainland. They would visit Glasgow on their way back to Menstrie, where Henry would see the great cathedral of St Mungo and hear the story of that saint, who had founded Glasgow, grand-nephew of the famous King Arthur, and of his noble mother Thania, who had braved all that paganism and its druids could effect against her and Christ's cause.

They spent two days at Menstrie thereafter, and then rejoined Mar at Stirling Castle, where a second batch of baronets was created, all the proceedings going satisfactorily. Then the long journey south, and back to normal living, with so much to tell Janet, Ailie and young Charles – and that would be good also.

The weather was distinctly more wintry as they went.

17

The festive season at Whitehall that Christmastide was especially festive for some reason, and Henry played his part in making it so. His mission to Scotland over the Ulster baronetcies seemed to have had the effect of maturing him; or perhaps, as Will wondered, could it have been the result of that experience on the ridge-walk of A'Chir that had done it? At any rate, quite suddenly, he had become a young man rather than a youth, and showed it in various ways, in especial in his recognition that he was heir to the throne, not in any vainglorious fashion but with the beginnings of an assurance and authority. Will had seen the like happen before, in some degree, with Archie Campbell.

As it happened, whether out of the king's awareness of this, or because of previous planning, on reaching his seventeenth year the official inauguration of the Prince of Wales was commanded. Henry had been known by that title for long, of course, but not ceremonially installed as such; and this solemnisation, and the celebrations which followed, all added to the air of festivity.

But it was the masques which made that Yuletide especially notable, at least for the Oatlands group, for Henry actually put on his own performance; and Charles, at his mother's insistence, took an active and prominent part in one of hers, his first tentative step towards princely behaviour. That masque was *Tethys Festival*, an elaborate one indeed, in which the queen played Tethys herself, the daughter of Uranus, and Charles was Zephyrus, dressed in green satin with wings of white cambric, eight little girls dancing round him, while Henry had to lead the thirteen river nymphs out of their cavern, Princess Elizabeth being the Nymph of the Thames, with Lady Arabella Stewart Nymph of the Trent. Charles had to kneel before Tethys and beg her to come down from her throne and dance with him, a part which must have taxed the boy to the full, but which he managed none so ill, comporting himself with a sort of staid dignity at odds with his years in the quadrille thereafter, the river maidens meanwhile chanting the charms of the rivers they represented. As a finale, Charles had to receive from his mother gifts, a trident to be given to his father and a jewelled sword for the Prince of Wales. So, to some extent, that was Charles's night.

Henry had his turn three days later, on New Year's Night, when he presented his own masque of *Oberon the Fairy Prince*, an ambitious production, King James however drawing the line at allowing horses to be ridden on to the set as the prince desired. Janet and Will had parts to play in this performance, indeed Henry would have had Ailie and the twin Alexander babes involved if their mother had permitted it. Despite elaborate side-effects of Henry's own devising which somewhat alarmed actors as well as onlookers, especially the monarch, fireworks shooting off the least of it, all went reasonably well. But Will, for one, was relieved when it was over, to acclaim.

They all stayed in London longer than usual that year before returning to Oatlands, this because part of Henry's official institution as Prince of Wales involved him being handed over his own establishment at St James's Palace, the traditional residence; he was also to get Woodstock as country seat. There not having been a Prince of Wales since Henry the Eighth was a young man, the palace was in a distinctly neglected state, and the Oatlanders were kept busy putting it to rights and seeking to make it habitable – good practice, Henry said, for a similar but more important refurbishment at Rothesay Castle.

Despite the January weather, the Prince of Wales asserted his new-found authority and independence by swimming almost daily in the River Thames – to the protests of his father and the astonishment of most others, the citizenry included. He also went riding daily in any open ground available, especially where he could find obstacles for his Spanish mare to jump over, practising in the palace tiltyard and running long distances. He did all this as meeting challenges, not in ostentation, save perhaps as demonstration to his sire of his rise to manhood and abilities in leadership which he felt the king failed fully to appreciate. Strangely, perhaps, all this had a marked effect on his mother, who was much more concerned with physical prowess and manifestations of character, as her love of masques showed, and Anne grew closer to the eldest of her offspring and became a more frequent visitor at St James's Palace than at Whitehall, from her own Somerset House or Greenwich. Indeed she was but seldom in the company of her husband, except on state occasions or banquets, James's interest in good-looking young men as frank as it was growing, with a new favourite from Scotland, Robert Kerr or Carr rivalling George Villiers and quite displacing Montgomery.

The newly acquired princely estate of Woodstock had to be visited also. Situated about eight miles west of Oxford, and so some sixty miles from London, it was one day's riding for Henry and Will. Here was an ancient manor-house rather than a palace, but it had been a royal property since Saxon times. Like St James's it had been neglected, although Elizabeth had been fond of it, and James had hunted here. Henry noted much to be put right, and saw possibilities in it – and he now had the means to put his ideas into effect, for as installed Prince of Wales he was also Duke of Cornwall, and had the revenues of that quite rich duchy at his disposal, a development which offended his ever financially embarrassed father with an extravagant wife. Woodstock was to be set to rights; but it would not oust Rothesay in Henry's priority.

Soon after their return to Oatlands they were all summoned back to London for Charles to be installed

238

as a Knight of the Garter, much to everyone's surprise. There was much discussion about the reason behind this, for the boy was still only in his twelfth year, certainly less than knightly interested, and it seemed an odd and scarcely suitable appointment. One theory was that James was ordering it as something of a warning and rebuff for Henry, indicating that the king was becoming ever more displeased with his elder son's independence and attitudes, particularly, and strangely, in that Henry was now showing distaste for James's chosen form of hunting, despite his earlier eagerness to take part; he did not like the acceptance that the monarch should always have the privilege of being first at the kill, and the wretched business of paddling in deer-guts. So now it was to be shown that royal favours could be bestowed elsewhere. Another theory was that James wanted to please his new favourite, Robert Carr, for whom his affection was becoming embarrassing, by giving *him* the Garter; and that to instal him alone would have looked too obvious a gesture and draw adverse comment, especially from Queen Anne. If Prince Charles took part in the same ceremony, it would seem less exceptional. Will thought that both might well apply, and that it might help to keep the queen quiet.

So they all went to witness the glittering scene at Westminster, Charles behaving himself with his almost detached dignity as though it was all happening to somebody else, in marked contrast to Carr, now suddenly created Viscount Rochester, whose attitude was not far off swaggering, however disapproving the other Knights of the Garter present managed to look.

Fairly soon thereafter a much more significant event was celebrated, the publication at last of King James's Authorised Version of the Holy Bible, culmination of so much study, debate, controversy and labour, the first sample copies actually printed by Robert Barker at his own expense, a notable gesture which, of course, more or less ensured for him the great and ongoing production contract for all future editions, which would amount to thousands.

Will was summoned personally to Windsor, without Henry, to be shown this milestone in the advancement not only of the nation's worship and the furtherance of the Christian message, but of the English language itself, of which this was intended to be an enduring monument and model – a strange preoccupation perhaps for a monarch who made a point of almost always speaking braid Scots to the partial mystification of many of his hearers. James proudly showed a copy to Will, especially pointing out the flowery dedication, indeed reading it out aloud, in case any point of it was missed:

To the most High and Mighty Prince James, by the Grace of God, King of Great Britain, France and Ireland, Defender of the Faith, the Translators of this Bible wish Grace, Mercy and Peace through Jesus Christ our Lord.

"Yon's only the beginning, mind," the king went on. "They couldna say less. But it improves, aye improves. Hear you this."

Great and manifold were the blessings, most dread Sovereign, when Almighty God the Father of all mercies bestowed upon us, the people of England, when first He sent Your Majesty's Royal Person to rule and reign over us . . .

"England, they say – hear that? Just England! What aboot Scotland? Aye, and Ireland forby. Och, they'll never learn, these English. Mind, they hae some sense wi' what follows."

Now at last by the mercy of God, in the continuance of our labours . . . we hold it our duty to offer to Your Majesty . . . the principal mover and builder of the work . . .

240

"Wha else could hae done it, eh? Och, but it's right enough that they should put that in, d'you no' agree, Alexander man?" He tapped Will's shoulder. "Noo, heed this."

The Lord of Heaven and Earth bless Your Majesty with many happy days, that as His heavenly hand hath enriched Your Highness with many singular and extraordinary graces, so you may be the wonder of the world in this latter age, for happiness and true felicity . . .

"What think you o' that, eh? The wonder o' the world! Mind, only the English-speaking world, belike! But, och, they couldna put that in. Hoo think you o' it a', man?"

"It is . . . very full, Sire." Will almost said fulsome, but stopped himself in time. "Appreciative. As to be sure it ought to be." That was the best that he could do.

James waited for more and, when it did not come, frowned. "Mind, I've a'ready uncovered a few inaccuracies. Aye, and misconceptions. Man, they've crept in despite a' my warnings – aye, even in your psalms, I've noted!" He began turning over pages. "Here's a right notable one. It's in Exodus, no' the Psalms. Here, chapter twenty and verse fourteen. They've got doon 'Thou shalt commit adultery' instead o' 'shalt not'. Guidsakes, even Barker's printer-man shouldna hae missed that not!"

Will's unsuitable grinning drew another frown, and more turning over of pages.

"You translated the Book o' Ruth, did you no'? Here you are, then. Chapter three and verse fifteen: 'and *he* went into the city,' when it should hae been she. Och, it's a' Satan's daeing, mind. Yon Beelzebub, or Belial, ca' him what you will. He'll work on thae printers o' Rob Barker's. But Rob should hae read it a' ower after them. Aye, I've had plenties o' experience o' Satan's damnable powers in yon witchcraft trials at North Berwick. There's some as dinna believe in him,

241

but I dae, and hae reason to. Sae wipe that smile off your face, Alexander!"

Will went back to Oatlands pondering over his liege-lord, as so often, but without a presentation copy of the Bible. At least no more translations were demanded of him.

They all made frequent visits to Woodstock that summer; and on one of these Janet announced that she was pregnant again. In 1612, she asserted, she would present the Laird of Menstrie with an heir.

18

The year of 1612 was indeed notable, for more than the birth, in February, of another William Alexander, to the delight of all concerned, and after a much easier delivery. But from then on, events went less joyfully.

It proved to be the hottest summer in living memory, and the plague struck London again, with dire results, victims numerous. But one of the casualties could not be blamed on *that* scourge. Robert Cecil, Earl of Salisbury, had been less than himself for months, overworked all agreed, except his sovereign that is, who used his services at all hours of day or night. His condition deteriorated, with Queen Anne frequently visiting him, for she had conceived a great regard for the Secretary of State, especially for his ability to find financing for the needs which her husband did not, indeed could not, supply, including her ever-increasing love for fine jewellery. In March the sick man made the exhausting journey to Bath, to take the waters, on the advice of the queen's physician, de Mayerne; and next month, on his way back to London, got only so far as Marlborough, where he died, to the nation's major loss.

So now England was without a Secretary of State, for James did not appoint another, declaring that he would be his own amanuensis and protonotary, adding that he had ruled Scotland for nine years from the back of a horse; down here, now, as the Lord's Anointed, he would do the same for England – after all, he was doing it perfectly well without a parliament, was he not?

Will and Janet saw a great deal less of Henry that year, for now having two establishments of his own to see to,

243

and a staff to assist him, he was much away at St James's and Woodstock, and Will, as Gentleman Usher to Charles, his new style, had to remain with that prince fairly consistently. The fact that the plague was raging in London did not inhibit Henry from spending much time in the heat-stricken city, where his all but legendary activities, particularly his midnight swimming in the Thames, were the talk of the town. But as the summer wore on, when Will did see him at Oatlands or elsewhere, it was to note a growing listlessness on occasion, fought almost fanatically, but so unlike that young man as to be noteworthy indeed. Urgings to see the royal physician were at first ignored; but eventually he did call in the man Mayerne and was told that he was suffering from tertian fever, no doubt brought on by walking at night and swimming in the polluted Thames. Blood-letting was prescribed, which Will for one thought counter-productive; but when this produced no improvement, at the queen's pressure the physician had the prince's head shaven, and newly killed pigeons applied to his brow while still warm. Henry did not take this treatment, as it were, lying down; indeed he sought to keep up his activities, and in fact rode to Belvoir Castle, ninety-six miles away. Anne, losing faith in Mayerne, called in other practitioners, but to no better effect. The prince's condition steadily worsened and eventually he was confined to his bed in St James's Palace. Learning of this, Will went up to London to visit him, and arriving at St James's found the Princess Elizabeth and her betrothed, Count Frederick of the Palatinate, at the bedside. Henry, clearly very weak, made a major effort at greeting his friend, but could not keep it up, and relapsed into a sort of torpor, out of which he had not roused when the princess indicated that they all should leave, calling the attendant physician.

Next day Will called again, to find the prince breathing but unconscious.

Henry Stewart, Prince of Wales and Duke of Rothesay and Cornwall, died that November night.

Appalled, all but shattered, Will returned to Oatlands with the harrowing news, more distressed than he had ever been. Henry had become an integral and important part of his life, of all their lives, the sense of loss like a grievous weight upon them. Prince Charles became more silent even than usual.

Not only the Oatlanders felt stricken, the nation at large mourned, for Henry had become popular in a way his father never would be. The queen sat in darkness in Somerset House for days on end, so much affected as not even to attend the funeral; nor did the king, who was hunting at Royston and who loathed all such occasions. The principal mourners were Charles, still-featured, tearless, but to those who knew him clearly much moved. Also the Princess Elizabeth, weeping, and Count Frederick. Westminster Abbey was filled with the highest in the land, barring king and queen, every ambassador and envoy present, the Archbishop of Canterbury conducting the service. Will and Janet, the children left in Ailie's care, strangely were aided to get through the ordeal by their concern for Charles doing so.

Henry Stewart was interred beside his tragic grandmother, Mary Stewart, Queen of Scots.

So the grim year ended, with no Yuletide celebrations at Whitehall, and with England wondering where the next blow would fall, although Scotland and Ireland, more distant from it all, were less affected.

Life became very different for Will and Janet. Charles suddenly was all-important to the nations, Prince of Wales and heir to the throne now, the more heedfully considered and watched over because of his early weaknesses and slow development. If anything happened to him . . .!

St James's Palace and Woodstock, with the duchy of Cornwall's revenues, were now his, a twelve-year-old. Oatlands was no longer considered a suitable permanent domicile, and much more time was spent at the palaces, and at Windsor and Hampton Court. Quite a little court was provided for the boy, under the governorship of Sir Robert Carey. Will remained his Gentleman Usher, and accompanied the prince on most occasions; but fond of him as he was, because the lad was so undemonstrative and quiet, contemplative rather than active, he never won so close to him as he had been to his late brother. Indeed Janet it was who was nearest to Charles, perhaps fulfilling a mothering need, although they did see a lot of Anne now; but the queen, although greatly concerned for her surviving son, was not of the motherly sort. Charles did not see a great deal of his father, therefore nor did Will.

As it transpired, it was poetry again which occasioned their first significant association after Henry's death. When the pain of it all had settled into what amounted to a permanent sense of loss, Will set himself to write an *Elegy for the Prince*, in which he was able to translate some of his feelings into emotional and emotive words, a very real help and comfort for him, whatever it might be for others. He gave this, in due course, to Robert Barker to print, and presumably that individual sent a copy to the king. At any rate, a summons came to attend at Windsor.

The monarch was alone, for once, neither Robert Carr nor George Villiers with him. His reception of Will was less than encouraging.

"You should hae tell't me o' this, man!" he declared, holding up a folder of papers and wagging it. "It's aboot *my* son, is it no'? Should I no' hae scanned it afore you gien it to the printers, Alexander?"

"I did not wish to trouble Your Majesty. It is no great writing. Just my own feelings for Prince Henry. A sort of salve for the hurt I sustained at his death. I intended to offer you a copy in due course, Sire. I did not judge it worthy of your royal attention beforehand."

"A' the mair reason I should hae seen it. You were remiss, man, remiss. Mind, it's no' bad, as far as it goes. Bits o' it. But I could hae improved on it, had I seen it first."

246

"You still could, Sire, if so you wish. It is still with Robert Barker. That must be just a printer's proof you have. It can still be amended."

"I'ph'mm. Aye, weel, we'll see. Hae you been scrieving onything else, man, these days? Your muse is a gift o' God, mind, no' to be neglected. And this bit elegy wouldna' tak that lang, I jalouse."

"I have been working on a large poem, Sire. On the Last Day. *Doomsday*, or *The Great Day of Judgment*. It is a theme which has always intrigued me, hard indeed to visualise. A vast canvas to paint, but a challenge. I am near the end of it – or was. Prince Henry's death put me off it, quite. Perhaps I should never have attempted it in the first place. Too great a conception."

"I should say so! The Day o' Judgment! What does the likes o' you ken aboot that?"

"That is just it, Sire. What set me on to it. None of us know, or can know. The size, the vastness of it all. Think of the numbers involved! The thousand times thousands! How are all the dead to be judged, and the living also? Truly and fairly, as God would require. A loving, forgiving God, yes, but still making judgment. It challenges the imagination. That is what set me at it. Henry and I used to talk of it – *Prince* Henry. But, since his death, I have not felt the urge . . ."

"Och, it was ower large a theme for you, onyway." James dismissed the subject in favour of a larger one still. "I'm aboot to issue a right important book, see you. On the *Nature and Attributes of God*. I've been at this for some time, mind. Yon Conrad Vorstius, a Netherlander, has had the effrontery, aye the effrontery, to publish a work, if you could ca' it that, on sic a mighty theme – a bit Dutch clerk! And they've made him a professor o' divinity at Leyden! Sae I've scrieved a condemnation o' his fallacies and notions, a large topic, see you. When it's printed and bound, I'll hae it issued to the clergy here, and in Scotland and Ireland, and hae the Dutchman's book burned at yon Smithfield. The insolence o' the man!"

Will reserved comment.

"Speaking o' Ireland," James went on, "the plantation is going weel. Aye, a'most ower weel, if you get my meaning. It's thae Undertakers – the Englishry, envious. Ower mony o' them want my baronetcies. No' ower mony for *me*, but for the Scots colonists. They dinna want to see Ulster flooded wi' English, for it's set to become a sort o' new bit Scotland! Sae there's a wheen mair Scots plantationers enrolling for it, the Hamiltons and your Campbell freends in especial. I'm thinking I'll hae to be sending you up to Stirling again for another investiture, for I'm no' haeing them a' coming doon here, to hae to be put up and fed at my expenses, wi' their wives and families. I am not!"

Will looked doubtful. "It was Prince Henry who did the investing, Sire, myself only as an attendant. And I cannot think that Prince Charles is yet old enough, or able to make the long journey."

"Na, na, I wasna thinking on Charlie. You'll dae fine, man, to take up the parchments. Johnnie Mar can present them, as representing mysel'. The pair o' you'll dae fine. No' yet, mind. Jamie Abercorn is to send me the full list. Aye, and their moneys! Then I'll hae the scrolls made oot, and you can be off. I'll send for you when a's ready. You may retire, Alexander man . . ."

As time passed thereafter, Will, however much he enjoyed returns to Scotland, began to assume that the king had changed his odd mind on the matter of the Scots baronetcies, or at least on himself having to play a part in the matter, for the winter was over and spring 1614 well advanced before a call to Royston taught him otherwise.

James was hunting again – he ignored seasons in his chosen sport – and, with his favourites and courtiers thronging him, had little time to spare for Will Alexander. When, late at night, he was ordered into the presence – although he had seen James eyeing him from a distance at the evening meal – only Carr was with him, Viscount

Rochester. In his bedroom and in a bedrobe, the king did not beat about the bush.

"There you are then, Alexander." That sounded as though Will had been deliberately absenting himself. "It's a' ready for you noo. You're to be off, forthwith. Eleven new baronetcies o' Ulster. Scots ones. The parchments are a' signed and sealed. Robbie, fetch them frae the desk ben yonder. You'll tak them up to Stirling and present them. Johnnie Mar will hae the men a' there."

"Yes, Sire. But *I* cannot present them! I am no great one. These new baronets would take ill out of a mere small laird representing Your Majesty. The Earl of Mar, yes, as you said. But . . ."

"Och, you're aye the one for buts, Alexander man! I scarce ever gie you a task but you start butting! You're Gentleman of the Bedchamber and Usher to the Prince o' Wales, are you no'?"

"Yes, Sire. But it is not Prince Charles I will be representing, but your royal self. And I am . . . inadequate."

"Man, you're right obdurate – aye, obdurate! But I suppose I'll hae to gie you a bit mair confidence, like." Carr had returned with the scrolls. "These men up there are making request to me for baronetcies, and I'm granting them. Sae you're the instrument o' the granting, that's a'. I'll mak you Maister o' Requests – that's a style they hae here. Elizabeth Tudor had one. Maister o' Requests. Tae mysel', mind – to me. Will that suit you?"

Blinking, Will wagged his head. "Will they know what that means, Sire? *I'd* never heard of it."

"Och, you're right ignorant in some maitters, man. But Robbie, awa' ben again and fetch a sword. It seems we're to need one! See you, man, you'll be handing ower these scrolls wi' my signature and the seal o' the United Kingdom on each. I'd hae thocht that would be sufficient authority for ony man! But no' Alexander o' Menstrie, eh? You're a right stubborn critter – obdurate, as I say. I dinna ken why I put up wi' you."

249

"I do not wish to seem to act above my station, Your Majesty."

"Your station is what *I* mak it! Mind that. Aye, here's Robbie. *His* station is improved, eh? He's a viscount noo."

"None so great an improvement, Sire," the young man said boldly. "After all, I am the son of the chief of the Kerrs."

"Ooh, aye, Border mosstroopers, just! Cattle thieves! But gie's that sword." Gingerly James took the weapon, for he had a lifelong fear and hatred of cold steel, said to have been brought about by the stabbing to death of David Rizzio before Mary, Queen of Scots while she was pregnant with James, this on the orders of Darnley his putative father, while Rizzio, Mary's Italian secretary, was believed by many to have been his real sire. "Aye, weel, kneel, Alexander man."

Astonished, bewildered, Will took moments to obey, but that sword waving and poking in his close vicinity convinced him and he sank down on one knee. The blade, wobblingly held, all but missed one shoulder and only just avoided an ear on coming down hard on the other.

"William Alexander, be a guid and true knight until thy life's end. Aye. Arise, Sir William Alexander o' Menstrie, Maister o' Requests!"

Unsteadily the new knight arose, biting his lip. "I . . . I thank you, Sire. I, I . . ." His voice faded away.

"Aye, then. Knighthood's your station noo. Robbie, tak this awa'." Thankfully James handed over the sword. "Noo, leave us in peace, Sir William. And be off north at the soonest. Tak these scrolls."

In something of a daze Will backed himself out of the bedchamber. He had heard of carpet-knights, as distinct from knights-bachelor, more properly knights-battler, created in the field; but never of a bedroom-knight. Not that he could take in his abrupt change of status anyway. Just by that momentary tapping with a steel blade. Could that really translate him into something different, more lofty, at least in the eyes of men?

He made his way in the darkness to a humble couch in the stable block.

Next evening, back at St James's Palace, when he kissed Janet and his baby son and two little daughters, he smiled up at his wife. "I see you looking as beautiful as ever, Lady Alexander," he said. "Always a joy to behold. And to hold!" And he embraced her more thoroughly.

"You are very fulsome, Will!" she remarked. "Have you been up to some mischief? And seek to atone? Perhaps among the court ladies at Royston?"

"Mischief. I'd scarce call it that. But odd doings, yes."

"I thought so. Such as?"

"It is a long story, my lady. You will scarce believe it."

"Try me."

"I suppose that I must obey the Lady Alexander! Hear you this . . ."

"That is the second time you have called me lady. Is this to reassure me over the other ladies I spoke of?"

"It is because you *are* Lady Alexander now, my dear. And I am Sir William, Master of Requests to the king. Can you believe it?"

It did not take Janet Erskine so long as it had done her husband to accept their new status, as she flung arms round him and kissed him. But then women are like that, the practical sex.

19

The second baronetcy installation at Stirling Castle went smoothly, even though the new Master of Requests merely read out the names and handed the scrolls to Mar, who presented them to the recipients. There were three more Campbells among them. Will was very much aware of the absence of Henry at his side, and thankful when the little ceremony was over.

The Lady Minnie congratulated Will on his knighthood even if her son did not.

Later, it was good to be back at Menstrie, even alone. Will felt that he had better pay a call at Castle Campbell; for nothing was more certain than that word would reach Argyll that he had been home, even if he did not already know about the investiture, and he would expect a visit. The problem was, of course, Agnes – should Archie not be there. Will still was uneasy over his relationship with Aurora, glad as part of him would be to see her. He devised a ruse, therefore. If Archie was away, temporarily at least, he, Will, would say that he must leave and then call back; that he had to visit Cardross and the Erskines, and that his time in Scotland was sadly short, but that he required to see Argyll. If the earl was away at Inveraray, he must needs go there, tight as the timing would be. He was not proud of this device, but saw it as better than amatory complications and possible conscience-stricken regrets later. Was he a moral coward, as well as something of a moral weakling where women were concerned? Or at least, with these two women?

As he had feared, he found Argyll absent in Cowal, but expected back in the next day or two. But he need not have worried and devised, for Agnes Douglas was also from home, gone to visit her father and mother at Lochleven Castle, leaving her little boy in the care of a nurse. Whether he ought to feel relieved, or just a little disappointed, Will turned tail for Cardross.

There, his news of his little family was well received. Sir William was less than enthusiastic over Will's knighthood and new royal appointment; perhaps he saw it as a challenge to his own superior status, he who had been a knight for thirty years, two Sir Williams in the family. Also he saw his hopes of having his daughter return to Scotland, to be near them, receding, with this appointment of her husband to be Master of Requests. But there was no ill-feeling, and Will passed a pleasant couple of days before returning to Menstrie, and thereafter to Castle Campbell.

He found both the earl and countess back, and pleased to see him in their so very different ways, Agnes pregnant again. Her method of congratulating the visitor on his new style and title was typically demonstrative and physically so, with Will exchanging glances over her shoulders with a head-shaking Archie Campbell. Presumably he was getting used to his wife's uninhibited expressions of her feelings. Will wondered whether she behaved thus to other menfolk. He thought it unlikely that he was unique in her approbation.

The earl's wonderings were otherwise. What did Master of Requests mean and imply? Were there any requests which he, Argyll, might pass on to the king through Will? For instance, a marquisate? Huntly, that damned Catholic, was a marquis. And so was Hamilton. As Lieutenant of the North and admiral, surely he was entitled to such elevation. What had these others ever done to merit their advancement? Will promised to raise the matter with James, if suitable opportunity occurred; but he did not know how far this appointment of his went. It might well be merely a nominal one, meaning little.

He discussed the Ulster situation with Archie, who was

well pleased with the Campbell involvement there, both his own and his clansfolk's. He wondered whether James had plans to extend his colonising efforts further south, into the rest of Ireland. There was ample scope, after all, and the Catholic nobles and chiefs there were disunited, at each other's throats, like so many of the clans in their own Highlands. It ought not to be too difficult to turn all Ireland Protestant, and at the same time win large lands for enterprising colonists. Will agreed to pass on this enquiry to the king also.

That night one fairly brief but comprehensive embrace was achieved, not vigorously rejected by the man, with Agnes now making something of a joke of it all, which somehow had the effect of easing an awkward conscience.

In the morning he was off southwards, making for Edinburgh. He had brought with him the manuscript of his *Doomsday, the Great Day of Judgment* writing, for he felt that with James's evident lack of approval for him tackling such theme it would be unwise to send it to Barker for printing, or indeed any of the London printers. But he had put a lot of thought and effort into this work, and was determined that it should be published. So, some Scottish printer, and James would never set eyes on it.

At Edinburgh he went to consult the Earl of Dunfermline, whom he remembered as friendly, and who would be interested to hear of Prince Charles's progress, he who had been the little boy's guardian.

Dunfermline was indeed glad to have news of the prince, and to learn how his former charge would measure up to his responsibilities as Prince of Wales and heir to the throne, he who had been so backward. Will was able to give him some reassurance, saying that, although Charles was so very different from Henry, he believed that he would do none so ill, that although quiet still, and withdrawn, he was thoughtful, indeed studious, responsible and nowise lacking in wits. It was strange how King James had had two such different sons, and both so very different from himself. They did not actually discuss the king's oddities.

Dunfermline recommended a printer named John Orr, with a workshop off Edinburgh's Lawnmarket, and thither Will repaired, finding no difficulty in arranging with the man to print a limited edition of the work and have it suitably bound, samples of his productions shown being satisfactory.

That dealt with, Will faced the long journey back to London.

On his return, he found that he had missed the wedding of the Princess Elizabeth and the Elector Palatine. Also, that there was talk of another match, or at least betrothal: that of Prince Charles to the Spanish infanta, which had previously been planned by his father for Henry. The thought of Charles marrying was all but unimaginable; but any wedding would be years off, the match being purely an exercise in James's statecraft. A further indication of the monarch's priorities was his founding of a new study centre at Chelsea, the College of Controversial Theology, an enterprise only James would have thought up, allegedly to provide answers to Papists and Puritans. Will hoped that his liege-lord would not propose any duties for himself in this connection.

Charles was quite movingly glad to see Will back, for although he now had his own small court as Prince of Wales, with Carey as his governor, he clearly looked on the Alexanders as his closest friends – indeed probably the only such, for the boy's reserved nature was not apt for making friends. As a consequence, Will was kept very busy, Charles wishing to have him with him always. His wife also had to act frequently as his hostess, although Lady Carey was helpful, and with three young children to rear, Janet had her hands full. Ailie Graham was invaluable in this of course; but she too found herself with court responsibilities barely thinkable for the miller of Cardross's daughter.

Will saw little of the king for which, on the whole, he was grateful, for James's demands on him did complicate life. Without analysing it, he was aware of a curious dichotomy of feelings towards his sovereign. He probably understood him as well as anyone did, with a kind of affectionate regard, mixed with exasperation; yet he also deplored certain aspects of his so diverse character, his deviousness, his assumption of almost divine status and wisdom, the cruel streak in him, his unsavoury personal habits, his treatment of his wife and family, and his so-frank fondness for compliant young men.

Will's Mastership of Requests at least proved to be no onerous position, for no single duty as such came his way, and therefore no opportunity to seek a marquisate for Archie Campbell.

It was the young man preoccupation which produced a crisis that autumn. For reasons best known to himself, James had arranged a marriage between his favourite, Robert Carr, and the Lady Frances Howard, divorced wife of the Earl of Essex, a slightly older woman of very doubtful reputation, and daughter of the Earl of Suffolk. The Howards were a very powerful family, having the earldoms of Arundel, Surrey, Suffolk, Northampton and Nottingham, as well as the proscribed dukedom of Norfolk; and James required their support. At any rate, he celebrated this odd marriage by attending it and, not to demote the lady's style, elevated Carr from Viscount Rochester to Earl of Somerset. Little did James realise, when he devised this arrangement, the troubles he was storing up for himself, indeed for the nation, that he was to some extent going to alter the course of history. It was Frances Howard who saw to that.

Strangely, it all hinged on another poet, Thomas Overbury, of whom the king had approved and knighted, an ambitious character. He had seen the advantages of being close to Robert Carr. He in fact made himself almost indispensable to Carr, who had the most effective approach to the monarch in all the land, and so used his

256

influence there to gain position and promotion for many, at considerable financial advantage to himself. But he had offended Frances, Countess of Essex, and tried to prevent her divorce and remarriage to Carr, actually blackmailing her, or seeking to, a dangerous activity against a Howard. James was not aware of all this, but on complaints, and becoming disillusioned with Overbury, thought to get him out of the way by sending him as ambassador to the Low Countries. However, the poet saw greater advantage to himself by remaining close to Carr, and quite abruptly refused the royal appointment. James, unused to being so treated, clapped Overbury in the Tower of London. The marriage of Carr went ahead, and that might have been the end of it all. But Frances Howard saw to it that it was not. She arranged with an apothecary named Reeve to poison Overbury in the tower, and the poet died. Suspicion fell on Reeve and, under question, he confessed to having the Earl and Countess of Somerset as his paymasters. Great was the outcry, especially when it came out that the countess had earlier tried to poison her previous husband, Essex.

James was horrified, for he had all his life been afraid of being poisoned, just as he feared cold steel. And at the behest of the many great ones who hated and feared the Howard family, the king's second favourite, George Villiers, played on James's dread by suggesting that he might be poisoned also, so that young Charles would succeed to the throne, and the boy would be manipulated by Carr and his wife, who would then in effect rule the land. How much truth there was in all this was doubtful; but James took no chances. It was the new Earl and Countess of Somerset's turn to be clapped in the tower. Robert Carr's reign as favourite was over, and George Villiers took his place, and, being a much more shrewd operator, was in a position to change the course of the nation's affairs, which he proceeded to do.

All this Will learned as the months passed, and was thankful that he was nowise involved in these unsavoury ongoings, and that, because the king distanced himself from his son, he, Will, could remain that way. Fortunately it seemed that James had forgotten that he had made a Master of Requests.

The year 1615 came and went, and Janet presented her husband with another son, Henry. He was becoming quite a family man. And he was coming to look upon Charles almost as a son also, a very different relationship than he had had with Henry.

He had not much time for composing poetry, but did not altogether "neglect the muse", as his sovereign put it. And he received copies of his *Doomsday* from Edinburgh, but did not seek to present one to the king. Oatlands had now become merely a refuge they could occasionally visit for spells of escape from Woodstock and St James's, Charles enjoying these as much as the Alexanders and Ailie.

20

The death of James Hamilton, Earl of Abercorn, who had largely masterminded the Plantation of Ulster, as it were on the ground, was a blow, although the enterprise was proceeding fairly well, with no real Catholic uprising and no lack of settlers. But with new areas to the south being surveyed for development, especially Armagh, some sort of viceroy was required, for the parliament idea was stillborn, as was probably as well. Who to appoint to succeed Abercorn? It had to be a Scot, or there would be trouble. No individual sprang to the monarch's mind – and it was very much his concern – save Archibald, Earl of Argyll; but he was Lieutenant of the North and admiral, and needed in Scotland to keep the Highland clans and the Isles in order.

James surprised all by announcing that he himself would pay a visit to Scotland. It was now fourteen years since he had come to England, and he had never been back to his native land and original throne. Many in the north considered such visit to be overdue, to say the least.

When they heard of this, Will and Janet were pleased. They assumed that the king would take his son and heir with him, and that they would accompany the prince. But no, James would go alone – that is, with only a small train of courtiers under his now indispensable Steenie, as he called Villiers, this because he saw a resemblance between his favourite and a picture of St Stephen – not even the queen to be taken. No lengthy stay was intended. It was to be purely a stock-taking mission, and to find a replacement for Abercorn.

The Alexanders had to swallow their disappointment.

259

Charles did not seem to be concerned; he had no real feeling for Scotland, however often Will reminded him that he was Duke of Rothesay. That castle looked like now going unrestored.

So in May 1617 the king and no large entourage set off northwards on an unhurried journey, leaving, to the surprise of many, another poet and essayist, Sir Francis Bacon, the Attorney-General and Privy Councillor, as Lord Keeper of the kingdom during the royal absence, many great lords being offended thereby. Will hoped that while in Scotland nobody would present the monarch with a copy of his *Doomsday*. The king's party was away in fact for almost five months, one of them spent on the journeying north and south.

Word of what transpired did trickle down to Woodstock in some measure, James making his presence felt apparently in typically odd fashion. The first they heard of was on his arrival at Edinburgh, becoming impatient with the ceremonial welcome, he spurred his horse away from the speech-making provost and magistrates, thus getting detached from his party, and actually being arrested in the Grassmarket by the Moderator of the High Constables for insulting behaviour, so unmajestic had been his appearance. Another story reaching them was of a rousing debate, all but a wordy battle, with the Presbyterian divines, with the king giving them Almighty God's point of view, and the ministers the Kirk's. Who had won was unclear. Most dramatic of all his adventures, however, seemed to have been what he thought was an assassination attempt, when Sir George Bruce of Culross, in Fife, had taken him underground to inspect a new development on the coast of Forth, a coal mine which pushed far out below the firth, and at its furthest limit brought the monarch up by a hoist or lift on to a wooden platform-structure erected on stilts from the sea floor. James, not realising that they would appear, as it were, out of the waves, immediately took fright, assuming that he was to be cast off to drown almost a mile from the shore, yelling for help. He had apparently taken a deal of calming thereafter.

It did not sound as though the so-long-delayed return to Scotland was being a great success. The fact that George Villiers had been created Earl of Buckingham in the process was perhaps of more significance in the long run.

When in September the royal party arrived back in London after all the adventures, Will learned, through the Duke of Lennox, who kept in touch with Charles as he had done with Henry, that James had indeed not forgotten the Ulster situation while in Scotland and had, to general surprise, solved the problem of a successor to Abercorn in his own individual way. He had selected to take charge someone of whom few in either kingdom had ever heard, although he was of Scots extraction, indeed descended from the ancient Lords of the Isles and with royal Stewart blood in him, one Sir Randal MacSorley MacDonnell of Dunluce, in Antrim; this not only on account of his ancestry but because, although a Protestant, he was married to a Catholic, the daughter of the displaced and exiled Earl of Tyrone. James judged that this should help in healing the breach with the Irish Catholics and contribute towards harmony, not all agreeing with him, especially the Kirk divines. He had created Sir Randal Viscount Dunluce, and promised him, if he did his work in Ireland well, to make him Earl of Antrim in due course. Surely never had a monarch of England, or for that matter Scotland, created so many peers of the realm. The older established nobles did not hide their disapproval.

Charles's eighteenth birthday made an important milestone, not only for himself but for the United Kingdom as a whole. James's health was deteriorating, scarcely to be wondered at in the way he lived, his unconcern with personal cleanliness and sanitation, his consistent over-drinking – although no one had ever seen him drunk

261

– his lack of any other exercise than hunting, and even at that his legs were now so weak as having to be tied to his saddle lest he fall off his horse. He was now aged fifty-two and appearing more, growing heavy and fatter. So the further-sighted in court circles began to perceive that it might be politic to establish good relations with the heir to the throne, with a view to the future.

Will, accordingly, as closest to the prince, found himself being approached as a go-between, an introducer, little as he relished such situation. When even Steenie Buckingham came to him one day, seeking Charles, he realised just how times were changing, how unwantedly influential his own position was becoming, and how much Charles required to be protected. The all-but-despised and backward prince could be liege-lord of them all in the not too distant future; and he was still very much of an innocent.

His royal father was no innocent, at any rate, and with an all-seeing eye appropriate to Christ's vice-regent here upon earth, as he was now calling himself, surprisingly little escaping his notice. He sent for Will, at Windsor, and saw him alone.

"Aye, then, Alexander man," he greeted him, "I havena seen you for lang. No since before I went up tae Scotland." As ever, he made that sound like an accusation.

"I have ever been with your son, Sire. As appointed." Will did not fail to note how the king had begun to show age.

"I'ph'mm. Charlie's right growing up, is he no'? In body, that is, I hear. But, in his wits, eh? Hoo dae his wits measure up these days? You tutored him, and should ken."

Will felt like saying that if the father saw more of his son he would not need to ask such questions.

"He is well advanced, Sire," he said carefully. "Nowise lacking in ability. He makes much progress. He has become a good horseman. He is of a kindly nature, although he does not talk much. He has, I think, a quiet mind."

262

"Uh-huh. It's no' given to a' to hae a quiet mind! Monarchs canna just afford the privilege! And mind – *qui tacet consentit*! Aye weel." In a different tone. "He's seeing a deal o' my Steenie, I'm hearing?"

"The Earl of Buckingham not infrequently calls on the prince, Sire."

"M'mm. They're becoming friends, eh?"

"I would not put it just so far as that, Your Majesty. But Lord Buckingham behaves well with him."

"Aye. Steenie taks the lang view, maybe! Mind, Steenie's as guid as a son to me. Sae they're no' that far off being brothers, eh? Aye. Weel, you'll keep me informed, just, on that, their friendship, see you. Hoo they get alang. I need to ken. And you can best tell me. It's fell important that I ken."

"Yes, Sire." Will did not like the sound of this. It looked as though he was being directed to be a spy. To report on Buckingham's relationship with the prince. Possibly the king was jealous of his favourite showing favours towards his own son, the son he himself had neglected?

"Noo, there's another maitter. I want you to go to Ulster, see you. To gie me a right report on what gaes on there. Jamie Abercorn did nane sae badly. I've appointed a new man, MacDonnell o' Dunluce. I've made him Viscount Dunluce. You're to go and seek oot hoo he's daing, hoo the plantation's coming on. I'm consairned wi' a' Ireland, see you, no' just Ulster. And the rest o' Ireland's a' Catholic. If I'm to bring a' Ireland to peace and right government, I dinna want trouble between the Scots Presbyterians and the Catholic majority, no' permanent trouble. That's why I appointed this MacDonnell, for he's married to a Catholic, the O'Neill Earl o' Tyrone's daughter. But I've heard tell that their son's being reared a Catholic. Sae, you're to find oot hoo it gaes, Alexander."

"But, Sire, why me? I'll have no authority over there. *I* could not question and interrogate this Lord Dunluce. Surely some of the settlers already there could inform Your Majesty? Lord Abercorn's Hamilton brothers?"

263

"Buts again, man – aye buts! I'm sending you because you hae been in this ploy frae the first. And you've naething to gain by geing me a right inform, as ithers might. Forby, you're close to Argyll, and he's got a wheen Campbells planted ower there noo. Wi' his backing, you'll dae fine, and learn plenties."

"I cannot both look to Prince Charles and do this, Sire."

"It'll no' tak you ower lang. I'll hae you put on a boat sailing frae Bristol, whaur they trade wi' Ireland, and you'll be in Ulster in but five or six days. A week there and you'll be back three weeks frae noo. Dinna mak obstructions, man – aye, obstructions."

Will, perforce, retired defeated, as ever.

Royal orders ensured that the coastal trading vessel *Salutation* was waiting for him at Bristol, two days' ride from Woodstock, with instructions to deposit him at Dunluce on the north coast of Antrim, and to pick him up there again a week later, or otherwhere that he might choose. Charles would have to put up with Sir Robert Carey, now Viscount of Falkland, as immediate attendant meantime.

Will enjoyed his sail northwards, however little he looked forward to his mission at the end of it. Accommodation on the ship was basic, but no worse than much that he had had to put up with on overland travel; and this was a new experience, the late October weather being none so ill for voyaging. After the first two days, which required much tacking and sail adjustment as they headed into the prevailing south-west wind, they made excellent time when they turned northwards, with the breeze steadily behind them. Sailing up between the Welsh and Irish coastlines was interesting, and on past the Isle of Man, of which he had heard much. Will had not realised how close he found parts of Scotland to be to Ireland, the Mull of Galloway being only twenty-five miles, the shipmaster told him, from Donaghadee in County Down, and they were even closer when they passed the Mull of Kintyre, this only fifteen miles from the Fair Head of Antrim.

The fifth day out of Bristol they passed that Fair Head, between it and Rathlin Island, where the Bruce had taken temporary refuge in 1306, and turned the corner of north-east Ireland, from the North Channel into the wide Atlantic. Some sixteen miles along that coast, ploughing into much greater seas now, past the great Benbane Head and the famous rock feature of the Giant's Causeway, they came to a bay with a harbour and a large castle towering above, Dunluce itself. The skipper, in putting Will ashore, said that he was now heading back for Belfast Lough, but that he would be able to return here to pick up Sir William again in eight days' time.

So there was Will Alexander, on Irish soil for the first time, alone, and not a little unsure of himself and his errand. Admittedly Dunluce looked like any West Highland coastal village, save for its castle, and there was no foreign feeling, fishermen at the quayside greeting him in a tongue sufficiently like Scots Gaelic to be understandable.

He made his way up to the castle.

He had no difficulty, at least, in gaining admittance – indeed he had to walk on into the courtyard, since there was no one on guard to challenge him at the gatehouse. At the keep door, open, his shouting did at length produce a female, who greeted him cheerfully, again in the Erse tongue, and after commenting on his odd Gaelic amusedly, announced that his lordship was from home but that her ladyship was in the orchard gathering the last of the apples.

So Will, directed, found his way out of a postern door from the courtyard and down through a pleasance-garden to a walled orchard, where a woman in her thirties and a boy of perhaps ten years, he up a ladder, were picking fruit.

The lady, good-looking, tall and smiling, set down a large basketful of apples she had been holding up to catch her son's pickings, called to the boy, and turned to Will.

"A good-day to you," he said, bowing slightly. "My name is Alexander. William. Sir William." He still could feel a little embarrassed naming his title. "You will be the Lady Dunluce?"

"Yes, I suppose that I am, sir, although I still think of myself as MacDonnell. How can I help you?"

"I seek Lord Dunluce, lady. I come from the king." He tried not to make that sound lofty, pompous. "From London town. I have come by ship. I understand that my lord is from home?"

"He but visits one of the new farmers, not far off. He will be back shortly." She looked up. "Randy, come down and meet Sir William. Alexander, was it?"

The boy swung himself nimbly down from one of the branches of the old tree, proud to display his agility, a grinning lad. His mother told him to take one of the handles of the basket while she took the other; but Will quickly stooped to grasp them both and pick up the quite heavy load to carry it for them.

"Ah, a gallant gentleman!" Lady Dunluce said. "Come. Randy, run ahead and have Bridget ready some refreshment for our visitor. You have had a fair voyage, Sir William? The weather is good for the time of year. You come from King James, you say? Our royal master!"

Will glanced at her sidelong. That was said lightly but could indicate no light attitude towards the monarch. After all, this was the Lady Alice O'Neill, daughter of the Earl of Tyrone whom James had forfeited and exiled, and descendant of the long line of the High Kings of Ireland, from the famous Niall of the Nine Hostages, of the fifth century, a line which could make even the Stewarts seem upstarts; and despite her pleasant manner, she carried herself with an inborn authority.

"His Majesty sends me in goodwill, Lady Dunluce. He is concerned for the well-being, the peace and prosperity, of Ulster, of all Ireland."

266

"So my husband assures me."

"Yes. His desire is amity, collaboration between the native Irish and the new settlers from my Scotland, and his. I come with that message, and to see how it may be advanced."

"A noble pursuit, Sir William." That again could mean other than it sounded. "Welcome to my husband's house, then. Pray put the apples down on that bench."

Whatever Lady Dunluce's private feelings as to developments in Ireland, her attitude to Will was attentive and entirely hospitable, her son friendly, vocal, full of questions. Two little girls also appeared, much more shy. For his part, Will forbore to ask whether the children were being brought up as Catholics.

The viscount arrived after a couple of hours, a big, hearty character, red of hair and beard, somewhat overpowering at first, and a notable contrast to his quietly assured wife. He did not seem to find Will's visit in any way objectionable, indeed looked upon it more as a mark of the king's esteem than otherwise.

Over their evening meal, he held forth on the plantation situation. All in all it went fairly well, he asserted, Lady Dunluce raising one eyebrow at that. The new settlers mostly were effective and industrious, bringing much hitherto neglected and unused land into productivity. There was no real trouble with the native and Catholic landowners, such as remained. The problems were the vast areas to be settled; probably this was scarcely understood over in Scotland, almost certainly not in London. For instance, he himself had been granted three hundred thousand acres; others, particularly the Hamiltons, even more – Abercorn himself had had over five hundred thousand. It took many, many new settlers adequately to develop these great tracts, most of which had been little cultivated previously, or even grazed, the Irish being less than industrious. Again the wifely question, unspoken.

One of the biggest difficulties, Dunluce said, was the fact that many of the new baronets and hoped-for colonists just did not come over to Ireland at all. They might pay the occasional visit to inspect their landed acquisitions, but thereafter returned home. Some did send tenant farmers and cattlemen over, but only a proportion actually stayed themselves. So there was a lack of oversight and control, his greatest problem. He was seeking to improve the situation by establishing new burghs and parish areas, to exert some local authority and control; but this was a large task, lacking an Irish parliament to draw up the boundaries and allot the responsibilities. Almost inevitably these tended to be based on existing townships and villages, where of course the inhabitants were mainly Catholics. There was a great lack of Protestant divines prepared to come over and man parishes. And the English settlers, the Undertakers, wanted their Episcopalian ministers, even calling for bishops.

When her husband paused for breath his wife raised her lilting voice gently to point out that certain difficulties arose from the way the senior colonisers themselves behaved, seeing themselves as almost little kings on their vast estates, and accepting no superior authority: the Hamiltons for instance, the late Abercorn's brothers and their kinsfolk. Sir Frederick was as good as King of Derry, Sir Robert of her native Tyrone, Sir Claud of Longford and Toome. These tended to make her husband's task less than simple.

Dunluce had to admit that this was so. King James's instructions to him were to act more or less as viceroy. But without some greater and evident overall authority he was scarcely in a position to do so.

Will promised to convey all this to the monarch. He said that he himself had a special interest in the Campbell settlers. Were these proving helpful, or the reverse?

The Campbells and their like, Lamonts, Colquhouns, MacNaughtons and so on, were among the best, he was told. Will was able to claim that this would be partly because of instructions from their chief, Argyll. That great clan and its adherents always had a tradition of discipline, however aggressive they could be towards neighbours.

That was understood.

In the morning, Dunluce took Will on a tour of his own neighbourhood, to show him how the new settlers were doing. Being of Highland extraction himself, most of those he had introduced were Islesmen and Highlanders, and therefore not used to the larger Lowland-type farmery, small crofting holdings, herding and sea fishing being their backgrounds; indeed along this North Antrim coast many of the newcomers appeared to be more concerned with the fishing than with land cultivation, a preoccupation which Dunluce was seeking to amend. Even inland, where there was no fishing to distract, the farmers tended to be more interested in cattle- and sheep-rearing than in agriculture, and here the viscount was ever urging the tenants to till greater acreages of oats, and to grow potatoes, something new to most of them. But there were still great areas unoccupied and undeveloped. The further inland they went, the fewer settlers and the more indigenous Irish peasantry were to be found, these content apparently with very modest living conditions and a minimum of tillage, a few cows and a goat or two being as far as their ambitions seemed to go. Dunluce proudly showed Will mills he was establishing, along the Rivers Bann and Main, although when there would be sufficient grain to keep them busy grinding was another matter. This colonising was a slow process, he kept explaining. By the end of the day, Will was better informed, understanding but scarcely impressed.

Next day they rode westwards a score of miles, across the River Roe and into Derry, along the shores of Lough Foyle. Here they were into Sir Frederick Hamilton's territory. The holdings were larger, being run by Lowland farmers from the Hamilton lands of Lanarkshire and Ayrshire. But even so there was more emphasis on cattle than on tilth, and there were vast areas untouched, the native folk seemingly unaffected by the new dispensation.

Will had not anticipated that Dunluce would accompany him on his tours of inspection, but that man insisted on so doing. The visitor was grateful, for the other was proving good company; and since hereafter he would be progressing ever further away from North Antrim, and would have to find overnight accommodation, the viscount's influence and knowledge would be of considerable help.

They went south by the Glens of Antrim and the River Main to Ballymena and then Castle Toome, the seat of Sir Claud Hamilton. Like his brother, Sir Frederick, he was from home, but they were able to stay the night in his new castle on the shore of Lough Neagh. There was little difference in conditions here than at Derry, still more emphasis on cattle in the Glens area, but most of the picturesque countryside in a state of nature – fine hunting country Will was assured. And Lough Neagh was good for the fishing.

Eastwards now they made for Larne and Belfast Lough, spending the next night at Carrickfergus Castle, where the chiefly Conn O'Neill had been imprisoned, and freed in exchange for his lands. Here Will saw his first Campbell settlers, and was pleased to find most of them making good farmers, some setting up their own mills, tanneries and even a brewery. There was quite a colony of them around Larne and also south of the lough, in the Bangor area.

Thereafter it was westwards, south of Belfast town, by Lurgan and Dungannon, in Tyrone now, where not a few English Undertakers were settled, although only one baronet was in evidence, the rest conspicuous by their absence. It seemed clear that this colonising was being done only in name by the lofty ones, leaving the actual settlement and development to their underlings and tenants.

Still further west they were into the late Abercorn's great territories of Omagh and Strabane, and here the settlements were longer established and more productive. They spent the night as guests of Lady Abercorn and the new young earl, and Will learned much of value to his enquiries, for the widow was an intelligent and practical woman, as became a daughter of the Lord Boyd, of a family which had all but ruled Scotland in James the Third's day.

With his time running out, for he could not expect the *Salutation*'s skipper to wait indefinitely for him at Dunluce, they headed north again by Dungiven and the River Roe, meeting more Campbells and even a MacAllister, who was far-back kin of Will's own, and learning not a little of problems and conditions from him, from the working farmer's point of view. Now, in fact, Will thought that he had gleaned a sufficiency for the king, and need not trouble the viscount further, even though that man asserted that their tour had been valuable for him also, however much it made him more aware of his responsibilities.

So it was back to Dunluce.

The *Salutation* was already berthed in the harbour there, having arrived the day before. So Will had only one night more of Lady Alice's hospitality, and left in the morning, assuring his hosts of his gratitude and that his report to the king would be that the viscount made a very good and able acting viceroy in Ulster, and that the appointment should be made permanent. But he would also stress the problems and difficulties of the situation, that these should be recognised and understood, and greater authority and powers given to his representative.

They parted on excellent terms, and the vessel commenced its return voyage to Bristol in distinctly colder and rougher weather than heretofore. But, however boisterous the seas, the shipmen did not complain, for the wind had reversed itself, from south-west to north-east, and this would much hasten their journey home.

Will kept sea-sickness at bay, just.

21

At least James was at Whitehall when Will got back to London, so that he did not have to leave Janet and the family to go in search of the king. James received him less accusingly than sometimes, obviously eager to hear how his great colonising project went, for of course it was all his idea in the first place.

Will sought to make his report, not without many interruptions and hectorings, some shrewd, some fatuous. He emphasised the problems of development, especially the tendency of the new land-holders, baronets of Ulster as some of them were, to absent themselves. Having got what they wanted they returned to their preferred localities.

"Is that a fact! Yon's no' responsible – it is not! We'll hae to see aboot that," James declared. "I want thae lands exploited, see you, no' left as they are. To create wealth, just. Prosperity. There, but here tae. I hae that duty to my subjects, a' my subjects, no' just the few whae hae possessions and lands – my royal duty, aye. The Irish tae, they're my subjects, are they no'? Hoo did *they* seem to you, Alexander man?"

"They appeared to be but little affected, Sire. Little concerned with the new settlers, living their own simple lives. Content with little in goods and possessions."

"They're Catholics, mind, a' Catholics. There's nae religious bicker wi' the new folk?"

"Not that I saw or heard of, Sire. I saw a few priests, but they did not assert themselves. I was with the Lord Dunluce, of course, always. And they would not wish to cross him. And he is not hard on them."

"Aye, hoo's he daeing, the man? Did I mak a guid choice?"

"Your Majesty did, I judge. I found him able, understanding, very responsible. He seeks to carry out your wishes. But he lacks the needful authority over the landed men. They can, and do, ignore him. The Hamiltons and others. And of course the absent baronets and lairds. He has nothing to enforce his orders and sway."

"I'm no' wanting armed men sent ower there. Cauld steel's no' the answer, mind. I'm no' ruling my realms wi' armies."

"No, Sire, not that. But some greater powers. Some way of making your royal will known and carried out. Of insisting on more land cultivation, clearance of scrub."

"If I was to mak him Earl o' Antrim? Would that aid him?"

"I would think so, yes. It would help his authority. The only other earl now in all Ulster is the boy, son of Abercorn. The Catholic earls all banished. If Your Majesty named him viceroy and Earl of Antrim, I believe it would be of much assistance."

"The woman? His wife, yon daughter o' Tyrone? She doesna hinder him?"

"No, I think that she is a good influence. Helps him to understand the Catholic concerns. Useful at keeping the peace between the two religious opinions. A notable woman."

"Aye, that was pairt o' my notion in choosing MacDonnell. I want nae religious bicker. Hoo did you find your Campbells daeing?"

"Well, Sire. The best, probably. My lord of Argyll had given them good and firm instructions. He has a strong grip on all his clansfolk."

"Uh-huh. I'd hae made *him* viceroy, mind. If I hadna needed him in Scotland to keep thae Hielants in order. Does MacDonnell need a bit helper, think you? An assistant, just. Would that help?"

"It might well, Sire. Yes, I think so. Ulster is a large

273

province, many counties. A deputy viceroy would aid in its rule."

"It's no' only Ulster, mind. I'm wanting a' Ireland put to rights. Ulster's just the start o' it. A great task. This colonising and settlement is a duty laid on me by the Almighty, see you. As His vice-regent here. Aye. And I'm consairned aboot yon Virginia tae. It's no' being right done by, developed. Elizabeth Tudor didna ken hoo to go aboot it, forby she gien it the name o' her virginity – and that's naething to be proud o'! Och, maybe that's what's wrang wi' the colony! A fause start! And gieing it tae a company. The Virginia Company's nae way to run a colony. It should be a royal dominion, no' the property o' a company. Mind, they're ca'ing their principal settlement after mysel', Jamestown, on the James River. Aye, but I'll hae to dae something aboot Virginia. A' we're getting frae there meantime's yon pernicious and obnoxious weed, tobacco! Much guid that does us! I've put yon man Raleigh in the tower – he brought it. But the hairm's done. An offence to the nostrils and a right threat to the lungs! You've never smoked the weed, hae you, Alexander man?"

"No, Sire. Never."

"Then dinna start. That's my royal command!" James, who had been, as so often, sitting on his bed throughout this audience, suddenly seemed to have had enough of it. He scowled, and jabbed an ink-stained finger towards the door. "Aye. Hae Steenie sent in tae me. I've made him a marquis noo, mind. But he's no' sufficiently grateful! And tell Charlie I keep an eye on him! Sae, off wi' you!"

Not ungrateful to escape from that odoriferous royal bedchamber, and wondering whether the offensive tobacco might even make a preferable aroma, Will made his bowing exit.

That Yuletide was no festive season for the court circles, for the queen was very ill, coughing blood. Charles, who had grown close to his mother these last years, was very concerned, indeed moved from his own quarters in nearby St James's to Somerset House, Anne's London palace, to be nearer her still, sleeping in an adjoining room. James was worried also, but for a different reason. Like others, he feared that she would not live much longer, and was concerned over her will. For the queen, although always in debt to Geordie Heriot the royal banker, had been buying jewellery all her days, and was reputed to have amassed a collection worth four hundred thousand pounds. The king was afraid, not only that she might will it away to someone else than her husband, to Charles, or the Ladies Huntly, Bedford or Arundel, her favourites, but that some might well be stolen by her close servants, especially Danish Anna and French Pierrot. James himself had debts of over seven hundred thousand pounds, despite all his sales of knighthoods and baronetcies and colony lands, this largely because parliament was not in a position to grant him funds. Ruling three realms from the back of a horse could be expensive for the rider, lacking regular state revenues. The king actually visited his sick wife on three occasions, and planted a watcher in Somerset House to keep an eye on those servants.

Will and Janet, with their family and Ailie Graham, were affected, because Charles was. Christmas celebrations were subdued.

Then, in February, with the queen weakening and her physician, the man Mayerne, declaring that she had dropsy as well as lung trouble, they received dire news from Scotland, via the Duke of Lennox, who was ever more frequently visiting in the north to see his beloved mistress, Mary Gray, and their young son John Stewart of Methven; he could not marry the lady for she was herself illegitimate, daughter of the Master of Gray, and after Charles and the Lady Arabella Stewart, the duke was in line for the throne and would have to marry only a woman suitable to be a queen. But the Scots tidings that he brought them were otherwise. Agnes, Countess of Argyll, was dead, dying in childbirth.

Will and Janet could scarcely believe their ears – Aurora no more. It seemed somehow impossible, totally unacceptable, that so alive and positive a woman, so vivid a character, could have passed away. They were all but stunned. And whatever sense of relief, in some respect, came to them both, that was only mere flickers at the back of minds, they knew a great and abiding sense of loss.

There was, however, a release also. They could now talk about Aurora together, and did so, as they had not been able to do previously.

Lennox brought them other strange and disturbing news. Argyll himself was behaving oddly. Not that he seemed to be plunged into any deep mourning, but that he was as though quite unsettled, as it were come adrift from his former active and masterful life. He had left Castle Campbell and his children and was not thought to be at Inveraray. In fact nobody knew where he was, rumours being even that he had actually moved south into England. Those in power in Scotland, Dunfermline the Chancellor, Mar, Haddington the Secretary of State, and others, were concerned, for, after all, Argyll was Lieutenant of the North and admiral. Will wondered whether he could have gone over to Ulster, to visit his settlers there. Lennox said that there was no word of that.

The Alexanders pondered over it all, grieved and mystified.

They were also concerned about Charles, not only the effect of the queen's illness upon him but his growing animosity against his father, which was not like that young man who, however withdrawn and undemonstrative, was seldom unfriendly. Will was afraid that he was seeing too much of Steenie Villiers, Marquis of Buckingham, which could have the effect of upsetting the king. And as well as his father's attitude towards the queen, Charles had a specific complaint. This was that James was emphasising that he wanted his son to marry the infanta Anna of Spain, and Charles had no such desire. The king's long-term preoccupation with Spain was strange, so unlikely in a Protestant monarch. But it persisted. Spain was, of course, the richest nation in the world, with its vast overseas possessions and colonies – part of the reason behind James's interest in colonising. Money, or the lack of it, was always on James's mind, and he seemed to see Spain as Eldorado indeed, and hoped that the infanta would bring a dowry of at least six hundred thousand pounds with her. His friend Count Gondomar believed that Philip of Spain could influence the Emperor Matthias over the succession of the Princess Elizabeth's husband Frederick as Elector of the Palatinate, about which there were distinct doubts because of that prince's Calvinist leanings.

There was a very unexpected and curious development of this Spanish situation with, of all people, Archibald, Earl of Argyll involved. The Alexanders were still at St James's, not at Woodstock or Oatlands as normally they would have been, for Charles would not leave his mother's side, and she was growing ever weaker despite – or partly because of, Will feared – Mayerne's prescription that she should get out of bed daily to saw wood, to encourage her lungs to function better. Late one evening, as they were thinking of bed, Argyll presented himself, to their astonishment.

His manner was as abrupt as his arrival, not his normal towards Will. "I come to say farewell," he announced. "I am for Spain."

Will gasped. "Spain! *You*, Archie? What, how comes this? I do not understand. What takes such as you to Spain?"

"The king's affairs." That was brief. "I may be gone for some time. I have sent my children to Inveraray. I want you, Will, to take heed to them. Seek to win back to Scotland soon. Give guidance to young Archibald, in especial. He may need it. He has become strong of will, over-strong for his years. Sees himself as almost a man. As you know, I have a brother Colin. Of Lundie, in

Strathmore. But we were ever at odds, never see each other. I cannot ask him to see to Archibald."

"But, Archie, why this? Why *you* to go to Spain? On the king's affairs or other? You, Lieutenant of the North and with a great clan to oversee. James could send many another . . ."

"There are good reasons why His Grace chooses myself." Argyll jerked a hand to dismiss further questioning. "Will you seek to visit Inveraray and keep an eye on my son?"

"I will try to. But I have Prince Charles, here, to attend on. The king is pressing that I remain close to him. It is not simple to win leave to go."

"James has other matters also to concern him, connected with his son. That is why I go. Charles himself may be going to Spain shortly. I cannot say more, indeed, I should not have said as much. But find you cause to go to Scotland. There is this of Ulster – it is much on James's mind. Tell him that I am concerned about some of my Campbells there, while I am away. Encourage more to go there. That I would have you visit them. That will reach him. And you can sail over from Antrim to Kintyre in only hours. And so to Loch Fyne and Inveraray."

Janet, who had been listening to all this in silence, spoke. "Your wife, my lord. Is this because of her, in some way? Was it . . .?"

"That is no concern of yours. My wife comes with me, to Spain."

They stared at him, wide-eyed. "But, but . . .?"

"I prefer no questioning over this matter, woman."

"But, Archie! We understood that your wife was dead!" Will got out.

"Agnes died, yes. But I have married again. Anne Cornwallis. Now, I must be gone. I have much to see to. But look you to young Archibald, Will. Of your kindness."

Bewildered, they saw him out.

"What means all this, Will?" Janet demanded, when they were alone. "It is scarcely to be believed. How long since Agnes died? But months? Now, married again! Leaving his children, his clan, his duties as lieutenant. And going to Spain. MacCailean Mor! This is beyond all acceptance."

"It seems to have something to do with the king and Charles. It can only be the proposed marriage to the infanta. But what concern is that of Argyll's?"

Mystified and concerned, they went to bed.

In the morning, Will announced that he was going over to Whitehall. He could not very well request audience of the king, but he could ask the Duke of Lennox if he knew what it was all about. He was usually helpful as well as well informed.

Lennox was indeed able and willing to enlighten him – and astonished Will the more. What was behind all this was that Argyll had become a Catholic. He, the Protestant leader who had been the scourge of the northern Scottish Catholics, had himself turned to Rome. Just why was not clear. But he had married again, so soon after his wife's death, and Anne Cornwallis was a Catholic, and a strong one. That almost certainly had something to do with it. He must have known the Cornwallis woman long before Agnes Douglas died to have wed her so quickly afterwards. How this came about there was no knowing. But there it was. And as a Catholic, of course, James could no longer allow him to remain Lieutenant of the North, indeed to hold any office of state. So Argyll had to be summoned south to be told so. But the earl was obdurate and would not give up his new faith. So the ever-ingenious James had typically made use of the situation. He was sending Argyll to Spain as a special envoy, a Catholic – which the British ambassador there was not – to the most Catholic monarch Philip, to help negotiate the hoped-for marriage of Charles to the Infanta Anna. That was James Stewart for you! Argyll was to be a special envoy instead of being Scotland's leading soldier, and all but an exile into the bargain!

In wonder, Will returned to St James's.

*   *   *

Queen Anne died on 2nd March, 1619, of a massive haemorrhage of blood. By royal command her body was embalmed to await her husband's decision what to do with it. He was annoyed, for it was discovered that in her will she had left all to Charles, her jewels which James had wanted, but also, to be sure, her debts as well, and the one could cancel out the other. And she had died professing the Catholic faith, which was itself no small complication.

Charles was greatly distressed, even though he had had ample warning, for all knew that his mother had no hope of life.

These were not the only matters of controversy to hold up the funeral. James ordered an inventory of her assets, and it was discovered that at least thirty thousand pounds worth of jewellery was amissing, and money also – and so were Danish Anna and French Pierrot. A fruitless search was instituted. Then there was the dispute over the funeral itself, who should be the principal mourners, the composition of the procession, the route it should take, the actual interment in Westminster Abbey, and just where therein. The debate got no help from James Stewart.

In fact it was mid-May, over two months after the death, before all could be arranged, and even then not to everyone's satisfaction. At least there was no problem created by the monarch, for he was away hunting at Royston and so could not attend. It added up to a long progression, nevertheless, to wind its way through London's narrow streets. The hearse, drawn by six black horses, bore the coffin with an effigy of the queen on top. Charles, alone, walked in front. Then came Anne's favourite horse, led by the Master of the Horse, followed by the eventually decided three principal mourners: the Countess of Arundel, Ludovick, Duke of Lennox and the Marquis of Hamilton. Then came Anne's other ladies and a long line of nobles, peers and bishops, led by Buckingham and the Earls of Pembroke, Oxford and Arundel, with the officers of state, followed by the judges, the Lord Mayor of London, the masters of the trade guilds, representatives of practically every official body in the land, and ending up with two hundred and eighty poor women, with anybody else who cared to join in. Will and Janet managed to insert themselves somewhere midway in all this. It took four hours for all the parade to wind its way through the city, and, starting at noon, it was six in the evening, after the service and the Archbishop of Canterbury's sermon, that finally Anne of Denmark was left to be interred at the east end of Henry the Seventh's Chapel. She was aged forty-five, had been married for thirty years, and, wed to James Stewart, had inevitably led a strange life. This was her final masque, at least in this one.

22

Will had no difficulty about contriving another visit to Ulster, and thence to Inveraray in Argyll, for James actually sent him to Ireland with special instructions for Dunluce, indeed to carry with him the documents elevating that man to be Earl of Antrim and appointing him viceroy, with all necessary powers. Again he sailed from Bristol, although in a different vessel this time.

The Dunluces, now Antrims, greeted him in friendly fashion, and received the instructions from the king relayed to them, some of these with raised eyebrows. James's notions as to conditions in Ulster, in the rest of Ireland also, were less than accurate, however much Will had sought to inform him. However, in general, the royal commands were such as could at least be attempted; and the new earl was pleased with his increased status, however much his countess remained prouder of being the O'Neill's daughter.

James's wish that there should be less animosity against the local Catholics, and even attempts at bringing some of them into modest positions of authority, was accepted and approved, even though it was to be done with a view to impressing Spain and the Pope rather than out of any religious togetherness. How much co-operation there would be from the Protestant settlers remained to be seen. But Antrim did inform that there had been a quite notable increase in numbers of priests observed recently, especially in Derry, these coming from the south. It was to be hoped that this did not presage trouble.

The earl considered that his rise in station would much help. He had been calling himself Lord Deputy, but viceroy sounded much more authoritative, and implied that Ulster was a royal territory and protectorate, not just a group of northern Irish counties. Will mentioned that the king had been deciding that the American colony of Virginia should be known as a dominion, and cease to be run by the Virginia Company; so this of Ulster was in line with the royal thinking.

His host had an item of news which he thought would interest the monarch. He had discovered that there were great deposits of rock salt along this North Antrim coast, and he was intending to exploit this, make an industry out of it. Salt was greatly needed in both Scotland and England, especially for the trade in salt fish and salted meat; and the process of heating sea water to gain the salt by evaporation was laborious and costly. Rock salt, crushed, could greatly aid the trade. A royal monopoly in rock salt in England would much contribute to the king's finances, and a similar monopoly for himself in Scotland would be appreciated and at the same time assist the Ulster development, as a trading venture.

Will saw the point in this, and said that he thought James would be much in favour. He did not comment on the self-interest aspect. The king had granted a number of monopolies in various commodities in England, to the major advantage of those so favoured. Antrim was probably on to something of a silver mine with his salt-mining.

They made another but shorter tour of the new settlers, with Will seeing some progress developing, visiting Campbells as a token towards Argyll. Then, four days later, he had a Dunluce fishing-craft sail him over the North Channel to Scotland, promising Antrim that he would try to prevail on more Scots Presbyterian divines to come over to Ulster, where they were much needed, especially in view of the influx of Catholic priests.

The short sea voyage past Rathlin Island to the Mull of Kintyre, a mere twenty-five miles, again emphasising for Will how close the two realms were, landed him at

Kilkerran, now being called Campbeltown, round the more sheltered east side of the Mull, in four hours. There, rather than buying a horse to ride up the sixty-mile-long Kintyre peninsula, the longest in all Scotland, he decided to seek another fishing-boat to take him on up the east side of the Mull, through the Kilbrannan Sound and into Loch Fyne, to Inveraray. With that destination, and using MacCailean Mor's name as authority, he had no difficulty in finding a craft and skipper for the next morning.

It took considerably longer to get from Campbeltown to Inveraray than it had done from Ulster to Scotland, all day in fact, which made Will recognise how readily the Irish Celtic Church missionaries, Columba and the rest, had come over to convert the Scots or Albannach, but how much more travelling they had to do once they got here, yet were able to remain in touch with their home abbeys and monasteries. And now here he was with a mission to reverse the process, to have Presbyterian Protestant clergy go to Ireland with *their* version of the true faith.

It made him wonder, as they sailed northwards among the heightening mountains, whether all this, and so much else, would have been necessary had the queen, St Margaret, not been shipwrecked at Jarrow in Northumberland in the eleventh century, been captured by Malcolm Canmore raiding there, brought to Scotland and married to the king, almost single-handedly to convert the nation from the Celtic to the Roman Catholic faith. Had she not done so, and Scotland had retained the Columban system of Church government, so very different from the Catholic, there might well have been no need for the Reformation, and none of the animosity between Christians – a sobering thought.

At Inveraray, Will found that Argyll probably had reason to be concerned about his children, or at least about his only son, Archibald, Lord Lorn. He proved to be a strange youth, odd son of a quite good-looking father and a brilliantly beautiful mother, anything but

284

handsome, with a cast in one eye, pointed, sharp features and a sullen disposition. The four girls were otherwise, all quite attractive, one particularly so, cheerful and friendly. Clan Campbell looked like being unfortunate in its next MacCailean Mor, although that was perhaps too hasty a judgment.

The young people had as guardians here Campbell of Lochnell, a far-out kinsman, and his wife, from a nearby lairdship, a pleasant enough couple, but who could not quite see what role Sir William Alexander had to play in their affairs, even though they had known that he had been tutor to Argyll. Will himself found it difficult to explain, or indeed to see what he could usefully do. He did have talks with young Archibald – he somehow could not think of calling him Archie, and was certainly not going to my lord him – but did not feel that he was making much impression. He got on well with the girls, but that was not what he was there for. He wondered why their father had besought him to come. Something to do with conscience, probably.

At any rate, it was fairly quickly clear that there was little that he could achieve at Inveraray other than assert that more Campbells should be urged to go to Ulster as settlers, flattering the youth by indicating that he, as his father's representative, should interest himself in the matter, for there were great advantages for the clansfolk over there.

He took his departure after three days, buying a horse now, a sturdy garron, not fast but reliable, to take him southwards. Archie would have given him one, but not the present regime.

By the head of Loch Fyne and over the passes to Lochs Long and Lomond, he came in two days to the edge of the Highlands, at the Flanders Moss, east of Ben Lomond, being able to spend the third night at Cardross, where the Erskines were eager for news of their daughter and grandchildren. Then on next day to Menstrie, and his usual wish that he could return here for good and lead the kind of life to which he had been born. It was strange not to think of going to visit Castle Campbell when so near. He went instead to see the Earl of Mar at Stirling Castle next day, to pass on Antrim's requirement that more Protestant divines should be urged to go to Ulster. Mar was strong for the Kirk and could have influence. Lady Minnie was aged now, but still to be reckoned with.

Then it was on to Edinburgh, to try to further the Ulster objective. Tam o' the Coogate, Mar had assured him, was the man to see, Sir Thomas Hamilton of Binning, newly created Earl of Melrose – but, oddly, said to be anxious to change that title to Haddington – Secretary of State and Lord President of the Court of Session, who was now all but ruling Scotland, with old Dunfermline ailing. If anybody could persuade the senior clergy, he could.

Melrose was a large and lively character, now in his mid-fifties, with a hearty laugh but a darting eye, but shrewd enough to have become perhaps the richest man in Scotland as well as the most powerful, this because he, and his friend Sir Thomas Hope, the Lord Advocate, with George Heriot's help from London, had set themselves up, not so much as bankers, as money-lenders. With the monarch in England, Scots who tended to seek appointments, promotions and honours had to go to London for them, and that was a costly business, especially when wives and families wanted to go with them, and clothing and appearance had to be suitably fine. But the Scots nobility and gentry were seldom rich, save in lands. So Melrose and Hope supplied the necessary moneys, and took mortgages of land as security, and so often the borrowers could not afford thereafter to redeem the lands, London proving highly expensive. So these two had become among the greatest landowners in Scotland. Melrose was Geordie Heriot's cousin.

At his splendid town-house in the Cowgate of Edinburgh, Melrose proved to be well informed, knowing not a little about Sir William Alexander and his doings. He promised

286

to bring what pressure he could on the Kirk leadership, to coax ministers to go to Ireland.

Duty done, Will faced the long road to London on his garron.

PART THREE

23

How involved can be the interplay of the forces of destiny, and how unexpected can be their results, so often completely lacking in portents. Certainly there were no hints or glimmers of warning, no harbingers or hints vouchsafed to Will Alexander over the summons to the royal presence, which was to change his entire life. He had not seen the king for a considerable time, and was not complaining about that, Charles's affairs keeping him busy, not so much tutoring now but seeking to manage his properties and entourage as Prince of Wales. Charles was coming to rely ever more on the guidance of George Villiers, Marquis of Buckingham, an association Will was not entirely happy about. When James sent for him to attend, at Hampton Court, he assumed that it might well have something to do with this matter, which he guessed might well be concerning the monarch.

And Charles did come into it, certainly, but in no way as might have been anticipated.

Will had the usual long wait before he gained audience, well into the night, and as so often it was in the king's bedchamber, James alone.

"Alexander man," he said, "I've no' seen you this whilie. What hae you been at? You, my Maister o' Requests. You been scrieving mair poetry?"

"Not much, Sire. Nothing of any import, if any of my work is. I am kept busy with the Prince of Wales's affairs. And no one has approached me with any requests to forward to Your Majesty."

"Maybe no', but there's plenties o' requests. They come at me elsewise, folk ay wanting something frae me. But

291

this o' Charlie. You'll no' hae to fash yoursel' wi' his affairs hereafter. I've got ither wark for you, man. Aye, ither wark – and tae keep you busier than Charlie does, fell busy."

Will blinked. "You mean, Sire, that I am no longer to attend on Prince Charles?"

"Just that. He's no' going to need you. He and my Steenie are going to Spain. Aye, they are so, the pair o' them. I'm sending Charlie in person, to yon Madrid, to seek the hand o' the Infanta Anna. Your Argyll advises it – he's in Madrid noo. I've been seeking this for lang. I'd hae had Henry wed her sister, mind. An alliance wi' Spain and against France maks guid sense. Nae warfare, mind, but a policy, an approved and chosen policy. Argyll, and my ambassador, Digby there, advise Charlie's visit in person. So's Philip o' Spain can see him, and no' heed tales that he's blate, backward. Steenie will go wi' him. Sae, no need for you, Alexander man, at St James's and Woodstock. They'll be gone months."

Will drew a long breath. "I shall miss the prince, Sire."

"Nae doot. And *I'll* miss Steenie. Sit doon, man, sit doon. Hear what I've got for you to dae, to keep you right busy. Hae you ever heard tell o' Acadia?"

"Arcadia? Was that not somewhere in ancient Greece? Some legendary paradise?"

"No' *Arc*adia – *Ac*adia, man. It's the name the French gie to their American colonies – forby, they're no' right colonies. In the north o' the Americas, Canada and Maine and that. Weel, the French havena done much wi' it a'. It's ower big for them – they're no guid at colonising. The main bit they tried to settle, the bit they ca' Acadia, is an island off the main Canada. Island's maybe no' the right word, for it's right sizeable, bigger than Ireland. Seven hundred miles long, they tell me, and a hundred wide. Guid land, tae. They're no' daeing muckle wi' it, a' but abandoned it. Wi' ower muckle to dae in mainland Canada, they havena developed it. Sae I'm taking it ower.

292

It's to be a new colony o' mine, in the Americas. Pairt o' the reason I want an alliance wi' Spain, so's the French'll no' think to retak it, no' wi' my Spanish allies at their back door! It's well north o' Spanish America, sae there'll be nae trouble wi' the Spaniards. That's Acadia for you. Or for Scotland, leastways."

"Scotland, Sire . . .?"

"Aye, Scotland just. See you, the English colony o' Virginia, that I'm ca'ing a dominion, hasna been right managed by the company frae the start. I want improvements there. And I want the Scots to show them hoo it should be done. Sae Acadia's to be a Scots colony. We'll change the name. And you're to see to it."

"*Me*, Sire!" Will all but choked. Almost appalled, he shook his head.

"Aye, you, man. You've had a hand in the colonising o' Ulster. You ken some o' the problems and pitfa's. Colonies are a right usefu' way o' creating wealth. Aye, and keeping my subjects oot o' mischief, daeing something usefu', no' just bickering amangst themsel's. But there's the difficulties, tae it a'. You've seen it in Ulster. This is to be a Scots venture, and you're the man to see to it."

"But, Sire . . ."

"There you are – buts again! You're an awfu' man for the questioning! You should be right pleased, gratefu'. Here's me making you the builder o' a great new colony, governor if you like, and a' you can say is but!"

"I am sorry, Sire. But I cannot find words, cannot feel worthy of this great task. Able . . ."

"Whae's mair able? Tell me that. I canna spare the MacDonnell man, Antrim. Or ithers there. They're needed at Ulster. You've been at the Ulster ploy frae the start. You ken what to dae and what no' to dae. And I'm ay here to guide you."

"You do not want me to go to this Acadia, Sire? Thousands of miles away!"

"Na, na, no' right awa', leastways. I'll send oot a pairty to tak ower the land frae the French, or what's left o'

293

them. There shouldna' be any trouble, frae a' I've heard. The Frenchies cleared thae Indians off, and then a' but abandoned it, mair consairned wi' Maine and Canada. Your task is to find the settlers and gie them their instructions. In Scotland. We'll mak mair baronets to encourage them. Parcel oot the land. Winning the price frae them, mind. Teach them the problems learned in Ulster. Och, I'll gie you fu' adhortations later."

"You mean, Your Majesty, that I am to return to Scotland? Live there again?" Will scarcely dared to ask that.

"Aye, you'll need to. I'm aiming to show thae Virginia Company folk hoo it should be done, show them the Scots can dae it. I've no' decided on a' the details yet, mind. But I'll let you hae them in due course. Meantime, prepare you to return to Scotland, this time to bide there – apairt frae visits doon here to hae my instructs and commands."

In a state of wonderment, alarm and joy mixed, Will returned to St James's with his news.

Janet, of course, was delighted to be going home, Ailie Graham likewise, although she would miss court life more than the Alexanders. Janet made light of Will's doubts about his abilities to tackle this extraordinary and enormous task. For him it would be simpler than Ulster, she declared. There would not be the religious problems. No background of ancient history to counter and traditions to seek to put down. And the settlers' conditions and difficulties would not be for him to deal with; a blessing that the king was not insisting on him going to the Americas in person. They were going to miss Charles greatly, but he was going to be away overseas anyway. The joy was that they were going back to live in Scotland, as they had all along wanted to do.

Charles was too full of his forthcoming journey to Spain with Steenie to be too upset about losing the Alexanders meantime. Not that he was eager to wed this infanta, or to wed anyone; but this would be the first major adventure of his life, the exploration of foreign lands, meeting strange

294

and different peoples. He and Steenie were going to travel as Mr John Smith and Mr Thomas Smith, going to France first, to Paris. He would see the Alexanders when he came back. That was the quiet, withdrawn Charles Stewart, come to full age this year.

So it was but a matter of planning ahead, making ready to make the great move, and awaiting the king's further instructions as patiently as they might.

These came in due course, by the hand of Lennox, who seemed more amused by Will's new responsibilities than impressed. He brought a sheaf of documents in James's own sprawling handwriting. These included a charter appointing Sir William Alexander of Menstrie, Master of Requests, to be governor of the former French colony of Acadia, this to be renamed; authority for him to sell parcels of land there, one hundred such to start with, each at a price of two hundred pounds, payable to the crown; recommendations of suitable persons to be appointed baronets of the said new colony; orders to encourage industry and all useful developments; and to aid in this, permission to establish a base currency of copper coinage, as means of exchange therein. All this in constant consultation with the king's Majesty, whose royal dominion that was to be. Issued at the Palace of Whitehall, dated 9th September, 1621.

As well as this resounding charter, there were pages of writing detailing James's advice, guidance and close instructions on innumerable aspects of the project, not all entirely practicable in the circumstances, but at least allowing Will to be able to quote royal authority for most of what he would have to do and order, and some hope of excuse and remission if things went wrong or just came to little or nothing, as seemed all too likely. Clearly Lennox, for one, saw it all in that light, and judged it one of his royal cousin's more crazy concepts. He informed that the Alexanders were to be off forthwith, no further royal audiences or interviews called for apparently.

At least Will had something for the duke to take back

to James, hopefully for his approval. Since this was to be basically a Scots New World colony, renamed, and New Scotland sounded rather too obvious and mundane, he suggested Nova Scotia, which might appeal to the king's poetic and linguistic inclinations.

So, it was packing up and farewells, at long last, after eighteen years of all but exile.

24

Transporting the young family, Ailie Graham and their belongings the four hundred miles to Stirlingshire was a major undertaking; and the Alexanders were indeed fortunate to have the help of the Duke of Lennox in the matter. That man was always glad of an excuse to get away from James for a spell and visit his beloved mistress, Mary Gray, and their son in Scotland; and he was able to convince the king that Will Alexander would require assistance, not so much with the travel as with impressing the Scots magnates as to his authority to start and control a colony over in the Americas, this being conceded. So they had not only Lennox's good company on their journeying but the benefit of the ducal guard, useful indeed in coping with the carriage, on pack-horses, of possessions and gear accumulated over the years in the south.

In fact, on that journey, Will and Lennox became firm friends. Always they had been on good terms, despite their difference in rank, but now their association grew to fellowship and warm regard, a satisfaction to them both.

In the circumstances, it took them almost three weeks to reach Menstrie, into October, the children's first sight of their ancestral home, Lennox going on to Methven Castle, near Perth, his Scots seat which he had put in the name of his son, illegitimate as the boy was. It was so good to be back among their own hills, the youngsters exclaiming at it all, almost everything they saw, all so different from what they were used to, so much more dramatic and colourful, even though the heather's purple was beginning to fade, the great rock pinnacles and craigs, the multitude of lochs, the cataracts and waterfalls of rushing torrents, the ravines and gullies, the scrub forests, bogs and mosses. Janet rejoiced.

Much of the settling in had to be left to her, for Vicky Lennox – he was insisting on first-name terms now – left Will in no doubt over the king's expectation of prompt action over the new project, Nova Scotia as he was quite happy to have it named. Admittedly, with the winter approaching, settlers could not be expected to sail off to the New World until the spring; but much fell to be done before that stage was reached anyway. Among the documents sent to Will had been two maps, not very detailed, nor probably accurate, of Acadia, from French sources; and these had to be studied closely and the territory, in theory at least, divided up into counties and baronetcies, greatly enlarged copies thereof made, and the first hundred parcels of land sketched in approximately, as per instructions. It was all exceedingly vague and fanciful, of course, for those who had never been there nor anywhere like there; but the monarch's ventures were apt to be like that. James had, for instance, by royal decree, made a corner of the tilting-ground in front of the gatehouse of Edinburgh Castle, atop its rock, a part of Nova Scotia, so that the new crop of baronets and settlers could receive their charters and documentation and be installed in their holdings there, without ever having been furth of Scotland, a typically Jamesian conception.

In a few days, taking Janet and the children and Ailie to Cardross, Will made his way northwards another almost fifty miles through Menteith, the Mounth of the River Teith, over the Pass of Leny and Strathyre to Loch Earnside, and so down Strathearn to where Methven Castle sat on a high shelf overlooking the wide and fertile vale. There he had the pleasure of meeting the renowned Mary Gray, a very lovely woman in character as in looks, and her son John Stewart of Methven, a lively youth, clearly the apple of his father's eye. The tragedy that his parents could not marry. Vicky had threatened to do so, royal opposition or none, but James had announced that he would have the marriage annulled forthwith if he did so.

Will now discovered that most of Lennox's detailed, extensive and very useful knowledge of what went on in Scotland, with the court in London, and which, where he felt it suitable, he could pass on to the king, came from Mary Gray, who was as able and discerning as she was attractive, as became the daughter of the extraordinary Patrick, former Master of Gray, who had died nine years before, the Machiavelli of Scottish politics as he had been called and claimed to be the handsomest man in Europe. The king had made a grievous error when he had refused to take Patrick Gray with him into England, and deprived him of continuing office in Scotland. Will now learned that James had been blackmailed by the master until the day of his death, to keep him quiet on a number of matters which the monarch preferred not to have broadcast, including the murky details of the Gowrie Conspiracy, the king's mother's Casket Letters and the activities of the late Logan of Restalrig, Gray's own cousin. Here were aspects of the royal career which Will had known nothing about.

But intriguing as all this was, it was not what he had come to Methven to hear. His discussions with the duke were concerned with how best to go about making known the new colonising venture and getting it started, or at least preparations made for a start. One of the problems was how to make it distinct from the Ulster project, for it was a very different endeavour and designed to appeal to a very separate type of colonist. Acadia, or Nova Scotia, was not just a score of miles away across the Irish Sea but thousands of miles over the ocean in what amounted to another world. There could be no hopping back and forth to see kin and friends for these hoped-for colonists. These would have to be prepared to commence a new life in strange and unknown conditions. They would tend to be, almost certainly, young men of an adventurous spirit who would volunteer, possibly some who might want to get away from trouble at home for one reason or another; younger sons of lairds with no likelihood of inheritance; and the like. Few men of substance and middle years could be expected to go. As for the new Nova Scotia baronets, these, it was anticipated, would pay the declared charge, and send out their dependants and nominees to do the colonising for them, not go themselves. To encourage such to take part in the venture, the sum demanded would be only two hundred pounds for the royal coffers, this for a parcel of sixteen thousand acres, as against almost six times that for the Ulster holdings – but with also, of course, vastly greater possible results from the investment. As well as this price, however, the new baronets – whom James insisted must be of suitable birth and standing to bear his titles, the standard being that their paternal grandfathers must have been arms-bearing, that is entitled to a heraldic coat of arms, and to have an annual income of at least one thousand pounds – must also agree to invest at least two thousand pounds in the colonial lands they were granted. How many would be prepared to fulfil these royal demands remained to be seen.

Will, it was decided, would see how the first hundred parcels of land were taken up, and something of results achieved, before deciding on further grants and payment levels.

So much for the policy of it all, as it were, however little Will, and for that matter Lennox, felt in tune with the entire proceedings.

Then there were the problems of making known this new project, and commending it to those who might be interested. The Scots parliament would be the ideal means of spreading the news, but it sat only infrequently these days. The duke thought that the Secretary of State, Melrose, Tam o' the Coogate – none seemed to call him other than that – would be the most useful channel to get it all known, especially if there was anything in it for himself, for he had his capable finger in every profitable pie in the land. Some small commission on every volunteer

300

enrolled by his efforts would almost certainly further the venture. His Lieutenant, Sir Thomas Hope, the Lord Advocate, would be similarly useful, especially in getting the lawyers, notaries and sheriffs informed. Mary Gray suggested that the Kirk could help, not in providing divines eager to go to this Nova Scotia, but in getting the matter known nationwide, for of course there were ministers in every parish who could announce it if they could be persuaded so to do. Again some inducement was needed. Mar could probably help here, strong for the Kirk. Will conceded all this, but pointed out that his authority in the matter did not extend to paying out any of the king's precious moneys. He had been given the right to issue some sort of currency for the colony, yes, but that was for the future; and anyway would not be of any immediate value in Scotland itself. Lennox promised to speak to James on this initial difficulty, and to suggest that some small disbursement would pay in the long run, indeed was probably essential.

So Will returned to Cardross more clear in his mind as to his tasks, but more than ever aware of the obstacles and stumbling-blocks involved. The Ulster development was simple compared with this one which had been landed in his lap.

He went to see Mar again, who agreed to use his influence with the Kirk to get the matter known widespread; but what could be offered to the ministers and elders to persuade them that it was any concern of theirs? Will had to admit that he could offer nothing specific as yet, save perhaps that the Kirk of Scotland should be established as the Church of Nova Scotia before any Episcopalian or Catholic influence gained a hold.

Mar, who had been quite prominent in the Ulster campaign, which of course was still going on, was concerned that the two issues should not get confused nor opposed, especially that the Irish development should not suffer; he had sent some of his Erskines over there. Will thought that there should be little of clash, the two endeavours being so different in scope and appeal.

He decided to put off any visit to the Secretary of State and others until he should learn from James what he might offer as inducement, if anything, for aid. Meanwhile he went to enlist the help of his father-in-law. Sir William Erskine's contacts in Glasgow should be useful, for that city had outstripped Edinburgh as the trading and merchanting centre of the land since the Reformation, and might well be a source of colonists, if scarcely potential baronets. Also Will urgently wanted to know something about his new territory which he had given name to, his ignorance of it all being shameful. Glasgow, and better still Dumbarton nearer the mouth of the Clyde, were the principal seaports of western Scotland; and if seafarers were to be found who knew something of the Americas it would be there to look for them. Sir William agreed to make enquiries. He could ride to either in a day, thirty-five miles.

The settling in at Menstrie Castle proceeded with satisfaction for all concerned. Janet was delighted to have a house of her own to see to, something she had never known hitherto, since her marriage, always having occupied quarters in royal establishments, Oatlands, St James's and Woodstock. Now she could make a home of Menstrie. It was modest in size admittedly but sufficient for the needs of even a growing family – for she was pregnant again. The children loved it all, the surroundings particularly, those nearby Ochil Hills for climbing and exploring, the Blairlogie woods to play in, the meanders of Forth for boating and fishing. Ailie Graham chose to remain with them, almost one of the family now. Will himself did not allow his preoccupations over Nova Scotia to spoil his joy at being home, to stay, at last. He recognised that this colonising effort must be a very long-term matter, impatient as the king might be for results, down in England. It was certainly not something which could be rushed, with no real start of any significance until the late spring, as even James had conceded.

At least Will learned something of the land he was responsible for that Christmastide. They had a visitor, sent by Erskine at Cardross, a youngish man named Duncan Drummond from Dumbarton, a shipmaster there, who had visited Acadia on voyages to Canada, a genial, hearty and down-to-earth character, who seemed nowise impressed by the company he found here but was in no way disrespectful. He was a skipper's son and a fisherman's grandson, bred to the sea.

Drummond's information about the new territory was invaluable, and enabled Will to fill in many large gaps in the two French maps he had been given by the king. The island was some three hundred and fifty miles long and one-third that in width, separated from mainland Canada by the narrow Strait of Canso. It was not unlike the western side of Scotland in character, its coast indented with innumerable bays, creeks and inlets separated by headlands, on all sides, with some hills inland but no mountains. It was forested with pine and birch and hemlock, and a tree called balsam. There were a great number of lochs inland and much marshy land. The climate was not unlike Scotland's also, but with much more fog. It had been discovered by the Cabots, father and son, Italians but operating from Bristol, but taken over by the French at the same time as Canada. But they had done little with it, apart from driving out the Micmac Indians, who had mainly fled to Maine and Canada. There was another island nearby to the north-east, Cape Breton. Was that part of Sir William's domain also?

Will thought not. Nothing had been said about that, and it sounded as though he had quite enough to cope with, lacking it. Were there many French settlers still on Acadia?

Drummond did not think so. There were much greater opportunities for them just across in Canada, and most had gone there. So Acadia was left very much as it had always been, save for the lack of its Indians – why King James had annexed it, no doubt. The new colonists ought not to find it difficult to take over.

How much land was suitable for tillage and crop-growing? Not a great deal, he was told, at least, not without much tree-felling, for most of the territory appeared to be forested. Not that Drummond had penetrated far inland from the coasts – he had had no call to – so he might be wrong. Why he knew what he did was because he had been storm-bound there twice, one time for a week. But there were great tracts inland of which he knew nothing. He had seen many deer, including great horned creatures which he had heard were called moose. And round the coasts the fishing was very good; indeed such Frenchies as remained seemed to be all fisherfolk and clinging to the shoreline.

This was all a considerable help to Will. And it occurred to him that this Duncan might well be of further aid. Was he likely to be going back across the ocean soon hereafter? Yes, he learned, he made constant voyages to Canada and Maine on behalf of the Glasgow merchants. Then, would Duncan do some exploring of Nova Scotia for him? He would be well rewarded. And while he was at it, if he could bring back with him on his next crossing some sackfuls of the local soil, this would be a help. For some soil deposited therefrom would enable the new land-holders and baronets to take sasine of their new properties in time-honoured Scots fashion by standing on the said earth and holding a fistful of it, while vowing the required oath of allegiance, in token that all land was held of the king. The shipmaster hooted at this request, but promised to do as required.

Drummond stayed three days at Menstrie, seeming in no hurry to leave. Undoubtedly this had something to do with Ailie Graham, to whom he appeared to have taken a fancy, without being noticeably rebuffed; indeed the third afternoon the pair of them went off for a walk, drizzling rain as it was, and were quite some time in returning. Will and Janet were nowise displeased at this development, for Ailie deserved some diversion; and a link between her and Duncan Drummond would help to make that man the more concerned to be helpful, making more visits probable.

Being governor of a colony, Will was discovering, could entail unexpected preoccupations.

25

If the spring of 1622 was looked forward to for some sort of start on the colonial initiative, it was still more personally so for the Alexander family, for Janet was delivered of another son, to great rejoicing, and a reasonably short and uncomplicated labour. The boy was born on St Anthony's Day, and so was to be named Anthony. So young William had a brother.

Soon thereafter his father acquired his first would-be baronet of Nova Scotia, and most unexpectedly. They had a visit at Menstrie from, of all people, Mary Gray from Methven, Lennox's lady, with her son John and a large, florid man of later middle years whom she introduced as a kinsman, William Gray of Pittendrum, in Angus, a cousin of her late father's, who had become a prosperous merchant in Dundee, laird or none. He was, she declared, prepared to consider investing some of his substance in the new overseas colony, and had a younger son and grandson who might be persuaded to emigrate to this Nova Scotia.

Will was much heartened, and grateful to Mary. "Here is a notable occasion, then," he said. "The very first to come forward. Few know about it all, as yet, to be sure. His Majesty will be much pleased to hear of your interest, sir."

"His Majesty isna apt to think well of the Grays, Sir William," the other announced thickly. "He didna act kindly towards my cousin, Patrick, Lord Gray, who did much to win him English Elizabeth's throne. You do not reckon that this will weigh with him against me? Prevent him from awarding me one of these baronetcies?"

306

"I am sure not, sir. When you are the first to support his project. I will strongly recommend your name. And I would think that the Duke of Lennox would do likewise." And he glanced at Mary.

She nodded. "I think that William need have no fears."

"You understand the terms of the grants? In moneys and to what you are committed?" Will asked. "You pay two hundred pounds to me, to transmit to the king. And agree to invest two thousand pounds in works in the colony. And to send out there settlers to develop your land, which will amount to sixteen thousand acres of the territory. You would accept these terms?"

"I will tell you that, Sir William, if you will tell me something of what I am getting. Sixteen thousand acres is a deal of land. But what is it like? What state is it in? How productive? How safe from French repossession? The settlers – will they be supported? Protected? I am a merchant, concerned with trading. What possible goods are they going to be able to deal in? All this and more I need to know."

"That I can well understand, sir. I myself have never been there, to be sure. But I am told by one who has been, twice, that there are large possibilities. The island, if it can so be called, extends to nearly five hundred thousand square miles, with over one thousand miles of coastline, excellent for fishing. So the export of salt fish could be important, as here, and the ships taking the fish could carry rock salt from Antrim on the outward journey. The land is heavily forested, so the timber trade could be valuable. The climate is like our own, so that grain can be grown and cattle and sheep raised. There may well be other products and yields, merchandise. From what I hear, most of what is produced here in Scotland could also be produced there."

"And Canada? So nearby. French Canada?"

"I do not think that there will be any danger from there. The French have far more than they can cope with in vast

307

Canada. Their Acadian settlers have almost all gone over there. That is how King James was able to take the island over. He is sending out a small force to ensure the safety of the colonists."

"And when will settlement commence? How soon?"

"I cannot think that there can be any real moves this year. Some prospectors, yes. A few to spy out the land, draw up divisions of properties, mark boundaries, restore abandoned French houses and townships. But the main plantation thereafter."

"And the moneys?"

"Ah, that is different! King James requires the baronetcy charges forthwith. He is ever in need of siller. But they are considerably less than the Ulster ones."

"No doubt with reason, Sir William!"

"On this of moneys," Mary Gray put in. "The duke sends word that King James is prepared to allow a small charge to be offered to such as may introduce a number of colonists – but modest, he insists! Also that James has learned that coal has been discovered in Acadia, readily available, it seems. And this should be an added source of wealth for settlers."

Gray nodded his acknowledgment.

Other news from Lennox was that the king had suffered some stomach ailment, the which threw him into a panic, assuming that he was about to die, although the physicians assured that he had merely over-eaten. As a result, Charles and Buckingham had had to postpone their visit to Spain in case the prince suddenly had to assume the rule – all a nonsense, but cause of much upheaval.

The visitors stayed overnight at Menstrie. Will was much taken with the young man John Stewart, discovering something that he had not known, and not mentioned hitherto, that he was in fact *Sir* John, not through any gesture towards the duke his father but because the youngster had been in a position to come to the king's aid during that eventful visit to Scotland, when the monarch was arrested by mistake, and in an outburst of thankfulness, had knighted the youth there and then. John was all but embarrassed by this gesture, for he was a modest young man.

Janet and Mary got on excellently together. The Alexanders were invited, pressed, to visit Methven whenever they felt inclined for a break, with or without their young people. They parted, already good friends.

Will was now in a position to call on the Secretary of State. He rode to Edinburgh in March.

Tam o' the Coogate, now in his sixtieth year, had heard something of the Nova Scotia project, but was interested to hear details, asking shrewd questions and perceiving the difficulties. When Will asked him to help make the endeavour known, and intimated that the king was prepared to allow some small commission on the fees of potential baronets introduced, the older man was quick to demand how much. The probably wealthiest man in Scotland was not past seeking to earn even modest further increments. Will was himself unsure of what James would consider allowable, and took a chance by asking Melrose what *he* judged suitable, to be told without the least hesitation that ten per centum would be his requirement, that is twenty pounds on each two hundred pounds. Accepting that here was a man who knew just what he was at, and that almost certainly, while driving a hard bargain, he would want to make the most of it, and was in a position to influence many, Will agreed, only mildly intimating that such candidates as were introduced through the earl should make this known, so that the due allowance could be calculated accurately and others not become involved. Nodding, Melrose said that was wise. He would see what he could do. And it occurred to him that his friend, Sir Thomas Hope, the Lord Advocate, might well wish to partake in this arrangement. Indeed, who knew but Hope, already a knight, might wish to take up one of these baronetcies for himself, so that he might pass the title on to a son. Will agreed that the earl should involve Hope in the matter. These two were, in fact, running Scotland to all intents, these days.

On the subject of governance, Melrose informed him that the former Chancellor, the Earl of Dunfermline, had just died, Prince Charles's early guardian.

So it was back to Menstrie, to await results from these tentative moves and probings. Will hoped that James, in London, might not become impatient. Would preoccupations with his health help in the matter, or the reverse?

That late spring, and well into the summer, Will Alexander, like everybody else, had more to worry him than matters colonial – the weather. Rain hit Scotland and Ireland, and to a lesser extent England also, rain, rain and more rain, day after day, week after week, heavy, cold, drenching rain, beyond anything in living memory. As a result, flooding was everywhere, fields could not be worked, cattle and stock were drowned, rivers out of all control. Menstrie did not escape, with the Ochils cascading torrents down to the hillfoots levels to such an extent that the little castle became all but an island, the salt tides of the nearby Forth stained brown with washed-away soil and peat. There would be hunger in the land after this, for without planting and little tilth there could be no real harvest.

In the circumstances little interest could be aroused over the Nova Scotia project, nor over the still ongoing Ulster one, for the word was that matters were even worse in Ireland. In Scotland lairds and landed folk were far too busy seeking to save their property and rescue their flocks and herds; travel was difficult with fords impassable and bridges swept away. Colonising was scarcely at the forefront of many minds.

It was July before the rains began to slacken off, and occasional glimpses of the sun illuminated a waterlogged land. Men commenced the mammoth and long-continuing tasks of trying to repair damage, drain off water, salvage gear, rebuild dykes, embankments, barns and sometimes houses, bury carcases of cattle and sheep. At least, for Will Alexander, there were no urgent commands from England, since the messengers' journeyings would have been all but impossible. Mary Gray and her son had to do without visits from Vicky Lennox.

In the circumstances it seemed strange that almost the first long-distance traveller they should welcome to Menstrie should be the furthest-travelled of all, none other than shipmaster Duncan Drummond, returned from a voyage to Canada and eager to report – or was it to see Ailie Graham? At any rate, he brought a pack-horse laden with sacks of good Nova Scotian soil.

He had much to tell them. He had visited Acadia both going and coming, and was thus enabled to explore something of the north and south sides of the island, and had much new information. There was more possibly cultivable land than he had thought, especially on the north, along the shore of the vast Bay of Fundy, which he had never before visited. There were many inlets there which would make excellent harbours. Small clusters of French settlers still hung on here and there, but not many overall. The innumerable inland lochs were rich in fish. Fruits grew. The forests were extensive, but felling would not be especially difficult. It all should make for good and profitable colonising.

Thanking Duncan, Will told him that he could be given a quite substantial holding for himself, to occupy if he so wished, or to sell to some other colonist. The shipmaster said that he would consider it, and added that he would consult with Ailie, which perhaps held its own significance.

Their visitor again showed a certain reluctance to depart.

There was practically no harvest to reap in Scotland that autumn. Moreover, so many barns and stores had been flooded, even demolished, that little of reserves of grain were available. And with stock drowned, and what had survived on the high ground in poor shape, meat was in short supply. Hunger stalked the land. But from Ireland the word was even worse. Famine reigned there, harsh famine, with folk as well as beasts dying.

It was a year which would not be forgotten.

It certainly was an inauspicious time to be recruiting colonists. Once the roads became passable, Will did visit various centres, Perth, Dundee, Cupar, Glasgow, Ayr, Kilmarnock, seeking to spread the news of opportunities and possibilities, enlisting, in the king's name, the help of provosts, magistrates and local magnates. He could not claim any enthusiastic response, but was grateful for any interest shown. He was only planting the seed, he told himself.

Then, in late autumn, he received a message from the Earl of Melrose to come to Edinburgh, for he had some potential baronets for him. Without delay he did as suggested, and was much heartened by what he discovered. He would have been quite pleased to hear of half a dozen possibles. But the Secretary of State had over a score of names for him, and, as far as he could gauge, of approximately the right standing and background to be baronets, or at least to satisfy the king. Tam o' the Coogate most evidently knew when he was on to a good thing and did not let the grass grow under his feet. If these nominees proved suitable, the monarch already owed him some five hundred pounds. Scanning the list of names, Will noted that there were three Campbells among them, the lairds of Ardnamurchan, Auchinbreck and Glenorchy. The last certainly would be approved by James, however much of a scoundrel was Black Duncan of the Cowl, for he it was who had put down the Clan Alpin, the MacGregors, in 1603, most bloodily, when the king had proscribed the Gregorach name for his own reasons.

A little uncertain as to the procedure now, when Will got home it was to learn that Lennox was at Methven, and suggesting that he should pay a visit there. Glad to

312

seek advice, he was off next day, Janet accompanying him, pleased to be going to see her friend Mary Gray.

The duke, astonishingly, announced that he had been married in the interim, saying that it was a marriage only in name, and seeming quite unconcerned over the matter, as indeed Mary Gray appeared to be. It was a mere formality, done to please James, who was worried about the succession, now declaring himself doubtful as to whether young Charles was sufficiently a man to bear a son. This wedding, to the widowed Countess of Hereford – it had to be a widow who had already borne a son, to satisfy the king as to fruitfulness – was not the first, for Vicky had apparently been married before, twice, again only in name, and as a young man, his second wife having died as long ago as 1596. Mary Gray remained, as she had always been and always would, his true partner and love, and seemed quite happy with the situation.

The duke brought instructions for Will from the monarch, who appeared to be recovered in health. He had sent to inform the young King Louis the Thirteenth of France – who incidentally had now married the Spanish Infanta who had been Prince Henry's hoped-for bride – that he was taking over the territory of Acadia, but not Cape Breton, and that any French citizens still dwelling there would be well treated and not dispossessed of their holdings. Will was so to direct his new colonists. Louis, already in trouble with Spain, despite the marriage, was seeking peaceful relations with England, and evidently had made no objections, Canada being more than enough as a challenge to hold and develop. James ordered that, to encourage involvement in Nova Scotia, there were to be monopolies granted, at a price of course, on certain imported commodities, such as the rock salt Will had mentioned from Antrim, whisky and sundry wines, gunpowder, paper, sailcloth and various other items which the colonists could not produce for themselves, Will to ascertain and assess these. Each new baronet was to be responsible for sending out at least six men, armed, to provide the necessary guard, these to serve for a minimum of two years. No land-holder was to own more than three miles of the coastline, so that the fishing industry would not be monopolised. And so on, Will taking due note, however uneasy he was about those monopolies.

Lennox was interested in the list of names supplied by Melrose, as well as the others which Will himself had produced, and Mar had suggested. He conceded that such candidates would have to be interviewed before any recommendation was made to the king, and at Will's suggestion agreed to assist in this, admitting that his ducal presence might possibly help to give the meetings some additional authority, and smilingly adding that it would give him a good excuse to remain longer in Scotland with Mary and John. So they would have to send out couriers to all these nominees, to have them come to be interviewed, and promptly. Where? Will said that here at Methven Castle would be more impressive than at Menstrie, and this also was accepted. The actual installing of the baronets, of course, would have to be done at Edinburgh on the tilting-ground, but that would be only after the king's approval of the names.

Fortunately Lennox had a sufficiency of guards and ser-vitors who could be despatched as messengers throughout the land. These were sent off to as far north as Moray and Banff, west to Argyll and Lochaber, east to Angus and Fife and south to the Borders. Ten days hence, then, and the first possibles should arrive at Methven.

It was an enormous help having Vicky Lennox there when the would-be baronets began to arrive at the castle, most of them being much superior landowners to this upjumped Laird of Menstrie. As well as being a duke, Lennox was Lord High Admiral of Scotland and Great Chamberlain of the United Kingdom, however little these titles meant to him, and so sufficient prestige was provided for even Campbell of Glenorchy and MacDonald of Sleat, chiefs of proud lineage. Most of the thirty or so who compeared in the three days allocated were rather less lofty, but all able to fulfil the royal requirement of at least an arms-bearing grandfather, lairds of some standing, indeed four of them chiefs of their name, of that Ilk, as they were termed, Napier, Riddell, Elphinstone and Nicolson. A surprising number came from Aberdeenshire and the north: Burnet of Leys, Johnstone of Caskieben, Leslie of Wardis, Forbes of Pitsligo, Turing of Foveran, Innes of Balvenie, Munro of Foulis, and others. To the south, Lothian and Ayrshire were particularly well represented, with even Sir Alexander Gibson, Lord President of the Court of Session, there in person. Melrose had cast his net wide.

Will felt highly uncomfortable, at first, interviewing all such, concerned not to make it seem like any form of inquisition or examination, but rather a friendly exchange, the duke assisting in this. But certain points and enquiries had to be put forward, conditions explained and assessments made and, of course, the financial aspects emphasised. By the third day it had become easier, simpler, particularly as Mary Gray had made all the visitors welcome to the castle, and sought to have a social atmosphere prevail. It was a great relief to Will that not one of the applicants was to be rejected, at least by him, although King James might have other views, to be sure. One or two did express their own doubts when they heard the fullest reports they could be given on the Nova Scotia conditions; but since obviously none was actually thinking of going there themselves, not to stay at any rate, these conditions were generally accepted. All agreed to make the necessary payments.

That first session over, the interviewers were reasonably satisfied. There would have to be others, of course, although whether they would ever reach James's suggested one hundred seemed unlikely. But meantime Lennox could return south and tell the king that progress was being made, taking with him a list which Will had made out of this first group. He, Will, would continue with his making known and advocacy of the entire

315

colonising project, seeking to enroll ordinary settlers also, not just prospective baronets. All one hundred and fifty land-holders need not be such.

That, and pray that 1623 would be a better year for the hungry lands.

26

That winter was a hard one, with gales and snow, but at
least there was no repetition of the deluge; and the spring,
late in coming, saw hardship widespread and prolonged.
But with April matters improved, and all began to hope
for a reasonable season of growth and the fair and so vital
harvest.

By then Will had accumulated another score or so
of baronetcy applications, including one from the Lord
Advocate, Sir Thomas Hope. His, with the Lord President
Gibson's name, commended the development to others, so
that the lists were looking satisfactory, as to quality as well
as quantity. Will meantime composed a pamphlet entitled
An Encouragement to Colonise, and had it printed and
distributed as widely as he could, this proving helpful.

In May young John Stewart brought a message from his
father, saying that the king was requiring Will to attend
on him. While he was doing this, and away from home,
why did not Janet and the young people visit Methven as
company for Mary? The duke also informed that Charles
and Buckingham had departed for Spain in February, via
Versailles, as Messrs John and Thomas Smith.

So it was off to England again for Will, but hopefully
not for long.

At Whitehall he had no difficulty, on this occasion, in
gaining an audience with his liege-lord. He was struck
immediately with the change in James's appearance, if
not in his manner and attitudes. He had grown very
noticeably heavier, more fleshy, grey, with his hands
trembling as he gesticulated. Never had he been agile,
with those legs, but now he was hobbling and unsteady.

At the age of fifty-seven he was looking much older than his years.

Although as far as greeting went Will might have been gone for only a week or two, the royal attitude as critical as ever.

"Aye, sae you've come then, Alexander man! You ay tak your time," he charged. "I've looked for you afore this. You may be no' bad a poet but you're a right sluggard tae, at times – aye, a sluggard." And the trembing hand pointed.

"I am sorry that Your Majesty deems me so. I came so soon as I received your command. And the roads are in a bad state for travel, Sire."

"Maybe so. But you've taken your time upby there in Scotland. Getting my baronets. Vicky Lennox brought me a pickle o' names back in October. Since then, naething. You'll hae to dae better than that, man, as governor o' your Nova Scotia."

"Conditions, Sire, storms, floods, near-famine, have not been apt for turning men's minds towards colonisation. I have done what I can to make the endeavour known. I have written and published a pamphlet to encourage it all." Will recognised that it was as pointless as it was improper to argue with the monarch. "Since my lord duke brought Your Majesty those names, I have gathered over a score more. My lord Earl of Melrose has been very helpful. As has Sir Thomas Hope. I have the new names here."

"Aye, Tam o' the Coogate kens hoo to fill his pouch, the man! Vicky tells me you're geing him twenty pounds o' every two hundred pounds o' the price. Yon's a fair scandal! Right iniquitous! Ten pounds would hae been mair than plenties."

"Those were his terms, Sire. I could not chaffer. It was that, or no recommendations. And he has done more, provided many more names, than anyone else. Made Your Majesty's project known. I judge the moneys well spent."

"It was *you* I sent to dae this colony-bigging, no' yon Tam Hamilton!"

318

"It is no easy task, Sire. I would say that we have been fortunate to enroll over fifty claimants for the baronetcies. And a number of other settlers who do not seek more than the lands. I am having to compete with the Ulster plantation, we must not forget."

"Dinna tell me what to forget and what no'!" Clearly James Stewart was not at his most amiable this day. Lennox had said that he was now suffering the pains of arthritis.

"I meant no disrespect, Sire. May I ask if Your Highness found the names the duke brought you suitable? Approve of these to be baronets? He, the duke, helped me interview and select them."

"Och, they're no' bad. Some rogues amongst them, nae doot. Especially thae Hielantmen! But they'll dae."

"The new list I have brought, Sire, includes the Lord Advocate himself, and the Lord President of the Session."

"Rogues tae, but mair clever ones! You still hae a lang way to go to your one hundred and fifty, mind."

"True. But *all* need not be baronets, you said. It takes time . . ."

"How go the monopolies, eh?"

Will had been rather dreading this question. He was not happy about these monopolies, bribes he would have called them, and apt to be to the disadvantage of most save the grantees.

"So far, none has asked for such, Sire."

"You'd hae won mair if you'd gien them the offer, belike! A bit cream on the milk! I've thocht on some mair to add. Commodities, just. Tools, aye implements. That they'll no' can mak themsel's, no' for lang. Metals. Axe-heids and the like. Saws. Scythes. Plough-shares. Och, plenties. Then there's cordage, rope. You'll maybe can think o' mair."

Will nodded, non-committal.

"This o' your currency – hae you done aught aboot that, man?"

"No, Sire. I am uncertain as to what is required. What it is for. The need for it. What to do with it . . ."

"I tell't you. Sakes, I'm no' haeing our guid siller taken awa' ower there! The settlers'll hae to hae their ain coinage. Base coinage'll dae – just copper. Yon tourners, or bodles. You'll need to contrive it. When the settlers gang, they're no' to tak my siller. We're short o' it as it is! Sae the moneys they tak wi' them will be your copper tourners, the governor's coinage. They'll gie their siller to you, and get copper in exchange, just. And you'll send me maist o' it! Keep a pickle for yoursel', but maist to my treasury. I can dae wi' it."

"Who makes this copper money, Sire? And how much?"

"You see to that. You'll need plenties. Coppersmiths'll mak it for you. In Edinburgh or Dundee or Glasgow."

"They, the smiths, will need to be paid. For the copper. And their labour."

Majesty eyed him levelly, however tremblingly. "You'll can see to that yoursel'. A bit invest, for you! You'll soon mak a deal mair than you pay for the copper!"

"M'mm. I am not a rich man, Sire, Menstrie no large lairdship."

"You *will* be, if you use your wits, man Alexander! Your settlers are to invest two thousand pounds each, at the least, in Nova Scotia. The moneys they tak there will hae to be in *your* coinage. So they'll exchange their siller for it wi' you afore they leave. You'll dae right weel oot o' it. Fix your rate o' exchange. I'm to get the main profit, mind. But wi' maybe ten percentum, you'll no' dae badly!"

Will blinked. This was something which had never crossed his mind, an entire new conception. Questions surged in him.

"The settlers – they will not invest their two thousand pounds right away," he pointed out. "They will tend to spread it out over the years."

"Ooh, aye. You'll no' get a' oor siller in ae lump, see

320

you. It'll keep on coming in ower the years. An invest, as I said. And you'll can think up mair monopolies, belike. Use your wits, man." James abruptly changed the subject. "You've no' seen Vicky Lennox o' late, hae you?"

"No, Sire. Not since the late autumn. He was not in his quarters here, when I sought him."

"I sent him awa' to tak the waters at yon place near to Windsor. He's no' right, is Vicky. No' the man he was, this whilie."

"The duke? Is he ill, Sire?"

"Mayerne – he's my physician – says he's got the dropsy. The right name's ascites, mind. It's to dae wi' the liver, I'm tell't."

"But . . . always he has seemed so well. Dropsy! Surely not, Sire?"

"That's what Mayerne says. He's no' been richt these months back. Gets weary, just. Ankles swollen. Nose bleeding. Och, we're a' mortal, mind! I'm no' that weel, mysel'. Colic and vomiting. It can be a sair fecht. It'll come tae you tae, ae day, Alexander man. We're no' immortal, no' oor bodies, that is, even the Lord's Anointed! Oor souls, that's different. They go on, aye – go on."

"But the duke is not old." Hastily Will added, "Nor are you, Sire, to be sure. He cannot be more than fifty years."

"Och, he's no' deid yet, see you! Nor am I! Thae waters'll maybe help, Mayerne says. I'd miss Vicky, mind. Especially wi' Steenie awa' in yon Spain. Aye. Weel, off wi' you, man. And get you your coinage started. I'm wanting to see some results frae this Nova Scotia ploy, some siller in my hand. Off wi' you . . ."

Sorry not to see Lennox, and concerned greatly over this of the duke's health, Will returned to Scotland without delay, but little enheartened by the prospects of possibly becoming quite a rich man one day, if James was right in his assessments. Did he desire wealth? Sufficient moneys for the comfort of his family and the well-being of his property and dependants, yes. But the sort of wealth suggested, and by the means put forward? The Nova Scotia project was, he judged, worthy, and might come to quite important results for many. But as a means of filling his own pockets, he was not so sure. Especially by this of monopolies. These he would not push, if he could avoid it. As for the currency, probably there was no ill in that. He could see why the king did not want the precious silver coinage of the realm to leave these shores, in short supply as it seemed to be already, the nation's coffers always empty apparently, although why that should be when the essential worth of the land, and men's skills, had not diminished, he could not understand. But copper would do equally well over in the colony – it was only a token of true wealth, after all. Any kind of coin would serve as well as siller. Yet why did not that apply here, at home? Setting his rate of exchange would be the problem. He would need guidance on that. How many copper bodles, or turners as James called them, to a merk or a bawbee? Or a pound Scots? Possibly Melrose could advise him on that – but at a price, to be sure! Lennox would be better. But . . .

The duke's state was never far from his thoughts. What was his new wife thinking of it all? Dropsy, if indeed that was what he was suffering from, was a serious ailment. It was said that was what Robert the Bruce died from, not leprosy as he had feared. Some failure of the heart's function, he thought. Will did not know much about such matters; but he was aware that folk could die of one kind of dropsy or another. But if it was caught in time it might not be so serious. This Mayerne, he who had treated Queen Anne, having her get out of her bed to saw wood, was he so able a physician? James apparently thought so, but . . .

Did Mary Gray and her son know of this illness of Lennox's? he wondered. If not, should he go and inform them? Would that be kind, or just the reverse? Worry them unnecessarily, when they could do nothing about

322

it? They might wish to go down to London, to be with him. James might have exaggerated. He would ask Janet what she thought he should do.

27

Will halted at Edinburgh on his way north, to consult
with the Earl of Melrose regarding the difficult matter
of currency and exchange, finding that able individual
very helpful, indeed spending the night at the very
fine town-house in the Cowgate. As ever, the earl was
unhesitant and definite in his advice, and clearly admiring
of what he saw as Will's shrewdness in contriving this of
the coinage, which he perceived as a notable source of
personal wealth as well as a wise policy. In fact Will knew
some discomfort when he realised that he had gone up
considerably in the other's estimation as a consequence.

Melrose declared that the rate of exchange for those
bodles or turners could go up or down depending on
the relative prosperity at home or in the colony. But
advised that a median rate should be set to start with.
It would be wise to link the Nova Scotian money with
the English penny, shilling, and pound rather than with
the Scots pound and merk, which had a much lower value,
three shillings and eightpence and thirteen shillings and
fourpence as against the pound sterling. Although most
of the settlers would undoubtedly be Scots, at least to
start with, their main trade would as undoubtedly be
with England, much the richer realm and with ten times
the population. A Scots turner was worth only one-sixth
of an English silver penny, so seventy-two turners to one
shilling. Make the Nova Scotian turner equal halfway
between – that would be fair, three to the penny, thirty-six
to the shilling. So, when the new baronets and colonists
paid their first instalments of the two thousand pounds
to be invested, they would get in exchange seventy-two

thousand turners for each one hundred pounds. But that would be worth twice that in Scotland. After deducting the cost of the copper coins and other expenses, and the amount sent south to the king, there would still be a sizeable sum left to compensate Sir William for all his trouble.

Will's mind reeled at the sound of these thousands, he who had never had to deal with large sums of money. Seven hundred and twenty turners to the pound sterling, seventy-two thousand to the hundred pounds! That was beyond all belief and coping!

The earl pointed out that they would not all be in single coins. Ten, twenty and even hundred turner pieces would serve, and cost a deal less to mint. Put that to His Grace in London, and he reckoned that it would all be well received. And the colonists, seeming to get double the value of the Scots turners or bodles, would make no complaint! So long as Sir William did not think to pay *him* his twenty pounds sterling on each baronet's fee of two hundred in anything but good sterling siller!

Obviously Tam Hamilton did not have much to learn from his banker cousin Geordie Heriot in London!

The earl also said that he could recommend an Edinburgh coppersmith in the Grassmarket to mint the coins at a reasonable price – no doubt at a reasonable commission also, for himself – Will to let him know what design he favoured on the pieces. They would all co-operate very well, he was sure.

Well content to leave all this in the Secretary of State's capable if acquisitive hands, Will passed a comfortable evening, and departed for Menstrie next morning.

It was good to be home, as always, even though he had been away barely a month. Janet had word for him of seven more potential baronets which, with the five Melrose had added to the list, made a dozen extra to please the monarch.

Janet was upset to hear about Lennox's illness, but advised against going to inform Mary Gray of it. She might already know, of course. But if not, it would be a pity to distress her when there might be no need, the duke possibly recovering his health. If he himself had not sent her word, he presumably would not want her troubled. Anyway, what could she do, other than fret? Now that Lennox was married to this new duchess, Mary could scarcely go to London to be with him. She could send young Sir John perhaps . . .

Will was in a way relieved not to have to be the bearer of ill news.

That summer was, on the whole, a good one, not only for Will and his family and his projects but for Scotland itself, and to a lesser extent Ireland. For the land redeemed itself with a bountiful harvest, and good weather to reap and store it. The mills got busy again, after long inaction. Conditions seemed to induce a better climate towards colonisation. Will had his pamphlets reprinted. Sample coins came from the coppersmith in Edinburgh, single, ten, twenty and hundred turner pieces, with the king's head on one side and a lion regardant, instead of rampant, on the other, which Will had judged was apt enough. The estimate of the cost of the many thousands of these seemed to him direly expensive, and he would have to pay at least a proportion of it before he could receive the first instalments. On a visit to Edinburgh to urge one or two small alterations, and to decide on how much to be produced as a first minting, he mentioned the payment problem to Melrose, who needless to say promptly offered a loan to tide over the interim period – for the smith could not wait for *his* payment; this at a modest rate of interest, of course. Sir William would amply recoup all in due course.

Never having been in debt before, that man was distinctly worried. But he did not see anything else for it. And with now over seventy would-be baronets, and almost a score of true settlers' applications for lands, there seemed to be no doubts as to the eventual financial well-being. He could ask for the baronetcy fees to be paid

326

now; but none of that money would come to him, all going to the monarch, who had not offered him any commission on this, save for Melrose's twenty per centum.

He wondered whether to take these moneys down to James himself, but was loth to do so for fear of more tasks and commitments being put upon him; visits to the monarch tended so to result. It was Janet who so proposed otherwise. Why not ask young John Stewart to go with the moneys? That would, as it were, kill two birds with one stone. If he and his mother did not know about Lennox's health problem, the son would then discover it for himself, good tidings or ill, and Will need not act the news-bearer. That seemed an excellent idea. Will would order the fee payments to commence, and then send a messenger to Methven, rather than going himself, to suggest the course.

So, the moneys having come in well, indication that the baronets-to-be were eager to assume their titles, in late September John Stewart, with three Methven men as escort, set off with his precious load of silver for London. He gave no indication that he knew that his father had been unwell.

Shortly thereafter Will took delivery of his first consignment of turners. He rode to Edinburgh to borrow one thousand pounds Scots – admittedly only one hundred and sixty-six pounds sterling – to help pay for it. He told the coppersmith to retain at his premises, presumably secure, further mintings rather than sending it all to Menstrie; he would call for it when necessary.

John Stewart came back at the end of October, clearly much worried about his father, whom he had found at Whitehall very poorly. The duke was undergoing various treatments prescribed by the physician Mayerne, but little improvement was being achieved. He could hardly walk, so swollen were his ankles; and with much nose-bleeding, the constant blood-draining by the chirurgeons seemed scarcely necessary, although perhaps this was devised to

327

get rid of diseased blood. Mary Gray would be much distressed.

The young man brought other tidings. The king was not well either, so much so that he had had to curtail his beloved hunting. But he was continuing to conduct the affairs of state, largely from his bed, where he had received the Nova Scotia moneys with satisfaction, although declaring that he had expected more. He had evidently been very distressed over the continued absence in Spain of his son and Buckingham – the latter missed more than the former, it seemed – indeed he had sent for them to come home whether or not the mission for the Spanish match was successful. Charles and Steenie had in fact arrived back just before John Stewart left again for Scotland, and with unexpected news. The prince was *not* going to marry the Infanta Maria, the Pope refusing to allow her to marry a Protestant, and also demanding that all penalties be lifted against English Catholics. But both on the outward and homeward journeys, the pair had visited Versailles, and Charles had taken a great fancy to King Louis the Thirteenth's sister, the Princess Henrietta Maria, and was now desirous of marrying her instead. Apparently he had gone so far as to suggest this, and Cardinal Richelieu, who was in effect ruling France for the young monarch, was prepared to consider it, again provided that laws against English Catholics were repealed; he did not seem to be concerned about papal permission. So this was the new royal preoccupation, friendship with France rather than with Spain. It was bound to tell against the hopes of Spanish aid to James's son-in-law the Count Frederick of the Palatinate, unfortunately.

Buckingham, now duke thereof, had come back very arrogant, feeling secure presumably in his influence over Charles, even insolent towards James, who wept over it all. He was making enemies of many at court.

Will was concerned to hear this last, worrying that Charles was in danger of being misled and his position prejudiced by this upjumped favourite.

There came a notable lift to the Nova Scotia project. One of the would-be baronets, already a knight, Sir Robert Gordon of Lochinvar and Kenmure, visited Menstrie, sent by the Secretary of State, and proved to be an enthusiast in more ways than one. He was prepared to go to the new colony and help in the actual settling, not to remain permanently but to stay for some time. A middle-aged man of sturdy appearance and obviously strong character, Will took to him at once. He was of quite a well-known line, one of the original Gordons from the Merse, who had moved over to Galloway, where Lochinvar and Kenmure were sited, inheriting quite large lands there. But presumably he sought a more adventurous life than merely managing estates, and the notion of helping to found a new overseas colony appealed to him. Will was more than glad to have a deputy who would go to Nova Scotia and assist the new settlers to move in and develop the colony. He had toyed with the idea of paying a visit there himself, but recognised that he had too many responsibilities at this end to risk being away from Scotland for any lengthy period; and the Americas were not a place where you could go over for a month or so. This Sir Robert's offer was a great support and service.

Gordon stayed with them at Menstrie for a few days, and much tentative planning was proposed and debated. Gordon would be deputy governor. He would sail over in the spring. He had his own ship in Kirkcudbright harbour, on the Solway Firth, and would take the first batches of colonists to establish a base settlement. Will would put Duncan Drummond, the shipmaster from Dumbarton, in touch with him; together they might achieve much. Sir Robert would send back a fuller list of the productions and commodities which Nova Scotia could produce for export, and detail requirements which would have to be sent out. They agreed to do nothing about the monopolies meantime.

Sir Robert left Will much heartened, a man after his own heart indeed.

Quite soon thereafter they had another visitor, the said Duncan Drummond. He had not been back to the Americas, having had two voyages to the Low Countries. His visit was for another purpose: to ask Ailie Graham to marry him. Was she prepared to be a shipman's wife, with her husband inevitably away for long periods? Ailie did not surprise the Alexanders by deciding that she was; she might even accompany Duncan on some of his voyages.

All at Menstrie were happy about this development. They had known that the couple much liked each other. And Ailie deserved a more fulfilling role in life. Duncan said that if all went well with the Nova Scotian plantation, he and Ailie might even settle down there themselves, he to organise the shipping enterprise which would become necessary if the colony prospered. Meantime, he would co-operate with Sir Robert Gordon.

Will foresaw the Drummonds becoming quite important folk in the new land.

In the circumstances, it was decided to hold the wedding right away, for Duncan had another voyage to the Netherlands lined up. So they all rode over to Cardross, where the Erskines were glad to arrange that the local parish minister married the pair at short notice. They managed to produce a quite festive occasion.

Glad as they were for the bride and groom, all at Menstrie were sad to see Ailie off for Dumbarton, for she had become practically one of the family, and something like a favourite aunt to the young people. But these save for the baby were growing up now, and would no doubt soon be making their own way into the world. Such was life.

Also life, or the reverse of it, was news of the death of Ludovick, Duke of Lennox and Richmond, at the age of forty-nine. The word came to them not from Methven but from the Earl of Melrose who, as Secretary of State, was required to find a new Great Chamberlain and Lord High Admiral for Scotland, to recommend to the king. Much upset, even though in a measure prepared for it,

330

Will and Janet waited for a few days before setting out for Methven to condole.

They found Mary Gray and her son grievously distressed but not making that too obvious. They were both strong characters and had known that this had been only a matter of time – as it was, indeed, for all. But Vicky had not reached fifty, and he had had so much to contribute. He would be succeeded by his brother Esmé, who lived in France, where their father had been Lord of Aubigny; for apart from the illegitimate John, Lennox had had no surviving offspring by his various arranged and unwanted marriages.

The sense of dire loss notwithstanding, life at Methven would continue more or less as it was, for the properties were all in John's name, and he was used to acting the laird, his mother accustomed to her peculiar status. But it was the end of a chapter, nevertheless.

28

With Sir Robert Gordon aiming to set off the following
May, it was decided to hold the initial investment of
Nova Scotian baronets just beforehand, so that, as deputy
governor, he could be present and add significance to
the occasion. Therefore, in March, John Stewart, who
was glad to co-operate, was sent off again down to
London to gain the king's assent and to bring back the
necessary parchments of appointment, duly signed and
sealed, and other relevant documents, for presentation to
the applicants. He took with him a further consignment
of moneys from later candidates, which ought to help in
the royal reception.

He brought back, in due course, the baronetcy scrolls
and papers, with the grants of lands in the colony; also the
news that King James was now a very sick man, having
passed three stones he had informed, being more or less
confined to his bed but persisting in conducting the realms'
business therefrom, even though the Prince of Wales was
taking an ever-increasing part in the government, under
the influence of Steenie Buckingham.

Messengers were sent out all over Scotland to summon
the candidates to Edinburgh.

So, in late April, the great day dawned, fortunately in
reasonable weather, for April rain could have made a sham-
bles of the occasion; and all assembled on the high-level
tilting-ground, before the great rock-top fortress, for what
was to be, in theory, the founding of a new state, Janet and
her eldest son on this occasion accompanying Will. The
soil brought from Nova Scotia was duly deposited at a
corner of the tourney-ground, and the Earl of Melrose,

acting for the king before a large crowd, declared this to be an integral part of the royal colony of New Scotland, to a fanfare of trumpets. Thereafter, he called forward Sir William Alexander of Menstrie, Master of Requests to His Grace, to stand on this spread of earth, and then read out the monarch's appointment of the said Sir William as governor of Nova Scotia, that man seeking to look suitably calm and dignified, however embarrassed by this play-acting.

Now Will took charge. First he summoned Sir Robert Gordon of Lochinvar to his side, and proclaimed him to be deputy governor of the colony, saying that he would be sailing therefor within the month, with the first permanent settlers. He also announced that the King's Grace had granted to Sir Robert, as well as a baronetcy, the first *barony* of Nova Scotia, this to be named New Galloway.

Then, flanked by Gordon and the Secretary of State, with young John Stewart behind, Will declared that the king had graciously been pleased to raise to the rank, style and title of Baronet of Nova Scotia a number of his Scots subjects of suitable quality and leal service, who were prepared to invest in and assist at the settlement and development of the said plantation by purchasing lands there and providing a number of resident colonists, these all committed to the task of ensuring that the new colony flourished.

The long list of names was then read out, almost one hundred of them, nearly all of lairdly status, some even younger sons of nobles, with a few from the new prosperous merchant class anxious to advance themselves socially. Very few applicants had in fact been turned down, James being more concerned with the payments than with actual suitability and reputation, and Will, of course, having done his own enquiring, with Lennox's help, previously.

A little hoarse at the end of all this, Will called on the aspirants to step forward on to the carpet of earth, in alphabetical order to avoid any problems as to precedence, to be infeoffed on the soil of New Scotland, and to make their oath of fealty to the monarch for the lands thus granted them.

So, one by one, the long line of men presented themselves, to declaim the form of words required, kiss Will's hand as representing their sovereign-lord, and be presented with their baronetcy scrolls by John Stewart, who had been carefully placing them all in due order and now stepped forward, with a servitor to assist him, a process he had had to rehearse well, since any mix-up of documents at this stage would have been most unfortunate and embarrassing; and two of the applicants had in fact not appeared, which could have caused an upset, with that great pile of papers and parchments. Fortunately all went well, however long it took to work through the lengthy roll. Each new baronet was shaken by the hand by the Earl of Melrose and Sir Robert Gordon.

At length it was done and all repaired up into the fortress for refreshment provided at Will's expense, and for which he hoped to be reimbursed in due course. Climbing the steep flight of steps to the gatehouse and its drawbridge, and on up past the eight towers of the castle to the Governor's House next to the ancient Queen Margaret's Chapel, the large company celebrated, all agreeing that it was an auspicious occasion, especially the wives of not a few of the new baronets who had elected to accompany them, and were now able to address each other as my Lady this or that.

Will felt that he was perhaps spoiling the general con- gratulatory atmosphere by making a speech, especially on his subject. But the matter of the currency and rates of exchange had to be dealt with sooner or later, and it was simplest to do so when all were gathered there, rather than have to explain it individually. And having Tam o' the Coogate with them could help, if there were any objections, since he it was who had advised on it. So Will told them that no silver coin was to be taken out of the country, by royal command, but that a copper currency of turners was available for exchange, and the rate set at thirty-six turners to the English silver shilling, which was double the amount of Scots bodles. So for each of the hundred pounds of the two thousand the colonists had to invest, they would rate seventy-two thousand turners.

He had been quite prepared for protests and altercation, but there were none voiced. Indeed it seemed that most were quite pleased that they would be getting double what ordinary Scots bodles and merks produced against the English pound and shilling, even though the intrinsic value of the actual copper coins was minimal. A weight off his mind, Will was able to gain some satisfaction from the occasion.

The Alexanders and John spent that night at Melrose's palatial house in the Cowgate, Sir Robert Gordon also, Tam thereof an excellent host. In the morning they said goodbye to Gordon, whom they would not see again before he sailed, wishing him very well, Will feeling almost guilty in that another was venturing on what he judged should probably be his responsibility, although none other seemed to see it that way. He said that they would keep in touch through Duncan Drummond.

Nova Scotia was no longer the mere conception of two men's minds but an actuality, however uncertain and hopeful.

Without Lennox to inform him, Will had very little idea as to how matters went with the king, and court generally, only rumours and tales reaching him, strange after being so close to the sources of power. James sent no messengers, nor did Charles, which rather distressed Will, after having been the prince's guardian and friend. Melrose was the source of any information which came his way and that only occasional and scrappy. The word was that the king hung on, very ill, even though clinging to his royal authority. Nevertheless Charles was inevitably taking more and more of the kingly duties over, and, as inevitably, men were looking to him for decision and preferment rather than to his father, which meant that, to quite a sizeable extent, Buckingham was now ruling in England.

Worse than that, Buckingham was advocating war with Spain. Seemingly he considered that he had been insulted at Madrid, and claimed that Charles had been also. And the Spanish lack of enthusiasm for the marriage of the infanta was an insult to England. France was now at war with Spain, and if the French Princess Henrietta Maria was indeed to marry Charles, then an alliance with France would be advantageous. The king, of course, was always against war, and would not hear of it, even from his beloved Steenie. But Charles was said to be prepared to consider it. And, strangely, the common folk of England were in favour, always had been anti-Spanish since the triumphant days of Drake, Hawkins and the rest, with much rich booty to be captured from laden Spanish treasure-ships returning from the Americas, even the parliamentarians acceding, although parliament was not sitting.

All this, if true, was alarming, even if it did not greatly affect the Scots.

News from Ireland was better. Good harvests had put an end to the famine. The Ulster plantation was proving successful, and over the rest of the country the Catholics were presently quiescent. Indeed the comparative prosperity across the Irish Sea was having some adverse effects on the Nova Scotia project, a distinct rivalry developing in the appeal for colonists. Admittedly most Ulster baronetcy recruits were now English, the Nova Scotian financial inducements being much better for the Scots; but for ordinary settlers the pull of Ulster tended to be the stronger – as indeed was only to be expected, so near at hand, where the colonists would not feel so cut off from their kinsfolk at home.

A few more Nova Scotia baronetcy applicants, as well as major land-seekers not interested in titles, did come in, and probably would continue to do so, especially once the new colony was more surely established. But Will judged that the total was never likely to reach the one hundred and fifty for the sixteen-thousand-acre holdings. That figure, of course, had been only arbitrarily proposed by James in their first discussions, and held no especial significance.

That winter of 1624 saw Will receiving his first substantial returns from the copper currency investment, and to his great relief he was able to repay the Secretary of State his loan, plus interest. This was only the start, to be sure, for the new baronets would hold on to the bulk of their Nova Scotia investments for as long as was permitted. But the initial payments, or what proportion of them accrued to Will Alexander, were far from insignificant and augured well for the future. Tam o' the Coogate declared that Will would one day be a rich man, and he was an authority on such matters. Although he had composed that poem on Croesus and the dangers of over-great wealth, Will thought that he could probably face that future without too much dread.

They all awaited word from Sir Robert Gordon, presumably via Duncan Drummond, but none was forthcoming.

Over Yuletide there was rejoicing in the Alexander family, with romance blossoming for the two girls. Mary had been seeing a lot of another Will, one Murray, son of one of the Nova Scotian baronets, Sir William Murray of Clermont; and now their betrothal could be announced, her parents happy with her choice. And, not to be outdone, her sister Jean declared that she was in love with Hugh Montgomery, of the Eglinton line, but son of another baronet, an Ulster one this time, now of Airds, County Down, and he with her. They were very desirable young women. Janet said that they made her feel old, which Will scoffed at; bonny as they were, they would never catch up with their mother in looks, he averred.

All these baronetcy interviews and meetings had had other results than mere colonisation, it seemed.

PART FOUR

29

It was the spring of 1625 before news reached Menstrie
of Sir Robert Gordon and his party. It came by Duncan
Drummond, who arrived from Dumbarton with Ailie
Graham, who was now looking distinctly pregnant, to
the congratulations of all. The report Duncan gave was
only partly good. Storms in the western ocean had not
only much delayed Gordon's ship but driven it well over
one hundred miles northwards to partial wreck on the
shores of Newfoundland, where major repairs had to be
carried out before the voyage could be resumed to Nova
Scotia. They had eventually reached their destination
and set up an initial base on the seaboard of what was
to be New Galloway, and there Duncan had eventually
found them. The settlers therefore had not had much
time or opportunity to do a great deal of exploring and
surveying; but Sir Robert was nevertheless well pleased
with what they had seen and discovered, encouraged that
the territory would make a well-doing and prosperous
colony. He urged the sending out at the soonest of sundry
necessary items, some of them very simple and obvious,
such as large quantities of axes, nails and tools, rope,
gunpowder, canvas, pots and pans and the like. Also, of
course, more colonists.

It was only a week later, with Duncan and Ailie still
with them, that the word came from the Secretary of State.
The king had passed away to a higher kingdom, where
he was unlikely to be Christ's vice-regent. James Stewart
had died, in as little dignified fashion as he had lived, all
but drowned in his own saliva and unable to speak, on
27th March, with his physician Mayerne diagnosing his

favourite disease, tertian ague, although a rival declared dysentery. He had been a monarch for fifty-eight years, all his life indeed, save for one year, albeit a strange one. So now Charles was the king.

Will found it difficult to accept somehow, even though, like Lennox, long illness had foretold it. James had by no means seemed immortal but his odd presence and influence was so much part of his kingdoms' scene as to leave a gap, a vacuum, which seemed unfillable. Certainly Charles was unlikely to fill it.

Will scarcely mourned his departed liege-lord, for their special association would hardly engender that. But he felt in a way bereft nevertheless, a major aspect of life removed. He would come to terms with the situation, of course, but it would take time.

There was now the question as to whether Charles would continue with his father's interest in colonisation, whether indeed the Nova Scotia project would go on at all. Could it be abandoned now, at this stage? The prince had never shown the least concern in the matter. He could hardly cancel the enterprise, with all the moneys which had changed hands over it and which he would certainly not be prepared to pay back; but he might let it all dwindle and die perhaps. Much would, unfortunately, depend on George Villiers, Duke of Buckingham, who would now, almost certainly, be very much the power behind the throne. And Will Alexander foresaw little good emanating from that quarter. Meantime, he could only continue as before, and hope for the best.

Duncan Drummond went off to prepare his ship for the transport of a new batch of settlers and all the stores Gordon required, which Will would organise, leaving Ailie at Menstrie to have her baby, in Janet's experienced and capable hands. He would aim to sail within the month.

In the end, Will did not have long to wait for answers to his questions. In early May a messenger arrived from Melrose to say that King Charles required Sir William

Alexander to visit him at his earliest convenience; that and no more.

So it was the road south again, after a lengthy relief therefrom. Will took John Stewart of Methven with him, who was becoming his assistant and lieutenant as well as friend. Lennox had always behaved kindly towards Charles; the new monarch might look favourably on the son.

On the way, they called in at Edinburgh to learn such news of what went on in London as Tam o' the Coogate could tell them. They discovered, among other things, that it had not taken long for Buckingham to have his way. With James barely cold in his tomb in Westminster Abbey, England declared war on Spain, and the duke was taking almost personal charge of operations, which, considering his complete lack of military and naval experience, scarcely augured well for results. The king who had boasted that he was the only monarch of any of his kingdoms who had never gone to war, had a different successor.

The travellers found Charles at Whitehall, and were well received. He had developed noticeably since last Will had seen him, become a tall, dignified, handsome young man, so very different from his father in every way, still quiet, slow of speech but no longer actually diffident. He welcomed Will with, for him, warmth.

"It seems long since we saw each other, Sir William," he said, in his slightly hesitant speech. "That is my loss."

"Scarcely that, Sire." It seemed strange to be calling Charles Sire. "I remain your humble servant and most respectful subject." It was hardly suitable to congratulate the young man on succeeding to the throne, when that was by his father's death. "And wish Your Majesty all satisfaction in your reign, and God's blessings and guidance in all great decisions you will have to make." If that sounded prosy, all but pompous, it was the best that Will could do. "Here is Sir John Stewart of Methven, son to the late and esteemed Duke Ludovick of Lennox."

343

"Ah. The duke was ever my friend. A sore loss to us all, sir, however much the greater to yourself."

"Yes, Sire. I am only his bastard son, but we were close. I would seek to serve Your Grace, not as he did, but in some degree."

"Sir John assists me in my efforts to establish the Nova Scotia colony, Sire," Will said. "Much effort is involved, much travel, even around Scotland. And he aids me in this."

"That is good. Your labours in this matter are most valuable, Sir William, as my royal father left me in no doubts. These colonising efforts bring in much needful funding for the realm. More needful than ever, now that we are at war with Spain. Much requires to be spent on shipping, and arms and the assembling of men. My good George, Duke of Buckingham, is even now down at Plymouth and Portsmouth havens directing the necessary preparations."

It was a relief, at least, to learn that Buckingham was not here present at Whitehall and liable to make his presence felt to who knew what effect.

"This war, Sire, it will be costly, in lives as well as in moneys. Is it intended that there will be much of battle, of the actual fighting of armies? Or mainly but attempts on Spanish shipping bringing treasure from overseas?"

"Both, as I understand it. But the sea warfare will be foremost for us, leaving the ground battling mainly to the French. But the provision, repairing and manning of ships is indeed costly, as you say. And parliament is less helpful than it should be, both houses in favour of the war but withholding the means. That is why I require as much help from Scotland as is possible at this stage. So I urge you, my friend, to pursue your efforts with all vigour, in both plantation ventures, Ulster and Nova Scotia. More baronetcies. Even peerages if that would help. At a suitable payment."

Will did not know whether to feel relieved or otherwise. The colonial projects were to go ahead, but apparently at added cost, labour and responsibility. This of peerages, lordships, was a distinctly daunting thought. How could he, *should* he, recommend for such?

Charles had evidently thought of this, for he went on. "I will consider raising you in dignity, in some measure, Sir William, that you may carry the more authority. I will consult the Earl of Melrose, Secretary of State for Scotland, to see what may be appropriate. I am too new to this of government to know what is available and suitable, especially in Scotland. But some advancement will be made, beyond being Gentleman of my Bedchamber and Master of Requests and, to be sure, Governor of Nova Scotia."

Will bowed, but shook his head at the same time. "I seek no higher ranking, Sire. It is only this of recommendation of possible peers, or lords of parliament. Perhaps that, if it is thought advisable, should be left to the Secretary of State?"

"But it is you, my friend, who seek out the colonists and persuade them, not Melrose. My father made MacDonnell Earl of Antrim, and Stewart of Ochiltree Lord Castle Stewart of Tyrone. These Irish peerages do not carry seats in the House of Lords. Something of the sort might serve for Nova Scotia?"

It was Will's turn to be hesitant. "I think, Your Majesty, not yet. The colony is too new. As yet scarcely a reality. Perhaps such lofty titles should be reserved for Ulster and the north of Ireland meantime? And that on the Secretary of State's recommendation, not mine."

"I will consider the matter. Now, sirs, I have the French ambassador awaiting audience. But I will see you again, and hear of what goes on in Scotland. Learn of the Lady Janet and your children. And Mistress Ailie."

They bowed themselves out.

Later they were summoned to the king's personal dining-chamber. Charles, it seemed, did not go in for great roistering banquets and drinking sessions, in fact avoiding public appearances wherever he could, preferring to dine alone, if not with Buckingham or especial guests. So Will and John had the new monarch to themselves for a fairly modest meal, and Will at least was able all but to forget that he was in the presence of his sovereign but in that of the young Charles he had tutored and guided towards manhood. They talked of the days at Oatlands, of Janet and Ailie, of Henry, of Charles's efforts to master sporting activities which he had never really enjoyed, his eventual success with horses, and the like. Inevitably Buckingham's name kept cropping up, but not dwelt upon; and James was scarcely mentioned. It was a pleasant occasion, at least for Will, person to person and differences of station all but forgotten.

Very little was said as to rule and governance, but they did gather that Charles was as assured as had been his father of the divine right of the monarchy, even if he did not declare himself to be Christ's vice-regent. He likewise was anti-parliament, at least the English model, so different from the Scots, and prepared to rule without it if necessary. The war situation was scarcely mentioned, so it was apparent that this was mainly Buckingham's doing and concern. Will kept off the subject of what James had called statecraft, as far as he could, but he did ask if Charles was planning to come north to visit his more ancient kingdom, and was told that he would do so but scarcely meantime, with so much to be seen to, learned and controlled here in the south. Give him time.

John Stewart took little part in the converse but was clearly interested in it all; and Charles did bring him in occasionally, and observed that they were related in blood, both Stewarts.

Charles mentioned that he had met the Earl of Argyll while in Madrid, and that man, now become a highly regarded general in the Spanish army, had asked kindly after Will Alexander, his old friend. He seemed to be very popular at the Spanish court. It would be a sorry outcome if, in this of war, he became involved in having to fight against his own people. Probably he would refuse, although it might well be different against the French forces.

When eventually Will felt bound to seek permission to leave the royal presence, it was with mixed feelings, a personal and enduring liking for the younger man, but doubts as to what sort of monarch he would make for the kingdoms, and some fears for the future, Buckingham's unfortunate influence ever in mind. Charles reverted to the subject of raising Will in dignity as they left, while reminding him of the need for moneys, by no means thus enheartening that man, who was quite content with his present position, and doubtful as to how he could advance the colonising efforts much further than he was already endeavouring to do.

There was nothing to detain the pair of Scots in London now, and with fears that Buckingham might appear and with no wish to see him, after one more day they returned whence they had come.

30

As it transpired, although another dozen or so major settlers were enrolled for Nova Scotia that year, not all of them desiring baronetcies, and none being offered peerages as an inducement, these of course to the advantage of Will's coinage exchange, the Ulster colonisation progressed more successfully, and really more profitably so far as the royal treasury was concerned. But this was now largely the concern of the Secretary of State and Sir Thomas Hope, money-spinners both. Will by no means begrudged them their gains, for he had a sufficiency on his hands. Apart from the Nova Scotia advocacy and arrangements, he had, largely at Janet's urging, started on the building of a new house, not at Menstrie but at the lower end of the tilting-ground before Stirling Castle, so similar to that at Edinburgh where the corner of Nova Scotia had been instituted. Menstrie Castle had never been large or impressive, a comparatively small laird's fortified dwelling; and these days, with the young people growing up and associating with loftier folk, and the many visitors coming to be interviewed for colonising from all over the land, and having to be put up and catered for, the place had become quite inadequate. Will reckoned that by erecting the new house at Stirling, with its many hostelries, inns and other facilities, it would simplify the business of receiving and entertaining all these visitors. And with his copper turners' earnings growing, he could afford a finer home for his wife and family. Alexander of Menstrie he still was, but few thought of him as that these days. The site he selected could not have been finer, high on the apron of the rock before the fortress, with magnificent views all around, close to the only other building apart from the castle itself, Mar's Wark as it was called, and that unfinished and no rival. This had been started by the present earl's father, when regent, but never completed, this allegedly because there was a curse on it, the regent having part-demolished Cambuskenneth Abbey nearby at the Reformation, and used the stones for his building, the curse not so much because it was a sacred building – after all, abbeys galore were pulled down by the Reformers – but in that it was the scene of Bruce's acceptance of the surrender of the English lords after the Battle of Bannockburn, and therefore sacrosanct. Will was careful not to use any such masonry but had his stones quarried from Abbey Craig nearer Menstrie.

He designed and personally superintended much of the erection, even although not as much as he would have wished owing to other commitments, for he found the task fascinating and a real challenge, his aim to make this one of the finest buildings in the land, his tribute to Janet and, in a way, to King James who had made it possible. James had been baptised, and indeed crowned, as a child, only a short distance away, in the Chapel Royal of the castle. Only Will's royal links, and friendship with Mar, made this site available.

The year 1626 proved to be inauspicious for England, and for Charles's first full year as monarch, this because the war with Spain more or less petered out in fruitless gestures and inactivity, yet at considerable cost in money if not in men. Buckingham's credit collapsed, and to some extent the new king's also. And the parliamentarians, who had applauded the declaration of war even though not voting it any funds, now turned hostile. There was much discontent in the land.

Not so in Scotland, where such concerns made but little impact. Certainly not for Will Alexander, for whom it was a very notable year indeed, however unexpected the developments. No one was more surprised than himself when, on a visit to Edinburgh in the spring for the infeoffment of the latest batch of baronets on the spread of Nova Scotian soil, Tam o' the Coogate assisting and supporting him, quite casually informed him that he had decided to resign as Secretary of State after thirteen years in that office. He was now sixty-three and had had enough of the burdens of responsibility, although he was still Lord Clerk Register and Lord President of the Court of Session. Visiting London recently to tender his resignation to the king, he had recommended that Sir William Alexander be appointed in his stead, Charles agreeing without hesitation.

Striken dumb, all but appalled, Will could only wag his head in something like disbelief.

Melrose seemed to see nothing strange about it all. Sir Thomas Hope was a year older than he was, and well content to remain Lord Advocate, his sons now appointed judges of the High Court. Who better for the task than Will Alexander? He had proved himself in the taxing matters of Ulster and Nova Scotia. Here was a new opportunity of great influence. And the office carried with it a stipend of one hundred pounds per year.

"But I know nothing about the duties of Secretary of State!" Will declared, bewildered. "With the king in London, *you* have been to all intents the ruler of Scotland. I am in no position to succeed you. How could your lordship have suggested me?"

"For very good reasons, man. You are a responsible and able carl. You have dealt effectively with the many problems that have come your road. You have shown that you can handle men. They respect you. And you have close connections with the crown, closer than have I. Who better? And I will be available for advice, see you."

Helplessly Will stared at him. Not since he had been handed the gift of Acadia had he been so overwhelmed.

Melrose promised to write out a list of the duties, functions and privileges attendant on the office. Will would have to be in Edinburgh fairly frequently of course, where were the law courts, where the Privy Council met, and where parliament usually sat these days. He would always be welcome to put up at the Cowgate house. And in return, there would no doubt be sundry little services which he could render in return.

That, at least, Will could foresee.

He returned to Menstrie, wits in a whirl.

Sure enough, two weeks later, not only did Melrose's promised catalogue of duties and responsibilities arrive, but also an official missive of appointment, signed and sealed by Charles, making Will His Majesty's Secretary of State for his ancient realm of Scotland, and dated three weeks earlier. So apparently he had already been in office for that time without knowing it, nor knowing what he was being let in for.

He was worried, if not alarmed. Janet told him not to be foolish, that it would all be less taxing than founding a colony. Melrose had done it all these years, and flourished on it. Was he a lesser man than Tam o' the Coogate?

Will studied that function list, and became somewhat relieved. In general, his duties seemed to be less daunting than he had feared. Much that he had assumed would be his responsibility would actually be done by others, and submitted through him. He would be a sort of assembly point, a central authority, to which others would contribute their findings, needs and proposals, these the officers of state, the councillors, the treasurers, the judges and sheriffs, the clerks and collectors, the commissaries and commendators and comptrollers, the provosts and magistrates and deacons of guilds and trades, even the churchmen on occasion. He would have to receive these, select, act the arbitrator, advise, encourage, reprove, even condemn, yes, and submit his findings to the monarch. He would have to attend many meetings, of course; but most of the office-bearers and responsible folk could come to him. Which would make his fine house up on Stirling's rock the more useful, indeed essential.

Will's first appearance as Secretary of State did rather reinforce his doubts about the task, for it so happened that the occasion was one where his position was less than clear-cut and simple. It was a meeting held in the great hall of Edinburgh Castle, under the Great Seal, to validate grant-charters of land to various inheritors and purchasers. In theory all the land in Scotland was the king's, as feudal superior, and could not be sold or transferred, not so much as a single field or oxgate, without the royal permission, granted under the Great Seal, and registered. The Keeper of the Great Seal was the Chancellor, in effect prime minister, who chaired parliaments, and who, at this juncture, was Charles Seton, second Earl of Dunfermline, son of the king's former early guardian, and married to the late Aurora's sister, the Lady Mary Douglas. He it was who presided at this meeting. But, with the monarch living outwith the country, and not present at the meeting, his Secretary of State, and Keeper of the Privy Seal, was his due representative. So Will found himself in the odd position of deputising for the king but not in charge of the gathering; and exceedingly uncertain as to his role. Fortunately Melrose was there, in his capacity of Lord President of the Council, and was able to guide his successor.

Not all present knew who or what Will was, clearly, and they made quite a large company, the applicants for charters, the granters of the lands and the witnesses necessary, and these last appeared to be all of lofty station, as indeed were some of the petitioners. The new Secretary of State was eyed somewhat warily, and was equally wary himself.

Dunfermline, a lean, youngish man with a searching glance, called the company to order and declared that they met in the name of the King's Grace and according to statute and long-established custom. They were, he said, pleased to welcome to the charter meeting, for the first time, His Grace's new Secretary of State, Sir William Alexander of Menstrie, Governor of Nova Scotia, recently appointed to succeed their esteemed colleague the Earl of Melrose, Lord President of the Council, who had

352

for so long held the secretaryship. He then gestured towards Will.

Rising, and hoping that this was the correct procedure, Will bowed to the Chancellor and then right and left, and sat down, unspeaking.

Melrose, who had presented Will with the Privy Seal, spoke instead. He said that King Charles had made an admirable choice in appointing Sir William, who had proved his worth in not a few regards, particularly in the skill and efficiency with which he had promoted the plantations of Ulster and Nova Scotia. He was close to His Grace, whom he had tutored and indeed helped to rear, as he had done formerly for the late and lamented Prince Henry. He was a Gentleman of the Bedchamber to King Charles, and had been Master of Requests for King James.

A latecomer, the Earl of Mar, Lord Treasurer, who had just arrived, added his commendation before sitting down.

Thus acclaimed, Will shook his head modestly, and the session proceeded. The first business was instructive as to how lands changed hands among the nobility and aristocracy, had Will required to be so informed. James, Earl of Home, was seeking royal acceptance of his taking over of lands in the barony of Newbattle and Dalhousie, come to him as dowry with his wife, Jean, daughter of the Earl of Lothian. And Sir John Preston of Penicuik, one of the new baronets, gaining the lands of Nisbet in Teviotdale, having married the former young woman's sister, the Lady Anne Kerr. Judicious marriages both, no doubt, and an indication of the cost to landowners of having too many daughters, who had to be provided with dowries. Lothian's heir would have to marry as judiciously, to recompense the Kerr of Ferniehirst family.

At a nudge from Melrose, Will indicated royal acceptance, feeling something of a fraud, for the king presumably knew nothing about all this. He held up the Privy Seal of Scotland as confirmation.

353

The next matter was similar, the Cunningham Earl of Glencairn, here present, with a daughter having wed James Hay of Tourlands and bringing him the lands of Corsbie, Mennoch and Gill, in the county of Ayr. This also was accepted.

There followed a somewhat different application. This concerned a merchant burgess of Edinburgh, evidently prosperous, one of the sort whose sons sometimes aspired to baronetcies, who had purchased the lands of Saughtonhall and Smithslands, with the manor-place and mills, in the barony of Broughton near to Edinburgh, these resigned to him by Sir William Ballenden of Broughton. The burgess, Alexander Watson, a frail-looking elderly man, obviously much embarrassed by having to be in this lofty company of earls and officers of state, muttered the required declaration of loyal service for the lands, this being acceded to in gracious fashion by the seller, presumably impoverished. The change of ownership was nodded through by the official witnesses, for it seemed that unless some objection was voiced, acceptance of these land transfers was almost automatic, which made Will wonder at the need for it all. He was aware of clerks' pens scratching busily at a side table, duly registering all.

The man Watson, bobbing bows all around, backed out from the chamber, obviously relieved to be gone.

There were another couple of land-purchase deals to accept, without any dissent. It was clear that all present were interested in who was selling land, rather than those buying, and why. In Scotland, land was the real wealth, rather than money. Even the loftiest were always on the lookout for pickings.

That concluded the Great Seal session, but not the day's business. As men were stirring, preparing to leave, the Chancellor beat with his gavel on the table and declared that the Secretary of State had a matter of some import to announce. Taken by surprise, Will looked at him.

Melrose came to his assistance. He said that since this matter had arisen before Sir William Alexander's

354

appointment, it might be suitable that he should speak to it, and the Secretary of State give his decision thereafter. Sir Archibald Napier of Merchiston, Treasurer-Depute and an Extra Lord of Session, much favoured by His Grace to whom and to his royal father he had rendered notable service over the years, was to be promoted to the dignity of Lord Napier of Merchiston. And in token of King Charles's appreciation and favour, he was to be granted, for seven years, the sole right to export from Scotland twelve thousand stones of tallow, to Ulster, Nova Scotia and to foreign lands, but not to England or English colonies, the monopoly of which resided elsewhere. This to be confirmed, under the Privy Seal. Another nudge.

So here was Will Alexander having to signal approval of one of these monopolies which, in fact, he deplored as an imposition and hindrance to honest trade, the enhanced prices having always to be paid by the common folk, the ultimate consumers. He knew this Napier, son of the famous inventor of logarithms, for he was one of the Nova Scotian baronets; perhaps this was partly why he had invested in the colony, knowing of the forthcoming monopoly. He was a notably clever man, in different fashion from his father.

There was murmuring round the table, of admiration rather than criticism, by the expressions.

Disapprove or not, Will could only signal acceptance, since this was the king's decision. Set-faced he raised the Privy Seal.

That was the end of the day's business, although thereafter Will undoubtedly achieved more in the way of recognition and acceptance of his status as Secretary of State in his conversations with the magnates present at a meal for which the Lord Treasurer would have to pay. There were six earls present, Dunfermline, Lothian, Home, Glencairn, besides Mar and Melrose. Also the Bishops of St Andrews and Glasgow, the Clerk Register, Hay, the Clerk to the Privy Council, Hamilton of Magdalens, a kinsman of Tam's, Murray of Elibank

355

and Ballencrieff, another Treasurer-Depute and Nova Scotia baronet, Napier, and sundry more. What sort of an impression Will made on all these he did not know, but at least his new position was more clearly established.

He went back to Menstrie next day more aware of his duties and what was expected of him, although not particularly happy about it all. It seemed that he had a lot to learn about string-pulling, and he was in a notable position both to pull and be pulled.

31

Ailie Graham produced a plump son for Duncan, to due rejoicing; and soon after, that autumn, the proud father returned from Nova Scotia to claim mother and child. He brought good news from Sir Robert Gordon. A base had been established on the northern shoreline, being named New Glasgow, and a subsidiary one on the more exposed southern side. The entire peninsula – for it was really that, not an island as it was usually described – had been mapped out and its hundred and fifty great parcels of land more or less defined, and some of them allocated to major settlers. Ordinary colonists were being active, felling trees, clearing scrub, erecting dykes to control the tides which could rise as much as fifty feet and which created vast salt marshes; and of course building houses, although themselves having to camp, or stay at the base communities meantime. Seed for crops was now in demand and Duncan was to take back a shipload by return. He also would take Ailie and the baby Pate, for he had started to build a house for them on one thousand acres near this New Glasgow, given to him by Sir Robert, and it should be finished by the time that he got back. So he was now a landowner, and could look forward to giving up seafaring, and settling down as a farmer, bonnet-laird and possibly even a shipbuilder, for there was obviously going to be a great need for boats and ships, and suitable timber was there in plenty.

This was all good to hear, although they would be sorry, at Menstrie, to part with Ailie, probably for good. But they wished her very well in her new life, and perhaps she might contrive a return visit in her husband's ship on occasion?

Occasional couriers arrived from London, sent almost it seemed haphazardly by Charles, with commands and enquiries but mainly requirements for money, especially over the selling of new monopolies. The news they had brought varied between good and bad, mainly the latter. The Princess Henrietta Maria had duly arrived from France, and was now queen, and the marriage a happy one. But, oddly, this happiness was in despite of a complete turn-around in the national situation, and a declaration of war on her France, of all things. This again was Buckingham's doing. He had become very much aware of his growing unpopularity over the feeble warfare with Spain, and decided that going to the aid of the persecuted French Protestants, the Huguenots, would please English Protestant opinion. In this he was again supported by the members of the House of Commons, but once more without funding. Not that much in the way of hostilities appeared to be taking place again, one of Steenie's "paper wars". But this situation much concerned Will Alexander for, with French Canada so close to Nova Scotia, it could possibly result in an attack on the colony and put an end to all their efforts. This did not seem to have occurred to Charles and Buckingham, for they were still urging new settling and emigration, for financial reasons.

Despite the French declaration of war, Charles appeared to be still at loggerheads with his English parliament, and declaring that he could and would rule without it, hence the crying need for moneys, since parliament all but controlled the national purse-strings.

These tidings were distinctly upsetting, even though Scotland itself remained more or less unaffected.

In November Will found himself appointed Keeper of the Signet, presumably on Melrose's advice, an office which he knew naught of but which turned out to be a sort of lesser Keeper of the Privy Seal, and useful, in that it allowed him to give assent to and institute many matters which did not require the king's approval and seal, in other words on his own authority rather than the monarch's specifically. With this appointment came the licence to raise his two landed properties of Menstrie and Tullibody to the status of baronies, which gave him certain privileges, such as to charge toll on any of the king's highways which might pass through his land, the right to hold fairs and markets, of which the baron could charge a tenth of the profits, all grain grown on his estates to be ground only at his own mills, at appropriate commission, and the like. These Scots baronies, which were so different from the English titles of the same name, the latter being in fact peerages, were much sought after by the lairds.

Will was glad enough of any increase in funding, for this war with France could possibly dry up his revenues from the Nova Scotia coinage; and the building of his fine house, now almost finished, was costing more than he had anticipated, as such developments were apt to do. But he was concerned to be a good laird to his tenants and common folk, and not mulct them of their hard-won earnings. Tolls were a different matter, apt to be paid by those who could afford to travel.

He himself was doing a deal of travelling these days, all but wearing a trail to and from Edinburgh, and, fortunately, because of his position, not having to pay tolls to the baronies he had to pass through on the way. He was unable to spend as much time as he would have wished in superintending the completion of the Stirling lodging, and wondering where he could cut back on the costing. Had he been foolishly extravagant, in the first fine flush of all that turner exchange? The hundred pounds per year stipend as Secretary of State did not go very far.

Oh, that Charles Stewart had been as dead set against wars as was his late sire!

Needless to say the French war had the effect of drying up investment in Nova Scotia almost entirely, Will not being the only one to foresee possible trouble and even expulsion there. But when Duncan Drummond arrived back in the spring he reported no difficulties with Canada as yet, the French over there apparently having their hands full in repelling other attacks, mainly from natives but some from New England colonists who saw opportunity for increasing *their* territories. But in these circumstances, Will asked, might not the French Canadians decide to retire to the former Acadia, from which the Indians had all but been expelled and English colonists from Maine and New Hampshire would be unlikely to invade? Duncan thought not, Canada was so potentially rich and vast. They would, it was likely, seek armed help from France to maintain and extend their hold there, rather than attempt to retake comparatively small Nova Scotia.

Otherwise news from the colony was satisfactory. Gordon was staying on meantime, and requesting more settlers, stores, tools and grain. So Will would have to try to revive his campaign of recruitment despite the international situation, England at war, in name at least, with both France and Spain, these realms, however, each at war with the other.

He was finding his duties as Secretary of State demanding much time, but less taxing and burdensome than he had feared. He was learning, thanks to Melrose largely, the wisdom and art of carefully delegating authority. There were many, over-many, officers of state and their deputies in Scotland, not a few hereditary. Let them earn their positions, and spare him all but the final authorisations.

The news from England in the summer of 1628 was depressing in the extreme. Cardinal Richelieu, who with the Queen Dowager Marie de Medici was governing France for the young king, was clamping down fiercely on the Protestant Huguenots, and was in person leading an army against their stronghold, the port of La Rochelle, besieging that city. Buckingham thought that he saw an opportunity to win glory, and had led an English squadron to relieve the Huguenots. This had ended in fiasco and humiliation, near disaster, and the city had fallen. So now the favourite's reputation was at its lowest, and inevitably Charles's with it. Demands that the duke be dismissed from all offices, indeed imprisoned in the tower, were rejected by the king, who stood by his friend. The parliamentarians were up in arms, and the people now critical of their monarch. Charles, however admirable in his private life, was making a poor king.

At a meeting in Edinburgh to debate the appointment of a new Chancellor for royal approval, Dunfermline having resigned, Will learned that he now had to address Tam o' the Coogate differently. He had become Earl of Haddington, not of Melrose, Charles having acceded to this, a most unusual circumstance. Apparently the earl had always wanted to be so entitled, for Haddingtonshire was where his principal estates were situated; now, on the death of John Ramsay, Viscount of Haddington, leaving no heir, the style was available. And, to be sure, Melrose was only a burgh, albeit a renowned one, while Haddington was a county.

The meeting decided that Will should recommend Sir George Hay, Viscount of Dupplin, to the king as the new Chancellor.

In due course the appointment came back, duly confirmed; and with it extraordinary tidings. Buckingham was dead. He had been assassinated.

It seemed that he had been in Portsmouth again, actually planning another naval expedition to assist the Huguenots, when he had been waylaid and stabbed to death by a naval officer named John Felton, presumably put up to it by unnamed others, this on 23rd August.

It is to be feared that few mourned George Villiers, other than Charles Stewart. Seldom had a royal favourite and adviser been so universally unpopular and condemned. Will agreed that the end of his influence could be only for the good.

At a meeting of the Privy Council soon thereafter, which the new Haddington chaired as Lord President thereof, Will took the opportunity to advise that the council send a recommendation to the king that the state of war with France should be declared over and

361

normal relations resumed. Scotland had always had a special understanding with France, the Auld Alliance, admittedly originally as a means of keeping the English aggressions towards either at bay; and this seemed to be a suitable time to emphasise it. The Nova Scotian position might thereby be safeguarded.

As it transpired, it was not. For Wentworth, Earl of Strafford who, with Bishop Laud of London, seemed to be taking over as principal advisers to the king, had scant interest in Scots Nova Scotia; and they concluded a treaty which, among other concessions, in name at least, returned Acadia to French sovereignty, although it was accepted that the Scots settlers should not be expelled.

At first Will was badly shaken. Was this the sorry end to all his efforts? The collapse of so many hopes? But gradually it began to dawn on him, and on others, that in fact little had actually changed. The French were not doing well against the Spaniards, and were unlikely meantime to get involved in armed aggression against the Scots, who were, after all, their ancient allies, for the colony which was being called Acadia again by them but still Nova Scotia by the new settlers. Whether any French colonists would arrive, from Canada or elsewhere, was questionable, with so much to be consolidated and exploited in those greater territories. Another visit from Duncan Drummond reported no untoward developments, no influx of Frenchmen. Sir Robert Gordon, he said, had little fear of trouble in the foreseeable future, and urged a resumption of immigration and store-sending.

Duncan had brought with him to Dumbarton the colony's first exports to the homeland, including salted fish which he was going to take on to an English port – since this was one of Scotland's own main exports – salted moose flesh, which should prove a delicacy for those able to afford it, dried fruits which were something equally new in Scotland and seemingly an Indian production, honey wine, and other items. This represented something of a milestone.

Gradually the word got round – Will saw that it did – that Nova Scotia was still worth investing in and colonising. Even a few more baronet applicants came forward. He sought to encourage this by raising the rate of exchange for his copper turners in the investors' favour, which reduced his own benefit therefrom, but that was better than having no commission at all. So he was able to send some moneys down for Charles's empty treasury.

The king, for his part, was raising funds in his own way. He was selling peerages. And since the parliamentarians, especially the lords, would never agree to this giving of seats to upjumped newcomers, Charles had hit on the idea of creating these Lords of Parliament in Scotland, Englishmen as they might be, this carrying no seat in the English House of Lords. So one Sir Edward Barret of Bellhouse became Lord Barret of Newburgh, in Fife; Sir Thomas Fairfax of Denton, Lord Fairfax of Cameron; Sir Walter Aston of Tixall, Lord Aston of Forfar; even Elizabeth Beaumont, wife of the Chief Justice of Pleas in England, became Baroness of Cramond. The Scots nobility, of course, were upset at this cheapening of their ancient status, but there was nothing that they could do about it. Will, as royal representative, came in for not a little complaint.

It was late autumn before Will received a double shock, which demanded his major decision. Duncan Drummond was the bringer of one, on another return shuttle from Nova Scotia. Sir Robert Gordon, who had been intending to make a return visit to Scotland, had suddenly died, a dire and quite unexpected tragedy. So now there was no deputy governor over there, no one to take charge of the colony's development on the spot. The second jolt came in a letter from King Charles, thanking Will for the latest contributions sent, urging further efforts at colonisation, and, to help in the process, granting him the governorship of any part of Canada which he might be able to take over. Just like that! Canada was his for the taking. And this despite the peace treaty with France.

363

Will wondered whether his liege-lord had gone mad. He declared that he must go south to see the king.

So now it was for a much-needed and possibly awkward interview with Charles Stewart in London, and the sooner the better, little as Will relished the prospect or the journey down. He would endeavour to be back before Yuletide. Scotland would have to do without its Secretary of State until then.

32

At Whitehall, in mid-November, Will discovered that Charles was presently staying at Windsor. So that well-known extra journey had to be made. It had been a long time since he had gone that way.

At least, with Charles, there was no problem of having to wait for audiences; he had not been half an hour at the great castle when the king actually came seeking him. Charles grew more handsome each time that Will saw him. His stiffness of manner soon melted with his old friend, the said friend worrying about what he was going to say to his sovereign.

He did not seek to broach difficult subjects immediately on their coming together and, after a fairly casual chat, he was led off to meet the queen, of whom Charles was obviously very proud and fond.

Henrietta Maria was an attractive young woman, not beautiful but with good features, wide eyes and a long nose in a notably round face. She greeted Will amiably in fluent if heavily accented English.

"Ha, I have heard much of Sir William Alexander of Scotland," she said. "My husband's good friend and teacher. My Charles ever speaks well of you, sir. Scotland – you have come all the way from there? I have never visited that far land, but have been told much about it."

"It is none so far, Your Majesty. I have come here in ten days' riding time, two of them within Scotland itself. Our ancient links with France mean much to us there. His Highness and yourself should visit, so soon as may be."

"I would so wish, Sir William. But, as you perchance can see, I am *enceinte*, pregnant is it? So, it must be later.

You have many mountains and lakes, no? Much – how do you say? – wilderness? Not desert, no, but much of the wild. Much of boar and wolves and eagles?"

"It is scarce so wild as that, Majesty! It is hilly, yes. And the Highlands are mountainous. But much of the Lowlands, the south part of the country, is more level and fertile. Fair to see. The Highlands have great beauty."

"And the air? The weather? The rain and snow and wind?"

"Less ill than many here in England suppose, Highness." Will glanced at the king, as it occured to him that Charles would probably know little more of Scotland than did his wife, despite his tutoring, since he had left there as a child of four and never been back. "His Majesty is the descendant of a long line of kings, the longest in all Christendom it is said, established long before there was an England, or indeed a France, long before the Romans sought to conquer our land." He stopped himself. This was no occasion to enlarge on one of his favourite themes.

"Sir William sought to teach me all this long since, at the Oatlands you have seen," Charles said, with one of his rare smiles. "We shall go to Scotland indeed, when you are able to travel, my love. For I must have my coronation there, as King of Scots. But meantime, I have a meeting with my lord bishop and Strafford. They await. My friend, you will dine with us later."

"Monsieur Claude is to dine this day," the queen reminded.

"Ah, yes. But no matter. He and Sir William will suit each other very well, I think. Claude de la Toure is a friend of the queen from childhood days. A Huguenot, he is now exiled from France, but a notable man."

When, in the evening, Will was admitted to the royal dining-chamber, it was to find there only the queen and a tall and handsome youngish man, who was introduced as Claude de la Toure, from Normandy, friend of long standing.

"Of Normandy no longer, you will understand, Sir

William," he was told, but cheerfully. "Banished therefrom for offending against the good cardinal's teachings and commands, Her Majesty here graciously overlooking them!" His English was excellent. "I have been hearing of all your great activities, and am much interested. For I have considered going to the Canadas myself, where they take their religion less . . . vehemently!"

"*I* say that we should worship the good God each in our own way, to our best endeavour," the queen declared. "I, now, must use, profess, the English faith, Bishop Laud instructing me! Our cardinal, no doubt, disapproves. You in Scotland, Sir William, accept neither the Pope nor the Church of which my husband is the head? It is all so confusing!"

"We are Presbyterian, yes. More severe, I fear. Myself, I agree with Your Highness, that we should worship in the fashion that we think best, not be marshalled like sheep! Christ's flock is not a regiment but a wondering, aye and wandering, host that loves its shepherd!"

"That is good, good!" de la Toure exclaimed. "So say I. Ah, His Majesty."

The two men bowed as the king came in.

"At last!" Charles said. "So much of debate and advice and signing of papers!" He went to kiss his wife and then to tinkle a silver bell to order the servitors to produce the waiting meal. "Monsieur Claude, you find Sir William Alexander, my good friend, admirable? As do I."

"Yes, Majesty, indeed. We have been discussing religion, and are agreed on much."

"Ah, a difficult subject, I find. At least, that should not produce difficulties in Nova Scotia."

No other guests invited, they sat down at table, and Charles said grace before meat. Thereafter, the conversation reverted immediately to colonisation, although Will would have preferred to discuss his problems alone with the king. But Charles was full of it, and clearly of the opinion that Canada represented great opportunity, and that there were a sufficiency of territories there for British as well as French exploitation. A start should be made, he suggested, on the New Brunswick coast opposite the south end of Nova Scotia, which, he understood, was all but ignored by the French. What of Cape Breton Island? It had been part of Acadia. Were the Scots settlers on fair terms with the French there, so nearby?

Will said that as far as he knew there had been no trouble between them. After all, fishing was the main activity there, and the seas around were ample opportunity for all. Sir Robert Gordon had made a point of allowing no friction between the two colonies. Grievously, he had died, a serious loss. Meanwhile Will had sent out his own eldest son to take his place until a new deputy governor could be found and appointed. This was only a temporary measure.

The king was much concerned over this news. Had Sir William anyone in mind to fill this important position? He understood that Gordon had sons. Would one of them perhaps be prepared to take over his father's duties?

Will confessed that he did not know the Gordon sons, and whether one would be of the stature to manage a colony, which would demand much ability and decision. Especially in present circumstances, with the French situation so delicate. He himself was unsure of how secure the Scots settlers were, with apparently Nova Scotia reverting to Acadia under this peace treaty.

Charles corrected him. The treaty declared that Acadia survived, yes, under French sovereignty; but that the established Scots colony of Nova Scotia also remained in existence, side by side, as it were, and neither was to interfere with the other. Actually the French were more interested in Cape Breton Island as part of Acadia. So it was important that there should be no disharmony between the two. That was why he was urging this of Canadian expansion. Nothing had been said in the treaty about Canada. And *it* was surely sufficiently large to accommodate provinces of both nations. Even the Dutch, who were said to be seeking a foothold there.

Will's anxiety was to some extent eased. But still he was unhappy about being termed governor of Canada. He indicated as much, tactfully he hoped.

"I named you that of set purpose," he was told. "To allow for what may be possible. I could have said of but New Brunswick. But that effort might not succeed. Or you might go beyond, elsewhere. Who knows? And how far? We must look to the future, my friend. So Canada is best, as style."

"Sire? I fear that it may be difficult to live up to your . . . expectations. Nova Scotia is still itself but very partially settled. So much to be done there yet. So many new colonists required. When we may be able to reach out to further plantation, I know not."

"We must provide greater inducements to settlers. Moneys. Baronetcies and Peerages. Offer them greater opportunities."

"Huguenots, Your Majesty, might well be interested. Or some of them," de la Toure put in. "Many, exiled from France, are seeking some new life. As indeed am I! If some could be encouraged to settle in Acadia, or your Nova Scotia, might that not serve to good purpose? Offer them a new opportunity, and provide worthy colonists. Moreover, being from France, they could serve to create good relations between the Scots and the French."

The queen clapped her hands. "That is most admirable, Claude! To be used. Is it not so, Charles?"

"Indeed yes. Think you that there are many who might go, monsieur?"

"If encouraged, yes. Most will have little money to purchase lands. But if granted plots, they would make good settlers, I swear."

"Here is something to consider well. Perchance to build on. How say you, Sir William?"

Will nodded. "To me, it sounds most hopeful. This of the French linking would be valuable indeed." He took a chance. "You, monsieur, *you* would be prepared to go, perhaps?"

"If I could serve His Majesty there, yes."

"How say you, then, if you were to be the new deputy governor of Nova Scotia?" It was at Charles, however, that he looked.

The queen clapped hands again. "Bravo!" she exclaimed. "That would be most splendid! Oh yes, yes!"

The king looked from one man to the other. "You would have this, Sir William? A Frenchman as your representative? However able and reliable?"

"Who could be better, in these circumstances, Sire? To assist in our good relations with the neighbouring French in Cape Breton and the Canadas? To encourage other Huguenot settlers. And a friend of Your Majesties. If he will do it?"

De la Toure spread his hands, Gallic fashion. "It would be a wonder for me. I would be honoured, sir. If thought worthy."

"How think you they would say in Scotland?" Charles asked. "It is a Scots colony – New Scotland."

"We think kindly of the French, Sire. There was much sorrow when war was declared with France. We have been allies from ancient times. Indeed, we have been apt to prefer the French to the English! And Huguenot, *Protestant* French. I foresee no complaint."

"Very well, so be it. Indeed, I rejoice in it. My only question was this of possibly offending the Scots."

Will took another chance; he was becoming expert at it. "Sire, this of offence to the Scots. I fear that some offence was indeed created by Your Majesty making Englishmen into Scots lords of parliament. This displeased many, who felt that it lowered the dignity of the Scots lordships."

Charles frowned. "Do they think Englishmen of less worth than themselves?"

"Not quite that, Sire. But these Scots lordships do carry a seat in the Scots parliament. So these new English lords could sit therein, which many felt unsuitable. When, it is understood, you did not want them to have seats in the English House of Lords."

"M'mm. I shall consider the matter."

There was a silence round the table, but not for long. The queen broke it.

"Inform us as to your Nova Scotia, Sir William. Where will Claude make his new home? Is it a country of good airs, weather? What is done there, how do men engage themselves? We know so little of it all."

"Sir Robert Gordon founded the township of New Glasgow, Highness. He came from the west of Scotland. No doubt Monsieur de la Toure will base himself there. On the north and more sheltered side. The climate, they say, is none so different from that of Scotland, but more of mist and fogs in the spring. Little of snow or great cold. The land much forested, but fertile once more of the trees have been cleared. As on Cape Breton, fishing has been the main occupation. But in time farming will, it is hoped, overtake it. Fruit grows well, and is dried and exported. With all the timber, wood-working, even boat-building, should flourish." He turned. "Sire, Ailie Graham, whom you know, has married, and her husband, a shipmaster, intends to become a ship*builder* there."

"Ah, yes. I remember Mistress Ailie kindly. She has gone there? I wish her well. You told me once of much flooding. Is this being conquered? Drained?" If Charles had been displeased at the criticism of his lord-creating, which of course had been done for the money, he appeared to have got over it.

"Partly, Sire. Drainage is a major work, yes. But a great part of the trouble is the very high tides which flood the south-west coast. They can rise as high as fifty feet at times. This water floods inland and sours the soil. So Sir Robert began the great task of building high dykes, earthen banks and walls, heavy work and lengthy. But it will be worth it all. The Annapolis valley there could be the most productive part of the colony."

"I note my duty, then, Sir William," de la Toure said. "I will have much to learn."

"I suggest, monsieur, that you come up to Scotland to

371

see me, when you are ready to sail, and we can consider it all . . ."

They discussed many aspects of the Nova Scotian situation, Will a little concerned that the queen would find all this boring. But she showed no such signs, and indeed asked questions. He judged her an excellent wife for Charles. There was an uncomfortable spell when the king got on to the subject of monopolies, and Will, after his protest about the lords, felt that he could hardly launch another attack on this separate issue. But perhaps his expression and silence spoke more loudly than he realised, for Charles eyed him thoughtfully and left the subject alone.

There was, however, a reversion to it before Will left the dining-chamber that evening, and in a distinctly personal application. On their feet, and Will preparing to bow out, the king made his announcement.

"Sir William, I have been indebted to you all my days. This of Nova Scotia makes me the more beholden. My father knighted you, but I must do better. And you are my Secretary of State and Keeper of the Privy Seal and Signet. You not only deserve but are entitled to higher station. So I have decided to ennoble you. This will give you the greater authority. I am going to create you the Viscount of Stirling. And I trust that your fellow Scots lords will not complain!"

Will had caught his breath, speechless. What was there to say? He could only stare.

"As a viscount, my friend, you will have a secondary title and style. You have two Scots baronies, I recollect. Menstrie and another. I forget the name. Tulloch? Ah, yes – Tullibody. Menstrie is but a small property but this Tullibody, I am told, is a village and parish. So your subsidiary title will be the Lord Alexander of Tullibody, my lord viscount! How say you?"

Will Alexander did not say much. He could not. "I . . . I . . . Your Majesty, I, I cannot say . . . I do not know what, how to, to . . ."

"Do not say anything, then. And to help support your new dignity, I have thought of a highly suitable source. You aided my royal sire in his rendering of the Holy Bible into the English tongue by translating the Book of Psalms. You told me often of that. So now I give you the right to revise the psalms, if so you think fit, and the licence to you and only you, to print the King's Version of that book exclusively for thirty-one years, that is until the year of Our Lord 1660. Is that not a just and proper monopoly?"

Struck dumber than ever, Will's wits reeled as, head ashake, he backed for the door.

33

Janet Erskine was much less excited about becoming a viscountess than by the fact that the Alexander lodging at Stirling had reached completion at last, and that she could move in. Or not quite completion, for over the doorway thereto had to be inserted a handsome heraldic panel, carved in stone and painted in the appropriate colours. Will had already designed such panel, indeed it was all but finished, the work of a local and talented stonemason, showing the arms of MacDonald, the famous galley of the Lords of the Isles, differenced for MacAllister, a sept thereof, from which came the surname of Alexander. This now fell to be altered and enhanced, remade indeed, to measure up to his new style and dignity. So while Janet was busy arranging the furnishings of the fine establishment, ordering new plenishings and fitments, choosing paintwork and carpeting, Will, among the host of his official duties, occupied odd moments of peace in devising an apt and significant coat of arms for over the doorway, which he could submit to the Lord Lyon King of Arms for due ratification.

Now that he was a viscount and lord of parliament, he was entitled to bear a quartered, as distinct from a simple, single shield; that is, divided into four sections. The first and fourth quarters would show the Alexander family arms, as before, this divided down the centre, argent or white on the one side, sable or black on the other, with a chevron superimposed, an inverted arrowhead, with at its base a crescent. Then, on the second and third quarters, would sail the renowned galley of the Isles, with its sail furled, black on gold, between three cross-crosslets, having the badge of the Nova Scotia baronets on top – not that he himself was one, but this the only way he could record his connection with the colony. For the necessary crest above, over the viscount's coronet, he chose a brown bear, to indicate far places, deciding that a moose would be too difficult to carve and be recognised by folk used only to red and roe deer. Supporters were also required, at each side of the shield, and he thought that an Indian would be apt on the left, for he had been anxious for the Micmac natives not to be harassed or driven out; and on the other side a mermaid holding a mirror and comb, this partly as a gesture towards Janet, with whom he had swum in the Loch of Menteith, but also as indication of the MacAllisters' origins on the shores of the Sea of the Hebrides, the mirror and comb being the ancient Pictish symbol for fair womanhood. There remained only a motto; or two of them, as was now his entitlement. He chose for the main one, on top, *Per Mare, Per Terras*, By Sea and Land, which seemed applicable; and for the other, at the base, *Aut Spero, Aut Sperno*, meaning the triumph of hope over despair or rejection.

Will, strangely, got much satisfaction out of deciding on all this, scarcely vital as it was from any material point of view. But it all meant something enduring; and long after he was dead and gone his heirs and descendants would bear this heraldic device and perhaps remember how it all had come about.

Janet was concerned that the sculptor of the panel did her figure reasonable justice as the mermaid.

Claude de la Toure arrived in the midst of all this furnishing and embellishing, and brought with him the news that the queen had been delivered of a fine son, to be called after his father, and all was well there. The Frenchman stayed with them at Menstrie, the town-house being scarcely ready yet for entertaining visitors, for the best part of a month, while Will made arrangements for a ship to sail him across the ocean, Duncan Drummond being presently in Nova Scotia. The prolonged stay was nowise unwelcome, for their guest made himself very popular with the Alexanders; indeed, a man of taste, he much assisted Janet in her house-plenishing, Will pretending to become jealous of their so close association. But discussing colonial affairs with him, he came to the conclusion that he could scarcely have found a more suitable and useful deputy, in the fairly delicate French situation.

When at length a ship was made available at Dumbarton, and Anthony Alexander was given the duty of conducting de la Toure thither and seeing him off, he promised to send brother William home on the vessel's return voyage; also to inform him that he was now entitled to call himself Master of Stirling, as son and heir to the viscount thereof.

The new house was finally finished and furnished to Janet's satisfaction in the spring, and a house-warming party was organised. Will, on his official duties, had been at the receipt of much hospitality from magnates and others all over the land; and he decided to take this opportunity of offering some acknowledgment. So a great assortment of the grand and the less so were invited. Probably Stirling had not seen such a glittering assemblage since its fortress-castle had ceased to be the Scots royal headquarters. Even the eleventh Earl of Angus, Chief Warden of the Marches and head of the proud Red Douglas line, attended, perhaps partly to assess the suitability of the family his daughter desired to marry into, and no doubt somewhat mollified by the fact that the Alexanders were now ennobled, even though very newly so.

The Old Countess of Mar had died, so the Alexanders were spared her critical appraisal; but her son, the earl, was there, and seemed to approve of all, although Will had been a little afraid that he might be otherwise, with this palatial establishment being put up so very near his own father's never-completed lodging. Tam o' the Coogate, who clearly looked upon Will as all but his own protégé, was loud in his praise, indeed acted as almost second host to the company.

It was all a great occasion, and went on for a full twenty-four hours, for, with most of the guests coming from long distances off, they had to be put up for the night one way or another, not all in the house, large as it was, but quarters found for them in the town, an expensive business altogether, Will did not fail to recognise but, he felt, essential. His concern, in that regard, was scarcely eased by one of the guests, a judge and Lord of Session, Sir John Scott of Scotstarvit, in Fife, noted for his acerbic tongue, who, in departing, glanced up at the fine heraldic panel above the door and observed that *Per Mare, Per Terras* might reasonably be translated as By Metre and By Turners, poetry and base coinage! The laughter which greeted this sally did reveal some criticism as to how Will had scaled to these heights. That man sought not to resent it, recognising that it was a way of looking at his career, however superficial. But Janet was hurt.

The discussions with Claude de la Toure had crystallised in Will's mind something of the problems, difficulties but also opportunities of the colonising process. So now he thought it worth while to try to set down on paper a summary of his findings, challenges and experiences, and those of the people on the ground, this for the benefit of further attempts at settlement, which, if King Charles had his way, would probably be not long in developing, this of the Canadas in especial looming. He arranged to have a limited edition printed

It was the spring of 1631 before William arrived home from Nova Scotia, having been gone a year. It was extraordinary what that year had made of him. Adventures, responsibility, decision-taking and sheer challenge had brought him back a man of strength and judgment, suddenly seeming older than his years. What the Lady Margaret Douglas would think of him now remained to be seen; but his parents were much gratified and proud.

He had much to tell his father of the colony, most of it favourable. There had been no trouble with the French so far, and de la Toure's arrival was going to assist in that situation. He had established an excellent rapport with that man, and seen that he would make a good and wise governor. Development went ahead on almost all fronts, with most settlers active and industrious, although there were exceptions. Duncan Drummond was a great asset, and Ailie most evidently happy and supportive. The dyke-building along the south-west shoreline was almost finished, and the drainage of the marshland in hand. Large areas of forest had been cleared, even though only a small proportion of the whole, and the problem of digging up the tree-roots being tackled, so that the crop and fruit growing could flourish. Houses were going up all over the peninsula, but the majority, so far, along the coastal areas, and fishing-havens established. Drummond had commenced building his first vessel. But they could do with many more settlers. This of Huguenots was good, the more the better. He, William, proposed making a tour round Scotland to seek to encourage emigration, explaining to ordinary folk, farmers, shepherds, smiths, millers, craftsmen and the like, what great opportunities there were for them in Nova Scotia, to raise their way of life most notably. Kirk ministers were particularly needed; could his father do anything about that problem?

With the young man's assistance, Will drew a much more detailed map, to go with his *Encouragement to Colonise*.

Needless to say, however, William went off on a visit to Douglas Castle, in upper Clydesdale, to see his hoped-for bride, before commending his tour of settler recruitment.

There were still a few baronetcy applicants coming forward, and William was instructed to advocate this aspect of affairs also on his visiting. King Charles would be grateful.

The monarch's gratitude for benefits received did show itself later that year. Will had sent a copy of his *Encouragement to Colonise*, with map, and Charles

378

acknowledged this by sending it to his own printer in Oxford, to be made available to potential English settlers. He reminded Will of the psalms revisal and monopoly, and ended up by appointing him an Extra Lord of Session, that is, an auxiliary High Court judge – not that this greatly gladdened the recipient, who had already over-many positions to fill.

He did seek to do something about the psalms, even though the idea of selling the revised version scarcely appealed. He had been fortunate in discovering that one of his fellow-poets, William Drummond of Hawthornden, in Midlothian, had written an elegy on the late Prince Henry and had expressed an interest in the Bible translation. Meeting him at a Court of Session conference in Edinburgh – Drummond was a lawyer – Will had little difficulty in persuading him to go over the earlier version of the psalms, with the original Latin rendering, and suggest possible amendments. His comments and improvements were excellent, although he took some time to produce them, a man of leisure, which was perhaps no bad thing. The final version was sent to the king for approval and printing, since it was to come out under royal warrant. Will was able to repay Drummond, to some extent, with helping him on details of a history of Scotland he was writing, dealing with the reigns of the first five James Stewarts, a major work.

While he was at all this composition and penmanship, at Janet's urging, Will assembled all his poetic writings together, or such as he judged to be worth perpetuating, into one large volume, a lifetime's labour of love and sometimes of agonising, entitling this *Recreations of the Muses*, and despatched it to his own printer in Edinburgh. His wife pointed out that, on this occasion, he had no need to dedicate it to Aurora!

34

It was June of 1633 before Charles and Henrietta Maria eventually came to Scotland for their second coronation; this because the queen had meantime produced another child, a second son, to be called James after his grandfather. They came with a vast concourse of the English nobility and senior clergy, including William Laud, newly appointed Archbishop of Canterbury although not yet enthroned as such, who was said to be urging the king to turn the Scottish Kirk to episcopacy – an ominous proposal. Laud was now Charles's supreme adviser, Strafford having disgraced himself and been more or less banished, as Lord Deputy of Ireland.

As Secretary of State it was Will's duty to meet the monarch at the borderline and welcome him and his consort to the more ancient kingdom. Not only himself, of course; sundry other representative folk were present, notably including the Chief Warden of the Marches, the Earl of Angus, who clearly considered himself to be the senior welcomer. They assembled at the Reidswire Stone, which marked the border, high among the Cheviot Hills south of Jedburgh where, it had been announced, the royal cavalcade would enter Scotland.

They had a lengthy wait, but fortunately the June weather was kind, and it was not unpleasant to dismount and relax there in the heather, listening to the carolling larks, with stupendous views all around, the Merse, or East March, of the Scottish borderland especially lovely, indeed spectacular, however blood-drenched its history.

Angus did not ignore Will but paid considerably more attention to loftier-born individuals, particularly Kerr of

Ferniehirst, Earl of Lothian, at whose castle nearby the king and queen were to spend their first night in Scotland. This Earl William's ancestor had been Sir Thomas Kerr, whom Mary Queen of Scots had called her Protector, and had suffered therefor. He was Warden of the Middle March, and an amiable character. Angus, no doubt, would have preferred the monarch to spend the night at his castle of Douglas, but that lay almost one hundred miles away to the west.

Lothian congratulated Will on his viscountcy, and declared it well deserved. He was interested in the progress of the colonising efforts, although strangely the borderland had been the least productive area of all Scotland for settlers. Will wondered why.

"I think that we are too much thirled to our own lands, territories, roots as you might say, to consider leaving them. We fight each other, of course, always have done; but we are all very much Borderers, and tend to see ourselves as a folk apart – with however little reason!"

"You could say the same of the Highland clans," Will observed. "Yet they have provided many colonists."

"Small wonder," Angus put in. "Any change would be an improve on the barbarous Hielants! What sort of settlers they will make over there, the good Lord knows!"

"Has your lordship ever visited the Highlands and Islands?" Will asked, mildly. He had to remind himself that this man's daughter was due to marry his son William, tact therefore called for.

"No, nor wish to!"

"My own family came from those parts," Will mentioned.

"Then they had the good sense to get out of a barren land, where even the language is uncouth and not to be understood by honest men!"

"I am surprised to hear you saying that, my lord! For your own name comes of that Gaelic tongue." Was he wise to come out with that?

"What do you mean, man?"

"Only that Douglas, or *Dubh Ghlas*, means dark grey. I would have expected you to know that. Aye, and to be proud of it, so ancient a style. And Angus is called after Angus mac Fergus, High King of the Picts, whose daughter married Kenneth mac Alpin, who united Picts and Scots and formed Scotland." In for a turner, in for a merk!

Lothian grinned, and Angus turned to find somebody else to talk to.

Their waiting came to an end at last, with the outriders of the royal cohort, almost a host, appearing afar off down the valley of the Catcleuch Water, on the English side. They would have come this day from Rothbury, one of the Earl of Northumberland's houses, and companies of that size, with women and clerics included, did not move very fast.

Although they sent messengers to meet the newcomers, the Scots lords were meticulous not to move a foot beyond the line of the actual border, so that they might welcome the monarch on to Scots soil precisely.

Charles and Henrietta Maria both looked somewhat weary as they came up, after their long riding, and did not dismount as they drew rein. Nor did any others of the great company.

Angus was the first to stride forward, to reach up to take and kiss the royal hand, although it was Will's face there, behind, which lifted Charles Stewart's handsome features.

"Welcome to your kingdom of Scotland, Sire," the earl said. "And your gracious queen. We greet Your Graces proudly. I am Angus, the Douglas!" He went over to kiss the queen's hand, in turn.

"Ah, I have heard of the Black Douglas, my lord," the king said, still looking over at Will. "My good tutor taught me the rhyme, so long since. How went it?"

Hush ye, hush ye, do not fret ye,
The Black Douglas shall not get ye!

382

That was unfortunate, however well meant. Angus was chief of the Red Douglases, not the Black. And however great a hero the original Black Douglas had been, of the verse, scourge of the English, he was scarcely looked on kindly by the Reds, who were, far enough back, actually of illegitimate blood however lofty.

Sundry eyebrows raised at this, Will approached to take the royal hand. He did not presume to tutor still his liege-lord, but he did think to advise in some degree.

"Your Majesty's leal and devoted servant. I rejoice to see you." And, lower-voiced, "Sire, you now are on Scots soil. It is customary to dismount and kiss the ground, in such event. At a first entry."

"Ha, is it so? I did not know." Charles promptly dismounted and knelt to go through the required motions.

Suitable and traditional as this was, it made a major impact, if hardly in the desired fashion. For there was another enshrined custom, in England as well as Scotland, and that was that none should ever seem higher than the monarch; so that when the king dismounted all others should do so also. There followed a confusion, therefore, as the first ranks of the large company, who could see what went on, hurriedly got down from their saddles, while the scores behind, unable to see the situation, looked surprised, some dismounting, others not. None of those now on foot sank to kiss the ground, however.

Charles, grasping Will's arm, looked at him enquiringly, to see whether there was anything else he ought to be doing. "My friend!" he said.

Other Scots notables were now coming up to bow and kiss the royal hand. Will went over to the queen's horse, she remaining in her saddle.

"Ah, Sir William," she said, smiling. "I think of you as that, not as *vicomte*! Here is a joy, to come to you here in your own land. How fair, how beautiful!" She waved her hand, which he was seeking to kiss, at all that prospect. "You said that it was so. I see that you spoke truth."

"Highness, my humble and admiring greetings! You

383

are as well as you look? And not over-weary with the travel? And your sons? You have had two sons since last we forgathered."

"Forgathered?"

"Saw each other, Majesty. A Scots word."

"Ah, I will have to learn much more language now! And see much. You will show me, teach me, Sir William. Yes, I have two fine sons for Charles. The pity that I could not bring them. Too young for the journey. I am tired, yes. We have been a month on the road, so much of being entertained in great houses, *châteaux*, abbeys, as well as the progress, the travel. For I am *enceinte*, once more! Hala – who would be a woman!"

Not knowing whether to congratulate or not, Will shook his head. "Not far to go now, Highness. To Lord Lothian's house at Ferniehirst, only a few miles. Then you can rest. Here is the Lord Lothian . . ."

The king remounted, which was the signal for all to do so, and the move northwards, down the long, green hillsides, was commenced. Charles beckoned Will forward, to ride between himself and the queen, which would not please the Earl of Angus, who found himself partnered with Archbishop Laud whom, as a stern Presbyterian, he would deplore.

Will discovered, on the nine-mile ride to Ferniehirst, that he was expected to be the royal guide and adviser during this Scotland visit, and hoped that he could cope. No doubt Tam o' the Coogate, not in this company today, would help when they got to Edinburgh.

Ferniehirst Castle, on the lip of its ravine above the Jed Water valley, although sizeable, was not nearly large enough to accommodate all that company; so many of the less important were sent on another mile or so to the town of Jedburgh where the Earl of Lothian had a commodious town-house, actually built for this very purpose by his ancestor Sir Thomas Kerr, to provide lodgings for Charles's grandmother's courtiers when Mary came to Ferniehirst as she so often did.

The present royal entourage would more than fill this convenient building. Other quarters in the town would house the escort guards.

So congenial proved to be the hospitality at Ferniehirst Castle, so excellent a hostess was the Countess of Lothian – whom Will knew well from long since, for she had been Lady Annabella Campbell, sister of his friend and student, Archie – that the king and queen stayed there for two nights, glad of a rest from their long ridings, which rather upset the schedule planned by Angus, who had intended them to spend their second night in Scotland at his own brother's house of Mordington in the Merse, on their way to Edinburgh. There would have to be adjustments, for the coronation ceremony was all arranged, at Holyrood, for 18th June, and this was the 15th. It was too far to expect the royal party to ride to Edinburgh in one day, so another resting-place, nearer the city, would have to be provided. Much beard-tugging by Angus.

The Lothians told Charles much about his grandmother which he had not known. He, and his wife, were duly impressed with details of Mary's extraordinary ride from there to Hermitage Castle in Liddesdale, thirty-five miles away, and back in the same day, this to see the Earl of Bothwell, whom she later married, who lay sick of a wound there. This journey of seventy miles across trackless hills, moors and bogs, indicated something of the vitality, courage and determination of a queen renowned for her beauty if not for her judgment. It certainly made the present royal ridings seem but moderate, even though these were of a more prolonged nature.

On the second day, they visited Jedburgh Abbey, part demolished by the Reformers but still magnificent and impressive, on its mound above the river. It had been one of the finest buildings in the land. Here Lothian related to the royal couple the dramatic story of how Sir Thomas Learmonth of Ersildoune, the famed Thomas the Rhymer, courtier, seer and prophet, had, during a masque staged in the nave in celebration of Alexander

385

the Third's second marriage, to Yolande de Dreux, and in which the king and queen were dancing, seen death, in the shape of a grinning white skeleton dancing behind the royal pair, this foretelling the forthcoming death of Alexander, who fell over the cliff at Kinghorn in Fife soon afterwards, leaving Scotland without an heir to the throne, this resulting in the dire Wars of Independence, Wallace, Bruce and the rest. Charles and Henrietta Maria eyed each other a little apprehensively at this account, before moving on to inspect the Kerr family burial-place.

The next day, then, they had quite a lengthy ride for such a cavalcade, down the Jed Water almost to its junction with the greater Teviot, there to swing off to Ancrum, where they picked up Sir Robert Kerr thereof, kinsman of Lothian, and on, climbing now out of Teviotdale and over Ancrum Muir, where Lilliard's Edge was pointed out to the royal pair, and it was related how Maid Lilliard had helped to fight the English at a battle there, "receiving mony thumps; and when her legs were hackit off, she fought upon her stumps!", the queen declaring disbelief.

On northwards to St Boswells and Lessudden, and over the easternmost shoulder of the three Eildon Hills, where they saw the Trimontium of the Romans, from which the terrible invaders had sought to conquer and occupy what they named Caledonia, and failed. Down to Melrose, which interested Charles not only for the ruined abbey where the famous Bruce's heart was buried, likewise the Black Douglas, but because this was the place that Tam o' the Coogate had rejected for his earldom in favour of Haddington.

Up long Lauderdale they proceeded, none being able to explain to the king why it was so named when the river was called Leader, to halt for rest and refreshment at the Maitland Castle of Thirlestane, where the Earl of Lauderdale was no more knowledgeable about the naming of his twenty-mile-long valley, but was able to show Charles a letter, written in his own hand by his royal father to his own grandfather, Sir Richard Maitland, twelfth of Thirlestane, acknowledging gratefully his leal service to "his grandsire, goodsire, good-dame, mother and himself" representing at least seventy years of faithful attendance. The earl continued on with them.

Presently they began to climb to the great barrier of the Lammermuir Hills, which cut off the Borderland from Lothian. At the lofty summit moorland the now wearying visitors were shown where, at Soutra, Malcolm the Fourth had established the first great hospital in Scotland, in the twelfth century, much interesting Charles. His wife wanted to know why choose such isolated and exposed spot; and Will explained that it was for that very reason, that infection and disease should not spread therefrom, and the bracing air should aid the sick, according to Malcolm.

The views from the northern mouth of the pass were stupendous, and had all, even the most supercilious of the royal train, exclaiming. For here the road dropped steeply to the Lothian plain, and thence to the Firth of Forth's gleaming waters, with the green Fife hills stretching behind, and far, far beyond, the blue ranked summits of the Highland Line, peak upon peak. Henrietta Maria declared that she had never seen the like; and Charles asked to have pointed out to him where, in all that, lay Dunfermline in Fife, where he had spent his first four years.

Many of the company tired indeed, they eventually reached Dalkeith, about halfway between Soutra and Edinburgh, which Angus had chosen as their halting-place for the night, instead of his brother's house, and had sent a messenger the previous day to warn and prepare. It had been something of a bitter pill for him to swallow, for Dalkeith Castle was the only large Douglas house on the way to Edinburgh, but it was a *Black* Douglas establishment, one of the seats of the Earl of Morton. This intrigued Will Alexander, for it had been Aurora's home. Now her brother was earl here.

Dalkeith was a fair-sized town, its castle rather oddly sited below it, but in a strong position nevertheless, on a cliff at a bend of the River North Esk, long a Douglas place. Once again, the size of the royal entourage had demanded a worthy establishment close to a town, for the necessary accommodation.

This Earl of Morton, a man of about Will's own age, whether he thanked the other Douglas for landing him with the entertainment of this great company, welcomed the royal visitors suitably and offered handsome quarters and excellent provision, despite the short notice. This branch of the Black Douglases had been based here for centuries, and far enough back had twice married into the reigning house. The king and queen were shown the oldest known will and testament in Scotland, that of Sir James Douglas of Dalkeith, dated 1390, in which, among other provisions, he requested that all books borrowed from his library be returned, and that all books that he had borrowed be given back to their owners, including romances. He left half of his free goods to pay for his funeral expenses, stating that the vicar of Lasswade's funeral fee was to be his best horse, stipulating that he was not to get any more than this – presumably knowing his vicar. But he did endow the Collegiate Church of St Nicholas in Dalkeith, providing for a provost and five prependaries, each to have suitable manses, to reside there continually and to be dressed decently in gowns and black hoods furred with lamb's wool, but that should any of these chaplains keep a concubine openly, he should vacate his charge. His own eldest legitimate son got his second-best horse, along with heiring the landed estates; but his wife, the Princess Egidia, sister of Robert the Second, got only a jewelled brooch, which she herself had given him; which looked as though he had found marrying into royalty less than rewarding. Actually Sir James had died in 1420, thirty years after making his will.

Fascinated with this, the queen forgot her tiredness.

While the guests were at table, sundry callers arrived

from Edinburgh, these including the Earl of Haddington, the Lord Lyon King of Arms, and senior Kirk ministers, these to inform of the arrangements for the coronation ceremony next day. It would be held in the chapel of the former Abbey of the Holy Rood. The newcomers were found an extra table and provender. Glancing from the soberly gowned divines to Archbishop Laud, otherwise clad, Will wondered whether feathers would fly.

Charles, who no more enjoyed speaking in public than he did eating in public, as the meal ended had a word with Will, whom he had sitting on his left, even though others were undoubtedly better entitled to that position than the Secretary of State, and possibly resented it. Their host was on the king's right, next to the queen.

"I have announcements to make," he said. "Is this as good a time to make them as any? Before all, rather than in private, I think. I am concerned, my friend, that my Scots people should esteem me as well as may be. They do not know me, and I have been long in coming north. Tomorrow will be all ceremony and formality, I think. So, now?"

"To be sure, Sire. But your folk here are loyal, and proud to have provided the monarch for the other kingdoms, proud to have Your Majesty here among them, where your royal line stemmed so long ago. Have no fears as to esteem."

"Nevertheless, some words, gestures, on my part now may help, I judge. How do I go about thus speaking, here? In Scotland. Is there some procedure to follow?"

"Yes, Sire. You should be duly announced by the Lyon King of Arms. He is here. Come from Edinburgh. I will go fetch him up."

Will rose and went down the hall to where the newcomers sat, among them Sir James Balfour of Kinnaird, Lord Lyon, beside Tam o' the Coogate.

"My lord, it is good to see you," he said to the earl. "His Majesty will be glad to have your good advice on a number of matters hereafter. But meantime, Sir James, the king would make announcement. Will you come forward to declare it?"

Balfour, who had had no opportunity to practise his duty of introducing and proclaiming the monarch since his appointment three years before, and that on Will's recommendation on the previous Lyon's death, looked a little disconcerted, but did as he was bidden. Up at the dais table he bowed before the king, then the queen. Will resumed his seat.

Not having brought his baton of office with him, Balfour had to make do with an empty silver wine-flagon. Reaching for this, he banged it on the table vehemently, to gain silence.

"I, Lyon, command all men's heed and attention," he called. "His Majesty, Charles, by the Grace of God King of Scots, will address this company." He bowed again.

Charles was in no hurry to speak, eyeing the gathering with that considering gaze which he had had since childhood, and which many thought to be haughty and was not. He sat forward, as though he would have preferred to stand, but must not, for if he did everyone else must stand also.

"My lords, councillors, officers, and friends of all degrees," he began slowly, carefully. "I rejoice, with my dear consort the queen, to be here with you in my native land this day, after long absence. I come to be crowned, yes. But also to see and learn and, I hope, to receive the affection of my people. And to show my concern for the well-being and weal of my Scottish realm and folk." He paused, as approving murmurs arose.

"It is my wish," he went on, as deliberately, "before the morrow's rituals and solemn occasions, to show something of my appreciation, yes appreciation and thanks, towards some who have aided and supported me hereto, some here present. That they may be recognised as my, my champions and friends, on the morrow." Sitting beside him, Will perceived that Charles's hands were trembling slightly, and recognised something of what

390

this speech-making was costing the essentially silent and retiring character he had helped to rear.

The king turned right-handed in his seat. "First you, my lord of Morton, our host this day, representative of a long line which has played a notable part in this kingdom's past, and has indeed inter-married with my own royal house, I have learned: you, my lord, High Treasurer of Scotland, I hereby nominate to be a member of the Most Noble Order of the Garter."

There were not a few indrawn breaths at that, including Will's. This was a great honour, indeed, but it was an English one. Unfortunately, the Thistle, the Scottish equivalent, had been put down at the Reformation.

Morton rose, biting his lip, and bowed deeply.

Charles went on. "Another Douglas, of ancient line also, my lord of Angus, Lieutenant of the Borders and my Chief Warden of the Marches, has recently married a good lady here present, who, however modest in bearing, now outranks her husband in degree, for she is the daughter of the Marquis of Huntly. And my lord is but an earl, although the eleventh, I understand. Therefore I now redress the situation, and appoint my lord to be Marquis of Douglas!"

That drew more gasps. Angus was scarcely popular, especially in the Borders where his hand had been heavy; and there were not a few Borderers present. Will wondered.

Charles waved a hand to the bowing new marquis, only the second in Scotland, and went on.

"A Douglas of yet another line, who has served my royal father and myself well, William, Viscount of Drumlanrig and Lord of Hawick, I promote to be Earl of Queensberry, in appreciation."

That drew applause, for Drumlanrig was well liked and friendly, and as Warden of the West March had frequently toned down the dictates of Angus.

The king stroked his trim, pointed beard. "My friends, lest you think that I am concerned only with the House

391

of Douglas, I now would pay tribute to another line and family which has played as notable a part in the life of Scotland, that of Bruce. The hero-king was *my* ancestor, as well as, as antecedent of Lord Bruce of Kinloss. My lord is not here present, I think, but I wish to show my acknowledgment of his illustrious house, as well as of his own services rendered. And I now declare Thomas, Lord Bruce to be Earl of Elgin."

That also went down well. Will thought that he could see what Charles was at. The names of Bruce and Douglas were folk heroes in Scotland, had been since the Wars of Independence; and by linking them with himself thus, at this early stage in his Scots visit, he was seeking to win popularity with the people. Was this the effort of a man unsure of himself, reigning by divine right as he claimed? Will, who had taught the boy about the Bruce, the Douglas and William Wallace, perhaps bore some responsibility?

His ponderings on this were brought to a halt by the words Nova Scotia. Charles was continuing.

". . . Nova Scotia and the Canadas. Colonisation overseas is highly important to us all, in these days, a source of prosperity and wealth and dominion. The nations compete in this. For us, none has contributed so much to this excellent end as William Alexander, not only in New Scotland but in the Ulster plantation. And so my final appointment this night is that of my old friend and tutor, William. He is raised to the dignity of Earl of Stirling and Viscount of Canada." And the king actually turned and patted Will on the shoulder.

It was the queen's hand-clapping which brought home to Will that what he had heard was reality, fact, not some meanderings of his wits, the effect of Morton's wines, perhaps. Also that his staring at Charles was highly unsuitable, deplorable. Somehow he got to his feet, gripping the table, and stammering he knew not what. Fortunately, following the queen's lead, applause was general, and what he said would go unheard.

Probably the king was thankful to have done with all

the oratory, and as well pleased as his neighbour to bring matters to a close at this effective stage. He rose, Will still on his feet and seeking words – and all must rise with the monarch.

The royal couple turned to withdraw from the hall, arm-in-arm, to much bowing and cheering, Balfour the Lyon, who had stood behind Charles throughout, striving to make himself heard.

It is to be feared that his Secretary of State did not contribute much to his sovereign-lord's advising and guidance, for what remained of that evening, amid all the congratulations and comments. Will could still scarcely believe what had happened. Strange, how much more this new elevation seemed to mean to him than his previous honours and appointments. After all, a year ago he had been made a viscount, a lord of parliament, this only the one step below an earl. But this rank and title was especial, different from all others. Marquis admittedly ranked higher these days, but that was a new importation from the south, only thirty years old; whereas the style and status of earl always had been the position of the very highest in Scotland's long story, stemming from the seven great mormaors, the *ri*, of lesser kings of ancient Alba, under the High King, the Ard Righ, the title becoming changed, or translated, to earl in the twelfth century. At first there were only the seven of them, relating to the provinces which succeeded the mormaordoms, but gradually they increased in number, to be linked with the counties of the land. There were now perhaps some forty holders of the rank. Nevertheless it was a highly prestigious step up, an entering of the topmost grouping of the nation, extraordinary advancement for one born a small laird of Highland extraction. Was he foolish to be so affected?

What would Janet say?

Will did not in fact see his wife until after the coronation, for next day he had to accompany the king and queen on their seven-mile ride to Edinburgh and all the celebrations which followed. And these were quite elaborate, and more time-consuming than was perhaps desirable before the actual coronation, even though they made an early start of it from Dalkeith, warned of something of the city's preparations to receive the monarch.

First of all they had to add to their journey by encircling the town, south-about, in order to reach the West Port entrance to the old walled city, the traditional entry-place for royalty, this because hitherto such had always come from the west, Stirling or Linlithgow, not from Dalkeith, to the south-east. At this West Bow arched gateway, the great cavalcade was met by the provost and magistrates, and on a decorative stage, a scantily clad lady representing Edina – whose links with Edinburgh were surely equally scanty. She proclaimed a welcome in flowery verse, prompted by none other than Drummond of Hawthornden, who stood behind, and had no doubt composed the eulogy; indeed after she had finished, he himself launched forth into a panegyric on the descent and virtues of Charles Stewart. The king responded briefly, and bowed to the lady; and then the provost of the city came forward with the keys thereof on a cushion to present to the monarch, with a large bouquet of flowers for the queen, which on horseback she had difficulty in coping with. Speeches of loyal greeting followed, again acknowledged with only a word or two from the less-than-eloquent Charles, and they were able to move on through the gateway and down to the Grassmarket below the towering bulk of the castle-fortress. Here, at the Over Bow, there was another halt, while a second nymph, but of ample proportions, announced that she was Caledonia, and represented to its liege-lord the most ancient kingdom of Christendom which even the Romans could not conquer. More verses, presumably by Drummond. Then on, climbing now to the long spinal ridge of the city, which stretched from the castle a mile down to Holyrood, where, just below the High Kirk of St Giles, at the Tron, was an extraordinary conical mound made out of rocks and turf and flowers, which a spokesman, dressed to represent Dionysus, declared was Mount Parnassus, the favourite resort of the muses – which of course required more versifying. Even Will's love of poesy was beginning to flag, and he, and no doubt others, was considering the passage of time, with noon intended to see the start of the coronation ceremony. The deacons of the guilds and crafts were gathered here, and had to have their say, but fortunately these were less wordy than hitherto, men of their hands rather than tongues. But still they were not finished with welcome, for proceeding on down the Canongate, at its tolbooth, they were held up by an apparition who declared himself to be Fergus mac Erc, who had first come from Ireland as initial King of the Scots, in the year of Our Lord 500, earliest recorded ancestor of their gracious Charles. Good advice on the role of monarchs was given.

At last, the fidgeting company was able to trot on the remaining few hundred yards to Holyrood.

Once again, not all the entourage could be accommodated even in the house which James the Fifth had erected as an extension of the former abbot's lodging, this beside the semi-demolished abbey, one wing of which had been left intact by the Reformers, as a quite large chapel, although stripped of much of its decorative internal fittings. There had been some question as to whether this would be of sufficient size to be used for a coronation, but the Kirk was concerned not to make too much of it anyway, and Charles, consulted, was all for simplicity and a minimum of fuss. But clearly, even limiting the numbers of those entitled to attend, there would not be room for all of the company that had ridden with the monarch. Much selection was going to be required on the part of the Lord Lyon King of Arms, his heralds and officers, inevitably much turning away and disappointment.

Within Holyroodhouse itself, after the necessary changing into suitable clothing by all concerned, there did develop what Will had rather feared, friction between the Kirk divines and Archbishop Laud over the forthcoming ritual, late in the day as this was – indeed late in every respect, for owing to all the city welcoming and speech-making, it was already past noon and the ceremony was going to start well over an hour after it was planned. There had not been a coronation in Scotland since 1513, the year of Flodden Field, when the two-year-old James the Fifth came tragically to his father's throne, and that had been a much-reduced affair. His grandson, the late James, had been crowned after a fashion as an infant at Stirling Castle, but that was no true coronation. And the Reformation had changed men's ways of thinking about such matters, especially on the religious side. Certain of the temporal procedure was clearly laid down by statute and custom; but with the putting down of so-called papistical practices, the anointing with oil and the like, there were gaps to be filled. The clerics had their own ideas as to what should be done, but Laud viewed it all differently and, close adviser to the king as he was, dissension arose. Laud saw all this as very much a secondary and less important event than the Westminster Abbey coronation of eight years earlier, all but unnecessary indeed, and certainly not such as to have the monarch involved in unsuitable Presbyterian rites and forms, he who was head of the Church of England. The archbishop was anything but a conciliatory prelate, and much heat was generated, even in the royal presence, and this so soon before the actual enthroning was to take place, direly improper and deplorable as it was. Laud actually called the divines dissenters. Will, much troubled, made use of his own personal influence with Charles, together with Tam Hamilton, to smooth things over and seek to preserve the decencies, along with the dignity and essence of the occasion. The pair were not alone in wishing a plague upon the clerics on both fronts.

Lyon, seeking to marshall all, found it a difficult task, back from overseeing his deputies ordering the admissions and refusals at the chapel doors. Recognising the problems and the arrogant attitudes of some of the company, Will excused himself from the royal presence and went to help. It was mainly a matter of precedence. Lofty and high-born folk were apt to have their own notions in this respect, the English ones, needless to say, not backward, even though they had no effective part to play in this event, being merely honoured guests.

Once these, and all with no actual duties to perform, however illustrious their rank, including a phalanx of the ministers representing the General Assembly of the Kirk of Scotland, were led off, the next group to go were the earls, these entitled to make a separate entry, such as were not officiating as officers of state. Here there was some exchange of views, not only as to seniority, for it transpired that the new Marquis of Douglas, not only insisted that he was a step above the earls now, but claimed that as Lieutenant of the Borders, as distinct from Chief Warden, he was an officer of state, which Lyon and others disputed. However, Will advised, rather than have dispute and delay, this should be accepted, if doubtfully. The earls paced off.

These officers of state now formed up, save for the four who were to bear the regalia. They included Will, as Secretary of State, who paired Haddington, leading the Lord Advocate, the Great Chamberlain, the Lord High Admiral, the Master of the King's Works and others. And to be sure the Marquis of Douglas. Led by the Albany Herald they were led out and to the side or vestry door of the church, where they entered in file.

That building made an odd chapel, for it was merely one of the transepts of the former great abbey. It had retained its roof, but was walled off from the ruinous remainder. So it seemed all out of proportion, far too high for its moderate length and restricted breadth, even its lofty clerestorey galleries remaining. It was now packed to overflowing. Choristers were chanting no very rousing refrain. The officers of state went to sit on the front row of benches reserved for them. They faced the chancel area, up its step, where a group of black-robed clerics stood, stern-faced.

They all waited, nobody very sure of the sequence of events. Will wondered what would happen about Laud. Would he deign to grace the occasion at all? And if so, in what capacity, since he had no least authority here. Tam o' the Coogate observed that they would be fortunate to get through the proceedings without pickle and pother, since none here had been involved in the like previously, save the king himself in a no doubt very different crowning. He did not sound distressed by the prospect.

Two heralds appeared from the side door, in their colourful tabards, to thump on the floor with their staffs. The chanting died away. Then in strode Lord Lyon Balfour, to halt and raise his baton high.

"The Honours of Scotland!" he cried.

All stood. After a brief pause, in came the four remaining earls, Keith, the Earl Marischal leading and bearing aloft the great sword of state. He was followed by Hay, Earl of Errol, the High Constable, carrying the principal sceptre. Then came the Chancellor, another Hay, the Earl of Kinnoull, with the lesser sceptre. Finally the Justiciar, the Graham Earl of Airth and Menteith, with the gleaming, glittering Scottish crown borne on a scarlet cushion. These paced along beside the single step and halted, to face the chancel with its greater and lesser thrones in front of the communion table.

The heralds thumped again, and Lyon raised voice. "Here enters His Grace, Charles, High King of Scots." And then, almost as though an afterthought. "And Her Grace the Queen." He turned, and bowed the royal couple in, stepping backwards before them, a hazardous proceeding, for he had to negotiate that step, in leading the pair up to their thrones. Will held his breath. A trip there would be disastrous.

Charles and Henrietta Maria however held all eyes, and worthily so, he handsome, dignified, all but aloof, she attractive and smiling slightly, jewelled hand on her husband's arm.

The progress up to the two thrones, past the clerics, was achieved without mishap, Lyon negotiating the step with care and, no doubt thankfully, gesturing to the chairs. Turning to face the congregation, Charles indicated that the queen should sit on the lesser throne, but himself stood for a moment or two, head high, as though quietly master of himself and of the situation, before seating himself.

After a pause, everybody else who could sat down. And as they did so, Archbishop Laud appeared, on his own, mounted to the chancel, bowed to the royal pair, and went to stand immediately behind the king's chair, this to sundry gasps, especially from the Kirk ministers.

The Lord Lyon was clearly troubled, for this was his traditional place. He hesitated.

Into the silence, a voice spoke, not loudly but clearly, a royal voice.

"The Earl of Stirling to come to my side. As is meet," Charles Stewart said.

Will was surprised, embarrassed, glancing at Tam and the others. But it was a royal command. He rose and went up, past the clerics and Lyon, to bow low and then go round to stand beside Laud behind the throne.

Balfour, glancing at the monarch, recovered the initiative. Stepping to one side, and turning, so as not to have his back to the king, he reached into a pocket within his magnificent lion rampant tabard, and drew out a paper.

"I present to you, as is my duty and privilege, the person of Charles, son of James, son of Mary, daughter of James, son of James, son of James, son of James, son of James, son of Robert, son of Robert, cousin of David, son of Robert, King of Scots." Having got that out, he paused, to glance at his paper, for here was the difficult point where relationships and due succession scarcely prevailed. Clearing his throat, he went on.

"Descended from Alexander, son of Alexander, son of William, brother of Malcolm, grandson of David, brother

399

of Alexander, brother of Edgar." He paused again, not anxious to go into the distinctly confusing order of the reigns of Donald Ban, Duncan the Second, Malcolm Canmore, Duncan the First and MacBeth, contenting himself with ending up, "All descendant from the longest line of monarchs in all Christendom, through Kenneth mac Alpin back to Fergus mac Erc." He sighed with relief, the Senechal's part of his office duly discharged. He turned to the clerics, and nodded.

The Reverend Andrew Ramsay, Professor of Divinity at Edinburgh's university, raised powerful and resounding voice, and announced in the name of God the Father, the Son and the Holy Spirit that they were there to worship the Lord of all, not the lord of this earthly realm, whose vassal Charles Stewart was, but on whom lay the duty and responsibility of sustaining and protecting the Kirk of Scotland as established, its supremacy and integrity in the sight of the Almighty, as enshrined in the Confession of Faith and the Book of Discipline. It was uncertain, to Will at least, whether this was a prayer or a homily, a petition to their Creator, a declaration of zeal, or a warning to the monarch – presumably Master Ramsay was not unaware of Charles's desire, at the urgings of Archbishop Laud, to turn the Kirk to the episcopalian forms of worship. At any rate, it went on for some time. On either side of him, Will sensed the stirrings of his two neighbours, Laud in offence and anger, Lyon in concern as to the timing of the programme he had to oversee.

During all this, Will, facing the congregation, was interested to scan all and observe reactions. And he noted four individuals in especial, towards the rear of the great company, noticed them because they were notably clad in handsome ecclesiastical robes, much contrasting with the sober garb of the Presbyterian divines. These were, in fact, bishops, who had been bold enough to attend; and although not recognised as such by the Kirk, could not be denied their titles however little authority they had. For the late King James, who had approved of the office of bishop, even in the Kirk, had nominated a number of such prelates, including these four: the Bishops of Brechin, Dunkeld, Moray and Glasgow. Laud would no doubt observe, and seek to use these later.

Will noted something else. Up there in the right-hand clerestorey gallery, among other watchers of the proceedings, sat Janet. Haddington had told him that she was presently lodging at his Cowgate house. He could scarcely wave to her, in the circumstances, but hoped that she perceived that he had noticed her.

When at length, with a vociferous series of Amens by the divines, Balfour was able to continue with his duties, he stepped forward, and raised his baton.

"The Honours!" he called. Everyone stood, save the king and queen.

The four earls who had waited, as patiently as they might, facing the thrones, now played their parts. Marischal came forward with the sword of state, to present its long two-handed hilt to the king, who duly touched it in acknowledgment, but left its heavy and lengthy bulk in the other's hands. The earl went to stand with it between the two thrones, as a symbol both of the power of the monarch and of his protection. Then Errol, the High Constable, came up, to hand the larger sceptre to Charles, on bended knee, this the king accepting to hold, its silver and jewels glistening. Then it was the turn of Kinnoull, the Chancellor, to bring forward the lesser sceptre to the queen, who received it graciously and laid it across her lap. Finally, the High Justiciar, the Earl of Airth and Menteith, came with the crown. Lyon took the cushion and the Justiciar went to stand before the king and, raising the crown high, placed it very carefully on the royal head.

"God save the King! God save the King!" Lyon shouted.

All there took up the cry. "God save the King! God save the King! God save the King!" On and on the shout was repeated.

Charles sat unmoving, necessarily so, for that crown, splendid as it was, balanced but precariously on his head, and for it to slip or fall would be catastrophe.

Probably most in that chapel knew something of what William Graham, Earl of Airth and Menteith, must be feeling as he stood before Charles Stewart thus. For he had been most unfairly treated by the monarchy. By right of descent he was holder of the ancient semi-royal earldom of Strathearn, stemming from the second of Robert the Second's marriages. But because there was a theory, almost a tradition, that Robert the Third, son of the first marriage, had in fact been illegitimate, the Strathearn line had a more lawful right to the throne than its present incumbents. So on the advice of Laud, no doubt, and other mentors, Charles had withdrawn the senior earldom of Strathearn from him, even though he had volunteered to surrender, for himself and his heirs, any possible claim to the crown, and had made him instead Earl of Airth and Menteith.

Having allowed the crown of Scotland to adorn the royal brow for the necessary few moments, the earl bowed, and reached out to remove it again, Charles gravely acknowledging; and Lyon brought the cushion back to receive its precious and so significant burden. The Justiciar turned to stand holding it, beside the now crowned monarch.

The congregation sat.

Although the coronation was accomplished, the ceremony was not over. The divines still had a part, other than homolitics and prayer, to contribute. Now the Reverend Ramsay, and another, the Moderator of this year's General Assembly, came forward, not to the king but to pass on either side of the thrones to the communion table behind. There all save the royal couple turned to watch them. A white linen cloth on the table was removed, to reveal a silver platter and goblet. These, presumably previously blessed and consecrated, the two ministers held high, the Moderator sonorously declaring them to be the duly sanctified bread and wine, which on their Good Lord's own institution became His Body and Blood, these now to be partaken of by the King's Grace and his queen, as representing all the realm, and a token of the royal duty and agreement to protect and maintain Christ's Kirk here on earth.

The sacraments were then brought round and presented to Charles and his wife, who, on a sign, rose to accept them standing, which of course, had everyone else standing also. They ate the bread and sipped the wine. Beside Will, Laud frowned and stirred. The divines returned the elements to the communion table and covered them with the linen. All who had seats resumed them.

Lyon raised baton for a final gesture and feature of the ceremony. "Fealty and allegiances!" he called. "By the earls of Scotland. In token of all." Clearly all there could not take the oath of homage to the newly crowned monarch.

In reverse order of the regalia presentation, the Earl of Airth and and Menteith led the duty. Handing crown on cushion to Balfour, he sank to his knees before Charles, reached out to take the royal hand between both his own, and murmured the oath of loyalty and obedience. Rising, he bowed to the queen, and resumed custody of the crown. Kinnoull did the same, then Errol and the Marischal.

Lyon was beckoning towards the earls' bench at the front of the congregation when the king, who had been so passive throughout all, took a hand. Turning in his seat, he gestured.

"My lord Earl of Stirling," he said.

So Will had to make himself conspicuous again, and distinctly reluctantly, by coming round from behind the throne and sinking to his knees to receive the hand he had so often had to guide and instruct in earlier years, and to speak the required formula, this while the other earls, led by the former Angus, lined up to offer each their own duty. On his feet again, Will turned to the queen and took *her* hand, to kiss it – and was rewarded with a warm smile from Charles as well as herself. He did not go back behind the chairs but stood beside Lyon.

This gesture towards Henrietta Maria apparently commended itself to the waiting file of nobles, who each in turn kissed her hand, after fealty, making Will wonder whether inadvertently he had initiated a new feature of the coronation observance.

At last it was all over, the ritual at an end. Lyon waved to his heralds, who thumped their staffs, and everybody stood, to bow towards the thrones. Charles rose, then his wife, and, led by Balfour himself, followed by the regalia earls, was conducted from the chapel, with the choristers raising their chanting once more.

The first real coronation in Scotland since 1408 was over.

Will was in some doubt as to his duty now. Would Charles be requiring his services further meantime? Probably not. He might well prefer to be private for a spell, to be alone with his wife, after all the public exposure. Forby, he himself had a wife, and a duty to her surely. Instead of processing out, he went off down into the body of the chapel to find Janet.

Eyed by many, greeted by some, he waited at the foot of the narrow turnpike stairway down from the clerestorey, as those who had watched from up there gingerly picked their way down. When Janet appeared, he held his arms wide for her, not caring who observed.

"My dear!" he exclaimed. "At last!"

"Will! Will! Who would be wed to a Secretary of State!" she demanded. "And one who makes himself so prominent!"

"Not makes, is *made*! Charles you must blame, not me."

"He appeared to be needing help, yes. Confused. However dignified. Twice he made a mistake, forgot your title, Will. Called you earl instead of viscount."

"M'mm. No mistake, lass. At least, not in the speech. I *am* Earl of Stirling now. He has made me that, for some reason. Earl of Stirling and Viscount of Canada, no less! So you are now a countess."

"A mercy! Countess! How will I live up to that? Viscountess was bad enough. An earl, Will – you? You do not cozen me? No? What will my father say to that?"

"He will purse his lips in the way he has, I fear. Deem me growing too lofty for a goodson! But, more important, how will our William take to being Viscount of Canada? What a style! Canada, half of the Americas!"

"So long as he does not think to go there and seek to grasp it, or any of it." She shrugged. "What now, my lord Earl? Have you got to go back to Charles? Or can you spare a little time for your countess? I am at Tam's house in the Cowgate."

"I think that the royal pair can do without me for a little time, lass. They will be glad enough to be alone together, I would judge. I will send one of Tam's people to Holyroodhouse to let them know where I am. So . . ."

She took his arm, to lead him off.

Will Alexander, Earl of Stirling, Viscount of Canada, Governor of Nova Scotia and Secretary of State, headed for the door of the chapel, turning to face, with his wife's support, whatever the future held for himself and her, for Scotland, and for those lands beyond the seas, a man concerned and, he hoped, faithful.

HISTORICAL NOTE

King Charles, a good man but scarcely a good monarch, the reverse of his strange father, in the end took William Laud's advice, not William Alexander's. He came north again four years later, in 1637, determined to ordain episcopacy on Scotland, and this while at loggerheads with his English parliament, and creating growing animosity from the Puritan and Calvinistic elements of English society consequent on the dominance of Laud in state as in Church. The Scots would not take it, and the National Covenant was the result, and the northern kingdom was plunged into civil war. Within a year or two, similar hostilities broke out in England, and Cromwell led the call to arms. But still Charles would not lessen his demands and withdraw his edicts. He paid for his obstinate insistence on his divine right, on the scaffold, in 1649, Laud having preceded him to a similar fate four years earlier.

William Alexander did not live to see the final outcome, dying in 1640, aged sixty. But four years before that he was given a further grant, by the king, of all the territory on New England, between the rivers St Croix and Kennebeck, and the lengthy territory which he named Stirling Island, later altered to Long Island, whereon rose the city of New York. The title of Earl of Stirling died out with the decease of the fifth earl in 1739. But a collateral kinsman, another William Alexander, a major-general in the American army, taken prisoner on Long Island in 1793, claimed the title, but his right was voted down in the House of Lords in London.